M.J. WOODMAN

DIVINE

PHILBERDS FILM & TELEVISION
LIMITED

For John D. Woodman

AUTHOR'S NOTE

This work is in no way a representation of historical fact. The world of Divine is one influenced by both Greek and Roman history and mythologies. The story takes place in an alternate reality where the Roman Empire still exists. There is use of both Latin and Ancient Greek language throughout, hence a glossary has been provided for clarity.

CONTENTS

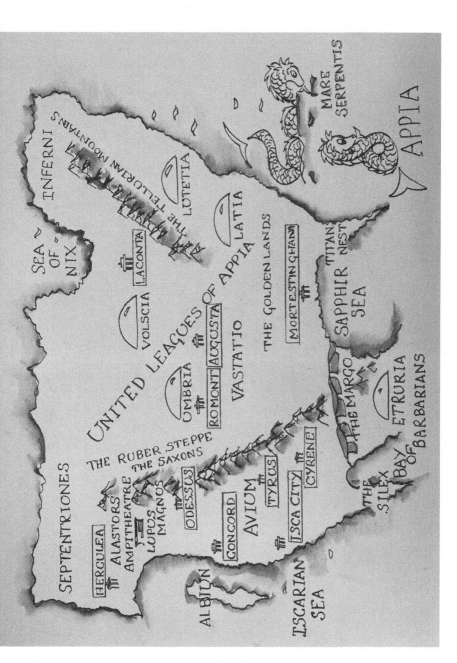

Map drawing by Stephana Martin

PROLOGUE
2010 A.D.

The sky bleeds. The rain is sticky and warm against his skin, and as the sun peers over the easternmost mountain-top, it glows, rutilant, turning the water of the heavens to blood. It wouldn't surprise Lysander if it *were* blood – he had seen enough death that day to make such a tragic miracle justifiable. On his hands and knees, he climbs, grabbing handfuls of wet soil in an attempt to reach the crest of the hill. His legs, out of use for some hours now, are deadweight behind him. Mud and sweat are all he can taste as his thirsty tongue laps over his lips.

None of this matters to him. His endurance for such physical conditions has always been strong. Serving in the Latian army had taught him resilience, pain and unyielding loyalty to his nation. But it hadn't taught him about loss or grief or love. His mind struggles to grasp any image of her but his last. Her bare, olive skin corrupted by death, turning blue from the cold snow that cushioned her corpse. Bile rises in his throat.

He clambers over the last incline. In the valley, the basecamp peers over the marsh. Lysander had spent three days on the run from Spartaca, terrorists who had slaughtered his legion and his betrothed. Safety is now finally within his reach, but the anticipated relief of his survival never comes. Instead guilt gnaws at him, a dull ache that rises until he is entirely numb.

He wades through the dirt. His trembling fingers scrape against something solid. He clutches at the branch hidden by the mud and yanks at it, tearing it from the sodden ground. With his left hand, he rips his red uniform and ties the rag to the branch then waves it around. His movements are frantic. As his strength abates, his arms collapse under the weight of the makeshift flag and the cloth made heavy by the rain. The warmth ebbs from his body, which is now slumped in a heap on a lonely mound of melting earth.

He drifts into a heavy type of sleep that some fear there is no returning from. His usual dreams are absent, but voices are calling him. *Lysander, stay with me. Lysander, breathe. Lysander, wake up.* These are men's voices, but his cruel mind transforms them. It is now Persephone who speaks to him. *Don't leave me, Lysander. Come back to me. I am waiting for you.*

He awakes to the gentle crackling of fire and the earthy scent of recently chopped wood. His clothes have been changed; he is dry for the first time in days and his wounds have been bandaged. He sits upright in his bed, his tent unchanged from the last time he saw it. He looks over, expecting to see another body curled up beside him, her small, neat body that nestled perfectly into his chest. But there is no one. She is gone. It wasn't some terrible nightmare conjured up by the demons of his mind.

"Where is she?" The emperor addresses him. Romulus Titus Ovicula has the sort of voice that could startle wolves. His presence had gone unnoticed until he rose from the seat in the shadowy corner of the tent.

Lysander's voice, which often comes so easily to him, falters, and the words stick in his throat. "Dead. They k-killed her," he manages to stutter. His words leave him cold.

Romulus had expected this response, yet he still shakes his head gently. The customary platitudes of consolation are absent. He rubs his palm over his beard, the bristles making a soft scraping sound. "Dominus will blame you for this…" His voice trails off, leaving Lysander with the barrage of thoughts he had been fending off for the past three days.

Romulus lifts his face up to the tarp, opening his mouth then closing it again, choosing his words carefully. "I am well aware that Persephone was the one who convinced you to abscond with her and you could have never been in a position to deny her. However, I fear our master will seek vengeance, and you, my dear boy, will face the full brunt of his wrath."

Lysander's face contorts in a near grimace; his fate is death, in spite of his survival. Dominus doesn't forgive; he doesn't forget. "I suppose there is nothing you can do." Lysander sighs as he speaks, the tone of his voice flat.

The emperor pauses, rolls his tongue over his bottom lip and smirks as if he just had some miraculous idea. "Not necessarily."

The war trumpet shrieks from outside the tent, the noise that rouses soldiers from their troubled sleep. Another day of the war. Lysander wonders if it will ever end, and if that trip to Rome would ever have been worth the trouble it has caused.

Romulus continues, as if uninterrupted by the disturbance. "The men and women of the Latian army believe you to be a hero, Lysander. The sole survivor of a legion of over five hundred men. You are also a general; the youngest general our army has ever seen."

A hero. Lysander had always dreamed of such a title, to mimic the great deeds of those men who had lived thousands of years before him, those epic heroes of the ancient world. Hercules, Aeneas and even the tragic Achilles. A boy from a broken home, without family, love and honour.

This dream of his now accomplished, seems superficial and false. The cost has been too high. Five hundred dead. *Hero.* Somehow the word seems smaller than it used to.

Romulus must notice Lysander's discomfort at his terminology, as he nears him, raises his hand and places it on Lysander's shoulder. "I am sorry, my boy. I truly am."

This display of paternal affection wasn't uncommon between the two men. For Lysander, Romulus was the father he never had.

Lysander doesn't allow himself to cry. He won't show weakness to his emperor, yet his expression tightens as if he ought to be in pain. His cracked lips tremble as he speaks. "Even you, my emperor, can't fix this mess."

Romulus stiffens his features, appearing more serious than usual, and leans forward so that he is only inches from Lysander's face. "I have a plan. You won't like it. But it may just save your life."

I

AB INITIO

From the beginning
2020 A.D.

My father says I am full of rage. He says I get that from my mother. I wouldn't know, as she left two years after I was born. In a letter, she told me not to mourn her; she believed in the legends that said people like her would be safe. I know better. The Institute stole my mother away at just seventeen. Tomorrow, they will take me too.

I bind my hands with tape, the thick kind that makes my fingers numb. My brother's army boots are laced on my feet, three knots, just in case. The hum of the Haven's skeleton rings out above me. It is a field of energy that keeps us caged in like birds, and no one else can seem to hear it but me. I hear it, and I hate it. It is a beautiful cage, but a cage still.

I take a pomegranate from the ground. The fruit is swathed with dirt and dust, not like those perfect things they sell in the forum. I tear away its skin with my teeth and suck out the seeds. The taste of earth lingers on my tongue, but I don't mind. It distracts me from the nagging thought of tomorrow, of the Choosing. Lana calls out from the glade that overlooks the valley. That's where we fight, where we pretend to be like the warriors of myth and legend. But we are just kids and we call ourselves the Grey.

I see a pair of bony legs stretching out beneath a child's body as it darts through the trees.

Lana.

She may as well be my sister, only fifteen and much smarter than I will ever be. I swore to her brother that I would look after her when he went to war, but the truth is, I have gotten her into trouble more times than I can count. Her talents include pickpocketing and illegal bartering. She steals denarii from the merchants' togas as they trade in the market. Her quick legs and slight frame

1

make it easy work. She bet a week's worth of earnings on me. It will be a bet wasted. I can't fight. I can't do much of anything worth a lick.

She drags me from the shade of the trees, and the sun stings my bleached skin. The high heat of summer in Ore is enough to send even the farmers from their fields. Sweat beads on my brow but I don't bother to wipe it away. Lana tugs at the rough fabric of my athletic vest, urging me onwards. The trees give way to grass and rolling hills that spread across the horizon. The sun spills light over Latia's heartlands, and it is golden, as if blessed by the gods.

Lana thrusts me headlong into a thick mass of bodies and my skin sticks to theirs. I shoulder through the crowds, breaking into the clearing where my opponent awaits. The boy has slender brown eyes, but that is the only thing small about him. A low grumble ripples through the hordes that encircle us. My eyes fall on the boy's boulder-like fists, strapped just like mine. Suddenly, my mouth goes dry.

A look of satisfaction spreads over the boy's thickset face. Even as I roll on to the toe of my boots, the crest of my head falls just below his chest. The boy's friends stand behind him, and his name hangs in the air. His name is Magnus. *Big*. I almost laugh.

Lana is the only one who chants my name as she clambers atop a rock to get a better view. The others have seen me fight before, and they have seen me lose. A long time ago, I wanted to be a gladiator, and I foolishly etched my name into the fight rock on which Lana now stands. Once the name is in stone, it is in stone forever. Those of us whose names are on that rock draw lots once a month. It seems I have rotten luck.

Slowly, I draw my fists up in front of my face. Magnus counters, shuffling his heavy-looking feet towards me. The *cornu* sounds, and my legs are taken out from beneath me before the horn's shrill abates. I crash, face first, to the ground. Dust swells up from the arid earth. I blink, clearing my eyes as I choke on dirtied air. A boot lands in my stomach, and hot, searing pain spreads until it is in my throat and I can no longer breathe.

A small groan passes from my lips but quickly dies as Magnus grabs me by the scruff of my vest and hauls me up onto my feet. I throw a futile fist. He swats it to the side. The sharp stab of knuckles on my cheeks sends me hurtling backwards, and I pitch over. My skull rattles, and darkness edges into my vision. There are voices, indistinct but hushed like a prayer, the same voices that have haunted me for months. The heat of Magnus's breath falls on my face as he stands over me, and his boot smashes into my face. A bone cracks.

"This will help with the pain." Lana speaks softly as she sits me up against the fissured bough of an olive tree. She uncurls her fist, revealing crushed green herbs gathered up in her palm.

I swallow the herbs, and she laughs, pointing to my teeth. With my nails, I pick out the green residue, grimacing at the bitter taste that lingers on my tongue.

"Thanks," I mutter, rubbing my swollen nose.

Over her shoulder, the old *Horreum*, a ruined warehouse, is painted orange in the dusk light. The soft sounds of singing ring out.

A dark tendril of hair falls into her face as a gust of wind shoots up the valley. "We have to do something about your face before tomorrow," she says, brushing a finger over my temple. It is tender to the touch, and I flinch.

"What did I tell you?" I say with a coldness in my voice that she has come to expect.

She sinks back onto her elbows. "Don't talk about tomorrow."

"Exactly." I clamber up onto my feet, leaning against the bark to steady myself.

Lana springs up too, with surprise in her eyes. But she should know by now that while I often take a beating, I can always get back on my feet again. After all, what choice do I have? What choice do any of us have?

"Electa," she starts, her voice breaking.

I hate the sound of my name, especially now. It means *she who has been chosen*. Sometimes, I think it was some cruel joke my father played on me when I was born. People like us don't get Chosen. The only reason my father survived that fateful day was because he chose another path for himself – the war. I had that same choice, the choice that all children of military families do, but I didn't want to fight the faceless enemy that the Institute has never named. I didn't want to be their slave – even death is more appealing to me than that. Tomorrow, I will meet my fate head on. In some ways I think it makes me braver than my father, but he would never say so.

"Lana," I snap. "Stop your fussing. Even if I am Unchosen, they'll just send me to another Haven."

It is a lie, of course, one I often tell myself. It offers her a little comfort, I think, to know that the Choosing is not a death sentence for people like us. The other Havens, hundreds of miles from ours, have a Choosing just like ours, because they, too, are governed by the Institute.

Lana has two years until her Choosing, until she is seventeen. Those two years slipped away from me, and every moment of them I spent in dread. There was this dull ache in the pit of my stomach, an anxiety that made many sleepless nights. The only antidote, in my case, was this – the Greys, the drinking, the fighting and partying, everything the Institute hates. It is our little defiance, futile, but ours all the same. I suppose it is the only choice most of us ever makes.

She skips along in front of me, skidding down the berm on heels. "That's not what they all say," she says.

No one knows what happens to the Unchosen but there are rumours. Some say that they are sent to the barren wasteland outside the Havens and left to fend for themselves. Others tell stories of how they are executed in prison camps. The Institute doesn't want us to know because it is our fear of it that controls us.

I catch up with her, a limp in my step. "Well, they are all wrong. I know the truth."

She throws her head back, catching my eye with that cheeky smirk of hers. "But ... how? No one knows for sure, except the Institute, but they don't tell—"

"My father told me once, okay?" I interrupt, the lie passing from my lips as easily as my breath. "He was drunk one night and spilled all sorts of Institute secrets."

My father swears he doesn't know what happens to the Unchosen, but even if he did, he would never tell me. He is a faithful servant of the Institute, the government and the Imperials who serve as the heads of state, of our Haven and the League of Latia.

That sparks her interest, and she comes to a stop. "Like what?"

I nudge her, playfully, and feel the protruding bone of her shoulder beneath her rough tunic. But she is not some fragile little thing, even if she looks it. "If you *tace*, maybe I'll tell you one day."

She mimes sealing her mouth, and with a shove dashes off. The smell of crushed honeysuckle underfoot brings a smile to my face. It smells like home.

"Last one to the warehouse drinks two bottles of *Posca*," she shouts back.

Her pace quickens. I shake my head and, with a huff, break into a sprint.

The second bottle of *Posca* burns my throat until a numbness befalls my entire body. I squeeze my eyes shut, wincing at the taste. A boy sits across from me, sharpening a knife on a whetstone. The sound of the blade scraping against the stone makes me shiver. We are the only two left. Others vomit in the bushes or fall over themselves, scrambling for the last few bottles of liquor. I crane my neck, looking over into the warehouse. Flames lick from the brazier, spilling red light over the concrete floor. Lana clumsily dances with Felix, the boy she claims to love, but we don't know what love is – we're only kids, and soon we may die.

The radio plays Latian folk music, the kind only we Plebeians listen to. The Patricians who live in the marbled city, in glitzy townhouses and sprawling country villas, frown on such behaviour. The blond-haired boy across from me smokes on a pipe. He exhales, closing his eyes, and his features soften. He is blissfully unaware of the sobbing girl that is slumped up against the log beside him. I study him, and for a moment I forget where I am and what tomorrow will bring.

His hand flies away from him and sends the knucklebones gathered beside him tumbling to the ground. He swears under his breath and blinks, catching my stare. His skin is darker than mine, scorched from working in the fields, his broad hands tell me so.

He coughs, the smoke spilling from his nostrils. "How was your Assay Day?"

The question makes me go cold. It is a question you should never ask a Plebeian. Assay Day was months ago, but the memory of it lingers like a bad taste on my tongue.

I tear my eyes away from his. "I don't like to talk about it."

He laughs. "You don't give much away, do you?"

No, now leave me alone, I want to say but bite my tongue.

He stands on two unsteady legs and moves to sit beside me. His shoulder brushes against mine, and the music dies inside the warehouse; someone has probably tripped over the radio and snapped the transmitter.

"I have never seen you around here before," I finally say, breaking the still of the night.

"I'm from the Infra province. Felix invited me." His voice trembles with unease, an anxiety I recognise so well. I am not the only one who has lived in fear.

I take a swig of *Posca*, scrunching up my eyes. "You're seventeen?"

He gestures to the log he had been sitting on just moments ago. "I thought the two empty bottles and sharpened knife made that quite clear."

I manage a smile. "So, you're planning on slitting your throat before the night is up?"

He offers me his pipe, but I quickly decline. I don't want to embarrass myself in front of a beautiful boy on the last day of my life.

His lip curls. "Perhaps. I haven't decided yet."

"And your Assay Day?"

He pushes his curls back with a calloused hand. The pink scars on his knuckles are bright against his skin. "I don't remember much of it. I suppose we never really stand much of chance, do we?"

I sigh at the flash of an unwelcome memory. Even if I hadn't fainted on Assay Day, the fates wouldn't have been on my side in the face of such overwhelming odds. They say only ten percent of Latia's seventeen-year-olds are Chosen, and most are Patrician children who attend illustrious academies in the city. Plebeians can't afford such luxuries, and few survive. The Institute's interviews, academic and physical assessments on Assay Day are something we spend our entire lives studying for. *But for what?* As the blond-haired boy says, we never really stand much of a chance.

"I stopped coming to the meetings, tried to study," I say, remembering the time I swore to my father I had put the Grey behind me. I did, for a while at least.

He looks at me, dazed, the alcohol slowing his movements. "But here you are."

One last night, what harm could it do? I had said to myself. The meetings are rarely broken up by the vigilites, the Institute's armoured police force. We are breaking their laws, but they allow our hopeless resistance, because that is just what it is – *hopeless*. We talk of rebellion and freedom from the Institute, the Choosing and all it entails, but it is no more than faint grumblings around a campfire or drunken speeches on top of tables.

My alcohol-drenched lips tremble as I wipe my mouth with my forearm. "What does it matter now? Our fate is no longer in our control."

The fates are not kind to people like us, not anymore.

"The Institute could catch us, and we would be sent away. Imagine that, a day before the Choosing, and then, well … blacklisted," he says, struggling with each word.

There are rumours of Grey kids being taken from their homes and sent to the world outside the Haven, before getting the chance to face their Choosing.

"You believe those stories?"

He shrugs. "Kids go missing all the time."

I catch myself believing him, even if for a moment. But such talk is treason.

A mosquito whines in my ear. I shake my head. "I won't be Chosen, so none of it matters."

"But imagine if you were? And you threw it all away for one last jaunt with the Grey."

I baulk at the suggestion, even if it is true. "I could say the same to you."

He bobs his chin and casts his eyes skywards, taking a long, drawn-out breath.

"Do you hear it?" he whispers, his words fervent like a prayer.

I look up at the glittering, limpid sky. "Hear what?"

"The sky," he breathes.

I thought I was the only one who heard it – the dull electric hum of the Haven, the domed force field that protects us and cages us both.

"Yes."

He rocks back and forth on the log; the motion seems to calm him.

"Why are we here?"

I frown, surprised. "What do you mean?"

He looks at me, the blue of his eyes holding mine. "Have you never thought about it?"

"No," I mumble. "We are not supposed to think about it."

I have always wondered what lies beyond the Havens, but never why the Havens existed in the first place.

"There was a world before ours, the myths say, a world before the Havens, before the United Leagues of Appia," the boy says, with a mystical quality to his voice.

The myths say it was a terrible world. The earth was soaked with blood, the old heroes were dead and monsters roamed in the darkness. Is that the world I will face when I am Unchosen, or will I die before I get the chance?

He snatches the bottle from my hands, gulping down the last dregs of *Posca.* "The Institute knows the truth."

"But they'll never tell." My voice is so faint, I am not sure he even hears.

Eyelids drooping, his head sinks into his lap. "Dominus, bless us."

The fire flickers one last time and then dies, the coals reduced to glowing embers. The girl no longer cries, and the sound of drunken teenagers spewing in the shrubbery is strangely absent. I jolt up from my seat, hushing the blond-haired boy who mutters indistinct prayers beside me. Fluorescent lights rove along the bank. *Stercus.* I swallow the lump in my throat, but my legs are motionless.

I shake the boy, trying to rouse him, but there is no time. The screams pierce the metal structure, echoing out across the valley. I hurtle through the warehouse doors, tearing Lana from the arms of her inebriated dance partner.

"We need to go, now," I stammer between the heavy breaths that rasp in my throat.

Lana takes a look back at the searchlights descending from the groves. "Vigilites." She chokes on the word.

We run, breaking through the back door of the warehouse, the metal rattling behind us. Shrieking children spill from each side of the building, darting into the trees. Engines groan behind us, but we don't stop; even if we hide, they will find us. The blue light of the vigilite's scanners is on our heels.

Lana stumbles, tumbling over onto the ground. I drag her to her feet, but she slows, like a deadweight behind me. Startled sobs escape her, her eyes wide and wet with tears. I urge her onwards, and we climb the hill. The wheat beats in the breeze, shuddering under the stars. I cover Lana's mouth with my hand, stifling the noises that escape her.

"The tree, we need to get to the tree," I whisper, my heart lurching in my chest.

She dashes to the old oak, cowering behind it. I follow, keeping my head low. She is pressed up tight against me, her small body in my arms. Gunmetal grey visors jut out over the wheat, and gloved arms swat the plants aside. *They're close, too close.* Blue light crawls towards us, and with it a dark, monstrous shadow. A hand reaches out, then the crack of a gun, a shot reverberating from the other side of the valley. The vigilite collapses with a thud, his blood staining the wheat.

Lana trembles, and we don't breathe. Moments pass. We remain still, but the searchlights encroach and we have to run once more. I take Lana to the watermill at the foot of the hill, where the engines of vigilite vehicles are but a faint growl in the distance.

"You need to go home; follow the river to Hedera," I say, doubling over as I catch my breath.

"Not without you," she says, her voice childlike. I often forget that she is only fifteen, young and afraid.

I shake my head. "It is better if we go alone, like children lost in the woods."

She nods slowly and disappears into the shadows.

I should go straight home, but I never do what I *should*. Instead, I hide in the watermill, my back against the dank stone walls, and doze in and out of sleep. Hours pass, and daylight breaks over Aventine Hill. The numbness of alcohol wears away and I rub the sleep from my eyes. I return to the wheat fields, hoping to understand what had happened there – how the vigilite was killed and by who.

The body is gone. I think it must have been a dream. But then I see the red blood on the wheat beside the great oak tree. I blink twice, but the blood remains. *It was real.*

The grass is sticky with morning dew and cool against my baked skin. The thickness of the air thwarts my breathing as I clamber over the bank. I follow the scent of sweet honeysuckle, and it guides me to the olive groves where the others hid.

The *Horreum* is deserted, the only remnants of the night we had spent there are the smoking coals of the brazier and abandoned satchels of schoolchildren. But then I see him, the blond-haired boy, and I wish I hadn't come back at all.

The boy is strung from the bough of an olive tree, swinging in the southern breeze. His corpse is half-illuminated by the red dawn of the horizon. I never even knew his name.

I retrieve his knife from the log, his knucklebones too, but I am greeted by another terrifying sight. At the centre of the warehouse, which was empty just minutes ago, a body is hung from the girders. The burnished chest plate of the vigilite lies on the floor, and the bare chest of the corpse steams, branded with a symbol I don't recognise. *Two crossed swords.*

My stomach roils, and I stagger backwards. The Grey couldn't have done this, but if not the Grey, then who? In the shadows of the corner of the warehouse, I see two blue eyes glowing in the darkness. My body turns to ice. The blond-haired boy's possessions fall from my hands, clattering on the concrete. And I run.

I burst through the doors of my villa. An uneaten meal is set out on the table. I was supposed to be home in time. Fresh food is a luxury item we can't afford. The Institute provides every citizen with pre-prepared meals containing all the vitamins and supplements we need. The bitter-medicated taste is something I can't pretend to bear. My father had saved for weeks to prepare a final feast before my Choosing, and I didn't even show up.

A figure emerges from the kitchen, shrouded in thick smoke. My father puffs on his pipe, a dull look on his aged face. I notice the spilled wine on the countertop and how the red liquid leeches into the wooden cabinets. I rush to clean it, but before I can grab the cloth, father catches my wrist. He blinks, and a tear slips from his eye.

"Where were you?" His words are slurred, and I can barely make sense of them.

I snatch my arm away. "With Lana."

I scrub the wine-stained wood furiously, as if that somehow makes up for my absence. My father's expression says otherwise. He is a military advisor in the city these days, and once a commander on the front. He gave it all up to spend more time with us. A little late for that. I will be dead tomorrow.

"Two Institute officials stopped by this morning looking for you." He stands over me, watching my futile attempt to remove the stain.

My breath sticks in my throat. They know I was there last night, at the warehouse – they know I am a Grey. A slow sinking feeling pours from my throat into the pit of my stomach. I am blacklisted out of the Haven, no questions asked. The small hope that had rooted itself inside me for all these months is torn away in a single breath. But I already had my death sentence. I don't think of myself but of Lana, who still had two years, two years to study, to survive, to live. I have to fix this.

I turn, looking up at my father. "What did you tell them?"

His fists ball at his sides, his face turning ruddy in ire. "The truth. I didn't know where you were."

His coppery eyes rake over me. They were soft once, but now there is a coldness I no longer recognise. He changed when he returned from war. He never speaks of it; he is forbidden by the law. But one thing I know about this war is that it makes monsters of good men.

"Electa, what were you thinking?" He slams his fist onto the marble countertop, soaking his hand in the spilled wine. "This Grey nonsense was always going to be your downfall."

I toss the cloth to the side and it lands on the counter with a wet smack. "No, Father, my downfall is that I am a Pleb!"

He hates that word. He used to say it was disrespectful, a slight on all Plebeians.

"Do *not* use that word."

It is hard for me to remember how he used to be, the Cassius Steel who would bring us baskets brimming with edible gifts when he would visit us every three months. There was no biting fury or a single wrinkle on his golden skin. But now his butterscotch-coloured hair has greyed, frown lines crease his forehead, and there is an unrelenting fury that makes me cower at his feet.

I look down. "I'm sorry, Father."

He grips me by my shoulders, the wine on his hands cool against my skin. "Electa, you could have been great; you could have lived the life your mother never had."

I hate it when he says that. The terrible anger he always speaks of froths inside me, and I can restrain it no more.

"My mother is dead because of you, your precious Institute and their fucking Choosing," I shout, my words lashing him like whips. He steps away, his arms wrapped tightly around his torso as if injured.

I brace myself for a rage to match my own. But a silence floats in the air between us, and silent tears spill from his eyes.

"Why would you throw your life away like this?" he finally says, sinking onto the couch.

He made me promise I would try to pass Assay Day and live. He couldn't bear to lose both me and my mother. But I would never be perfect enough for them, for the Institute, even if I tried.

"This is no life. I will not be like you, I will not be their slave," I say, and the room suddenly turns cold.

He gathers himself, wiping his cheeks with his linen sleeves. "Better their slave than their enemy. That is what you are, what the Grey are – traitors, enemies."

When I was young, when he was a different man, he told me stories of the Grey and the myths that inspired them. He used to go to the same *Horreum* when he was a boy. He used to speak of the mosaic on the wall of the warehouse, a remnant of the old world. It shows children fighting with swords, training how gladiators might. Those tiles are sacred to us, and the Grey exist because of them.

"You were a Grey once," I say softly. "Have you forgotten?"

He clutches each side of his head, shaking it in quick, frenzied motions. Anyone would think he is going mad. Maybe he is.

"All your dreams wasted. Look at all that." He points to an old crate in the corner of the room. Costumes and props spill out from the box. Those were mine. "You wanted to be a gladiator once, instead you chose to be a dissident."

My heart drums as the rage churns within me. I was young and foolish – I had hope. But people like me aren't gladiators, they are Unchosen, and I almost feel like I deserve it.

I square up to my father, unable to bear the weight of his disappointment any longer. "You once told me that I should worship Laverna because the only thing I was any good at was lying. I had no talents, you said that much yourself."

In the old myths, Laverna was the goddess of thieves and cheats. To my father, I was a good liar. He was never home and believed me when I told him I went to school, trained at the gymnasium, came home and that was all. I fooled him for years, but eventually the truth sent him to the bottle, and it has been like this ever since.

He screws up his nose and huffs. "I never said such a thing. Polytheism is dead. There is only one god now. I pray to him every night for your survival."

He pretends he doesn't remember who he was before and the things he once said, but he does. There are just layers of grief between him and the person he used to be.

"Your beloved Dominus won't save me. I couldn't even save myself." I turn away and begin to climb the stairs.

His voice follows me. "Get some rest and use your regenerator. You have a long day ahead of you."

The regenerator hums in the corner of my room. Prisons of the night, my brother and I used to call them. I never use it, but disuse is punishable by law. The Institute claims it teaches us and heals us as we sleep. I used it when I was young, and it stole away my dreams. The glass chamber is uncomfortable, not at all like the plush linen of my bed. Rather strangely, I am impervious to the crippling tiredness that afflicts those who don't use their regenerator.

In my anger, I kick the glass, hoping it will crack. It doesn't. I suppose the Institute thought of that, too, when it designed these stupid machines. I collapse to the floor beside my bed, pressing my head into my hands. I fend off the terrible thoughts that come crashing down all at once. Lana's life may be stolen away, and I have only hours to fix it before I am gone forever.

I scrawl letters to my family, and to Lana, my thoughts spilling onto the paper. This will be my goodbye. It is the only goodbye I can bear. An intense throbbing pain pulses at my side. I peel away the fabric of my athletic vest. A large bruise has formed on my torso. It seems I took quite the beating.

From the rack, I take the golden tunic, the only feminine attire I own. I pull the garment over my head and mask the scent of dirt and sweat with my mother's old perfume. Today, all must wear gold, the nation's colour, spare a token representing your family colour. Plebeians wear white, and I tie a simple ribbon around my wrist. I stare at my reflection in the dust-ridden mirror and fight off the urge to gag. When I see myself like this, conforming to their rules, their laws, it disgusts me in a way I can hardly describe.

The Choosing will take place in the city of Ore at the heart of the Haven. But I still have five hours before my name is read out among countless other Unchosen ones. First, I will go to the Institute building and find out if Lana is truly blacklisted. Somehow, I will fix it, remove the label in any way I can, even if it is my last act upon this earth. I will not be the reason she dies.

I creep towards the doorway. The soft padding of my steps doesn't rouse my father from sleep. He remains on the couch where I left him. I place the letter for him, my brother and Lana on the table. I tell them that I love them and to be brave in a way I never could. Half a step out of the threshold and a weak voice rises behind me.

"You would leave without saying goodbye?" Vel is softly spoken, not at all like me or Father. But we have the same olive skin, golden, sun-bleached hair and deep-set brown eyes.

I can't bring myself to look my brother in the eyes. "I thought it might be easier that way."

He stretches out his arms with a yawn. He is bare chested from sleep; I must have woken him as I passed through the corridor. The Imperial army tattoo emblazoned on his chest is the only thing I see when I look at him, and it makes me sick.

"I heard the argument. Electa, why would you?"

I back out of the doorway, facing him still. "Please, Vel. Maybe you would understand if you hadn't joined the army." There is a harshness to my voice that I didn't intend.

He is only fifteen, but towers over me. "You had that choice, Electa."

I press my lips together, swallowing the urge to cry. I must be brave for once, for him. "I won't be their slave."

He shakes his head, not furiously like our father does, but instead it is a slow, measured movement. "I am not a slave."

"You might as well be." There is a bite to my tone. I can't help myself.

He narrows his eyes, studying me for a moment, trying to understand whether I am feeling sadness or anger. "Is this really how you want to say goodbye?"

"No." My voice breaks, and a tear rolls from the corner of my eyes onto my lip. The taste of salt makes me feel human, for the first time since Assay Day, when I swore to cry no more. "Look after Father when I am gone, okay?"

His forehead creases. "Didn't he tell you?"

"Tell me what?"

"There was a notification from the Institute. He is being sent back to war. And you know I will be off to Cassida at the end of the month."

Cassida is a military training fort, a boarding school for soldiers. Terrible rumours whisper through the Grey *bacchanals* that speak of that place.

"So last night?"

"Was the last time we would all be together, yes." Vel has confirmed my worst fear.

I am a terrible sister, a terrible daughter, but I won't be a terrible friend. I must save Lana.

I pull my brother close into an embrace that warms my bones. All those years we spent together, alone with no parent to help us, has brought us closer than most siblings could ever be.

"I am so sorry, Vel," I breathe into his chest.

"It doesn't matter now." He grips me tightly. "*Bonam fortunam.*"

Good luck.

"*Vale,*" I say, tearing away while I still can.

13

The hourly shuttle comes to a halt beneath the dirt track. I glance back at my home one last time. Our small villa is the only one on this lonely hill that over-looks Chrysos Valley and the town of Hedera. It is made of crumbling stone and twisted vines, and crests the hill like a second-rate crown. There is something beautiful in its imperfection. It is the one thing I will miss when I am gone from this place. The memory of it, of my family and my friends, will be a flicker of light even in death, even in the darkness.

II

FACILIS DESCENSUS AVERNO

The descent to hell is easy

The hallway pulses with a fluorescent light, and the whine of electricity sings out from above. I don't know how I found myself here, on the lower levels of the Institute's monolithic dome structure. The signs for candidate enquiries lead me one floor down, but I have continued, hoping to find what, I am not quite sure. I am not supposed to be here; I know that much. In hindsight, this is not one of my better ideas.

I turn a corner, quickly glancing behind me to ensure I am not seen. With a thud, I land against what I think could be a wall but is actually a chest that feels as though it is made from iron rather than flesh.

Asher Ovicula towers over me, his brow creasing as he examines my eyes then my face and then my whole body. I feel stripped, bare and vulnerable as I stand before Latia's prince. I expect a critical remark and then for him to turn his back and briskly walk in the opposite direction. Instead, he smirks.

"Lost, are we?"

I don't think I have ever been at a loss for words, but the prince's simple question paralyses me. The possibility of me being caught out was high, but by Asher Ovicula of all people. Reality slips away, I can feel the vein on my forehead throbbing as I try to find my tongue, yet it lulls in my mouth, and no matter how hard I try, I can't move it.

The prince prompts me once again, his voice tinged with sarcasm. "So you're deaf and blind?"

Finally, I find my voice. "Excuse me?" I manage to choke out.

"Well, it's very difficult to get lost with all the signs."

He obviously thinks he's funny. I fake a laugh and roll my eyes. He narrows his eyes in response, either surprised or disgusted by my demeanour. I force myself to remember who I am standing before and what is at stake.

15

"You know it's common courtesy to bow in the presence of your future emperor ... Miss?"

His arrogance is infuriating. He probes for a name and I can't control my tongue.

"Electa Steel. I apologise, Prince, I didn't recognise you without all the make-up." I pronounce my words more than I ever have in a natural response to his pomposity.

The prince's complexion burns fiery red. I can almost feel the heat radiating from his skin and the sweat beginning to form on his brow. I doubt anyone has ever had the gall to question him, let alone treat him with such disdain. I hate bullies, and I fear he is the worst kind. His gaze ensnares me. I wait for him to haul me off before an Institute official for such a display of petulance, but now the prince surprises me again, and he smiles. He grips my wrist with a sharp tug, then softens his movements as he places a delicate kiss on the back of my hand.

"Pleasure to meet you, Electa Steel." He fakes charm, refusing to rise to my insult. I should know by now there are some fights I will never win. "You have some nerve addressing your prince in such a manner. That nerve must have landed you in quite a bit of trouble. I suppose that's why you've somehow managed to get yourself here, in the most restricted part of the Institute building. It's impressive, I must say."

Each word he utters is sugar-coated, too sweet to be real and too loaded to be trusted. His voice is stained by a distinct accent, a more refined language that only serves to bolster his pretension.

I respond by matching his masked ferocity. "It took days of planning, but I'm pretty good at breaking into places I don't belong. It's a skill of mine."

"Not the only skill, I'm sure." His mouth twists in an almost sadistic expression. It's strange how harsh his features are, but his eyes are the exception. The pools of molten brown are soft and endearing, the kind of eyes that could lure you into their darkness and their depth and before long there is no escape.

"I wonder how you were planning on getting out alive. I'm sure a smart girl like you is aware that the penalty for breaking and entering is severe."

I fire back. "I haven't got much to lose. I am a Pleb and today is the Choosing, and unlike your sort our chances of survival aren't particularly high."

He glances down at the floor for a second or two and his smile fades leaving a severe expression, perhaps even an apologetic one. He pities me. He must be thinking, *Poor little Pleb, you will be dead soon enough.* Just as quickly as the smirk waned from his face, it returns – and so does his attitude.

"Today's your lucky day, Electa Steel. I'll help you get out of here without getting caught but there's a catch."

"Why would you help me, Prince? I have the distinct impression you don't like me much."

His lip quirks and forms a half-smile, his eyes softening once again. "My dear Electa, you are mistaken. You intrigue me. Most girls bow down and kiss my feet, and I think it would be fair to say you have done the opposite."

"I'm not most girls," I quip.

"I can see that."

I tilt my head to the side as I contemplate his offer. I managed to get myself into the Institute unnoticed. Surely it wouldn't be impossible to do the same on my way out. But it would be more sensible to take Asher Ovicula's offer, no matter what it entails.

"So, what is this catch then?"

He answers almost immediately. "I'll let you know when I see you again, how does that sound?" His casual tone almost endears me to him, as if we are childhood friends reuniting at last. His charms are impressive, but I can't be fooled. Asher Ovicula has an agenda, I am sure of it.

My fate is no longer in my control.

"You won't be seeing me again, or have you forgotten what day it is," I remind him.

He chuckles, his chocolate waves bouncing gently on his head in sync with the slight movements of his expression. "Today is the day I will meet five girls, one of which is going to be my future wife."

Imperial Panore. The biggest event in a generation. Panore is the grand festival of Latia, which follows the annual Choosing ceremony. It is a celebration of talent and the opportunities of life that recognise the privilege of being Chosen. This year, the prince happens to be turning twenty-one and Panore has a whole new purpose – to find him a wife and empress.

"I highly doubt you'll be seeing me again, Prince." I won't be fooled into believing there is the slightest chance I might still survive.

Asher moves closer to me, so close that I can feel the warmth of his breath on my skin. "I suppose you will just have to trust me that we will meet again, and sooner than you think."

Asher ushers me along the corridor, directing me to a side entrance that he conveniently knows the code for. He instructs me to continue down the passageway, make two lefts and then I will be outside and will have avoided any Institute patrols. I mutter a forced thanks for his help. He turns on his heels and walks in the direction we came from with confident strides. He looks back with a motion so quick that I think I must imagine it. He flicks his head up, still smirking.

17

Out of the corner of my eye, I spot a man I can't help but feel I know. He is watching me. My curiosity sparks, and I stop in my tracks. We make brief eye contact, before he turns and walks away.

"Excuse me," I shout after him.

No reply.

"Stop!" I say louder this time.

And he does.

"Who are you?"

His eyes fall upon me, and his cool blue gaze pierces every inch of my skin.

"Aren't you supposed to be somewhere?" he says, indifferently.

"Why have you been following me?"

"Electa, if I was you, I'd not be late."

Before I can get out another word, he is gone. *He knew my name.*

I am in a half-mind to turn back and follow that strange man, but with half an hour until the Choosing I have no choice but to make my way to the Theatrum Victoria. The walk is short, but my pace slackens with every step. I allow myself to be swept away by the current of children all marching towards their fate. Yet I don't want to face what is behind those towering marbled walls.

The Via Sacra takes the crowds right up to the Theatrum Victoria, which is nestled beside the legendary Circus Maximus that makes the amphitheatre appear small in comparison. Every street in the city centre of Ore is paved in dazzling white marble and lined by cypress trees on each side. The Institute believes in perfection and that is reflected in every part of the Haven but especially in the cities. I look down, expecting the pavement to be stained by the dirt of thousands of shoes that have trudged down the street this day alone. But the marble is glinting with the high-noon sun and, as you inhale, there is the slightest smell of sterility as if the streets had been washed only minutes ago.

The city shuttle weaves and glides its way through the skies above the forum, carting hundreds more candidates to the Victoria. In spite of the heat, the air doesn't shimmer with humidity as it did at home. The dehydrators protruding on the rooftops take care of that.

Dainty Patrician ladies stroll about the streets with pastel parasols and glittering fans studded with jewels. They are the proud mothers of the Chosen. My father and brother, along with most Plebeian families, will watch their children from the comfort of their modest abodes on the live broadcast. Sometimes I envy the lives of the Patricians, their freedom. These ladies, parading themselves as a peacock would, have little care in the world. They survived their Choosing and will live long happy lives. I hope Lana and Vel will get that chance.

There are large signs marking the registration desk in the distance. I edge my way closer but pause for a minute or so, looking up at the sight before me.

Palatine Hill dominates the horizon, the backdrop of the largest amphitheatre in the five Havens. The palace glows white as it is illuminated by the fiery sun that has now reached the highest vault of the heavens. Mist shrouds the hill and makes the palace seem transcendent as it crowns the white mountain. I squint from the brightness, closing my eyes, the darkness dancing with light spots.

I join the orderly queue of candidates at the back entrance of the theatre. The ironclad gates peep open so there is no disruption to the single file of seventeen-year-olds who nervously chatter or stare at their feet as they are herded off into groups of fifty or so and then escorted into the building. The identification process is thorough, ensuring that every candidate in Ore is present today. There has never been an incident of a no-show. It would be futile. Even if you ran, they'd find you – there is only so far you can run in the domed Havens.

After I leave the registration box, I turn back and catch a glimpse of the official's monitor. On it is my identity card, but something is different. The usual green border has been replaced with black. My heart sinks into my chest; the sensation is slow and excruciating. As suspected, I am blacklisted. They know who I am. They know I am a Grey.

I thought I was so careful. I am already doomed today. I came to terms with this on Assay Day months ago, but if I am blacklisted, there is a great possibility that Lana has been too. Not only have I destroyed my own life, I have destroyed hers. Blacklisted means you are out, Unchosen by default, no questions asked. They could have already taken Lana. She could even be dead.

I follow the signage leading me to my delegated group, Gamma. I push through the throngs of bodies that stick together in the sweltering air. I find myself wedged in the corner of the crowd, the only space remaining in the segment. The boy standing beside me extends a hand.

"Warren Shademoore," he says. His voice is burly, more that of a man than a boy.

I look him up and down and my eyes widen a little at his appearance. He looks about twenty-five, not seventeen. He towers above me, the top of my head barely reaching his shoulder.

"Electa," I say, surprised that his grip is gentle for someone of his size. The uniform barely fits him; no adolescent is that muscular. It looks as if his pants could rip at any second.

There is an air of familiarity about him. His smile, the blue eyes and pale skin. He must not be from around here, with a name like Shademoore. He must be an immigrant from another League, perhaps Volscia or even Umbria.

"How are you feeling?" Warren grins and exudes warmth, making me at ease for a small moment.

"Not quite feeling myself today," I admit. I suppose no one is. Well … except the Patricians.

"I can understand that." He smiles.

As we are led individually into the theatre, I take a deep and calming breath in the hope of masking my shaking hands. I refuse to be one of the whimpering children who wail and sob like a puppy taken from its mother. Those type of kids would never survive in Latia where the people pride themselves on being ambitious, steadfast, ruthless and cold. There is no place for those who cry in Latia.

Thousands of feet of marble tower above us, the seats etched into the stone. The half-theatre is filling up and by the time we reach our seats there is not a single seat unoccupied. I wipe the sweat from my brow with the sleeve of my golden dress, the material scraping against my forehead harshly. I wish the last outfit I will ever wear could be at least a little comfortable. The fabric rubs my skin, leaving me itchy and irritable. I take another breath. I will not be shaken.

Gold, the national colour, is everywhere in the theatre today. The roses along the marbled walkway are swathed in aureate paint. The flag of Latia adorns the entire back wall of the edifice. Its emblem is the Golden Sun, with a winding green snake inside, a representation of the eternal life and the almighty power, our Haven.

The midday heat blazes down upon us inside the unroofed theatre. Sunglasses are prohibited by the dress code and everyone squints at the brightness that reflects off the mirror-like broadcasting panels that seem to levitate above the central stage. The separate panels transition with each frame, forming a larger full-screen image displaying the Institute emblem and the words, *Achieving Perfection*, beneath it. A recognisable anthem begins to play over the images that follow on the screen. The same tune drones at the end of every broadcast and commercial break. It gets tedious. I suppose this will be the last time I have to hear it, but I almost wish it could last forever.

"Since the formation of the Institute…" speaks a woman's voice over the changing pictures of the screen around us.

These pictures show our civilisation, traditions and culture. From the festivities of Panore to Snow Day. Civilians working in the city; bankers, pilots, senators, lawyers – they happen to leave out the soldiers, of course. And also images of what the Institute considers to be menial tasks, such as farming, production goods in factories, maintenance, cleaning; these are all executed by the Plebeians who survive the Choosing. The images of farmers with baked skin and crippled backs from the toil of labouring. The caretakers whose hands are worn away by chemicals of the stringent cleaning products, and the production-line workers with soulless eyes and minds dulled by mundane work.

"…our world has never been more perfect," the woman continues. "We live in peace. There is no hunger, natural disasters, crime or unfortunate accidents. People live in equality, in unison. There is no poverty, nor suffering, nor murder. We owe our perfect world to the Institute and our Choosing. The Choosing allows us to control our population and our society to ensure our Havens remain in their perfect state."

Most of what the woman says is true. There is no famine, or car accidents or murders. We are all given a house, our fair share of food, a job and a decent salary. Everything is in balance. But the Grey think differently, corruption runs deep, especially with the war and the Choosing — you might as well call it murder. Equality is virtually non-existent. Our lives are an endless cycle; a cycle you can't escape. The advertisement ends in the same way it began, with the Institute emblem and its slogan, then black.

Warren chuckles under his breath so that only I can hear. I give him a look.

"Ironic, isn't it?" he says, his voice almost a whisper.

"What?"

"No murder."

I haven't known Warren for long, but he seems like someone I can relate to. My mouth curls, but my smile is not one of humour or agreement, it is sad. Maybe the Institute is telling the truth. There is no world outside ours. My heart wishes that weren't true. For my sake.

A man suited in emerald green strides onto the platform beneath the flag and the hovering screen. Lysander Drusus, the Institute director, the most famous and recognised man in all five Havens. He stands tall. But if it weren't for his enlarged image on the screen before me, he would seem the size of an ant that I would be eager to stamp on.

"Please stand for Institute director, Lysander Drusus," a faceless commentator instructs us.

Trumpets blare from either side of the walkway as he takes his place centre-stage. His serpentine eyes flicker around, scanning the crowd. Lysander is Latia's playboy, the richest man in the League and the cruellest. He has few friends and hundreds of enemies, but no one would dare cross a man with power like that. They say the emperor rules the League, but in reality, it is him, Director Drusus, who rules the emperor.

"Welcome." His honeyed voice resonates from the speakers beneath every seat. "Candidates. Ladies and Gentlemen. Today, many of you will be welcomed into our prestigious society. Only the elite, those who will offer their talent and prestige to the Republic of Ore, will be Chosen."

21

He sounds so cold. His lack of any acknowledgement for the lives taken on this day is apparent. He is a Latian through and through, void of emotion and adopting a charisma that makes you believe every falsehood he utters.

Lysander turns and bows. "Now please stand while we honour our mighty emperor, Romulus Titus Ovicula, his heir, prince of Ore, Asher Romulus Ovicula, and the princess Shauna Diana Ovicula."

The Institute director's voice is drowned out by the orchestra of instruments that ushers in the Imperial family. All three Imperials are carried on their own litters. All wear gold, and with tradition each wears a red token. The emperor is adorned by a red crown, the princess with a red rose and Asher with a red headband that pins back his lengthy curls. Bold statements.

The prince has changed his clothing since I saw him just an hour ago. He is dressed in gold robes; he looks less boyish than the prince in black clothing I met in the back corridors of the Institute building. I am certain he wasn't supposed to be there, much like me in that sense, yet he was surprised to be caught and I was not. No one would dare to question the prince, yet I, of course, managed to walk straight into him.

The Imperials take their seats on an elevated dais behind the director. They are shielded from the high noon sun by ruby red tarp, which is draped over four ornate colonnades on each corner of the dais. Asher is sullen, sitting slumped on his little throne as if he were wishing to be anywhere else. The princess, Shauna, is upright, poised, almost uncomfortable looking, and I am still yet to see her blink. She looks more like a statue than a girl.

Director Drusus continues with his address, his voice commanding attention. "This year marks a once-in-a-generation event – Imperial Panore." The director has a crooked smile on his thin lips. He stands like an emperor. Shoulders back, spine straight. He elongates his neck with every inhalation, giving him an undeniable presence, even among the Imperials on the stage. Strangely, he wears no token. Instead, he dons his trademark gold serpent brooch that is always fastened to his left collar.

He continues, "The top five preforming female candidates on Assay Day, some four months ago now, will not only be Chosen but will also have the chance to become the next empress of Ore."

At this hardly unexpected announcement, the girls in the theatre jostle in their seats at the excitement. I sit still, more focused on the floor than this pageantry, a clear demonstration of Patrician power. There has never been a Pleb in the top five, male or female, and there never will be. The system is rigged. The Patricians get the best schools, training and nutrition because they can afford the luxuries on offer. The Plebeians are offered the basics from the state, which is hardly second-rate but does make all that difference at the Choosing.

"The five girls will compete against one another to marry our beloved prince, Asher Romulus Ovicula, who shall succeed his father to the throne later this year," the director elaborates. He speaks as if his words were lyrics in a song.

The Patrician girls in all their shades of colour giggle and gush. I wonder how anyone would want to marry that pig. Warren laughs along with me, imitating their high-pitched drawl.

Lysander Drusus takes a step back behind the lectern, ushering Prince Asher to the centre-stage. The audience erupts into the din of applause and cheers of his swooning female admirers. Asher takes his place in the limelight that he so obviously craves.

"Welcome candidates." The prince smirks. "It has been thirty years since our last empress was Chosen, my mother, may she rest in peace."

I knew the empress had died but no one knows how. Rumours circulated for a few years; some suggesting suicide, others believing she had been afflicted with some rare and incurable disease.

Asher opens a sealed envelope and a small smile forms, creasing his nose. "The first candidate is…"

He leaves the audience waiting in anticipation, every girl sitting a little forward in their seats, eyes glued to the proceedings. I slouch in my chair and even let out a small yawn of boredom. The prince suddenly looks up, scanning the audience for the face belonging to the name.

Asher rolls his tongue over his bottom lip. "Electa Steel."

III

ALEA IACTA EST

The die is cast

A ir catches in my throat, but with all the cameras on me I don't dare splutter. I cover my mouth with my hand to muffle the sound that escapes me.
Thoughts rush to my head all at once, and others follow in quick succession. *I
must be dreaming. This can't be real.* Time stops for a moment as my eyes are daz-
zled by the spotlight and my ears drum with the hollers of the mob. I bite down
hard on my lip, bringing myself back to reality.

"That's impossible…" I mutter under my breath.

Warren grips my arm, shaking me in the process. He, unlike me, is not at all
fazed by what is happening around us.

"Electa, it's you. You've been Chosen," he whispers. He urges me to stand.

An official stands over me for a second or two, expecting me to follow him to
the stage. But I can't move. Before I know it, the official hauls me from my seat.
Eyes follow me as I walk, and then the audience falls into an unsettling silence
when the camera catches an angle, revealing my white ribbon. The displeasure
of the female candidates becomes apparent as they grumble under their breaths.
"But she's a Pleb," I hear more than once.

Strangely, I feel no anger towards the Patricians who glare at me like a circus
animal on parade, but rather agreement. I am not only a Plebeian, but I didn't
complete the Assay Day testing. There must be a mistake. When they realise,
I will be sent packing to the outside world where my life will be conquered by
the cruel fates that are only mentioned in the legends of old. But I put my fear
aside for now.

I am positioned in front of the prince by the official who compels me to
bow. This is no time for another argument with the prince, so I abide and lower
my head. Asher grins, and I realise that he expected this all along. He was so
insistent we would meet again. He must have seen my name on a list before the

ceremony. Asher grabs my hand a little too violently, as if to warn me that I am being watched by millions of people in Latia, on live broadcast.

He presses his lips to my hand for show. He must maintain the façade of the dashing, charming and handsome prince of Ore. My immediate reaction is to recoil but I stop myself. If I want to survive, I have to play the game for as long as I can. The prince then moves his mouth to my ear, the gesture bordering on inappropriate. My body turns to stone.

"I told you we would be seeing each other soon. Congratulations," he hisses.

The official pushes the small of my back, ushering me to the side of the stage. I keep my eyes on the ground, so I don't meet a thousand stares. Asher continues to read out names, standing so tall that he might as well be a god. In the people's minds, that is just what he is, what all the Imperials are. They may be mortal – they breathe, live and die just as any human would – yet they are idolised, prayed to and for, control armies and lives.

A female official stands to my left and at a whisper explains what will happen next. "Once the other five girls have been Chosen, you will be escorted to the Palatine immediately."

The Palatine, with its floors of marble and walls of alabaster stone. I will go there and live among the Imperials and Senators. The Palatine is no place for a Pleb. They will think I am a fraud, or probably already do.

I am joined by another girl on stage, who takes her place beside me. Trinity Messalla from the family of Valerii, the bigwigs of media and publishing in Latia. Her violet fascinator is the first thing that catches my eye. It veils her face and draws attention to the artificial blonde locks that reach her waist. She throws me a disapproving glare and swats her ponytail to the side as if I am a fly and she a horse.

The third girl is Valentina Sylla, another Patrician of the Cornellii family. The red-haired girl joins us on stage, expressionless. She seems tolerable, at least. The fourth is promptly called up. Aria Glycias of the Claudii. Unlike the others, her token is far less conspicuous. A small sapphire rests against her neck, and as she smiles demurely I realise just who she is. The Glycias family produced the last winner of Imperial Panore and, clearly, they hope to again. Her family beam down at her from the private boxes above, with their distinctive thin white hair and bright blue eyes.

I can't make out the name of the fifth and final girl called to the stage over the noise of the crowd. Her name promptly appears on screen – Ember Hadrianus. She is from the family of Fabii, the family of the Imperials, and the noble house with the most superior and preserved heritage of them all. You can tell she is the immediate favourite; even the emperor applauds her as she approaches the stage. She is certainly striking, with wintry blue eyes and lengthy black hair. She has a smirk not so dissimilar to the prince's. Her nose, daubed by dark freckles, crinkles when she gets a close look of me.

I am no competition for these girls. I am plain, with no make-up or jewels or fancy tokens. I have no talent. I can haggle, brawl and steal but that is about it. I am better suited to a life in the army than a life in the Palatine.

Along with the other four girls, I am hurried away into a limousine from the back of the theatre. I find myself wedged between Valentina and Trinity, both angling their bodies away from me as if I were some disease. The electromagnetic wheels pulse beneath us, resounding with gentle rhythmic beats. The noise is a welcome distraction from the silence of the girls who barely talk to each other, let alone to me. They nearly all smile, except for Valentina who seems to wear a constant frown. They must be excited; maybe I would be too if I was supposed to be here. We are going to the Palatine, after all, yet I want no part in this competition, being Chosen would have been enough for me. I wonder what Vel and Father must be thinking; they must have seen me on the broadcast.

"Electa? Was it?" Ember's voice grates on me and, despite her feminine features, she sounds almost boyish.

I meet her stare directly. "Yes, Electa."

She grins so wide that it can only be fake. I think it must hurt to smile so much. Her voice, just like her smile, is sickening in its charade. "What an unusual name. You must not be from the city," she says, twisting the ruby ring on her finger.

"No, I'm not." I respond with a blank expression, which I quickly realise is a mistake. It is clear Ember was expecting more respect from a Plebeian, but if I don't bow for the prince of Latia then I certainly won't be bowing to her.

"Then where are you from?" Her smile fades, her eyes narrow and her lips pursed. This is all an attempt to provoke me, prod me, maybe even scare me.

I maintain my composure; expressionless, as I say, "Hedera."

"Never heard of it."

"It's a beautiful place." I turn away from her, as I have no patience for idle chit chat.

Ember huffs, angered by my refusal to engage with her little games.

"What in Dominus happened to Plebs showing a little respect to their superiors?"

I take a long steadying breath to calm myself. I bite so hard on the inside of my cheek that I draw blood. The tang of metal on my tongue is enough to remind me of the consequences of fighting with a girl like Ember, who has trained for years in the gladiatorial arts.

Valentina chimes in. "Don't get your hopes up, Electa. People like you never have and never will win Imperial Panore. Honestly, I'm surprised they let you compete."

I restrain my temper. My nostrils flare and my muscles clench, but I don't rise to them.

"Well, my prospects can't be that bad if I was in the top five. Can they?" I say, my cheeks flushing red with ire.

The girls fall silent for the rest of the journey. Aria at least makes an effort to smile at me, in a half-reassurance that not all of them are the monsters they seem.

The Palatine is said to have been constructed and designed by an illustrious architect from some far-off land. Legend says he was executed after the completion of the palace to prevent reproduction of his work. I can see it now in all its splendour; the towering marble, the columns that seem to touch the skies and the green vines sprouting yellow buds creeping across the exterior. The view is of the city itself and of settlements dotted about in the distance among vast swathes of forestry and olive groves. They call the olive oil from the region encircling Ore "Liquid Gold" and say it is a blessing from the gods. The quality and colour are famed across all five Havens.

The entire south side of the hill is built up with levellings of marbled terraces and pillars. Glassy structures interweave amongst the verdant gardens and villas. Shrubs and trees shaped and trimmed to perfection sprout from the earth, and the scent of incense wafts in the light breezes. I step out into the court cobbled with white stone. A doorman greets us and bows his head. The welcome is customary to these girls but not to me. The awe of the place strikes me with every glance. Even the smell is how I imagine the aroma of Rome, the home of Dominus and the gods, would be.

The lady official who escorted us here ushers us through the courtyard around the fountain and through arched mahogany doors. The atrium is just as imposing as the exterior. Our footsteps echo on the marble floors. The sound bounces off the vaulted ceiling, filling the room. Colonnades, supporting the many floors above, line the walkway as we make our way to the far end of the hall. I am starting to understand why the prince behaves as he does. If I lived in a place such as this, maybe I would look down on everything else and consider it mediocre in comparison. The Palatine is a place fit for gods.

Aria is so light on her feet that she almost skips along the floor, and her voice is just as light, like a mother singing a lullaby to her newborn child. "How lucky are we?"

Lucky. No. If being Unchosen wasn't my punishment, this will be. Trinity and Valentina nod in agreement with the white-haired girl. Ember walks backwards to face us.

"My family visit all the time."

Not only is she trying to intimidate me but the other girls too. She is in the prince's and emperor's favours, I am sure. I wonder if she and Asher are friends, and if there is any point in the other four of us even competing. It seems to me like this marriage is a done deal. All the girls here are from the most prestigious of noble families but even amongst the Patricians there is hierarchy.

We are led to a reception room with soft white couches draped with grey linen and plush cushions. The stone cools the room, a relief from the torrid heat of the afternoon. The official instructs us to make ourselves comfortable while we wait for Mr Falto, the *Princeps Officius* of the emperor. I expect an aged man to meet us. The *Princeps Officius* is the highest office in the land and the right-hand man to the emperor himself.

Mr Falto is not at all what I had expected. He looks not a day over thirty-five and is scholarly in appearance. His large green eyes are accentuated by an oversized pair of black-rimmed glasses, and he blows a stray piece of his unkempt hair from his brow as he approaches. His lively red suit is almost nauseating in its vividness; he, too, must be a Fabian. The other girls rise as he enters. I follow suit so I don't look as out-of-place as I feel.

"Girls, please, sit." He brushes aside our courtesy and laughs as if we were silly to stand in the first place. "Now." He claps his palms together and steeples his fingers. "I apologise; I am terrible with names. Would you mind introducing yourselves?"

One by one, we relate our names in full to Mr Falto.

"My name is Cosimo. Mr Falto is too formal for my liking." He kneels on the carpet to address us.

It is a skill to make people feel so at ease. I believed Patricians to be conceited and often choleric of temperament but that is not so for Cosimo.

"Firstly," he begins, "congratulations on being Chosen." His wide smile suddenly fades. "However, I'm sure you know the Choosing was the least of your worries."

I feel a sudden lurch in my stomach. *What does he mean?* I almost fear that this is directed at me, a blacklisted girl who has mistakenly been Chosen.

Cosimo continues, his expression now passive. "You may or may not be aware of the process of choosing our future empress."

I certainly am not. The other girls, however, have trained for this their entire lives.

"Each of you will compete in a series of gladiatorial-style live battles."

I shuffle uncomfortably in my seat. This doesn't go unnoticed by Cosimo, who throws a disapproving stare in my direction.

I grew up watching gladiators fight in the arena. Gladiators are the celebrities of our age, considered the bravest of heroes, but to me the fights are more brutal than brave. More often than not, they end in injury and occasionally even death. Fame comes at a price for most gladiators.

"These battles will be similar to what you may see on your viewing screens at home or even live at the Dome," Cosimo elaborates. The girls nod. They know what they signed up for. I, on the other hand, look terrified. The Flavian Dome is iconic, the largest arena in our world, where the rich and famous gather in their masses. My father could never afford tickets.

"Only one of you will be victorious, however. The fights will not be the sole test of your eligibility. There will be a series of public voting rounds, which will determine your draw for the arena," he says, and then pauses for a moment to pour himself a glass of water from the jug on the coffee table. "If you want to be the empress, you will have to learn to sell yourselves to the people of Latia." Still Cosimo's tone doesn't falter. Every word is sugar-coated and far too friendly. He is talking about battles and gladiators, glory and gore. The things our shallow society value above all.

The other girls don't flinch. Valentina even manages a smile. They are confident, assured in their abilities. I am not. I can't fight. I note Trinity's lean fingers, sculptured from years of drawing a bowstring. Aria's arms are thicker than her svelte figure, primed for hurling an array of weapons. Valentina's cunning smile. Ember's brawn, height and pink scars against dark skin, fresh from sparring. They all know about this obscene competition and all it entails; they are all prepared. I am far from it. I am a mistake.

My thoughts come all at once. *I need to leave. I can't do this. I am not supposed to be here.* Lost in my own head, Cosimo's voice becomes a low and constant drone. He coughs to bring me back to attention. Valentina whispers to Ember and they laugh.

Cosimo speaks, louder this time. "In the first few weeks, you can expect a series of social events, interviews, parties and so on. You will be scrutinised by our public who will then cast their votes, which determine your lot and advantages in the fights."

"The impression you make on the senior figures of our society will be paramount. Their votes will hold the most bearing. The vote of one senator equates to one hundred Plebeian votes." Cosimo looks away from me as he says this.

Of course. Voting only exists to feign the utopian notion of democracy.

"You will all be assigned with a specific team of professionals dedicated to your welfare, training and styling throughout the next couple of weeks. They will make you aware of your schedule immediately. Each team will be led by your personal advisor; they will be here shortly to meet you. Are there any questions?"

Silence descends upon the stone room. The girls don't speak, and I know I shouldn't either.

"Is it compulsory that we compete?" I say this a lot more frankly than I had intended.

Cosimo peers over his glasses at me in either shock or disgust – I can't distinguish between the two. The simple question makes the eloquent man stutter and falter on his words.

"No. However, you will have to seek approval from the prince. With his consent, you may join the Unchosen outside the Haven."

Either way, I lose. My chances of survival here are higher, albeit not by much. *At least I will live longer,* I tell myself.

I ask my second question: "What happens to the losers?"

Even the others sit a little forward in their seats.

Cosimo has his response prepared. "Well, that very much depends on the fights. In the past, the loser has rarely come out alive. If neither competitor is dead after forty minutes, it will come down to scoring."

This is even more brutal than I had imagined. There is only one gladiatorial tournament with conditions such as these. No rules. Kill or be killed. "So, it's like the Skull League?"

"Yes, except you have the right to concede during a fight."

A small mercy. The room seems to get a little colder. A nervous ache tugs at every inch of my body. I shake a little too. Overwhelmed. Scared. Angry.

Five elder-looking men and women enter the room. Cosimo introduces us to our future advisors – Lucella, Roxon, Ivandus and Marion. Only four. Not enough for all the girls.

Cosimo stands and forces a wide grin. "I will also be an advisor this year and will be working with one of you lovely young ladies over the forthcoming weeks."

This seems a little unusual. The *Princeps Officius* undertaking such a role. I think nothing more of it but note Cosimo's charade of joviality. He doesn't want to be doing this.

"Your advisors will be allotted at six. In the meantime, you will be escorted to your chambers and an *Ornatrix* will be at hand ready to bathe and dress you in preparation for this evening." Cosimo bids us farewell for now, leaving us with expressionless guards as escorts.

The Palatine is larger than I had imagined it. Ten minutes of following a guard and still I am not yet at my room. I distract myself from the day's events with thoughts of my brother and father who must be joyous at my survival. Then I remember Lana, who is likely blacklisted and doomed, and I am sad again.

The guard speaks, to my surprise. He tells me that my room is in the west wing tower, third floor up, although the marble staircase seems to spiral to the heavens. The halls are lit dimly, as if by candlelight, and a shadowed figure nears.

"I can take her from here."

The guard bows and takes his leave. I am left with the prince, his voice now familiar to me. He has the kind of voice you would expect a general to have. Loud and unwavering.

"Looks like you're here to stay, Electa Steel." Even in the darkness I see him smirk, and it is insufferable.

My response is simple and direct. "Not for long."

If it were possible, I would be out of here quicker than he could count to ten. But of course, it is not. I am stuck here for now. Asher walks a few steps in front but then turns to face me.

"Why do you say that?" he asks, tilting his head, as if surprised by my response.

"Maybe because I don't want to be here."

If he is shocked by this, he doesn't show it. He lets out a small, choked laugh. "This is an opportunity every single girl in the League would give her life for."

The prince is not mistaken, even in his arrogance. "Firstly, I don't even know how I am here. I fainted on Assay Day. Secondly, I don't particularly want to be married to you."

It is obvious he is still not accustomed to my honesty. His eyes bulge and his mouth lulls open. "Well, you must be the only woman in Ore who doesn't."

I roll my eyes. "Then don't look too disappointed," I scoff.

The prince chuckles a little too loudly, more a roar than a laugh, and the longer it lasts the falser it seems. He is theatrical in his facial expressions, frowning, feigning a disappointed smile, and he even pushes out his bottom lip.

I let out a small laugh. It is the first time I have smiled all day.

By the time the prince has finished pulling the sort of faces a five-year-old would make, we are at my chambers. Asher opens the curved door with its marble panelling and drops a key in my palm.

"You knew this morning at the Institute that I would be Chosen. How?"

"What did you think I was doing at the Institute in the first place."

His response is cryptic, but I don't pry further. The prince smirks again.

"I think you want this more than you realise, Electa."

"What makes you say that?"

He pauses for a long moment before answering. "I know girls like you. You may not be interested in me, but I know you are interested in power."

I struggle to understand how he could have come to such a conclusion in the six hours we have known each other. I look down at my feet, lost for words, then back up at the prince, who stands a little too close to me now. I step back into the safety of my room.

"Your Highness, if you believe that, then you don't know me well at all."

My room is even grander than I had imagined. Hues of blue and white dominate, and there are long billowing curtains at every window. The room extends beyond the initial entrance hall, with velvet recliners and bespoke artwork on the walls to a double bedroom, walk-in wardrobe and the biggest bathroom I have ever seen. Marble coffee tables prop up bouquets of exotic flowers, and the stone floors are heated beneath me. There are no regenerators here, in this room or in the entire Palatine, I believe. The Institute laws seem not to apply at all.

I stroll out onto my balcony, which juts out of the hollow west-wing tower. Tens or maybe even hundreds of rooms encircle the courtyard all the way up to the tower's steeple, several flights up. I wonder if the other rooms are just like this, reserved for Palatine guests.

The dressing room and wardrobe are my favourites. I allow my hands to trail across the folded clothes in the glass drawers and the dresses hanging on the railings. There are even jewels in a locked cabinet and crowns of varying colour and metal. Every individual drawer of my armoire is brimming with folded clothing, all labelled accordingly from day to night and sleep wear.

There are gowns on one railing, the majority in white, my family colour. The fabrics are delicate and of better quality than anything I have ever worn. I change out of my Assay Day dress into something more comfortable from the loungewear drawer. I pick out some linen trousers and a plain shirt. As I undress, I notice markings on my torso again, the bruising from the fight and the Institute raid the other night. The bruises have grown darker in colour and throb, turning my skin hot to touch.

I soothe the dull pain with a damp, cool towel and climb into bed. The satin sheets envelope me, and already weary I drift into semi-consciousness. My head is swallowed by dizziness. Light spots illuminate the darkness of my vision, and the spinning follows. I experienced this feeling many months ago during the Assay Day testing, just before I fainted and experienced a strange dream. No, it was more like a vision than a dream. A vision that I still don't understand. This time I can see and there are no voices. There is no noise at all, and my senses are limited to patchy vision that fades in and out of darkness.

There are two male-shaped figures in a dull room, illuminated only by candlelight. There is one man seated, his face in shadows. The other glows in the light of the fire. His face is chiselled, defined by a close-trimmed beard. He is middle-aged, youthful in appearance, with ice blue eyes and woody hair that falls to his shoulders. A menacing coolness seems to glaze over his presence as he raises a gun at the man sitting opposite.

IV

NECESSE EST AUT IMITERIS AUT ODERIS

You must either imitate or loathe the world

I wake to the doorbell. My *Ornatrix* arrives with cases of make-up. First, she attempts to undress me, and assist me in washing myself. I decline as politely as I can. It is strange to me that Patricians are bathed by their servants. Instead, she runs me the bath and perfumes it to my satisfaction. She provides sponges, flannels and herbs for decoration. The girl, Lucia, is only small, even shorter than I am, with the limbs and weight of a pre-pubescent child. She doesn't talk without encouragement; she is servile, just how the Patricians like their slaves.

She paints me for an hour or so before she allows me to dress. I make no conversation, but my politeness seems to catch her by surprise. There is a small glimmer in her eyes when I thank her. Lucia makes me a little less Plebeian-plain. She is most likely a Plebeian herself. Most *Ornatrixes* are; those who aren't rich and famous with their own fashion lines and make-up studios.

The dress code for the banquet is family colours and I am to wear white. My gown is tight-fitting with a long train and embellished by a glittering hue over a pearl white. My neck too is decorated by the *Ornatrix*, with swirls of silver glitter and long pearl beads. I barely recognise myself when I catch a glimpse of my reflection in the mirror. I look… Patrician.

A guard has arrived to escort me to the banquet. Lucia informs me that guard escorts are a temporary measure until we familiarise ourselves with the Palatine. I realise that I have only experienced a quarter of it, with four other wings and nine more floors. The guard waits in the reception hall.

I am met by a face I saw only hours ago. Warren. The boy who sat with me during the Choosing. I had wondered earlier how he fared in the ceremony. Now he is here in the Palatine, wearing the same scarlet uniform all the guards wear. The enlisting process once you are Chosen is usually quick, a matter of days. But no one begins their vocation on Choosing Day, yet Warren is here at my door. My eyes glance over his uniform for a second time – symbolic Praetorian red.

Vocations like the Praetorian Guard are open only to the elite, the Patricians. Before I can say anything, he flings his arms around me. His smile is a comfort in this sea of strangers and puts me at ease just as it did a few hours ago. His friendliness is unexpected but to my own surprise I enjoy the human touch far more than I ever have. I feel alone. Lost. Scared. Warren is a familiar face, a face I can place from some time and place in the past, although I am still not sure where.

"How—" I begin.

He cuts me off. "I was Chosen … I was taken aside with a few other boys and girls by the Institute, and they immediately enlisted us into the Guard."

The excited rush of his voice takes me by surprise. If only I had been that happy to have been Chosen.

"But I thought you were a Plebeian," I say.

"No. I'm a Patrician."

"You never said."

"You never asked."

He is right I never asked because I didn't think to. He wore no extravagant, coloured token, and his demeanour wasn't tainted by that typical superiority that most Patricians exude.

I shake my head. "I'm sorry."

He frowns. "You don't have to be sorry. Being a Patrician isn't something I'm particularly proud of."

His humble approach is unexpected, considering what I have experienced of Patricians today. "A Patrician who doesn't want to be a Patrician." I laugh.

Warren looks down at the ground, avoiding my gaze. "I was always the disappointment of the family."

Me too, I nearly say. But I barely know Warren, so my personal matters don't concern him. I expect his smile to slip but he almost seems to laugh at himself.

"Your family name is unusual. Shademoore definitely isn't of Ore or Latia at all, for that matter?" I ask, curious to hear of other Havens. It is not every day you meet a foreigner in Ore. Most Plebeians never get the opportunity to travel to other Havens, but the Patricians frequent in select holiday destinations in Lutetia, Umbria and Volscia.

Warren hesitates. "My family migrated from another League." He avoids telling me which League. Before I can ask again, he changes the topic of conversation. "You look wonderful, Electa."

I have never been able to accept compliments, so I blush and shuffle from foot to foot. He ushers me out of my room and leads me to the banquet. He offers his arm, which I take to steady myself in these ridiculous shoes. We continue to chatter as we walk.

"It's a strange coincidence you were assigned to me," I say in an off-hand manner, but Warren's response is almost defensive, muddled.

"They assigned me, and then after that I said I knew who you were, and they changed my assignment."

He is hiding something from me. There is something suspicious about his behaviour. Or am I being paranoid? This day has put me a little on edge. I put the thought to the back of my mind.

"Can you do me a favour?" I realise that Warren may now be my best chance at finding out whether Lana has been blacklisted. If she has, I may need his help doing something about it. Warren agrees immediately, so I ask, "My friend, Lana Russo, I am concerned she may have been blacklisted. Can you check?"

"Shouldn't be a problem," he says.

I promised myself that I wouldn't leave this Haven without saving Lana. I thought I had lost my chance today. This accidental Choosing gives me borrowed time, and that borrowed time can at least be used for some good.

"How are you feeling?" Warren asks, noticing my silence. For the first time in my life I am afraid, and this terrifies me. He must notice it. My hands haven't stopped trembling since the ceremony hours ago.

"I don't understand. This must all be a mistake. I fainted on Assay Day, and even if I hadn't there is no chance I could ever be in the top five."

"The Institute doesn't make mistakes," he says. I know in usual circumstances he would be correct. This has to be a mistake, though. Or a cruel practical joke. Warren continues, "Haven't you thought that maybe you're here for a reason. That the fates have led you down this path?"

Fate is something I have always believed in. The myths of old taught me to believe in all sorts of things that I shouldn't. The stories, the wonder, the imagination, it all twists the minds of children and turns them into little fools. My father was the same. Some families are different, they believe in the sciences and technology of the new world but not mine.

We come to the staircase, pausing to let a hurrying official pass. Warren steadies me as I clamber downwards, clutching at the thin glass railing.

"I didn't want this. If the fates are leading me down this path, then it is unwillingly."

"Walking away won't be easy," Warren muses.

I stop my descent to face him. "So, then I should just stay and die in the fights?"

"That's not certain."

Warren's confidence in me is misplaced. "I can't compete with these girls. They've spent years training for this. I am just a Pleb. Those girls have grace, strength and intelligence."

"You have more brains and strength than you think."

I shake my head. "You barely know me, Warren."

And he can't contest that.

Warren and I gather just outside the north reception hall. The other girls are there too, dressed in coloured gowns just as extravagant as my own. Trinity wears violet, Aria is in blue, Valentina yellow and Ember blazing red. They cast their eyes over me as I approach. They all dismiss me and focus their attention on Warren. They put on forced smiles, and Ember even gives him a coy wave before turning her daggered gaze on me.

I never took much notice of Warren's appearance. I suppose he is handsome. Blond, blue eyed with pale skin and large muscles. As he is a member of the Praetorian Guard, girls will throw themselves at his feet. The Guard is an elite profession with a salary to match. Many Patricians' families seek to marry their daughters to a Prateorian. Warren will have the pick of the lot. He mostly takes no notice of the girls and continues talking to me, although I do notice him glance over at Trinity once or twice.

The Guards escort us one by one into the reception room where a large crowd greet us with gentle applause. The orchestra plays delicate tunes from the dais beyond the crowds but is silenced by the simplest gesture – a raised hand – from the emperor nonetheless, but the applause rings out louder than before. The prince stands at the front of the thick of bodies preened with expensive garments and elaborate jewels. He exchanges a kiss on the cheek with each of us. I am last in line and move swifter than the other girls when it comes to my turn. I can't bear to be close to him for longer than I have to, and I don't want to encourage his already imposing behaviour.

The emperor and princess stand behind him and we greet them next. We bow and are led aside. They don't appear any less stone-like in real life than they do on those billboards. The only thing that moves on the emperor's taciturn face is his plaited beard in a draught. Shauna is the half-sister of Asher and they don't look at all similar. Strangely, Asher doesn't even resemble his father, who has much darker and more bulbous features than his son.

We assemble around a crystal bowl. Inside it are five delicate snippets of paper. The advisors all gather around. I am sure they are all hoping they are allotted Ember and praying not to be left with me. I go last and, by process of elimination, I know exactly who my advisor will be before the official can even read out the name.

Cosimo strolls over to me and pats me on the back as if I am a pet. The other girls are jealous, as everyone wanted Cosimo, although they try their best not to show it. Cosimo leads me away. As we disperse into the crowds, I feel the stare of Ember Hadrianus on my back.

Cosimo's face tightens as we move closer to the edges of the hall, away from prying eyes. I brace myself for a lecture. But his first words leave me stumped. "It is obvious you don't want to be here, Electa, but you do have potential. With my help, I'm confident you can win."

I struggle to take this comment seriously and choke back my amusement, only for a laugh to escape through my nostrils. This aggravates Cosimo, who lets out a long huff. He is deluded if he thinks I can win, or he is simply the most optimistic person I have ever met.

"I don't want to win, I want to go home," I say, almost hoping that I sound rude.

Cosimo turns to face me. "That isn't an option, Electa." His voice is firmer than I have ever heard it. "You're very lucky to have me as your advisor. I want to win this, but I have to make good of a bad roll of the die."

He only cares for himself and his reputation. *Typical Patrician.* I was wrong to have thought otherwise.

"What is that supposed to mean?"

"Making a Pleb popular won't be easy." Cosimo almost spits out his words. His anger almost seems forced and doesn't suit the poised man standing before me.

"Don't expect working with one will be either," I say and walk away before he can stop me. Trapped among the throngs of bodies that now twirl in partnership, I shuffle to the edge of the dance floor. The gentle orchestra hums and the buzz of people talking drones in my ears.

I look for an exit to escape from, or even to find Warren to offer some comfort. No such luck. A hand tugs at the hem of my dress, almost revealing my undergarments. I turn to slap the face belonging to the hand, but I stop myself. It is the prince. I know better than to attack him here in public. He chuckles.

"You're a child," I tell him, shoving his hand away. He doesn't seem surprised.

"I can't disagree." The prince grins.

The other girls are in the background, fluttering about, talking to complete strangers with ease. Ember appears to be having a serious conversation with a businessman of some sort, whose attire is similar to those who trade and deal in the forum. Pinstripes, a fashionable cravat and a tailored suit. I would have no idea how to talk to these people even if I wanted to. For a moment, I find myself wishing I were them. I notice Cosimo among the faces, peering over and around the graceful couples. He is looking for me, to encourage me to socialise, and even worse, dance.

I try to slip away again before the prince can react. But Asher is too quick for me; he tugs on the crook of my elbow before I even make two steps. The prince now extends his hand, wanting me to dance.

"I'd rather not," I say brusquely. Usually I love to dance. But only how we do it at home with traditional folk music characteristic of the outer provinces. The basements brimming with underage kids drinking liquor and smoking pipes they have stolen from their fathers. The way the girls' dresses billow as they twirl, and the raucous laughter of foul-mouthed boys wishing they were men. The festival days where the streets themselves seem to come alive with dancing bodies. I miss those things. I miss home. These fanciful arrangements are not to my taste, and neither is dancing with the prince.

"Now ... don't make me force you," he says, and I notice that the entire room has their eyes on us. "You can't refuse a prince."

"I don't want to dance." I raise my voice to make myself clear, even in the knowledge that others may hear. I care little what they think of me, they will already think the worst. To them, I am a Pleb and that is all.

The prince grasps my arm again, pulling me so close that our bodies touch. He is stronger than me and struggling would be futile. "Don't make a fool of yourself, little Pleb."

The nickname stings no matter how many times I have heard it today. I don't have much of a choice but to allow him to dance with me. I give in and let him guide me. Then he is getting too close, and my entire body shudders.

"You're making this very hard for yourself, Electa. Tread carefully. If you don't play by the rules, the Institute will be forced to step in. I will see to that personally."

"I'll play the game by my own rules, Prince." I almost spit at him. His haughtiness is grating on me.

A disembodied voice sounds from behind me, "May I steal a dance, Your Highness?"

The voice is familiar, coarse and gruff. I am surprised that it belongs to such a young-looking face. The man places his hand on my shoulder.

"Only if you promise to give her back," the prince jokes, his smile cynical.

The stranger grips the prince's wrist in gratitude. "I can see why you're so fond of this one, Your Highness."

Asher finally releases his grip. It is a relief, but the stranger who quickly replaces him has an even tighter hold. I stare at the man before me in shock. I recognise him from my vision, with his ice blue eyes and a gun. He is the man I saw earlier today at the Institute. *He knew my name.* He must notice my alarmed expression yet doesn't react. His glacial eyes cut me to the core, leaving me stripped, bare and vulnerable before him. We sway with the music, but my body stiffens.

After several minutes, he speaks. "Crew Gracchus. Pleasure to meet you, Electa Steel." His tone is barely a whisper, and his smile is unsettling. His facial features twist with every syllable. Though he is tall, his slender figure is cut in a way that makes him appear gaunt, and there is a starving look in his eyes. He is familiar to me beyond the past twenty-four hours. I have seen this man before, although I am not quite sure where.

"I would try a little harder if I was you…" he hisses, as he brings his mouth up to my ear. The bristles of his neatly trimmed beard scrape against my cheek. As I try to recoil, his grip doesn't falter.

"Excuse m—"

He cuts me off. "The lives of your loved ones depend on it."

I stop swaying. My entire body goes still. I am sure I even stop breathing.

Before I can find my voice, the man slips a balled-up note into my hand. "Tell no one." And then he vanishes.

A thousand thoughts cross my mind. Curious, I unfold the note.

9.00 PM Meet me in the Palatine Archive room. My guards will come to your room. C

I fold the note up and tuck it into my dress. I edge my way out of the crowds to the corner of the room to steady myself against a wall. Sweat beads my forehead, and my trembling fingers fiddle with the stitching of my dress. Waves of nausea almost overwhelm me, but I can't faint here in front of everyone. My stomach hollows but I hold myself upright until I spot a free seat by the bar. Crew asked me to try harder. He is referring to the competition. There is something strange afoot, and I am intrigued and terrified all at once. This strange, menacing man has been following me today, perhaps even longer, and now I sense I am being watched at every moment.

I have to make sure my family is safe. I find Cosimo socialising with some elder Patrician ladies with oversized wigs and unnatural lips. The dresses they wear look uncomfortably tight and their wrinkled skin is loose at the edges of the straps.

"Oh, Mr Falto, your project has arrived," the fake blonde trills.

I roll my eyes not so subtly. Cosimo turns with a stern look on his face. He must be less than pleased that I disappeared earlier.

"When can I contact my family?" My words rush out without warning. This day has been so fantastical that I have often thought I was dreaming. My life seems amplified, as if nothing is real. My only hope is that my family and Lana are safe.

"You will be able to contact your family from tomorrow but not in person," he tells me.

"Why not?"

"It's the rules, Electa. No outside contact."

This place is more of a prison than a palace. I brush my hand against my forehead in frustration.

"What is wrong, Electa?" Cosimo tries his best to sound sympathetic, and I can't tell if it is genuine.

I fire back, "Don't act like you care." I am too candid for my own good.

Cosimo winces a little but my comment doesn't appear to rile him. "I do care, Electa, of course I do. I apologise about earlier, I was rude. We must always look to the positives in these situations and I simply did not. I'm sorry."

Patricians don't apologise to people like me. I am good at holding grudges and not at accepting apologies, especially ones I don't trust. Cosimo's eyes go a little dark, and a smile twitches on his lips. He is sad for me, and this time I know it is sincere. I still don't know what to make of this apology, though. Should I accept it and move on? We are worlds apart, and it is unlikely we will ever see eye to eye.

"I'll drop by your chambers in the morning to run through tactics and schedules."

Tactics. It is a competition, after all. I am not in the mood to argue further, so I simply nod back at him.

The emperor stands on a dais to make an announcement. He urges the audience to take their seats for the banquet, and everyone makes their way into the adjacent dining hall. There are six elongated tables and one smaller elevated table in front. There is a seating plan, and people wander about for several minutes at an unhurried pace to find their positions. The smaller table is reserved for the Imperials and the five Panore girls, including myself, and our advisors.

Lively chatter commences from all corners of the room. A number of white pillars encircle our table to illustrate its superiority. Delicacies from every region of Latia are placed before us. The suckling pig from Palus in the south. Seafood from Pelagius in the north. Game meats from the hunting region of Nemus. Figs and olives grown on Palatine Hill itself. Each dish is explained by our designated server, who is dressed in an embellished white toga and wears olive leaves in his hair.

Tradition is of the utmost importance during Imperial Panore, and the meals are no exception. We are served wine from large mixing bowls that are wheeled around on a serving trolley. The drink is much more refined than the home-brewed liquor and unpalatable Posca served in the local taverns that I am accustomed to. I sip slowly, knowing well the effects alcohol will have on my already lashing tongue.

I barely say a word as we eat. I can't remember ever having finer food. The mundane Institute meals are bland. This feast is far from that, and I expect this how they eat regularly. I savour every mouthful while the other girls socialise with the prince and his family, not eating a bite. My mind is elsewhere. I glance at the watch on Cosimo's wrist every two minutes, my apprehension getting the better of me.

The emperor, evidently aware of my lack of contribution, addresses me, "Electa. This must be very different to what you're used to." His voice has such a tenor that it rattles the china on the table.

I am almost embarrassed to speak. My accent is so unrefined and abrasive compared to their eloquent manner of speech. But I find my courage. "Yes. Very," I say.

Valentina wades her way into the conversation. "I absolutely love it here, Your Highness, and you are so generous to host us in your home." Her tone is mawkish. I am sure they must see through the spuriousness of it all.

The emperor caresses his beard. "Well, I'm sure you all do. Asher simply adored growing up here. And Ember, my dear, you may as well have grown up here yourself."

Ember relishes in the attention. It is clear who the emperor's favourite is. I doubt there is any point in the rest of us even competing. Ember and Asher must have been close growing up, yet they seem so distant now – there is almost a tension when they look each other's way. Asher even appears irritated by his father's comment, and he is quiet for the first time this entire evening and plays with his food.

The princess, Shauna, also appears riled by her father's comment. Her eyes meet Ember's in a sharp glare, her soulless black eyes colder than ever. There is a complex dynamic existing between the two Imperial children and Ember Hadrianus, for what reason I can't yet ascertain.

An endless plethora of dishes keep arriving at our table, wine is still being poured and there have been at least a dozen toasts in honour of the Imperials and the Panore girls. The meal goes by slowly and the idle chit chat doesn't simmer down. It is eight-forty and time for me to get back to my room to meet Crew, but the evening shows no signs of letting up.

I whisper to Cosimo on my left, "I feel sick." A lie, and not a very convincing one.

Cosimo is discrete but a light chuckle escapes his mouth. "Too much to drink?" he scoffs.

"Perhaps." I smile to myself. If only he knew what my life was like back in Chrysos.

"You must request permission from the emperor. I will explain the circumstances later."

I ask the emperor if I can be dismissed, with all the courtesy I can muster. I even sound sweet, a first for me. I tell the table that I am feeling faint and wish to lie down. The emperor can only accept but his son immediately stands.

"Let me escort you to your room. It would be inappropriate for a lady to return unescorted at this time of night." Asher lifts his chin and pushes out his chest in an attempt to portray the gallant gentleman that he could never be. His chivalrous façade doesn't fool me especially after his behaviour earlier. But before I even have the chance to refuse, he has linked his arm with mine and is walking me out of the great vaulted hall. As soon as we are out of sight, I shake him off.

"So, you're feeling lightheaded now?" he mocks, obviously unconvinced by my charade.

I instinctively step away. "Yes, I had too much to drink."

He simply raises an eyebrow. "Why the hurry to leave?"

I start walking off down a corridor that I definitely don't recognise from earlier. The prince is at my heels, but I ignore his presence. "Look, Your Highness," I jeer at his title. "I can get back to my room by myself."

As I continue to navigate around the winding halls and passageways of the Palatine, the prince is at my side, not saying a word. After five minutes of hopeless meandering, I give in.

"Need my help now?" he teases.

"Just show me the way." I don't have time to get lost. I need to be back in my room by nine.

Asher escorts me through the maze of lavish rooms, magnificent hallways and flights of spiralling stairs. The shortcut means it only takes five minutes, when earlier it could have taken ten. We walk in silence, and it is comfortable for a change to have the prince by my side. I suppose he is not all that bad when he doesn't open his mouth. Yet that self-important smirk won't leave his perfect face. I know the quiet can't last much longer.

"So, Miss Steel," he begins, and I let out a long sigh in preparation for whatever comes next. "What is going on in that head of yours. I would say my best skill is reading people. You must be something special if I can't work you out."

I can't comprehend his curiosity. Perhaps it is because he has never met a real-life Plebeian before who wasn't his servant. I am fascinating to him; maybe it is the uncouthness, the accent or even my unrefined look. I am just some strange, foreign creature, and one of the few Plebeians he has ever made contact with. If I were him, I may too be intrigued. He will get bored of me soon, that is for certain.

"I can't understand why you are so interested in me."

"So now you're talking to me, huh?" He tilts his head and forms a lopsided grin. "I am determined to get a smile out of you by the end of the day."

I realise he has completely disregarded my question. "Why are you interested?" I persist, staring into his eyes searching for an answer. He gives nothing away, but I notice for the first time how similar our eyes are. I thought his were a deep chocolate before, but here in the torchlight they glow amber flecked with gold. They are soft eyes, which I didn't expect him to have. He has the same freckles on his nose that I do but his are darker.

We stand like this for a while. The direct eye contact is a little too personal, too invasive. Then he smiles, and for the first time it is not contrived, and I can't help but smile too. We both laugh out loud. I am not sure why I am laughing, but perhaps it is because I am not used to him being so serious in manner.

"You can't help but smile at my face, Miss Steel." He continues to chuckle as his typical demeanour returns, and I shake my head. "Here we are."

It's eight fifty-five, just in time. "Thanks." I force the word out. I can't stand his company for the most part, but he did get me back on time and more or less unscathed.

"Not at all, Miss Steel." As he bows his head, I don't imagine he has ever bowed to anyone before except his father. "I am trying to be a gentleman, in case you hadn't noticed."

I stare at him. "I hadn't but thanks for trying. Goodnight," I say with a small smile on my lips.

"Not going to invite me in for a drink?"

"I'm feeling sick, remember?"

I close the door behind me. I sit on the couch and fidget for a while, watching the large grandfather clock tick away the hour. *Tick. Tick. Tick.* The sound of time ebbing away into oblivion. I fear time. I always have. I have spent my whole life afraid of a seemingly impending doom. Years wasting away at a rate I was never prepared for. All to end up here. Tonight, I will get answers. This mysterious and strange day will be over. Whatever happens I will be glad for the certainty.

I have a bad feeling in my chest, though, something is not sitting right. The secrecy surrounding this meeting with a complete stranger who has been following me for however long is unnerving. I don't trust this man, Crew. I know nothing of him, who he is, what he wants, apart from the fact he made a veiled threat on my family.

My thoughts are interrupted by three knocks on the mahogany door. They sound urgent, in quick succession, so I quickly jump to my feet.

When I open the door, a man and woman greet me. They are both clad head to toe in the blazing red uniform of the Praetorian Guard. Am I being taken to the emperor? But then why all this secrecy? They instruct me to follow them and not to say a word. I abide, too nervous to talk anyway.

I am being led deep underground. With every step forward, my urge to run away as fast as I can grows. We go through clandestine passages and concealed trapdoors. They don't want us to be seen. I finally ask where they are taking me but am met with a lingering silence. We descend through darkly lit rooms with disconcerting gothic décor, rooms that don't appear to have been used for years. Each doorway we approach has layers of security – retina scans and passcodes. I am not being taken to the emperor.

Finally, it seems as if we are in an archive room. There is sparse lighting here, just from large monitors that emit a pale blue glow. Shelves are stacked high with ageing files and antique books. There is a stale odour of dust, paper and unpolished wood. It is unusual to see paper documentation, but I expect that this room hasn't been in use for some years. The floorboards creak beneath me as I walk. The guards knock just as they did at my door, three times, on a wooden panel between some bookshelves. To my surprise, the panel comes ajar with a creak. The female guard uses her tiny fingers to prise open the panel, revealing a dingy tunnel. A face emerges. Warren.

I stagger backwards. "Wh-what are you doing here?" I stammer.

"Keep your voice down, Electa." He hauls me straight into the tunnel and places his palm on the small of my back, urging me onwards. The tunnel is pitch black, and my eyes don't adjust. I am completely blind and at the mercy of Warren's guidance.

Before long, we reach a small opening into a square-shaped room. The lighting is dim with a single bulb dangling from the ceiling. The room itself is bare, resembling a prison vault, and both the floors and walls are plain, grey stone. A solitary figure huddles directly beneath the bulb in the centre of the room. As I near, all I can distinguish is a head of butterscotch hair matted with clumps of blood and dust. It is a boy. A boy I would recognise anywhere. Vel.

V

ET FACERE ET PATI FORTIA ROMANUM EST

Acting and suffering bravely is the attribute of a Roman

I lurch towards my brother. I crouch down, tilting up his chin so he can see me. His bright fervent eyes are dull, creasing with pain.

"Vel, what's going on? Are you okay?" I ask. My voice trembles and my whole body shudders as I caress his bloody face with my hands.

"I'm fine." His voice cracks although he is trying to sound brave. He was always the braver of the two of us. "Don't worry about me."

His slight frame is broken and bruised. His arm twists outwards in an unnatural position, and I realise how much pain he must be in. He is bound to a stake with ropes, immobilised and weak. The guards who escorted me drag me away from Vel, restraining me. I kick and scream but my struggle is futile. They grip me firmly as Crew emerges from the shadows of the vault, his blue collared tunic daubed with fresh blood.

"Glad you could make it, Electa." He snarls like a predator. I recoil as he nears me, as much as the guards will allow. "Don't be so afraid, my dear, you're about to become the next empress of Ore."

I stare him down, puzzled by his claim and laden with anger. Warren stands at his side with a similar smug expression. "What are you doing with my brother?" I almost scream the words at him.

Crew crouches down next to Vel and puts an arm around him as if they are friends. "Perhaps you recall our conversation earlier this evening, my dear."

"You didn't say much." Rage blunts my words. No one hurts my family.

"That frown really doesn't suit such a pretty girl." He seems thirsty for a reaction. If I could, I would tear out his throat. "Don't worry we won't hurt him. That is, if you do as we ask."

"I get the impression you're not asking."

Warren chimes in with, "I told you she was smart." I am yet to understand what part he has played in the deception but just seeing him here, standing proud in front of my tortured brother, repulses me.

"She certainly is." Crew sneers. They are both like hungry wolves, ready and waiting to devour me.

"What do you want?" I am tiring of their tactics. I am already afraid and willing to do whatever it takes to save my brother.

Crew steps up to me, inches from my face, breathing heavily. He smells of smoke and blood. "We," he gestures to Warren, "are part of an organisation known as Spartaca. We're from outside the Haven."

My heart leaps right into the pit of my stomach, my mind pulsing with questions. "That's impossible. The world outside is a radioactive wasteland."

Warren smirks and nods. "Or it's a land festering with disease. An uninhabitable desert. A war zone. It's whatever the Institute wants you to believe, isn't that right?"

I can't argue. I only know what the Institute has told us, what the rumours say, and the truth is that no one really knows anything but to fear the fate of the Unchosen.

As Crew continues to explain, I hang off his every word. "The Institute has been lying for years. The Unchosen mostly live, Electa, but the Institute makes them their slaves. This was commonplace for the first hundred years or so of the Havens' existence but now the population is becoming out of control and the Institute has begun to cull half of the Unchosen before they even get outside the gates."

I feel like my jaw has dropped. I can't move or think clearly. Crew doesn't give me time to register this information before telling me more.

"You have heard of this war. The mysterious war that no one understands much about. The United Leagues of Appia are at war with us. They are at war with Spartaca."

The war my father fights in, the war my brother would be shipped off to in just two years' time.

"Spartaca's aim is to liberate the Unchosen and the entire outside world from Institute oppression. We are the Institute's greatest enemy and we have been inside the Latian Senate and even the Palatine itself, planning a coup."

Warren takes over. "We need your help to accomplish this. We have chosen you, Electa."

For a moment, I question whether any of this is real. Could this be an Institute test? No, they surely wouldn't go to these lengths. I feel lifeless in the grasp of Crew's guards.

Crew puts his hand on my shoulder, and I instantly recoil. "We have been watching you for years. From Warren helping you get home after Assay Day, befriending you at the Choosing. Myself at the Institute this morning. We altered your result, Electa, so that you would be in the top five."

It all makes sense now. The familiarity I sensed when I met Warren at the Choosing. He was the boy who took me home from Assay Day some months ago. "Were you the reason I fainted?"

"Yes." Crew nods. "We knew you wouldn't perform well, and we had to fabricate your results. That was easier for us if your profile was blank."

I have no idea how they did that and I am not sure I want to ask. Perhaps Warren drugged me when I wasn't looking. It is best I don't know. I fall silent again.

"Electa." Crew's expression hardens and his jaw tightens, so I assume what he is about to say must be important. "We need you to win Imperial Panore. Marry the prince. As soon as he comes to power, you will kill him. Under Act Thirty-two of the Imperial Commission, you, an empress and his widow, will ascend to the throne."

I am speechless. A world outside, the Institute's lies, a conspiracy … and they want to use me. It is too much. My head spins in my confusion and waves of hot emotion tug at me. I glance at my brother, his torn clothes, his eyes welling with tears of pain. I can't refuse them, even if I wanted to. I have to save Vel.

Crew follows my gaze to my brother and then back to me. "I don't think I need to tell you what will happen if you refuse to comply."

I shake my head. I know what they will do, and I would rather not have a description.

"And if you even think about warning anyone, your brother will suffer a far more painful death than you could ever imagine."

I wince at the thought of my brother's death. It is something I could never allow. I swore I would always protect him, no matter the cost.

"Remember we are everywhere. There are many of us in Latia, people you may never expect, and rest assured you will be watched every moment of your time here."

Just how much power and influence does Spartaca have, I wonder. It has fooled the Institute once already. Crew has fooled everyone in Latian high society that he is somebody he is not. Then I realise, he has fooled me too. I have been seeing this man for years without realising it.

"It was you…" I stammer. "You, in the *Horreum* the other night, you shot that Institute official." It all finally makes sense.

"Warren saved your life the other night. If you had been caught by the Institute, our plan would be ruined."

Warren beams at me as if he were some type of hero. "Your friend Lana is blacklisted."

"But we can fix that," Crew says quickly. "That is, of course, if you do as we ask."

The only way I can save Lana and my brother is to agree to their terms. I only have myself to blame for Lana, this is a mess I got her into, and I promised to fix it. The only thing I am yet to understand is my role in all this. "Why me?" I say, faltering on every word. My voice wobbles but I try to keep a straight face. I don't want them to see me afraid.

Crew rakes over me with his eyes. "A Plebeian girl. A girl who doesn't have much to lose. A girl who would do anything to protect her family. You can relate to our cause. If it wasn't for us, you would be Unchosen, either dead or an Institute slave. Your government has lied to you for years about a war that they pretend doesn't exist. Most importantly, the people of Latia can relate to you, Electa. Your story will be like a fairytale, a legend."

I question their faith in me. I have no chance of winning. I am not a trained fighter, and that is really the most important part of this entire process. If I can't fight, I will lose, I will die. A dead girl can't become empress. "There is no way I can win. I'm sorry but you have the wrong girl."

"You will win. You have to if you want your brother to live, and if you want your friend to stay in the Haven." Crew's tone is insistent, cruel and calculated.

"I don't think you're understanding me. Your organisation is doing itself a disservice by choosing me. I can't fight. Those girls will eat me alive."

"Do you think it is a coincidence that Cosimo is your advisor and that he is even an advisor at all?" Crew raises his eyebrows. "If Cosimo's ego doesn't get you to win, then his advice will."

I hesitate. "Cosimo is a part of the conspiracy?"

Warren, still unable to look me in the eye, answers, "No. He has no knowledge of it."

I pause, considering my options. This could all be a ruse. Spartaca may not even exist. Crew may just be a politician looking to control the Latian state from the top. The entire explanation is so fantastical that it is hard to believe.

Vel screams out, "Don't do it, Electa!"

The guards release me and now kick my brother, who coughs up blood. I scream and flail myself at the guards. They quickly overpower me, throwing me to the ground. They tie a filthy rag around my brother's mouth, and he yelps out in pain. Crew yanks me up from the ground using just the sheer material of my dress. I expect it to tear, but it holds firm. With the scruff of the fabric in his fist, he pins me against a wall. His entire body weight presses against me and I can't move.

"I would keep that mouth shut if I were you. We will happily find you a gag, too." His spit is all over the side of my face. When I flinch, he smiles.

I compose myself, determined to stay strong, to not let him break me. "But you need me. If I refuse, you kill my brother, but your entire plan falls apart. You wouldn't risk it."

Crew's anger flares. "Oh, my dear, you wouldn't be so foolish." He squeezes my throat with his free hand, still holding me up with the other. He is stronger than he looks. I choke and splutter, gasping for air. My head tightens, and I feel all the blood drain from my face.

"Don't hurt her!" Warren tears Crew away from me.

Crew staggers backwards and looks shocked by Warren's disobedience. I expect him to retaliate but he stands still. He whispers to Warren now, but I can't hear the words they exchange. I can't understand this act they are playing out. Warren is merciful and Crew is cruel. Perhaps it is intentional.

Warren nears me now, checks over me, even straightening out my dress. I step away. I don't want or need his sympathy. He betrayed me, and any chance we had at friendship is gone.

"You may go. I assume you agree to our terms." Crew's voice sends shivers across my skin.

"I have a condition," I say, boldly. "If you want me to believe there is an outside world, you have to show it to me. Show me the world outside the Haven and then I'll do as you ask."

Crew contemplates for a few seconds. "Seems fair, Steel. Warren will take you tomorrow at twilight. You will return by morning. No one will know you're gone."

I wasn't expecting him to agree, or for it to happen so soon. But tomorrow night I will see the world I have always feared.

Warren escorts me from the vault. I am not even allowed to say goodbye to my brother. He leads me to my room in the same secretive manner by which I was brought here. There is not a person in sight. My heart rate remains at an elevated pace and I can't walk straight. Guilt claws at me like an uncaged beast as the unrelenting images of my brother gagged, beaten, and bruised strike me. They can do anything they want to him, and I am completely powerless. I already feel as though I have failed him. How can they expect *me* to kill a man? To kill the future emperor. That is, if I survive that long.

Warren and I walk in a harrowing silence. I swear he must feel the heat of ire rushing from my body, and I wish I could slap him. When we arrive at the room, he opens his mouth to speak but struggles to find the right words. I open the door and go inside but Warren follows me without permission.

"I don't know what to say, Electa, other than I'm so sorry." Warren's voice breaks as he speaks, and I can't tell whether it is for show or a display of genuine regret.

"I trusted you." I stare down at the ground, embarrassed by own idiocy. "You're just doing your job, I suppose…" My voice trails off and I turn my back to him.

He shouts after me. "No! It was supposed to be a job. Emotion isn't supposed to play any part. But it does. It does…"

"Emotion?" I almost laugh the word out of mouth. "No one with any emotion could stand by and watch an innocent fifteen-year-old boy be tortured."

"You don't understand. Crew would never allow it. Crew would never allow me to feel how I do. He would kill me too. I care about you, Electa, and despite what you may think I don't want you to get hurt." His tone sounds so desperate and wavering that I almost want to believe him.

"Warren, you barely know me," I remind him. He acts as if he has been a friend of mine for years.

He nears me. "This may sound strange, but I have gotten to know you after watching you for all these years. You want everyone to think you're tough, but underneath all that you're pure, innocent."

Those words make me ache. Any innocence I had was lost the moment I stepped foot in the Palatine. Warren's hands reach out to me, to touch me, comfort me, but I recoil and wonder if those were the hands that beat my brother. "How long have you been watching me?" I ask, my skin prickling with unease. It seems that I have been spied on for years.

"Me, four years or so now. Crew, longer. Yeah, this must be strange for you."

"That's an understatement." My voice descends to a whisper. "I'm guessing you aren't seventeen either or were really Chosen."

He can't look at me as his lies come to light. "I'm twenty-five and I've been in the Praetorian Guard for two years now."

I shake my head in disgust and walk away.

"Don't worry, I won't let them hurt your brother."

I won't take his word for it.

I don't sleep, as my mind wanders hopelessly over the events of the day. I drift in and out of dreams, not of my brother or of Warren but of Asher. His words play over and over in my mind. At three a.m. the last thing I see is Asher's ardent amber eyes morphing into Crew's. His voice transforms too, and it is Crew who now speaks to me. *We will be watching you…*

I wake to a cut-glass voice and know that I am no longer dreaming. "Miss Steel. Miss Steel. Miss Electa!" Cosimo stands over my bedside, screaming at me. "If you want to have any chance of winning, I strongly suggest you rise from your slumber. You can sleep when you're dead."

And if I don't listen to Cosimo, I will be dead soon enough. His words motivate me enough to quickly dress and splash my face with cool water from the faucet. Cosimo calls for my *Ornatrix*, Lucia. She does my make-up, despite my protestation that it is the daytime, while Cosimo cuts straight to the point.

"Now, Electa. Are we going to take this competition seriously or not?"

I remember my brother's blood-stained face so my answer comes easily. "I will do whatever it takes to win."

"Well, that's an unexpected change of attitude." The sentence stumbles out of his gaping mouth. I am not surprised he seems shocked. Last night I made it quite clear to him that I didn't want to compete at all. "Well, then we must get to work immediately. Today you don't have anything scheduled so I recommend you get your bearings with the Palatine. It will be your home for the next month. All our facilities are at your disposal. My recommendation would be the spa and the baths. I can organise a private session if you wish?"

I wonder if Cosimo is always this upbeat. It is beginning to irritate me. The last thing on my mind is using the spa. "I'm actually okay."

"Well, let me know if you change your mind." His brow furrows in response. "There are some rules I am obligated to recite. Firstly, you are not allowed beyond the Palatine gates without permission and supervision. You will be able to make a call to your family once every three days and that is all. You will not engage with the press and paparazzi without supervision. There will be no fornication with anyone on Palatine Hill."

The list continues for several minutes but I quickly lose interest and find myself staring at a wall.

"You will abide by the rules and any infringement of these conditions will be punishable by disqualification." Cosimo finally takes a breath. "As I said before, today you are free to do as you wish. However, since there is a grand ball and interviews taking place tomorrow night, I thought perhaps it would be best to spend this time in preparation for those events." Cosimo takes a clipboard out of his briefcase and starts fingering through the pages.

"Interviews?" Just the thought of such a thing frightens me.

"Yes, live interviews will be a chance for the voting public, Plebeians and Patricians both, to see you for the first time. If you want to win, you will have to appeal to the people of Latia."

I remember Cosimo discussing this yesterday when we first arrived. The first round is voting. The second round is the fights. I nod as he continues to explain the details.

"You, along with the others, will appear in a series of broadcasts, modelling campaigns and public events, all to vie for the favour of the mob and the elite. At the end of this two-week period, there will be a vote. The girl in first place will avoid a first-round fight altogether. The second place will choose their opponent for the first-round fight. The others gain no advantage. If you want to succeed you must get that early advantage by coming first or second in the voting round."

The explanation of the tournament makes my head spin. As he elaborates, I begin to think winning is even more of an impossibility. Cosimo continues, despite my fearful expression. "My job is to create a persona, a brand, an identity, a marque for you, Electa Steel. The other girls are already one step ahead in this regard. We will be working on this today."

What Cosimo is really trying to say is that I can't win by being myself. I squirm at the idea of playing a character, putting on a show. I have never been a good actress. "Surely the mob will vote for me. I am one of them, after all," I suggest, trying to wiggle my way out of the theatrics he has proposed.

"Yes, they may well, although it won't count for much. One vote from a member of Imperial family or Senate member is the equivalent of one-hundred Plebeian votes," he says, his tone manner-of-fact. This doesn't surprise me. The Patricians would never want people like me making the important decisions. I smile to myself and shake my head. "If someone like Director Drusus voted for you, it would go a long way towards securing a win."

Cosimo mentions Lysander Drusus, the young, attractive and slick Institute director. I remember seeing him at the Choosing. He is one of the most powerful men in the ULA.

"Someone like him would never vote for someone like me."

Cosimo clasps his hands together and gives me a knowing smile. "Now that's where you're wrong. I will teach you to charm them, Electa, to converse with them as if you have been a part of high society your entire life. It may take a few lessons, but you are a smart girl and will learn fast."

I remember how I felt last night at the banquet. Entirely out of place. I don't fit in here like the others do and I don't want to feel like that for the rest of my time here. I don't want to be the freak of Palatine Hill. The problem is I have no etiquette and I can hardly master diplomacy, let alone charm.

"I believe in you, Electa," Cosimo does his best to sound enthusiastic but I can see him form these words through gritted teeth.

"What about the fights? I will need training."

"That will commence in the third week of the first stage. I won't be much use to you in that department, but I know a few people who will," he says, and I realise now that Spartaca chose Cosimo for me because of his contacts. "Let's begin by thinking about your marque. I haven't known you for long so tell me a little about yourself."

I pause for a while to consider whether I have anything interesting to say. I don't. I simply recite my background. "Well, I grew up in the Chrysos Valley. I'm a Plebeian, obviously you knew that. I lived with my father and brother in a little villa in the countryside. My father was away fighting in the war for most of my life, so I looked after my brother."

Cosimo nods so much he must have a headache and stifles a yawn with his manicured hand. "Any interesting hobbies?"

"Um…" I bury my head in my hands. "I like reading, and I hunt sometimes." I definitely can't tell him about the Grey.

I see Cosimo cringe through his smile. "Right. Well, let me tell you about the other girls. Ember is strong, she exudes power and confidence. Aria is sweet, kind-hearted and good with animals. Valentina has an incredible mind, she is cunning, quick-witted. Trinity is athletic, a skilled fighter and charioteer, not to mention beautiful."

I sink back into my armchair, unable to look Cosimo in the eye.

"What about you, Electa? Who are you apart from a Pleb with a sharp tongue?"

I bite on my tongue, nearly drawing blood, to stop myself reacting to his insult. My eyes crease in frustration. He is trying to irk me, and I won't let him succeed. "Why don't you tell me since you seem to have so many opinions?" Anger edges into my tone but I strip it back. "Tell me what you want me to do and I'll do it. Tell me who you want me to be and I will be it."

Cosimo chuckles, his eyes brightening. "I think you could pull off the Nemesis story. The transformation from the poor Plebeian girl into an icon of class, sophistication and hope. Everyone loves an underdog, even Lysander Drusus."

"You want me to emulate Nemesis?"

Cosimo nods.

Nemesis was my childhood idol. I grew up wishing I could be like her. How hard can it to be to pretend? She came from nowhere and rose up from the blood-stained sand of the arena to become a goddess of Ore.

Cosimo stands and starts pacing around the room. He carries on like this for a while, lost in thought. "May I ask you a question?" he finally says.

"If I said no, you would still ask."

He chuckles, acknowledging my attempt at humour. "Why did you have such a sudden change in heart?"

Images flash through my mind. My brother bound by ropes. His proud head drooping over his withering frame. I wonder if they are even feeding him. He may have always been the braver one, but now it is my chance. "I don't really know. I suppose I'm doing it for my family. If I win maybe my brother won't have to go to war, and my father can come back. I could give them a better life," I explain. I am not lying to him, either. I am doing this for my family. To save them, when I couldn't save myself. I owe them that much.

"That's admirable," Cosimo says, and I detect his humanity, concealed by all that pomp and grandeur, for the first time. Perhaps he has family too. I suppose at the end of the day, we are all human, Patrician and Plebeian alike.

I sigh audibly. "Yes, I have to win, for them."

The prospect of losing my family is too much to bear. I always knew deep down that I would be Unchosen, and the one glimmer of faith in my life was that my family would still be there once I was gone. Now that hope could be torn away from me too. That is not the only thought that haunts me in my every waking moment. I think of the prince I will be forced to kill. A prince I don't care for, who I barely know but is human all the same. A life for a life. My brother for the prince. I will be playing god. It is not for me to choose who lives and who dies. That is for fate to decide. In just a few hours the roles have been reversed, the tables have turned. My fate is no longer dragging me. I am its master.

After much goading, Cosimo allows me two hours to explore the Palatine. I move freely through the halls of this imposing structure. I could use some time alone.

Instinctively, I head for the gardens and stroll down one of the porticos leading outside. I welcome the change in air, the tang of something other than incense and the warmth of the sun casting over me, my yellow dress now awash with an aureate glow. My heels drag on the gravel, the sound reminding me of the backstreets of home.

Moulded shrubs mark the footway but I stray from the path just for the sake of it. A singular act of defiance, if you could even call it that, in a world I don't belong. I pass fountains with cerulean water glinting with white light. I let my body feel the spray of moisture as I near, rubbing away my make-up in the process. Carved marble statues are elevated on podiums, embossed with gold lettering. The Imperials of old, even made of stone, share the haughty guise that their descendants so frequently project. I scurry down the banks abound with pastel lilies, passing the walled orchard and into the coppice below.

The landscape transmutes; it is rawer, the ground scabrous with rock. Olive trees erupt from the earth, their aged boughs fissured and bulking with wooden knots. I feel at home here. I take an olive from a low-hanging branch and throw it into the air, catching it in my mouth. I spit the stony pip onto the parched soil. There is lake in a clearing beyond, humming with life. I follow the strident chirping of crickets to the banks of the pond and the escarpment where rows of conifer trees sprout across the entire downwards-sloping incline of the hill.

I tumble onto the embankment, my head shrouded by the reeds. The shade is a welcome relief. Dragonflies cavort above me, and I reach out to them, letting them dance around my outstretched palms. I am alone, truly alone out here with only a breeze for company. I forget for moment why I am here, a mere mortal among gods. I forget about my brother, Spartaca, the prince and this Dominus-forsaken competition.

Until a voice startles me from behind. "It would be a shame to dirty such a beautiful dress." The accent is soft, softer than a Latian's would be. I must not be the only one here who craves isolation.

A sun-streaked silhouette hangs over me. I jerk upright. He has the type of face that could make any girl blush in an instant. Almost certainly foreign, his russet skin glows in the early-morning flare. His ash-blue eyes temper a natural pensive expression. The stranger unbuttons his vest and lays it down beside me on the bank, instructing me to take a seat.

"Apologies that I startled you," he says, squinting in the sunlight. He lowers himself down by my side. "Calix Lupus. Pleasure. Miss?"

He asks for a name that I labour to relate at first. Then I find my tongue. "Electa Steel," I say while Calix plants a delicate kiss on the back of my hand.

"I recognise you from somewhere," he says, examining me for a moment. "You're one of the Chosen, aren't you?"

I nod, studying his attire. His garments are far too formal for him to be a servant or guard. The sleeves of his plain linen shirt are rolled up to his elbows. The vest I now sit on is dyed with expensive Tyrian purple. "Are you a senator?"

"No." He bends his head to catch my eyes. "I'm from Umbria, actually. The prince of Echos, the capital Haven. I grew up here, though."

Another prince. A kinder one, it seems. I tip my head, practicing the obeisance that Cosimo had tried to instil upon me this morning. "Your Highness."

He hushes me. "No need for that, Miss Steel. Please call me Lix."

"Then please call me Electa," I say.

We exchange smiles, warm and sympathetic.

Lix twiddles with a chain in his hands. A small amulet is attached to it – a serpent, the symbol of Dominus. He must be religious. As he holds the silver snake within his palms, he closes his eyes, muttering indistinct prayers. Legend says that Dominus, disguised as a serpent, tricked the gods of old into relinquishing their kingdom to him. The totem of our chief god, our creator and guardian, has ever since been depicted as the divine serpent. That is, if you believe in any of that *bovis stercus*.

"I come here to pray sometimes. It's nice to have company." He beams, refastening the chain to his neck. I never thought the first person to be kind to me here would be a prince.

"May I ask why you grew up here in Latia?" I ask, as there are few Umbrians living in Latia. They are a race that keep to themselves, and few become a *Peregrinus* in a foreign Haven.

Lix shifts uncomfortably. His expression steels. "I'm in asylum. My father was killed by his own government and they wanted me, his heir, dead too. The alliance and enduring friendship between my late father and your emperor Romulus allowed me sanctuary."

You would never be able to tell he is an orphan. He carries himself well. Acting and suffering bravely is the attribute of a Roman. That is true of Lix. "How long have you lived here?"

"Since I was fifteen, some ten years now. I was brought up like a son by the emperor, as a brother to Ash and Shauna."

He looks younger than twenty-five, his wide, hopeful eyes reminiscent of innocence not yet lost. He could still be fifteen, if it weren't for his height. "Can you ever go back home?" I say, now realising I may be asking too many questions.

My father once told me it was not the place of a Plebeian to question a Patrician. Honour. Duty. Respect. Words he often liked to use. He has been the ULA's puppet for his entire life. But I won't be.

Lix doesn't seem to mind my interest. "Well, your League dispatched an entire legion tasked with overthrowing the despot regime several years ago now. They were unsuccessful. If I were to return, I would be executed immediately."

I clear my throat, trying to find the correct words for consolation. All I can think of is a simple, "I'm sorry." What else is there to say when such tragedy occurs?

"Don't be sorry. I'm very happy with my life here. The emperor is a good father figure, and Ash a good brother."

I can't help but scoff. "Asher is a good brother?" comes out before I can stop myself.

Lix mouths twitches into a shrewd smile. He stares up at the sky in thought. "There is another side to him, I promise," he finally says, though I can tell he is lying. "But I will apologise for my brother's behaviour. He isn't exactly tactful."

"Far from it." My tone edges from amusement to disdain. It is as if the prince was created solely for the purpose of tormenting me. I dare not relay my inner thoughts to Lix, though, as he evidently cares for his adoptive brother. As it approaches midday, the commencement of the *Ludi* can be heard in the valley. The festivities begin today. Hollers of an excited mob, the screeching of chariot wheels, the sound of clarion trumpeters.

Calix sinks back into the grass until he lies horizontal, his hands intertwined, cradling his head. "I'll admit he only reveals his true self to those he cares for, and there aren't many of those." He tosses a rock up and catches it. "What are you doing all the way out here anyway?"

"I had to get away. The guards. The politicians. My advisor. Patricians in general." I realise I may offend him and quickly put my hand over my mouth. I don't know what gets into me sometimes.

To my surprise, Calix laughs. "You and me both. The palace exhausts me. No matter how long I live here, I'll always be a *peregrinus*, an outsider. The ways of you Latians, they are nothing like those of my people in Echos."

"How do you mean?"

"The Umbrian people are kinder. We are a pious race. Morality to us is worth more than gold."

"And Latians?"

He pauses, choosing his words. "They're cold, ambitious and ruthless manipulators in pursuit of their goals. I'm sure you know this, but the Patricians here truly think they are gods."

"Maybe they are." I smirk.

Lix chuckles, his dimples creasing. "Latians, in spite of all their posturing are not gods. They are as human as any race."

Latians are Dominus's chosen race. That is what the Institute tells us on every Choosing Day. We are the superior peoples of the ULA and that is why our Choosing is more draconian than any of the other Leagues'. It is all *stercus*. Calix articulates this all in such a way that he neither criticises nor admires us. His indifference is not unattractive; he is simply an outsider looking in, a silent observer.

"There is this arcane corruption in Latian politics. The Institute is omnipotent, or rather its director is. The emperor bows to Drusus as if their roles were reversed."

Lix certainly seems to know a lot about the Imperial family and the Institute. The mention of Lysander Drusus piques my interest. I remember seeing him at the Choosing ceremony. The way his lustrous eyes commanded attention. The way he rendered an audience of thousands silent by placing a finger to his lips, not uttering a word. He is fearsome and magnetic all at once.

"Surely the Institute ruled in Umbria too?" I ask, knowing that every Haven is governed in some way by the Institute.

"Yes. But the director back then was far kinder than Mr Drusus." He hesitates, opening his mouth to speak then quickly closing it again. He sits up straight as if to say something of importance, his fists curling into balls. "Not that you heard this from my lips, but Lysander is unhinged, outright sadistic and probably the most demonic man I have ever encountered. Adored by the emperor, no less." Lix's soft accent warps just at the mention of the director. He clenches his jaw; his body stiffens and I wonder if there is more than plain animosity between these two men.

"I didn't know that the emperor cared for the director so."

"Like a son." Lix reigns back his disgust by releasing the balls of his fists, his knuckles returning from white to ruddy once again. "He loves Lysander more than his own bastard daughter, and perhaps even more than Ash. He doesn't even try to hide his favour for him."

Shauna, a bastard child. Asher, a son cast aside. And Lysander, the golden boy. These were things I never knew. Lix and I share an intrusive yet comforting stare. I notice the mystical silver flecks in his eyes.

"Know you have a friend here, if you ever feel alone." He speaks without malice or agenda, and extends a hand. I grasp his forearm and he mine. I even smile.

I never considered that I may make a friend here. Making friends was never something that came to me naturally, and Lana was my only close friend back home. My father always said I was too guarded and stubborn for my own good. In my mind, I was protecting people from the disappointment of my impending fate.

I bid the mysterious yet kind prince farewell, knowing Cosimo will be expecting me for lunch. I scurry back to the palace, my dress clean and my mind clear, for now. However, as soon as my strange ink-coloured bruise begins to throb, reality comes back into focus. I have too many unanswered questions, four girls who want me dead, and a brother being held hostage by revolutionaries.

VI

IN VINO VERITAS

Truth in wine

Five minutes late and, as expected, Cosimo mutters faint words of distaste under his breath. He questions me, relentlessly. "Where were you?" "What were you doing?" "Who did you see?" When I inform him of my encounter with the prince of Echos, his studious expression sours.

"Be careful around that boy." Cosimo's reference to the prince is derogative and his voice is less precise than usual.

My eyebrows quirk in surprise. "He seems fine."

Cosimo makes a tutting sound with his tongue, silencing me. "No, Electa. I should warn you that Prince Calix has a habit of wanting things that aren't his to have."

I pause, perplexed.

Cosimo stares at me. "This is for your own good. Stay away from Calix Lupus or endure the wrath of the prince," he says, and begins to walk. I follow, close to his heels. "There is a story, I'm sure you've heard of it, of an empire built on blood." Cosimo's hands cast about in every direction as he speaks. "Two brothers, Romulus and Remus, founded what we now know as the kingdom of Dominus, Rome, thousands of years ago. Remus jumped over his brother's wall. Romulus, in turn, killed him. You, my dear, are that wall."

Cosimo's effortless spiel confounds me. He has an analogy for every situation, it seems. But Lix is not anything like the jealous brother he describes from that banal legend. "I can make my own judgements, Mr Falto. If I remain in this competition, it will be on my own terms."

While I am speaking, Cosimo halts in the middle of the atrium, his eyes widening past the pearled rims of his glasses. "I pray to Dominus, Miss Steel, that you will be blessed with some grace and manners during your time here," he says with a huff, clearly tiring of my impudence.

I regret my tone but not my words.

"Where are we going anyway?" I finally ask.

"You are going to lunch with the other candidates. I am going to the temple for my midday prayers." His answer is curt. I wonder if it is only the Grey who don't worship Dominus. Everyone here seems to. The mysterious, omnipotent entity that endorses the Institute's reign simply doesn't appeal to me. It is actually forbidden by law to be agnostic. But I have never cared much for laws.

Cosimo delivers me to the morning room, as he calls it, where lunch will be served daily for the candidates. Pink hues soften the room with its granite slabs by means of furniture and the obsidian flagstones at my feet. The four other girls are sitting already, pushing the meal around on their plates. It is not surprising they are all as thin as twigs. I haven't yet seen one of them consume even a mouthful of food.

Cosimo deserts me, shouting over his shoulder that he will pick me up in an hour as if I am a child left at school. The others all look up from their plates and stare. The only empty stool is adjacent to Ember. Reluctantly, I take a seat.

Ember breaks out in abrupt laughter; her brassy voice reverberates in the marbled room and her ruby-jewelled hands prop up her chin. "Finished your etiquette lessons?"

And then the others snigger too. Except for Aria whose gaze is transfixed on the nearby wall with whimsical, wide eyes. I keep my head down, as if I don't hear them. My reaction, or lack of it, bores them, and they quickly forget I am here in the corner of the room, quietly eating my meal.

"You worried about the interview, Tina?" Ember questions the red-haired girl opposite.

Valentina bobs her chin but retains a confident smirk. "Who isn't terrified of Trixie Merula?"

I almost spit out my food. Cosimo didn't warn me that our interviewer would be the acclaimed Trixie Merula. The Latian talk show host is an urban legend, famed for her ruthless probing and humiliation of celebrities, politicians and gladiators across the ULA. She has ruined careers and blighted the dreams of countless emerging stars. She is a woman in her late fifties but is just as stylish and youthful in manner as the girls sat around this table.

In her career as a journalist and media magnate, she has always been able to prise the truth from even the most talented liars. Deception is a skill of mine, yet to Miss Merula I will be little more than an amateur. I fear she will expose me for what I am, an ill-tempered liar with nothing but a smart mouth by means of a defence.

"She could ruin your chances of winning with a single sentence," Trinity broods from the other corner of the morning room, her body language just as closed off as mine. Her upper body is hunched, wisps of blonde hair covering the majority of her face. Her voice is monotonic as she speaks. It is as if she doesn't want to be here, either that or she simply thinks she is better than anyone else in the room.

For such a beautiful girl, it is strange how she has chosen to dress in comparison to the other girls' feminine attires – cotton slacks and a shapeless navy sweater that drapes to her knees. When I catch a glimpse of her face, I can't help but notice the dark circles entrenched beneath her usually sparkling eyes.

"Isn't Merula your distant aunt?" Valentina barks at Trinity. "Surely that's an unfair advantage?"

I wish I could reach across the table and slap her. Her cloying Northern accent nettles me unlike any other I have heard.

Trinity narrows her eyes and throws Valentina a pointed stare, stifling her. "Trixie Merula takes no prisoners. Family means nothing to her. Once she sued her own daughter for ten million denarii." She shoves her plate away, and marches from the room without another word.

"What's her problem?" Valentina squawks to Ember, who just sits there, the picture of an empress, chin lifted, shoulders back, unblinking, god-like. She couldn't care less about Trinity's fit. These girls aren't friends. The only thing they are united in is their hatred of me.

After a while, Ember and her sycophant Valentina follow suit with Trinity and depart from the morning room. Aria remains, alone. As soon as the other girls are gone, I hear her speak for the first time.

"Hello." She waves from across the expansive granite table. Her wandering eyes fall on my white ribbon, unremoved from yesterday's Choosing. A reminder that I don't belong here. "I apologise for the way they treat you. The other girls, I mean." She strokes her braided white hair, tucking the stray bits back into her plait. She is clearly shy. "They're just jealous because Prince Asher likes you more than them."

"Wh-what?" I stammer, choking on my mouthful of venison.

"He kept asking where you were at breakfast."

I grit my teeth. Asher Ovicula has made me into a walking human target for my competitors, especially Ember, the darling of the emperor. I wouldn't be surprised if I woke with a dagger plunged through my heart.

"You know, Nemesis was a Plebeian." She fidgets in her seat, her bony stature and spindly legs are barely contained on the tiny stool. Her attempts at conversation are endearing.

I decide to humour her. "Yes, I do." I don't tell her that I have been instructed to embody her persona. Cosimo would be displeased if I let slip his big plans for me.

Aria crinkles her nose and grins. She has the demeanour of a ten-year-old girl and is unique in her beauty. Her pastel skin is just as pure as those mineral eyes that exude a youthful innocence I can only wish to project. I am her exact opposite in almost every way, rough and ready, cocky and even a little reckless. She is the kind of girl who did all her schoolwork, never returned home a second past curfew, and was the apple of her parent's eyes throughout her formative years. Could her chastity all be a façade? I shouldn't underestimate her. Her muscled arms suggest she could be anything but innocuous prey in this den of lions. She could snap my neck in an instant.

Our conversation is interrupted by a low growl originating from the doorway. I leap up from my seat. The prince leans on the doorframe, with Crew at his side and a tiger trailing just behind. I muffle my shriek with my hand but that doesn't stop Asher from roaring with body-shaking laughter. I brush myself off, feigning disinterest, my eyes still fixated on the animal at Asher's heels.

"What in the name of Dominus…" I mumble. I look over to Aria, who is untroubled by the sight of the beast. I cower behind my stool while the prince continues to chuckle at my expense.

"Electa meet Atlas. My only companion worth his salt."

Aria begins to pet the tiger, which welcomes the affection with a faint chuff. I knew the Patricians like to see exotic animals perform and fight in the arena. The creatures in the arena are feral and encouraged to be that way. It makes for entertaining a battle. Atlas seems the opposite, domesticated and good-natured. He has been reared from a young age to be a suitable companion for an emperor.

Asher clicks his fingers at the beast, who returns to flank him. "Don't worry he's tame and harmless unless I tell him not to be," he says, patting the crown of the animal's head.

Crew steps into the morning room, his chin lifted, and lips pursed. I assume he wishes to speak with me. I excuse myself and leave Aria in the morning room. The prince follows us out with Atlas just behind. The tiger approaches me and I back away, instinctively. I freeze as the animal nudges his head against my leg. The prince, noticing my discomfort, doesn't re-call his pet but rather smirks and laughs in unison, his back resting against a wall. I clench my fists, my face steels and I stare daggers at the prince.

"I bumped into the prince on my way to find you, Electa," Crew begins, his tone from last night softened in Asher's presence. He improvises, of course. Asher can never know the true nature of our relationship. "I was hoping to discuss the possibility of your sponsorship by my party."

His party. Crew is far more immersed in Latian society than I realised. He is a politician of some kind. Atlas sits at my feet, staring up, prodding me with his snout as Crew speaks. Asher still does nothing.

"Crew is the leader of the Populares, the opposition party in the Senate," Asher explains, and it begins to make sense. The Populares are the party of the people. People like me. Their aim is to give Plebeians power, an idea not well-received in this social sphere or in the Senate. The conflict of orders has never ceased even in our modern *utopian* society. "But I'm sure you already knew that, if he's proposing sponsorship."

I didn't know but I nod to maintain the charade Crew has me playing. "I would be honoured to be sponsored by Mr Gracchus." The lie comes easily to me, just as many have over the years, although this is by far the most convoluted of them all.

Crew hesitates, as if sensing an opportunity, and his lip quirks. "However, that is a discussion that can be had another time. The prince expressed his wish to show you around the Palatine, help you get your bearings."

Asher looks just as surprised as I am; his eyes enlarge and a singular eyebrow is raised, if only slightly. Crew wants me to seduce the prince. I can't talk my way out of this one. I am being blackmailed and I really have no say in the matter.

"That would be nice," I mumble, with a laboured smile that begins to hurt after a while. When I look at Crew, all I can see is my brother's bloodied face, his bruised arms and the unnatural dullness that occupied his eyes. I almost gag at the thought. But it is also a thought that keeps me here, playing this game and attempting to woo a prince I would rather do my best to avoid.

Asher runs his hand through his hair, then clicks his fingers, finally releasing me from my torment. Atlas returns to his master. "Shall we go then?" The prince gestures towards the glass-vaulted atrium just ahead. He sounds uneasy, my sudden eagerness to spend time with him must seem suspicious. I made my animosity quite clear last night.

I follow Asher and Atlas to the atrium; he proceeds to show me a few other rooms on the first floor. The gymnasium is vast, with respective indoor and outdoor areas. There are Sim-Cubes similar to the ones the Institute uses for Assay Day physical examinations. The prince points to a secure metal door, which he tells me leads to an armoury. There are three boxing rings, and sand pits to mimic the arena in the *palaestra*. Servants with cloths wipe down the equipment used during the morning session.

The outdoor area includes a mock circus for chariot racing and targets for archery and spear throwing. Atlas bounds around the grassy banks, while Asher hurls javelins for the tiger to fetch and return to him. His aim is faultless, and as he raises his arm, I notice a small, yet distinctive scar on his right wrist. It is triangular shaped with four faint lines. It is almost identical to my own.

"What is that?" I ask.

The prince turns, dropping the javelin to the ground. "What?"

"The scar on your wrist, how did you get it?"

The prince examines his wrist for a moment, then shrugs. "I've had it for as long as I can remember." He quickly turns the conversation, his expression more austere than I have ever seen it. "I'm throwing a party tonight to bid farewell to my bachelor status. A *bacchanal* of sorts – would like you to come?"

The prince picks up his javelin and continues with the activity, Atlas flicking his striped tail, growling in his impatience. I ponder his invitation, but I have plans for tonight already. I will be seeing the world outside. I have to think of an excuse, quick. "Um well…" I stumble over the words. "I don't like parties much." Another lie leaves my lips.

The prince whirls around, his training shirt's sleeves swelling with the breeze, his eyebrows furrowed. "You don't like parties? Then why are you blacklisted, Electa?"

Stercus. He knows. But how? Spartaca supposedly erased all the blemishes from my record. I shuffle, nervously. The prince stands so close now, I hang my head, unable to meet his stare. Maybe it is all over. He will report me to the Institute, and I will be disqualified. My brother will die, and I will be sent to the world outside. Each thought that washes over me is more terrible and nauseating than the last.

"You are going to the party tonight." His tone is imperious, a command from a future emperor rather than the twenty-one-year-old boy who stands before me. Yet I still see the boy beneath his princely pretence. He is a spoilt child who is still play-acting the role he was born to assume some day. Asher doesn't frighten me, not the way his father does, not the way Lysander Drusus does. He is not ready to be emperor, and I doubt he ever will be.

"With all due respect and gratitude, Your Highness, I won't be attending." I back away but he catches my arm, his grip firm and aggressive. There is barely an inch between us. He must notice the alarm in my eyes. "You can't make me come."

"I can do what I want Electa. I am the prince, remember."

I should just relent and surrender to him but I am just as stubborn as he is, if not more. "Do you even hear yourself?"

He is taken aback, and his grip tightens. He rolls a tongue over his bottom lip in contemplation. "You have some nerve, Steel, talking to me like that."

"And you have some nerve touching me without permission."

His reaction, of course, is to yank me even harder, twisting my arm.

The pain comes all at once, and if he turns it even just a fraction further, my bone will snap. So I don't think, I just act.

I stamp down hard on his left boot, hard enough to make impact through the leather, and slap him across the face. He doesn't flinch at all, and his skin feels like iron. My hand stings from the contact, so I shake it.

He howls with laughter and grips me again, with a strength I have never felt before. No matter how much I try, I can't get away.

"You're stronger than you look."

Strong is something I have never been. My only advantage in a brawl has been my quick legs and agile body. The adrenaline must be taking over – or my rage.

A calm voice resonates from a few feet away. "No need to be aggressive, brother." Calix is just as composed as he was a few hours ago by the lake. He has a towel around his neck, along with athletic gear, a golden chest plate and matching metal cuffs on either wrist.

"The Pleb hit me," the prince says, almost spitting out the word. I belong on the bottom of his expensive martial boots as far as he is concerned. It upsets me more than it should. "I don't believe this is of your concern, Lix." Asher is seething with anger. I can feel the heat radiating from his skin, searing against my own. His golden skin is turning red.

"Her welfare is my concern. She is just a girl."

"I've never seen *you* treat a girl with respect."

Lix grimaces as if Asher speaks the truth. I notice he doesn't refute the prince's accusation. "Just be kind with her. That is all I am asking." Calix is cool, and even the prince, who is becoming more and more incensed, doesn't seem to fluster him. If Asher continues to behave like this, I will happily kill him once I win.

"I think you like her a little too much, Lix. Remember what happened last time."

I wonder what transpired between the two brothers and if what Cosimo said earlier was true. I expect Lix to react, but he inhales sharply, grabs my hand and leads me back to the palace. Atlas growls dimly in the distance, and I can feel the scathing gaze of Asher on our backs.

"I apologise, Electa. He's probably drinking again." Lix hangs his head in a way that makes me believe this is a regular occurrence.

"At one o'clock in the afternoon?"

Lix presses his lips together. "He starts early..." His voice trails off, and I wonder if this is a problem he often deals with. I suppose it is one thing the prince and I have in common, drinking far more than we should.

"I never thanked you." I smile, knowing that if he hadn't intervened, I could have been thrown in one of the palace cells. My inability to keep my mouth shut is going to end poorly for both me and my brother. I have to try harder, I know I must, for Vel's sake.

Lix cups my hands in his own, a chivalrous gesture. "I must go. I have to clean myself up for a meeting with Rita Messalla. I daren't be late, she is one scary woman."

I faintly recognise that name from the *Acta Diurna*. She is a correspondent from the news broadcasting channel, *Messalla News*. She is also a Quaestor, I believe. "I didn't know you were political."

"I'm usually not, but I do like to make myself useful around here."

I manage to find my way back to my quarters through the palatial labyrinth. I wonder if attending the party would be the sensible thing to do. I could show my face for an hour or two and then leave in the darkness of the night with Warren. Everyone will be at this party tonight, making it easier for me to escape unnoticed.

I have to go; the stakes are too high. My life, more importantly my brother's and even Lana's too. And I can't say that I am not curious about these people, these Patricians, who live in marble palaces and threaten lives as regularly as they fake smile.

Evening approaches and still not a word from Warren. I wonder if he has forgotten that he offered to take me tonight. I emerge from my room hoping to see him. Instead, there is a large bouquet of red roses at my door, the colour of the Fabian family, Asher's colour. There is a handwritten note attached, the letters elegant, sloping.

He must have sent this. I imagine Lix encouraged him to do so. I throw them at the wall opposite my door, the petals splaying out across the marble flagstones, and rip the note to shreds. He can't behave like he did and simply send me flowers by way of an apology.

"Someone's had a bad day." Warren makes light of my tantrum out in the hallway for everyone to see. I should have known he was watching me. It is his job after all. There are three other Praetorians stationed at the end of the corridor, in front of another doorway. I assume one of the other girls' chambers. "You don't need to be discrete, they're with us," he says, sensing my unease.

The Praetorian Guard has been infiltrated and it is only now I realise how real Crew's threat was – I am being watched every second. "Who are the flowers from?" Warren eyes up the flowers with their crumpled stems and missing petals strewn across the hall.

"The prince. He wants me to come to his party tonight."

"The *bacchanal*?"

I nod.

"You should go," he says, abruptly. I know he is right, but I won't admit it. "It wouldn't be wise to spurn a prince."

I can't deny Warren's counsel. I spurned a prince once today; it would be imprudent to do so twice.

"Go for a few hours and then we can leave once you're back."

That is just what I wanted to hear. I had hoped he hadn't changed his mind about the trip.

"What time are we leaving tonight?"

"Late enough so that no one notices you're gone," he says, pausing for a moment to consider the logistics of it all. "I'll come by your room at one and I'll aim to have you back at five, before everyone wakes up. That is, if it all goes to plan."

"If it all goes to plan?"

"Yes, if we aren't caught," he says, without a smile. I had hoped he was simply toying with me but that is clearly not the case.

"I didn't even know that was a possibility," I say, wary. But I should have expected it wouldn't be as simple as walking straight out of the Haven.

Warren appreciates my trepidation and attempts to reassure me. "It's always a possibility, Electa, but I am an expert in getting out of the Haven undetected and back in again afterwards."

"And if we were to be caught?" I believe I already know the answer, but ask anyway.

A smirk spreads across Warren's face. "We'd be executed."

His laughter irks me. "You think that's funny?" His brazen attitude doesn't instil much confidence in me.

"You still have time to change your mind."

"No. I want to go," I say quickly, resolute in my decision. I have to see it, the world beyond ours. Then I will know where I stand, with Spartaca or against it. But I am selfish, and a part of me knows that I am only going to ease my conscience, to find a reason to kill the prince with my own free will. I want to choose. For the first time in my life, I have that power.

"Stubborn as ever." Warren shakes his head, smiling. "Are you still mad at me?"

"You are blackmailing me, remember?"

Warren stares at me, casting his eyes up and down. His entire body tenses; I can even see the large veins on his wrist, just below the cuff of his uniform, begin to throb. He is conflicted, that much I can tell. "I really wish this wasn't how things had to be," he says, his voice fading to a whisper. "I have no choice, Electa."

He is convincing, I'll give him that at least. That innocent smile and those baby-blues. But I will never forget, nor forgive him for who he is and what he is making me do. I prise my eyes away from him, letting my gaze slip to his brown leather belt, which is partly concealed by his martial jacket. There is a pistol in the holster, striped with cerise paint. Praetorian Guard weaponry. There is also a *pugio*, engraved with the serpent of the Latian flag. It is as if all his innocence suddenly drains and all I can see is a soldier, an insurgent.

Ice seems to spread across my body as a cool hand grazes my bare shoulder. I recoil. I didn't even hear him coming.

"Warren, I need a word." Crew's comment is barbed, and it is clear Warren is in some type of trouble. The slick man turns to me. "I have something for you, Electa," he says, opening a plain white box. Inside, there is a dress entirely emblazoned with crystals, or maybe even diamonds, I wouldn't be able to tell the difference. "I'm sure you will look divine." He leers, his mouth curling at one end, his attractive features twisting, serpentine. "And don't even think about not coming tonight. It starts at ten."

I don't argue. He is fearsome even without provocation. I bob my chin, then look to Warren and back to Crew, who glares at the younger man intently. "I better clean myself up then," I say, forging an excuse to leave before bearing witness to a tense altercation. I scamper back into my room, shutting the door behind me. I press my ear to the wood, their voices just audible, albeit slightly muffled by the barrier between us.

"Don't think for one moment I will show you any favouritism." It is Crew who speaks, his gruff voice is the more distinguishable of the two. "The rules apply to you just as much as anyone else."

Warren doesn't respond. Why would Crew show Warren favouritism?

"If Castel heard about this trip outside, he would kill you and probably me as well." Crew continues his tirade, unleashing fury, his voice reverberating through the mahogany door. "Your actions are putting both of our lives on the line."

"Our lives are always on the line, Crew," Warren finally speaks. "You don't scare me, neither does Castel." He converses with Crew in a way that surprises me. He sounds cruel, ruthless, just like his superior.

"You should be scared, Warren. Caring about the girl will only get you killed."

"I don't care about her."

Even I can tell he is lying.

"If this all goes to *stercus*, you will be the first one I throw to the wolves." Crew sounds more and more irate.

His threats are real, I don't doubt that. This is man who will do whatever it takes in pursuit of his goal.

Warren goes quiet. "I have given up everything for this, Crew. We are on the same side."

"If your feelings for the girl get in the way, I will ruin you. I know everything about you, Warren, lest you forget."

Crew's declaration makes me shiver, and my blood runs cold. I don't want to hear any more. I rush away from the entrance foyer and shut myself in the bathroom, running the taps to appease my nerves. I perch on a stool, soothed by the sound of running water. Once again, I open the box Crew gave to me and study the dress. The shimmering jewels muddle my sight, leaving me dazed with blind stupor.

My *Ornatrix* soon arrives to prepare me. She dresses me herself, the diamond ensemble clearly compulsory attire. She zips me up, the dress a perfect fit, as if it had been tailored for me, the hemline falling just above my knees. Unsurprisingly, Crew arrives to escort me to the party himself. Perhaps he heard of my scuffle with the prince earlier and wants to see to it personally that I attend.

The party is being held many floors below ground level. Crew and I emerge from an elevator to an expansive underground chamber. The ceilings hang low, and the walls are made from megalithic boulders. The space resembles an ancient shrine, but it is far from holy. Air vents jut out from each corner, pumping thick white smoke into the cavern that masks the bodies of the occupants. Silhouettes twirl in and out of the haze, some on tables, others on the rostrum at the far end of the room. Blazing spotlights dance across the ceiling, operated by drunken revellers dressed in vibrant togas. This is like nothing I have ever seen before. The Grey parties I am accustomed to are nothing like this debauchery, glamour and excess.

Servers carry trays overloaded with towers of champagne glasses, no mixing bowls in sight. The round table before me is bowl shaped, a turret of glasses overflowing with liquor at its centre. Passers-by dip their glasses into the pool of sparkling liquid, re-filling them before quickly downing the contents. Music fills my ears; electro-swing resounds from the bandstand. Trumpeters, organ, cithara and lyre players. There are singers too, well-known Latian performers, with their fashionable bobs and cascading jewels.

I can barely move in the perpetual throng of *bacchants* that swarm around the elevated bandstand. Professional dancers with nothing but chainmail to protect their modesty prance around in groups of ten, line-dancing. Crew, a man in his thirties, must be the eldest attendee. Everyone here is young, my age or slightly older, personal friends of the prince and the celebrities who fawn over him.

Topless courtesans parade themselves before Crew, who ogles them, oblivious to my discomfort. The chiming of their jewelled anklets ringing through my ears. I glance around in search for a familiar face. I spot the other girls; they are all standing together, huddled in a booth at the corner of the room. We are all wearing the same dress. They scowl at me as I march towards them. Ember is absent but Valentina shrieks with complaints about the attire we have all seemingly been forced into.

"Who in the name of Dominus's idea was this?" she demands, just as I come into earshot. "Making us all wear the same dresses." She huffs, knocking over her glass as she flings her arms around, spilling wine across the table.

Trinity and Aria bob their chins, their eyes glazed over, glassy. The party has only just begun and yet everyone is in this near trance-like state. I see Ember now, clinging onto the prince on top of a nearby table. She, too, wears an identical dress. Someone clearly wants to keep an eye on all of us. I stand still, unwillingly linked to the arm of Crew Gracchus.

"Looks like you have competition," he goads, noticing Ember and Asher carousing together. He presses his palm against the small of my back, urging me onwards, towards the prince. Atlas is beneath Asher, obscured by the ivory tablecloth. He growls at me as I near. I stick my tongue out. *Stupid tiger.* Asher finally notices me, and extends a hand, helping me clamber up onto the table. Ember is, thankfully, too drunk to care. Asher whispers to a servant below, who returns moments later with a microphone. He intends to make some sort of speech, the microphone in one hand and glass overfilled with champagne in the other. He taps the device a few times and then begins.

"Welcome all." His speech is slurred and varies in volume. He must be drunk already, but then I remember he has been like this all day. "We are Dominus's chosen race and if that doesn't give us an excuse to do whatever we want, I don't know what does."

The entire room roars back with the din of cheers and applause. They holler his name over and over again.

"Tonight, I invite you to join me in this celebration and revelry as a means of farewell to my old life and in honour of my new and my future bride, whoever she may be." The prince winks at me, and I am sure everyone must see. Crew will be pleased, at least. I blush hot red with embarrassment. The crowd shouts out the names of their favourite, the room as a whole overwhelmingly in support of Ember. But I do hear my name once or twice. Asher raises a glass, tips the liquid down his throat in one go, then throws it to the floor. Others join in with the strange toast, mimicking the behaviour of their prince. The shrill of breaking glass echoes throughout the cave. Clamour pervades from every direction, and my ears won't stop ringing. A server offers me a short glass of green liquor. I wonder if this is what is making everyone behave so strangely. I refuse the drink. I can't afford to get drunk tonight.

Asher shouts at me as if we are several metres apart. "Why are you not *drinking?*"

I pretend not to hear but he continues. "You look beautiful, Electa," I think he says, for he sounds utterly incoherent. I am in a half-mind to run away back to my room, but when I look into the crowds beneath, there is one man completely still amongst the frantic movements of the partygoers. Crew stares up, his gaze fixated on me and the prince. There is no going back now. "I am really really sorry about earlier," Asher says, getting closer and closer to me as the words spill out.

I hold back my tongue. "Apology accepted." I swear it even hurts to say it.

Before I can do anything to stop him, Asher is twirling me around on the tabletop. I feel my legs going weak beneath me, my entire body going lax. I haven't drunk a thing, yet my vision blurs, my head spins and all I can hear is the music, the repetitive melody over and over again.

I am jumping from table to table, being thrown around, caught in the arms of the prince. Drink is being poured down my throat by unfamiliar faces. I have lost all control. They cheer me on. It all becomes too much. I can't stop myself, no matter how hard I try. I am not in control of my own body, my own movements.

I see red. Blood. The boy in the olive groves. My brother. Asher. The strange visions afflict me, coming and going as I lose myself in the hordes. Bodies crush me as I stumble, their faces merge and transform into those from my vision. They all call out my name. Suddenly, one figure stands out, dressed entirely in black. I can no longer distinguish between what is real and what is not. The man in black stares at me for a while. His hood covers all but his eyes. Green. When he turns away, I remember falling, darkness and then Warren's voice.

"Let's get you out of here."

VII

BELLA! BELLA HORRIDA!

Wars! Horrid wars!

I jolt upwards. My head pounds and I am drenched with cold sweat. Someone guides my head back down to the pillow, holding a cool, damp cloth to my forehead.

"Warren?" I choke out his name. My lungs feel heavy, damp. "Where am I?" I cough uncontrollably. He eases me back, running his hand over the crown of my head.

"It's okay, Electa. You're in your room." His voice is soothing among the chaotic chiming in my ears. "I don't think it's wise we leave tonight."

"No." I gasp for air. "I want to go. I need to." Sitting up straight, I sip on a glass of water.

Warren bows his head into his hands. "I just don't think you're up to it."

"I didn't even drink anything until later, I swear." Not that I remember much of what transpired. Dominus knows what would have happened if Warren hadn't got me out when he did.

"That's the thing," he says, pacing about the room. "You didn't need to."

I lean forwards, propping myself up on my elbows, confused.

"They pump some sort of gas through the air vents to loosen everyone up." Warren is just as dismayed as I am. No wonder I feel so sick. The behaviour was not alcohol induced, although it may have played some part. Everyone in attendance was unknowingly or knowingly high on drugs.

"Th-that can't be l-legal," I stammer, but really, I shouldn't be surprised.

Warren hangs his head. "There are no laws in the Palatine, remember?" he says, trying to conceal his disgust, although not particularly well. "Asher Ovicula can do whatever the hell he likes, there's no one to stop him. It isn't the first time he's done it either. The elite in Ore can't feed their addictions any other way than by coming to his parties."

The Palatine is a lawless place, immune to the Institute's watchful gaze. I can't believe that someone like Lysander Drusus would allow such a thing to occur, Imperial family or not. There is no such thing as drugs in the outer provinces, and by the sounds of it, you can't access such substances in the city either. It is strange how the Institute rules with an iron fist beyond the Palatine gates and turns a blind eye to the hedonistic goings-on within.

"Well, I found an antidote, so you should be feeling better." Warren points to the small glass bottle at my bedside. It's an antidote for Porgy, an illicit drug that is known for its hallucinogenic side-effects.

"You're going to get in trouble for helping me, aren't you?" I say, expecting that Crew knew exactly what would happen tonight. He wanted me to be drugged, mindless and wanton. He wanted me to be with the prince in that state for as long as possible. The thought makes me sick.

Warren won't be treated kindly for retrieving me. I was exactly where Crew wanted me to be. I remember his threats from earlier and suddenly feel a stomach-turning guilt wash over me. Warren will pay the price for what he has done tonight. What he has done for me. I may not trust or like my personal guard much, but he certainly doesn't deserve whatever Crew has in store for him.

Warren's eyes shift downwards, avoiding my gaze. "Don't worry about me," he says, firmly. I don't press the matter further. I can only hope Crew, too, was too intoxicated to remember what happened this night. "Are you sure you want to go?"

"Yes." I won't change my mind. My curiosity overwhelms any sense of tiredness, or sickness that lingers from the drug.

Warren has me dress entirely in black – tight black trousers and a sweater to match. I lace the army-issued boots, like I used to do with my brothers, three knots, just in case. He then attaches a tiny circular-shaped device to my forehead, just below my hairline and another to the nape of my neck. He presses down to activate the tech. I feel nothing. He leads me to stand before a mirror. I stare at my reflection and I see raven hair, pale skin and two beady black eyes. I am not myself; a stranger's face has taken the place of my own. I look to Warren, mystified. I touch my new face and the virtual illusion pixelates, revealing my olive skin beneath.

"It's a Viscom, illegal tech. You have to keep it on until we leave the Haven. And for heaven's sake, don't touch it."

There is no one in the Palatine halls, apart from a few guards who Warren seems unconcerned to pass. Everyone is either asleep or still at Asher's *bacchanal*. The walk down the hill is quick, easy. There is no one, only the sound of crickets chirping in the undergrowth. The Palatine Hill gates are swarming with vigilites in their gun-metal grey armour and heavy-duty automatic guns in their holsters. The security checkpoint looms above the marble archway, its spotlights now on Warren and me as we approach. Warren shows a vigilite his identification card, along with my own forged documentations. The vigilite scans the documents, taking his time examining the in-built screen on the cuff of his uniform. He raises the retina scanner, the thin blue light dancing across my eyes. A green *confirmed status* illuminates on the screen.

"Where are you heading tonight, Mr Tanner, Miss Antonia?" The question is seemingly routine, his tone uniform, as if he has said these words hundreds of times this day alone.

"We are running an errand for Mr Gracchus in the forum," Warren says, his voice steady. He has done this before. The vigilite nods and signals the checkpoint supervisors overhead to open the gates. As we leave, Warren mimics putting a finger to his mouth urging me to keep quiet until we are a safe distance away.

"That was easier than I expected," I say as we walk the winding path adjacent to the Circus Maximus, the greatest athletic stadium in Latia, particularly renowned for its chariot racing. I didn't think it would be so simple to get out from the greatest fortress in Latia.

"I know the guards. They know Crew, he is an important political figure after all."

My *Ornatrix* tried her best to explain the political pecking order to me earlier this evening. Crew is the leader of the opposition party to the ruling Optimates led by Ember's father of all people, Marcus Licinius Hadrianus. The *Cursus Honorum*, the slippery pole of politics that you must climb to obtain power, even at the top, she said, and you are still shackled by the Institute's manacles. The family feuds and faction rivalries are just as vicious as any battle in the arena, apparently.

"I thought your name was Warren Shademoore?" I remember that the vigilite addressed him by the moniker Tanner.

"It is. My full name is Warren Tanner Shademoore. I leave out the Shademoore part on the official documents," he explains.

"Why?"

Warrens rolls his eyes skyward as he considers a response. "Well, let's just say my family are notorious around here and not for the right reasons." He is vague, and before I can press him further a car screeches up along the sidewalk. The vehicle is unlike any other I have seen. Four wheels. Military plating. This must be what they use in the outside world. In the Havens, every vehicle is operated by electromagnetic pulse technology, Maglev, which means, of course, no wheels.

The Circus's glass walls gleam in the moonlight, casting us and the car in an ethereal glow. Warren and I climb into the back of the vehicle. The driver is a woman, dark-haired, pale skinned. She is like Warren, a foreigner from a whole other world. When she turns, I notice her mismatched eyes, one bright blue, the other dull grey. The unusual feature is unmistakeable, and I find myself staring for a little too long.

"Electa, this is my sister Ciara," Warren introduces the woman, who must be at least five years older than him. He squeezes her shoulder, affectionately.

"Nice to meet you," she says. Her accent is heavy, less refined than those of the Haven dwellers, especially Latians, who seem to have more pomp in their voices and more attitude than any other race. Warren's accent is not so noticeable, so perhaps his time in Latia has played a part in that. "I was expecting you to look a little more Latian." Ciara scans over my now-pastel skin with her strange but beautiful eyes. Her hair has small, bedraggled braids beginning at her hairline and hugging her scalp. The thicker hair at the crown of her head is coiffed and adds height to her petite frame.

Warren waves his hand in front of my face, revealing my true identity beneath, the vision fading and re-appearing with his touch. "She's wearing a Viscom," he explains, leaning forward in his seat as Ciara pulls away from the side street. "How was the checkpoint?"

"Not too bad. The vigilites, well, they're no more scrupulous than usual."

Whilst the Praetorian Guard may have been infiltrated by Spartacan loyalists, I doubt any vigilites' allegiance sways from Director Drusus.

"How do we get out?" I ask, my curiosity now overwhelming. I am about to see the world that I have been told for my entire life doesn't exist. I take a long steadying breath, the adrenaline putting me on edge, as the realisation finally comes. I am escaping this marble cage.

Ciara laughs a little at my excitement. "Spartaca has lots of secret ways in and out of the Haven but tonight the best way is straight out the main gates."

Warren explains that we are posing as military intelligence agents on a recon mission. The military-issued vehicle and the all-black costume enhance the façade. My father has probably been driving cars like these his entire life. Of course, he never told me that. He was sworn to secrecy by the Institute. It would be a betrayal of his honour to discuss the war, even with his own children. Yet, I can't help but feel betrayed by him, by his lies. The years he spent doing the Institute's bidding – for what? His son to suffer the same fate, and a daughter who would have been cast away to join the ranks of his enemy.

We drive along the Appian Way, leaving the city of Ore behind us. The road takes us past my region, Chrysos, the small town of Hedera glittering under starlight. The hills where I grew up, climbing, hunting and playing, pass by in the window, the cornfields flickering in the northern wind, what our ancestors called the *Aquilo* and believed to be a god. Old warehouses and grain stores are the only buildings now at the foot of the monolithic statue I used to see from my window, towering over us, the silent vigil, the protector of Ore, a serpent-Dominus.

We reach the checkpoint soon after, a lofty marble triumphal archway that is incongruent with the rural surrounding. Over a dozen vigilites guard the threshold in a uniform line, visors down, gleaming in their grey suits of armour. The labyrinth of serpents stamped on their shoulder plates indicates their allegiance to the Institute and Lysander Drusus. The arch appears to simply be a thoroughfare to the horizon beyond, fields of poppies tremble in the twilight air. It is an illusion, a virtual image created by the Institute for our peace of mind, I suppose. They would never want us to see what lies beyond the Haven's skeleton, and neither do they want us to believe we are trapped inside a dome of their own creation. They want us to fear the world beyond. The unknown. The fear is what they use to control us. But I am not afraid anymore.

Four vigilites approach the vehicle, and it is only now that I notice the miniature loopholes in the skyline. Guns follow the vigilites as they walk towards the vehicle. The invisible parapets make me uneasy as Warren instructs me to get out of the vehicle. I can sense a sniper's aim as I stand out in the open, a metre away from the protection offered by the vehicle. The vigilites search the vehicle with scanning devices that resemble canes in their length and width. The devices emit blue light that fill the interior, pulsating one, two, three, four times before turning green. The car is clean.

Next, they pat us down, individually, confiscating Warren and Ciara's respective handgun and pugio for now. They continue with a retina scan, something that I am now accustomed to. They order us to stand still, hands outstretched while they scan our identification cards and examine the citizen profiles on an electronic tablet.

Warren even has a different identity; I suppose a Praetorian venturing outside the Haven is not commonplace. He is Cian Blake; I am Fleur Antonia and Ciara is Honour Grandus. The profiles flash all at once with a Latian legion symbol. We are tribunes of low rank, but our status is confirmed almost immediately. They return the weapons and, satisfied with their inspection, signal us onwards through the arch.

Marble gates open within the arch, splitting what seems a boundless horizon in two, revealing a tunnel and an abyss of blue lighting overhead. The car rattles onwards into the tunnel, leaving the world I know behind. My pulse quickens, and my hands tremble. How will the mythical world I had imagined as a child measure up to what I am about to see? I am not even certain that I am ready to see it. Ready to see what lies beyond. More than anything, I am scared. Scared that what I will see will change my world forever. Daylight escapes into the tunnel, my eyes blinded by bright light. I squint, holding my hands up to shield myself.

"Are you ready?" Warren says, his tone full of foreboding.

I take a deep breath, bracing myself, and the white haze lifts from my vision, revealing the new world.

The first thing I see is grey. Hills not dissimilar to those inside the Haven roll outwards to the skyline of sooty grey air. The landscape is barren; the only semblance of life are the tree boughs obliterated by artillery fire jutting out from the soaking earth. Gunshots ring and echo across the valley where the red and gold of Latian legionnaires provide the only colour in the ashen horizon that is heavy with billowing clouds of black smoke.

The Latian basecamp here sprawls across the basin below the foothills of the mountain range beyond. The land is contoured with military tents, shelters and heaps of bodies piled to the sky. Even within the vehicle, there is the potent smell of death, rotting and burning flesh wafting from the valley below. As I inhale the sultry, fetid stench, my stomach churns yet Warren and Ciara barely flinch. The air is stifling, and I take shallow, desperate gasps as I choke on the fumes of smoke and ruin. I gaze upwards through the sunroof to see the grey skies stained blood red with the dawning sun. It is as if I have stepped foot in the pallid realms of myth and at any moment the gods of the underworld will pluck me away, into the darkness forever.

"Who are we fighting?" I stumble over my words, coughing and spluttering.

Warren turns to face me. "Us. Spartaca," he says, the dull surroundings blanch his bright eyes. His lips don't tremble as mine do, his eyes don't widen at the sight of this war-torn land. He has seen this many times before. "*Exitus acta probat*," he mutters under his breath three times. It is an old saying – *The outcome justifies the deed.*

Here is the thing about war. You imagine the glory, the honour, the legacy but forget what you leave behind. Your innocence, your family, your soul. I picture my father down there among those soldiers. His scarred face and cracked lips quivering as mine do at what he sees. I can only hope he feels what I do, the horror, the disgust and if he doesn't, I can never call him father again.

We drive, for hours it seems, on a meandering, unmarked path into the hills. Mist spills from the mountain peaks beyond, rivers of white against lead-coloured rocks.

"Where are we going?" I finally ask.

"Somewhere that will show you that you are on the right side," Ciara says, her eyes on the road. Her driving is reckless; I jolt at every corner. She brakes harshly and accelerates far quicker than she should. Warren holds me back with his strong arms a few times to protect me from lurching forwards on every bump in the track.

"It looks like we are suffering just as much death as you are," I say, knowing that this can't be a one-sided affair. This is a war that has lasted for years, without an end in sight.

Ciara's expression steels. "You haven't seen anything yet."

She is right. I wonder how big this world is, how much there is to see and how much of it looks like this. We drive beneath a desolate aqueduct and begin the descent up another hill. Ciara parks the vehicle on a small knoll that resides above a concrete settlement in the valley littered with makeshift tents for shelter. As I emerge from the vehicle, the chill of the air is a shock to me. In Ore, the climate is controlled by the Institute, with limited rain and a temperature that never falls below twenty degrees centigrade. My boots scrape across the fine film of gritty snow that blankets the soil.

"You can turn off the Viscom now," Warren says, disconnecting the device. "In some ways, Spartacan technology is more advanced than the Institute's."

"Yet people live like this?" I say, gesturing to the simple huts and tents that make up the settlement below.

Warren squares his shoulders defensively. "Electa, you have seen nothing."

His vagueness begins to irritate me, but I can't argue, I know nothing of this world or its people. "Where is Spartaca based?" I ask.

Warren points to a city that stands like a skeleton, the buildings reduced to sharp, jagged edges, nothing like the marble curves and domes of the Haven. "That's Romont, one of the larger settlements in this region. Two thousand miles' westwards is Albion, the island from which Spartaca operates. The Institute has been trying to break our defences for years, unsuccessfully."

Ciara continues. "But that may not last much longer. That's why we need your help, Electa."

I bow my head, unconvinced, shying away from the task they ask of me. A poor Plebeian girl from nowhere, with nothing – no courage and no skills to speak of. I turn back to the Haven. I never realised the true extent of its expanse until now. It rises far into the clouds, taller than any mountain peak.

"How the world came to be this way is little more than myth," Ciara explains, tying her hair back taut as it whips in the wind. "The history of it all has been skewed over time; ask one person and they'll tell you something completely different to the next."

Warren interrupts. "The Institute knows the truth," he mutters offhand, and Ciara nods in agreement.

"Millions of Unchosen have joined the people out here over the years." Ciara has a certain urgency in her voice that makes you hang on her every word. "Most are made slaves, there are thousands of runaways of course, and the rest, well, are killed before they even get outside that marble archway." She is emotionless as she reels off the crimes of the Institute as if they were as simple as petty theft.

"Why?" I ask, remembering that Crew said the same thing just yesterday.

Warren answers. "The Institute doesn't want to lose its control; the population is getting out of hand. Spartacan forces outman the ULA's forces ten to one."

I wonder how ill-equipped and disorganised its forces must be to still be fighting this war against a much smaller population. The Institute's money and resources must play some part in its successful defence of the Havens, otherwise this war would have been over a long time ago.

Ciara doesn't relent from her tirade, almost looking irritated by Warren's interruption. *Siblings.* "Imagine if people found out the truth. They would lose their control of you Golds and lose their perfect society."

"Golds?" I question her terminology.

Warren shoves Ciara gently, smirking. "Ignore my sister. It's a derogatory term people use out here for people like you who live in or used to live in the Havens."

It is all starting to make a little more sense, but there is one thing I can't get my head around. "I just don't understand how so many people can keep this war a secret?"

Ciara jumps in before her brother can. She is eager to get me on side, perhaps more so than Warren who secretly wishes I weren't a part of this at all. "Anyone who has any knowledge of the outside, except for Lysander Drusus and the Imperials, have devices implanted in their brains that allows the Institute to control them and erase memories at will."

That would explain my father's forgetfulness, and those headaches he has suffered daily since he was a child. He truly is an Institute puppet and not even by his own will.

Now Warren speaks. "And of course, there are the regenerators. They do much more than educate you. They see your every thought, analyse your brains, your bodies. The Institute are always watching, even when you sleep. Don't you see? There is no escape."

The rush of his words sends me spinning. It is all too much. The Institute's lies and manipulation has gone far beyond anything I could have imagined. When I find my voice, it is small and squeaky. "You're lying. I don't believe it."

How much can I trust their words when they are counting on me to side with them? I don't know what to believe anymore. I realise that I have stopped breathing. I don't move, think or speak. I pray to Dominus that this is all just some twisted, horrible nightmare. But I know deep in my heart that it is not. I am shaken by sharp, high-pitched wails that seem to quake the earth beneath me. It is a siren.

"*Stercus.* We have to get out of here now!" Warren shouts over the deafening noise, grabbing my arm and hauling me back towards the vehicle.

"What in Dominus is going on?" My throat goes hoarse as I scream. I'm not sure they hear me.

"There wasn't a raid scheduled today. I don't understand," Ciara bellows over the chaotic pulses of the siren. She swings into the driver's seat, starting up the engine.

I tug back against Warren, the realisation of what is about to happen suddenly burning through me. "They're going to bomb the settlement!" Warren nods, refusing to release his grip on my arm.

"They have shelter."

I resist his strength but find myself being dragged closer and closer to the vehicle. I had noticed the small makeshift hospital at the foot of the knoll earlier, full of children and wounded soldiers who can barely walk. Nobody will be helping them evacuate and they could never make it to the shelters in time by themselves. "People are going to die," I scream at him, hoping that some anguished quality in my voice will make him feel something, anything for those people we are leaving to die but he doesn't loosen his grasp. For a moment I consider running down there and helping them. I could easily get there in time if I ran down the knoll. It can only be two hundred metres away. But, to do so I would have to escape the constraints of Warren's muscularity and that is no easy feat.

Suddenly, I remember the pugio on his waistband, concealed by his black leather jacket. Without thinking, I yank it from him with my spare hand. He yelps out in pain as I plunge the dagger into his thigh. As soon as he releases the pressure from my arm, distracted by the pain, I run as fast as I can down the hill.

At a sprint, I weave my way through the boulders that obstruct my path. I can hear Warren behind me; he has recovered and now chases me, yelling out my name over and over. He is desperate and frantic as he shouts for me to stop my descent. I push my way through the routs, the panicked settlement dwellers making a beeline for the concrete bunker, little more than a hole in the ground. My black mark throbs at my side, the pain coming in waves, but I can't let it slow me down.

Drones hum overhead. The sound makes me shudder and I feel my blood run cold. I look skywards, the green Institute emblem stares down at me from the underwings. Then the fire comes. The heat of the flames licks at my heels. Fire bombs rain down from above. Bodies catch alight in an instant and the air reeks of flaming flesh. I fear that I will never forget those harrowing wails that escape people in their final breaths.

Then the ground is torn from beneath me. The force of impact flings me backwards. My vision wanes to black and all I feel is the pounding in my head and the slowing of my pulse. Then there is nothing, I no longer feel my own body and succumb to the numbness. *This is it. I am going to die.*

Voices echo around me. I am alive, I know that at least. Warren stands over me, panting, his breaths ragged and sharp. He hauls me from the flames, slinging me over his shoulder, and runs for the knoll. The bruise at my side feels as though it is on fire, searing my skin. The bombs continue to fall on either side.

Warren chokes and splutters on the cinders and smoke that envelope us. He doesn't even slow his pace as he climbs the steep incline of the knoll and makes the final push to the vehicle, to safety. I can no longer hear his breaths as the explosions thunder around us, only a high-pitched pulse ringing in my ears.

Then we are in the vehicle, on the backseat. He doesn't let me go, and I lie in his arms. Ciara revs the engine, and we speed away back towards the Haven, a safe place. I can't breathe. The daze of the impact, the flames and explosions, paralyses me. The numbness ebbs away slowly and the ringing in my ear's lifts.

"Breathe, Electa, come on." Warren sits me up, shaking me. He holds my face in his hands and tilts my chin up. I cough and splutter, gasping for clean air. My skin is covered in heavy black soot but otherwise I am relatively unscathed. But the ache at my side doesn't relent and I wince at the agony of it. I feel hot and cold all at once.

"That was either the most stupid or bravest thing I've ever seen," Ciara mutters from the front. I have endangered them both and it is clear from her tone she is not best pleased. I couldn't even save anyone; it was all for nothing. If it weren't for Warren, I would have died for nothing.

"Brave." Warren speaks softly, and it soothes me to hear his voice clearly now. He guides me onto his lap while caressing my hair.

I almost forgot what I had to do to him to get down to the settlement. I notice the puncture wound on his right thigh. Although it wasn't particularly deep, his cargo trousers are wet with his blood.

"I'm sorry for stabbing you." My voice croaks as I push myself to speak.

"I don't think you feel that guilty about it," he says, and a small laugh escapes him. Although it is no time for humour, it somehow puts me at ease.

'You're right. I don't," I reply, and a smile forms on his lips. I can't tell whether he is in pain, but if he were, I am sure he would never let me know it. He bandages the wound to stop the bleeding and then it is as if it never happened.

The journey back is long. My mind wanders over what I have witnessed; the explosions, buildings crumbling to ash, steel frames buckling, bending, death, so much death. I wonder if I will ever be the same again. The Institute's lies, deceptions and brutalities. It is all too much to bear. It is not surprising that I am a liar, and a talented one at that. My world, my entire life, has all just been a *beautiful* lie – and now I am empty.

I have despised the Institute for my entire life. How can I stand by while it reigns supreme, slaughtering innocents, manipulating minds, turning children into soldiers to fight in a war they don't understand. This is an organisation that controls our minds, our feelings and memories, every part of us that should be our own. For the first time, my eyes are open and I will be nobody's fool. The ash on my skin will become my armour and turn to steel. I will be their Nemesis, the harbinger of the divine retribution that this retched world deserves. I will fight for the truth to be known. I will fight for the freedom to feel, to love, to live. I will fight with Spartaca.

I wake the next morning resolute in my decision to fight for Spartaca's cause. The trip to the outside world, as horrifying as it was, has allowed me once again to be in control of my fate. I am not doing this just to save my brother's life but the lives of millions snatched away by the Institute and its Choosing. Tonight, I will face off against the other girls in the live interviews with the vulpine woman Trixie Merula. For now, I spend my time with Calix, the Umbrian prince, who whisks me away to the forum to distract me from the competition ahead.

A Maglev limousine arrives at the Palatine gates to drive us into the heart of the city. Praetorians flank us as we roam through Ore's side streets bustling in the early-morning trade. Of course, we don't need the protection, it is a pointless spectacle, a façade just as much as any of it is. No one will give us any bother because they have been compelled by the Institute to be good, faithful citizens. The regenerators have seen to that.

Lix and I stroll side by side. While people gawk at the prince in his regal blue tunic from a distance, they barely notice me in my plain white garments. Cosimo would be horrified by my fashion choice.

The market stalls jut out from the marble pavements. Traders selling their wares haggle with toga-wearing old men and Patrician ladies still in their gymnasium attire from the first classes of the day. More established stores parade their overpriced, exclusive goods in shop windows. There are gowns made of Charmeuse silk, supple fur coats imported from the cold, wintry region of Volscia, not to mention wreaths of jewels dripping from the mannequins.

Calix offers me anything and everything as we pass but I decline politely. He knows just as well as I do that it would be uncomfortable for me to wear such things when all I grew up with was cotton and wool. I do sample the food, though. The garish purple carts are wheeled around by vendors with booming voices advertising their sweet pastries and delicacies at every street corner. Lix must consume at least twenty fig candies, just to prove he can. We both laugh as he struggles against the sticky sugar in an attempt to prise apart his teeth.

A gaggle of young Patrician girls, not yet seventeen, scurry up to the Praetorian pleading for an autograph from the prince. Before the hulking sentinel can shoo the girls away, Lix steps in, happy to oblige, with an effortless grin on his face. As I watch him navigate his adoring fans, I wonder how much the Imperials are complicit with the Institute's indoctrination. I wonder if they know at all. Lix is not like the others. There is a goodness in him that the Palatine doesn't deserve. I could never imagine Asher doting on civilians the way his adoptive brother does.

The smallest of the girls, who can be no more than eleven years old, totters over to me. She looks up at me, hopeful, twiddling with her fishtail braid. She hands me a flyer, and on it is my face, a picture taken at the banquet just two nights ago. Below it, the letters read: *Vote Electa Steel.* This is Cosimo's doing, no doubt. He had mentioned he would be advertising the *Steel brand*, as he calls it, to garner public support. "I want to make sure everyone knows who Electa Steel is," he said. The youngster hands me a pen. I have never signed my name before, and I stand there, confounded, for what feels like forever.

Eventually I just spell out my name, as I would normally. She beams. I suppose she is too young to understand the caste system that divides us. I was like her once. Full of adoration for the celebrities of our society. Their lives remnant of some glamorous fairytale that our parents read aloud to us as infants. I am now one of them, a goddess, a princess, a gladiator. I suppose, to her, I am all three. One day, this will be a distant memory. I will be remembered as a murderer, a terrorist, a usurper. Little girls will no longer see me as their hero. They will see me as a villain.

I sit with Lix on a bench in one of the city's gardens. If it weren't for that monstrous Institute Dome looming above the trees in the distance you may think you weren't in a metropolis at all. The park is the picture of a Utopia. Faces come alive with the effervescent glow cast by the virtual sun that shines over those who don't walk beneath the verdure's shade. I am smiling too but then I remember. My mind parries the images that threaten to drown me in terror once again. It is all a lie. If only they knew the truth. The truth is an ugly thing that would not suit our perfect, beautiful world. The words make me sick.

A hovering billboard comes to life above. The electricity hums, rattling the earth and the trees and flowers that surround us. An enlarged image of Director Drusus appears onscreen, in his trademark viridescent suit, more stylish than the traditional garments of regular politicians. But he is, of course, no regular man. "*Salve*, civilians, and a good morning to you all." His voice is amplified, all the billboards in Ore airing the same broadcast at once, and it seems to echo from every nook and cranny of the city. His voice is sweet to the ears in the most disturbing way.

"*Caveat Suffragator*. Let the voter beware. At nine o'clock tonight, any citizen over the age of seventeen will be able to cast their vote on their personal regenerators." The sight and sound of the man who is responsible for what I witnessed just hours ago turns my expression to stone. I can barely look at him without feeling frothing rage gushing from the pit of my stomach. "Remember that this is your chance to choose your future empress, an ambassador for our Haven and nation. The Chosen girls are the most distinguished ladies of Latia, I urge you to show them your support. I will cast my own vote this evening and encourage you all to do the same."

The address ends with an omniscient smirk that haunts me just as it did the first time I saw it. The image of the director glitches away in the skyline, and the billboard returns to its original display. Lysander Drusus is a strange creature, terrifying and enthralling all at once. His eyes have a certain hypnotic quality that compels one to believe each and every word he utters. But I know a monster lurks beneath his polished teeth and porcelain skin. Dominus knows what he would do to me if he uncovered the conspiracy. I have heard what he does to traitors – it involves a sack, a dozen snakes and the Titan river. A fitting end for anyone who dare dishonour the snake god, Dominus, with unholy deeds.

Lix seems equally disinterested by the broadcast. I look over to him. He is tense, as if a puppeteer was stringing him up, spine straight and limbs braced.

"Do you ever miss Umbria?" I ask, almost afraid to question him about his tragic past. Perhaps I am being insensitive but, then again, I have never been particularly tactful.

"Yes," he breathes, his voice getting lost in the tender breeze that whispers in the leaves. "When I was just a boy, the old Institute director Ajax Quirinus visited my family in Echos often. His favourite saying was *sol lucet omnibus, maxime Umbris* – the sun gives light to everyone but especially for the Umbrians. By that, he meant the Umbrian race were the kindest he had ever encountered. He was Latian, of course."

All the Institute directors are Latian, and it has been that way since the formation of the Havens some two hundred years ago. Although the ULA alliance is said to be equal, Latia holds all the cards and anyone who thinks otherwise is simply *stultus*.

"What happened to Quirinus?"

"He was old, fell ill and died. Umbria mourned for months. He was a kind man, respectful of our customs. That's when Lysander came to power." Lix's eyes shift downwards at the mention of the director's name. His past haunts him still. Time never heals, it simply puts a little distance between you and your sufferings.

"And that's when your government toppled your father's regime?" I remember him mentioning something along those lines the other day by the lake.

Lix's eyes darken. I expect to see sadness but there is only guilt. He hunches over, head inclined to escape my scrutiny. "When I said that I wasn't being entirely truthful…" He mumbles as if he doesn't want me to hear. "You may as well know the truth; if you become empress, they will explain all of this anyway." He speaks in hushed undertones yet there is no one around, the Praetorians have made sure of that. They encircle us, turning away anyone who steps foot inside a twenty-metre radius. "You must not speak of this to anyone. It will put you in danger."

I nod, intrigued and scared all at once.

"My family wasn't attacked by the government. The Umbrian Havens were invaded by a terrorist organisation known as Spartaca."

I bite down hard on my tongue and swallow the urge to gulp. I turn my head from him to conceal my expression. He can't know that I have heard of Spartaca, let alone that I work for it. *Act surprised*, I think. Now it is my turn to be a liar.

"Spartaca?" As I question the name, the lie tastes bitter on my tongue. Lix doesn't deserve to bear witness to this charade.

"I couldn't lie to you, Electa, it's nice to finally have a friend here. Shauna has never been particularly sociable and, well, Ash is too busy for me these days."

I am ridden with guilt and embarrassment and stare at the ground, unable to look Lix in the eye.

"They're from the outside world. They took control of Echos first, a year later the entire Umbrian League fell. They're working their way to Latia, Electa." His voice sounds bleak. "They tortured me for months. I knew nothing, I was a b-boy, a ch-child." As he stammers, the memory of what happened tugs at his jaw, pulling his features into a pained grimace. This is not the Lix I know. "They killed my father and mother in front of me." The usual lyricism of his voice is absent as he recounts the tragedy. "I discovered some months later that they murdered all three of my sisters too. The youngest, Persisa, was just five years old. Millions more died, and those they didn't kill became their slaves."

The horror in his eyes is painful to witness. I feel a solitary tear slip down my cheek, I quickly wipe it away with my sleeve. My head pulses violently, as I question everything I have come to believe. I nearly forget why I am on their side. The side of an organisation that has already brought down one League and who I am helping to bring down the next. But the Institute is just as violent, just as cruel. I have to convince myself of that.

88

How silly I was to believe this was a war in black and white. How foolish of me to think the Institute bad and Spartaca good. I should have known things weren't so simple, I was a Grey – once.

"Lysander did nothing. He watched while Umbria burned. He didn't want to waste his men protecting the *inferior* League. He thought only of himself, his people, his home, his precious Latia. I was the only thing they saved, and I wish they hadn't."

The sadness in Lix's voice dissipates and is replaced by blind rage. He hates Spartaca but I think he may hate Lysander even more. Lysander could have helped Umbria; he could have saved millions of lives, but he chose to only save himself. And Lix would hate me too if he knew the truth.

I raise my hand and place it on Lix's shoulder. I squeeze it gently, hoping to offer some comfort. Lix doesn't cry but his face is flushed with wrath. I ache to tell him the truth. Maybe he could help me and my brother. But I push the silly and selfish thought aside.

"You can't tell anyone."

This is an order from a prince, an Imperial, and one of the few people the Institute doesn't control. There are no regenerators in the Palatine.

"The Institute has been covering it up for a reason. If they discover that you know, they will kill you."

I don't doubt that. Maybe it is not the Institute I should fear, but one man who seems to be control of everyone and everything in the ULA. *Lysander Drusus.*

VIII

QUOD LATET ANGUIS
IN HERBA

A snake lies hidden in the grass

The Theatrum Victoria reminds me of a day that seems so long ago that it could even have been in a whole other lifetime. I remember standing not far from where I am now, under its cloisters, waiting to be registered for the Choosing. I was corralled into a section with hundreds of other youths. I suppose most of them are dead now. There is something haunting about it, empty of the bright young faces that once occupied its stalls.

The interviews will take place here in just a few hours, and I feel a different type of fear this day. It is no longer just my life hanging in the balance but my brother's, and Lana's too. I am escorted to a dressing room backstage where my *Ornatrix* and several attendants spend hours preening and primping me into a pretty little thing who could maybe just about look how an empress should. I stare at myself in the mirror and realise that I will never be the girl I once was, the girl with a bare face and scraped knees. I am a gladiator now, and I shall wear my mask proudly. It was all I ever wanted, after all.

Cosimo dismisses the attendants upon his arrival, bringing with him a floor-length steel-plated gown. It is more a suit of armour than a dress. The riveted metal scales descending from the neckline would barely protect my modesty.

"I'm wearing *that?*" It is the most outlandish thing I have ever seen. So much for Cosimo's promise that I can stay true to myself. Then again, I don't suppose that plain linen tunics will make much of an impression on the voting public.

Cosimo is, of course, disappointed by my reaction, and his smile slips. "I had it custom-made for you since your cognomen is Steel. It looks like just the kind of thing Nemesis would wear. Iconic, don't you think?"

I cast my eyes over the gown again. It looks impractical and uncomfortable and I think Cosimo must have forgotten that I have to spend the entire evening wearing it. The Grand Imperial Ball is taking place at the Palatine tonight following the interviews and I won't have time for a wardrobe change.

"I'm not wearing it." I cross my arms and pout. Cosimo already believes me to be a petulant child and there is little point in acting any different.

He lets out a long, drawn-out sigh. "Can you ever be pleased?" He hangs the dress on the railing and walks out. I half-expect him to slam the door but I know such boorish behaviour is beneath him.

It seems I am just as much a talented liar as I am adept at hurting feelings. I don't know when I became so bitter, so full of anger. I want to change. But how can I? My father taught me when I was a child to never rely on anyone other than myself, to be as cold as ice so that no one could ever hurt me with cruel nicknames or jibes. I am a product of my childhood, and of an absent war-torn father. Uncouth and too defiant for my own good? Check to both. But what can anyone expect from a girl without a mother to teach her softness, beauty, grace and all the things that girls are expected to be in this world.

I wear Cosimo's gown only to ease my conscience. He is a nice-enough man – for a Patrician. I should be kinder to him. He waits for me in the backstage parlour. The other girls are here too, made up as I am, but their dresses pale in comparison to my own. Cosimo was right. Before, the girls used to laugh when they looked at me. Now, they flinch. Cosimo grins, pleased with my submission. I roll my eyes, of course. I can't have him thinking that I actually have a heart.

"Look who is actually taking my advice for once." He presses his palms together and inclines his head, poking fun at me. He bows to me with his hands in the air several times. As he hails me, I shrink away, my posture slumps and my face turns ruddy in embarrassment. "Dominus has finally answered my prayers."

"Don't get used to it," I say, rearranging the chains of metal that hold the steel plates and scales together. "Can you ask your god to make this stupid thing lighter?"

He brushes my comment aside with a chuckle. He ushers me over to our reserved seating area, two plush velvet armchairs. "And look, we're matching." He unbuttons his striped suit jacket to reveal a waistcoat made from a material similar to my gown.

"How cute." I sneer at him but even my sarcasm won't wipe the toothy grin from his face. I wonder if this man can ever be sad.

Cosimo explains the format of the interview. I will be going first. At least that way I get it over with quickly, I convince myself. Even the poised Patrician girls seem a little on edge. Trixie Merula seems to have that effect on people. The technician instructs the mentors to leave so that they can begin airing the broadcast. Cosimo squeezes my hand before he departs and whispers, "I believe in you."

And with that, I am left in the room with the girls who would love nothing more than to see me fail. The exception is Aria. She manoeuvres herself closer to me. Her usual eccentricity is absent. I suppose she has been advised to turn the theatrics down a notch or two.

"Hey, Electa." She starts stroking my dress as if it were some type of pet. I force myself not to snap at her. She means well. I manage a half-smile, masking my nerves. I can't let them see me afraid. "I have some advice for you."

My eyebrows crease in my suspicion. Aria's voice is silver-toned, and a little cloying. It almost makes me want to put my hand over my ears to muffle the noise.

"Be sure to comment on Trixie's appearance before she can ask you anything. She likes to think of herself as a twenty-year-old still. Stroke her ego and it may soften the blows."

With all the surgery Trixie has had, she should look twenty. I will keep Aria's comment in mind, but I am still unsure whether to trust her intentions. "Why are you helping me?"

"Because I like you, isn't that reason enough?"

I suppose it would be if I were anywhere else other than this snake den. In the background, Trinity sulks in a corner, Valentina re-applies her scarlet lip paint in the mirror and Ember files her nails in the shape of claws. Is Aria really the angel she seems? I notice only now as I examine her expression how gaunt her face is, how her bones jut out from her taut skin. Before I can think much more about it, the technician summons me to the stage entrance.

"*Bonam Fortunam*," Aria says.

Good luck. I am going to need it.

The theme tune from Trixie's talk show thunders from the loudspeakers overhead. I can't hear my own breathing. I think I may even stop. Bile rises in my throat, and my whole body seems to sway beneath me. This is it. I have to pull myself together. *For Vel and Lana*, I tell myself over and over.

"Please welcome ... Electa Steel." The commentary plays as the music dies away. Then there is silence, anticipation, and my heart thumping against my ribcage. The technician thrusts me onto the podium.

I now stand in the basin of the amphitheatre with thousands of faces glaring down. *Click. Click. Click.* The sound of the camera shutters engulfs all other noise. The flashes come all at once and all I can see is dancing white light. Then comes the laughter and I realise I must have been standing here motionless for several seconds. They are laughing at me. This is bad, very bad. I picture Cosimo cringing from his seat in the upper gallery. I keep my spine straight and force my shoulders back. I wave to the camera as Cosimo told me. Deep breaths. One. Two. Three. My hands stop shaking. I stride over to Trixie. She stands to greet me, extending her arm. Her grip is firmer than I would have expected it to be. There is this certain rapier-like glint in her grey eyes. I feel as though she is about to eat me alive. I take the seat opposite her own, both couches angled towards the audience.

"You look wonderful tonight, Miss Merula," I say, mustering as much confidence as I can and filling my voice with it. I can't let her hear my nerves. She rakes over me with her cunning eyes, searching for a weakness, a flaw. Dominus knows I have many of them.

A smirk grows on her plump burgundy lips. "Are you trying to charm me, Miss Steel?"

Obviously. I hope Aria was right about this. "I'm hoping to soften the blows." I meet her gaze, and as much as I want to turn away, I can't. She can't see me afraid. The audience surges with laughter. Trixie purses her lips and tilts her head, ready to pounce.

"I have never met such a charming Pleb." Her sweet smile remains as she says this, and I don't even wince at the nickname. She is trying to break me, and I can't allow her the chance.

"I suppose the Patrician charm has started to rub off on me," I quickly counter, projecting my voice towards the audience. They clap gently, indicating approval. It is working. Whatever I am doing is working. My eyes drift across the tier upon tier of colourful Patricians. One figure stands out. His silhouette is nebulous and all I can make out clearly is a set of emerald eyes and the off-beat slow clap of his palms.

The squawk of Trixie's voice brings the theatre back into focus. "How are you getting on with the lovely Prince Asher?"

I knew this question was coming. This is a lie that won't roll off the tongue easily. "Well … we're very different. In fact, we're from two completely different worlds. I suppose opposites attract." The response comes out a little too quickly. I hope she doesn't see through my pretence.

An eyebrow quirks on Trixie's lifeless face. Perhaps all she can do is frown. She has spotted an opportunity to pick away at me again. I brace myself for what comes next. "In what way are you opposites? Surely the prince needs a consort who will complement not contradict him?"

I breathe slowly, taking in all the air I can. It is a hot mid-summer's evening and the humidity sticks to my skin. My brow is damp, and I fight the urge to wipe the sweat away with my forearm. That would not be lady-like at all.

"I think the best way I could put it is that the prince is like fire, and I am like ice. We are completely repellent to each other." As I say this, gasps resound from the stalls, and I know Cosimo must have his head in his lap right about now. I continue, "But I genuinely believe he is capable of melting the ice in my heart and I am capable of tempering his flame."

The Patricians, of course, lap this up. The women go "aw" in their adulation. The men clap. They believe meaningless platitudes just as often as they spout them. Trixie, however, is not convinced, but there is this flash of admiration in her eyes. She knows exactly what I am doing. In this moment, I am pleased with the person I am pretending to be. Cosimo gives me a subtle nod from the front row.

I see now why they call Trixie "the fox". Her eyes are stark grey, cold and sly. Her features are feline and her voice purrs. "Why should you be the empress, Miss Steel?"

I stand without thinking. The gown is heavy and weighs me down, but I force my posture upright. "As you can see, I may not be the most refined girl here, nor am I the strongest, or the smartest or the prettiest." The metal of my dress gleams in the spotlight. Cosimo made me wear this for a reason, and I will be damned if I don't show it off to the world. "But I am a warrior. I know a lot of you think I don't belong here. Truthfully, I don't believe that I belong here either. Yet, here I am, ready to fight for change. I want to represent Patricians and Plebeians alike. We are all fundamentally human and I am a living example that no matter where you come from you can make your voice heard, you can inspire and be remembered for something over than just living."

A pleasing hum of cheers escapes from the spectators. I sit down once again, out of breath and exhausted by the sheer weight of my dress. I spot Crew just behind Cosimo. He seems pleased and offers me a crisp nod.

Trixie narrows her eyes while examining me. "How stirring," she comments, and I note her insipid tone. I may have roused the audience, but she is undeceived by my posturing. She smirks – it is too crooked to be a genuine smile. "Thank you for your time, Electa," she says.

I tip my head in deference and take my cue to leave the stage. A thunderous orchestra of applause follows me as I disappear behind the red velvet drapes. Warmth spreads through my body, the energy of the encore thrills me. Cosimo was right. The Patrician high society are so accustomed to such hollow mendacity that they can longer distinguish between what is real and what is fake. He knows exactly what he is doing, and I suppose that is why Spartaca wanted us to be paired. He has a talent for oratory, fashion and is a master raconteur. All qualities necessary of his office and duty to the emperor he serves. Lucky for me, those qualities may just help me win.

Back stage, I am met with poisonous glares from Ember and Valentina. I quickly sidestep them and find Aria in the corner with the technician. She is up next and I thank her for the advice before she is hurried on stage. Cosimo flings his arms around me and holds me in an embrace for as long as I allow. I shrug him off after a few seconds, but in a kinder manner than I usually would.

"Thank you," I say, without even having to force out the words. Cosimo's mouth gapes in surprise. I think this may be the first time I have actually been nice to him.

He brushes my gratitude aside, waving his hand through the air in the space between us. "It was all you. That fire and ice metaphor. Brilliant. It was almost like looking in a mirror."

I press my lips together and nod comically. "Sure. I'm not quite a palavering dimwit yet thank you very much."

He laughs, warming his face with joy. His happiness is enough to bring a smile to my own face. But our laughter invites an unwelcome visitor. Ember approaches, flexing her lacquered nails, all black. Her cape trails behind her. It is made of red gossamer silk, sheer yet regal. She is the embodiment of an empress and she has dressed for the occasion. Her hair is pinned back with a golden olive wreath, the crown of the Imperial consort. "I was expecting a lot worse, Steel." She spits as she speaks to me. I am nothing but an ill-bred Pleb to her. "Perhaps I have a competitor after all."

She steps dangerously close to me. I bare my teeth like a dog. Cosimo grips my hand, just in case. If I hit her, it would mean immediate disqualification. I restrain myself – for now.

"What is your problem?" I can't understand why she bothers with me. I feel Cosimo's grasp tighten, and I clench my fists.

"You." She glowers, her eyes darting up and down over my body. She towers over me, but I am not intimidated. "You don't deserve to be here. We have worked our whole lives for this, and you simply walk in here and bewitch the princes with your vulgar Pleb charms."

A voice interrupts her. "Making excuses for when you lose?" Lix places his hand on my shoulder protectively. He has come at just the right time. I unclench my fists. "Such bad-sportsmanship is beneath you." His cunning smile makes her squirm.

There is a flash of envy in her eyes. "Find some other girls to bother, preferably ones that don't belong to your brother, Half-Prince," she hisses.

Lix's expression falls. The nickname must be one she has used before, many a time. There is history between the two of them. They stand across from each other, staring the other down with hard, cold eyes. Ember is taller than Calix in her heeled sandals, and he shrinks in her presence. Cosimo had mentioned Lix had a history with girls who belonged to his brother. Is Ember the girl he had referred to?

Cosimo steps between them. "Now, now, you two, let us all play nicely," he clucks, and both of them take a step back. He has diffused the situation, for now.

Ember is called onstage. She struts off towards the curtains and tosses her braided ponytail behind her. I turn to Lix, grateful for his intervention. I am aware, however, of Cosimo's presence. He wouldn't want me to acknowledge the prince, let alone show him gratitude.

"I can fight for myself," I say, immediately regretting the coolness of my words.

He pauses, confused. "I was just trying to help, El."

I am used to Lix being soft, gentle and kind. My reaction has made his stance stiffen, and his eyes darken in the dull lighting. He is not the boy by the lake. He is a prince now.

"I don't need your help," I quip, but I am not angry with him. I have no reason to be. I am angry at myself for lying to him earlier, for scheming with an organisation that killed his entire family. I am distancing myself from him, unwillingly. Maybe it is better for the both of us that way.

He runs a calloused hand through the tresses of his hair. I notice only now how scarred he is around his neck. These are not the wounds of manual labour but from a childhood of turmoil, a childhood at the hands of Spartaca.

"I didn't intend to upset you, Electa, and I'm sorry that I did." His voice remains soft, despite the coldness that now envelopes him.

"It's fine, I just…" I don't know what to say without risking my newfound peace with my advisor. "I just like to stand up for myself." I mutter a feeble excuse for my harsh words.

Lix seems unconcerned as he simply shrugs. "Remind me never to get on your bad side." He laughs a little to ease the strain between us.

"I lash out easily."

Lix doesn't seem to care much for my pathetic attempt at an apology. "I don't. I suppose that's why we get on. Opposites attract."

His is reiterating my words about Asher from the interview. Lix is jealous of his brother, that much is clear to me now – Cosimo had warned me. There is another side to Lix, and this is just my first glimpse of it.

Lix walks out of the side door that leads to the stalls and silence descends upon the room. Cosimo is restless beside me. The atmosphere has been pulled taut like the string of a lyre, and his slightest movement makes me jerk.

"What happened with Ember and Lix?" My voice sounds stern. At least he can't criticise me for showing any favour to the Umbrian prince.

Cosimo ponders for a moment, as if wondering whether to divulge what he knows. "Ember." He sighs. "She caused some trouble between the princes, that is as much as I know." His voice trails away, and I know a liar when I hear one. He knows much more than he is letting on.

Before I can question him further, my attention is captured by the monitor. Ember's interview is being shown. I move nearer to the screen. Trixie, the fox disguised as an old woman, eyes up her next opponent. Ember looks formidable but her popularity is still a mystery to me. She is not quite the beauty that Trinity is, nor is she as smart as Valentina. But she is striking, in the way an empress should be. She commands a room and makes others shrink in her presence. She is a Latian through and through, exhibiting the traits we value above all in our society – ambition, honour, resourcefulness, cleverness and cunning.

"Ember, I have heard that you enjoy a good relationship with the prince," Trixie purrs, testing the waters with her iron-faced foe.

Ember's eyes brighten at the mention of the prince. She said when we first arrived at the Palatine that she had visited often, throughout her formative years. "Yes." She beams, and I think it must be the first time I have ever seen her smile. The expression doesn't suit her dour features, and her mouth twitches in its new, unfamiliar position. "We have known each other since we were children. I suppose when you have grown up with someone, you know them far more intimately than anybody else ever can." She puffs out her chest like some sort of boastful exotic bird. Her dress is made entirely of feathers, dyed crimson red. The audience roar into applause, the din much louder than it was for me. The Patricians adore her. I silently pray for Trixie to tear her apart.

Trixie cocks her head as if she has spotted a chip in Ember's flawless mannequin façade. "Well then, I assume you're already the prince's favourite?"

This is a trap. A trap Ember is about to fall right into. Cosimo wears a smug smile beside me. He knows just as well as I do that Trixie is on the verge of mangling Ember Hadrianus live on an Appia-wide broadcast.

Ember plays coy, covering her face with her hands. "I'd like to think so. We are very close."

Her slight smirk suggests that they were much more than childhood friends and perhaps they still are. The thought bothers me more than it should. The prince and Ember are well-suited. Arrogant, spiteful, superficial, *Patrician*. They deserve each other.

Ember continues, digging herself a grave at Trixie Merula's feet. "I will let you in on a little secret. Since we were young, Ash had promised me that one day we would be married and very much in love." She wears a playful grin, although she seems to be straining herself with the niceties. Her eyes don't crinkle at the edges in the way a natural smile would allow. Her movements are exaggerated to draw attention to herself.

The camera pans out to reveal the audience, who extol her with their hollers and cheers of praise. A few even have handmade signs that read *Vote Ember Hadrianus.*

"I think the prince and I would both like to fulfil that dream," she blusters, clasping her hands together in a gesture of hope, or rather desperation. I roll my eyes as Cosimo jabs my side, playfully.

Much to my dismay, her comment has sent the audience into a frenzy of ovation, many of them stand, chanting over and over, "Empress Hadrianus." The euphony of a thousand voice, strident with the distinct twang of their Orean accents, is enough to rattle the stone amphitheatre to its core. The vibrations pulse through me, filling me with rage. How are people believing the *stercus* she spouts?

Trixie must be the only one in the theatre not fooled by her act. Much like how she wasn't fooled by mine. Yet, Trixie had this sort of strange respect for me but certainly doesn't for Ember. There is perhaps one other person who is impervious to Ember's charms. The green-eyed man who watched me intently is motionless. He is still shrouded by shadows in the far corner box of the upper gallery but seems distracted now, his eyes darting around the concave marbled theatre, not paying attention much to anything or anyone, it seems.

Trixie doesn't wait for the audience to settle. "Ember, what makes you better suited to the role of Imperial consort when compared to your competitors?"

Ember is too busy basking in her glory to even meet her interviewers' eye. "I want the throne more than the others do," she replies eventually. "It has been my ambition since I was a child. The ULA needs someone like me at the helm, someone with the drive and determination to oversee this great Haven of Ore and the Latian League." She is shouting as if she is a preacher, flailing her hands about. Her words seem to fall effortlessly from her mouth. "I am a daughter of Dominus. Trust in the Choosing. Trust in me. I will stop at nothing to become the next empress of Ore."

The rhetoric is masterful yet her composure slips. Ember has fallen into Trixie's carefully laid trap and whatever she says next will be meaningless.

"I get the impression that you want the title, rather than the prince." Trixie's features morph from soft to wolfish. She snarls as she ensnares her hapless prey. Her tone is matter of fact, but her tongue is a weapon, a sharp one.

"That's not what I meant," Ember snaps back but it's too late.

"You've had your eyes on the throne since you were a little girl, isn't that right?" Every one of Trixie's word is like a blow, knocking Ember down over and over. Ember flinches, her eyes blinking at a rapid rate. I can't help but revel in her discomfort. Now millions of Appians will see her for what she truly is – a ruthless, cold-hearted bully.

"Your father has been pushing you to this end since you were old enough to talk," Trixie continues. "Tell me I'm wrong."

Ember is left speechless, her mouth agape.

The cameras pan from the podium to the stalls where Ember's father is seated. Marcus Licinius Hadrianus is the richest man in Ore and one of the most powerful. The luminary of the Patrician elite. Of course, he would be the one behind his daughter's ambitions. He will climb the *Cursus Honorum* right to the very top even if it is by the proxy of his own daughter. His tawny skin is flushed red with ire. Ember's head hangs down as she twiddles idly with her raven braid. Monsters are made, not born. Ember is who she is because of her family and their expectations. Her failure means the loss of not only her life but the respect and reputation of her family. Honour is everything to the Patricians.

Trinity is called to the stage next. She steps out onto the podium in a violet *stola*, cinched at the waist by a snake fibula. The serpent is the typical insignia of Ore, appearing on our flags, statues and military uniforms. Trinity's traditional style is simple and serves to promote her beauty. She doesn't need to compensate for her looks with fancy jewellery or gowns. She sits across from the fox and is in her typically sullen mood.

"Royce, I presume?" Trixie gestures to Trinity's hairstyle. Her golden locks have been pinned back into a decorative up-do, with loose ringlets cascading from both sides of her fringe.

Trinity's look is the work of Royce Segal, the most celebrated *Ornatrix* in the ULA. She is a socialite, fashion icon and celebrity in her own right. Royce is from Lutetia but has been the High-Imperial *Ornatrix* for some years now. I am sure that Trinity's family have offered ample payment for her services.

Trinity runs her palm over the silk of her dress, flattening out any creases. "Yes," she answers simply.

Trixie poses her usual questions. Trinity doesn't say much of interest or step a foot out of line, and Trixie struggles to even make her sweat. It is not that Trinity is boring but rather that she has been so well trained that no question seems to phase her.

Trixie tilts her head to the side and purses her lips, tiring of the interaction. Her tone becomes monotonous and the questions sound as if they are being read from a list. "Tell me, Trinity, if you were to become Imperial consort, what would be the first thing you change?"

Trinity, who has slouched in her seat for the entirety of the interview, sits up a little straighter. "I would stop the Choosing." She doesn't even blink.

The whole audience gasps. Cosimo holds his hand over his mouth, and I am sure I make some sort of sound in my astonishment. This must be some sort of joke. No Patrician would ever want to stop the Choosing.

Trinity's mentor stands near us, a middle-aged woman with neat braids and masculine facial features. Her fingers brush her parted lips and I know this can't have been planned. The woman paces up and down the room, just behind us. For the first time this evening, the theatre has descended into silence. No one moves, and even the unflappable Trixie Merula is at a loss for words.

Finally, Trixie composes herself, bringing an end to the cold quiet that has enveloped the Victoria. "The Choosing is a two-hundred-year-old tradition, Miss Messalla, and you wish to stop it?"

"Yes, I do," Trinity answers, and her voice doesn't falter.

The Patrician spectators who have roistered all evening with goblets filled to the brim with wine and snack boxes beneath their seats are still. No one eats or drinks. They sit like statues, their stares falling on the podium in awe of what is happening before their eyes.

Trinity is passive, as if she is unaware of the effect of her words. "Our society divides people into better and worse at the young age of seventeen. We are all different, no better, no worse than each other. This is something that should be celebrated, not punished." Her expression hardens and it is now that I realise that this is no act, no play for attention. She is genuine, and the Institute will see this as treason.

Warren had said the regenerators manipulate unholy thoughts. If that were true, Trinity would have been cleansed of such ideology. But there are no regenerators in the Palatine. Trinity's mind is her own.

Trinity is a Patrician. She has never had to fear the Choosing and all that it entails. It is a mystery to me why she feels the way she does, let alone to voice it in front of the entire world. She has self-sabotaged any chance she had at winning. The Choosing is the rite of passage in our society and the backbone of Appia as a nation. Take it away and we are nothing. The Havens will be nothing. I can't help but admire her for the courage she has shown and the courage that I will never have.

Valentina's interview is uneventful and overshadowed by what came before it. Trinity's statement is sure to be the only thing remembered from this evening. Valentina is typically precise and uppity in her demeanour. She is clever with her words, albeit a little dull. Her steely blue eyes light up at the mention of politics and diplomacy. I am sure the Senate must favour her. She is the tame candidate from their perspective, talented, intelligent and not overly radical with her ideology. Her family are traditional, conservative politicians and lawmakers.

She flaunts her technical jargon and boasts of her feats in academic competitions in all four Havens. I suppose it is just three Havens now, with Umbria in ruin. The news broadcasts still show the League in picture-perfect condition, with its vast prairies and the cornfields of the Lowlands. It must be old footage. Latians believe Umbria to be a prosperous place, foreign, far-away, but peaceful. Another Institute lie.

Valentina ends her interview by noting the importance of the Choosing in the wake of Trinity's *treacherous* statements, as she called them. She would make a fine empress as far as diplomacy is concerned.

The Grand Imperial Ball is held in the Fabian ballroom. It is grand and monolithic by design. The ceiling is vaulted with pale marble. I stare up in awe at the painted frescoes depicting scenes from Appian mythology. The deity of Dominus personified in his serpent form is in the position of prominence, at the frescoes' centre.

Cosimo doesn't leave my side as he presses me to engage in conversation with the attendees, mostly politicians and socialites with whom I have little in common. I notice Crew among the crowds, he always has one of his ice eyes on me. He winks as our eyes meet and I quickly look away, revolted.

Cosimo parades me around the room, introducing me to everyone we come into contact with. The Patricians like to make a show of things, prancing about like peacocks, boasting about their feathers in a display of power to the lesser Leagues. A few of the men and woman I meet compliment my dress and others, the braver ones, dare to ask me about politics, a subject I know very little about.

Cosimo helps me as much as he can, whispering names in my ear and steering the conversations in directions that are simpler for me to understand. After what feels like an hour of idle chit-chat, Cosimo deserts me, finding himself a large glass of liquor to lessen his embarrassment.

I am left to my own devices with an old lady whose name I have already forgotten. She is pleasant enough, for a Patrician, but drones on about her grandson whose war feats she compares to the labours of Hercules, an ancient hero famed for his fantastical adventures. I pay little attention; my mind is elsewhere. The nagging thought of my brother in chains and the pain of my mysterious injury clouds my senses, and the woman's voice becomes all but a hum in my ear. That is, until Prince Asher saunters over in all his haughty glory. He embraces the stout old woman whose greying hair has been pinned back into a demure bun. I realise that she must be his grandmother, Helena Titania Ovicula, who ruled sixty years ago. I would never have imagined that Asher was the grandson she had spoken so highly of.

The prince takes my hand. His is surprisingly warm, and I force myself not to snatch mine away. "*Opposites attract.* So, you are attracted to me now?" He purses his lips, teasing me.

I hide the scowl on my face, conscious that his grandmother is standing beside us.

She presses the two of us together, wearing the same smirk that Asher does. "I will leave you two alone."

Please don't.

A canny smile forms on her thin lips. "See you later, Ashy," she says, kissing him on the cheek.

As she leaves, I attempt to stifle my laughter. "Ashy?"

His playful grin is gone for a few seconds and his cheeks flush red. "Don't ever say that again." Then he laughs with me, and his smirk returns. "Please tell me she didn't say anything embarrassing."

I press my lips together and tilt my head. A fearful expression forms on the prince's face. The enjoyment I get from teasing him surpasses any form of entertainment available to me in the Palatine. "No. Although, she has convinced herself you are Hercules reborn."

"Well, she's not wrong," he says, lifting his arm to flex his muscles. His face tightens as he tenses. I must admit his physique is impressive. I am beginning to wonder if all this vanity and pride is simply a front that he hides his true self behind.

I stare at him for a while. He shifts from one foot to the other, and the martial suit, which I have seen him wear before at state events, is now a whiskey-stained white. He has been drinking again. His clothes are dishevelled and the darkness beneath his eyes is a remnant of sleepless nights. "I never knew you fought in the war."

He pauses, his molten eyes cast downwards at his gleaming leather boots. "I fought for as long as my father would allow." His words stumble out in his inebriated state. "Most of what they say about me, about what I did, was either staged or fabricated. Sometimes I don't even know which. My father said it was good propaganda to have a miracle child." He rolls backwards on his heels, as if it offers him some sort of comfort.

I examine his skin. It is flawless. "You don't have the scars that soldiers do."

He lets out a small, choked laugh. "You really think my father would let anyone lay a finger on his heir?" His eyes burn with a fire I have never seen before. I am not quite sure whether to be afraid of the demons of the prince's mind. He is alight, crashing and burning, while the whole world cheers him on.

I do my best to sound polite, conscious of Crew edging towards the pair of us. "It seems like he really cares about you." I soften my tone, hoping to calm him in some way.

"Trust me, he doesn't." The words are cold, and his bright eyes are glassy with what can only be sadness. Then, as if it never happened, he grins widely at the thought of something. "So, you really think you can temper my flame?" he says, mocking me and my words spoken in the interview.

"Shut up. I just said what Cosimo wanted me to." I can't have him thinking I actually came up with that by myself.

He nods, narrowing his eyes. "That doesn't sound like the sort of thing Cosimo would say." He steps closer to me, but it is a step too far. "I think you're actually starting to like me, but you enjoy this game of cat and mouse far too much to admit it." His breath is warm against my cheek and the distinct stench of liquor makes me gag.

"I don't play games, Prince," I retort.

My tone must be much more biting than he expected, as he holds his hands up and backs away. "Will you ever address me by my actual name?"

"Probably not."

The prince reaches into one of his breast pockets and takes out a cigarette. He reaches over to one of the torches and lights the cigarette in the flame. I stare as he puffs clouds of smoke in my face. I am almost certain he is not supposed to do this, here in front of all these people. Tobacco is an illicit substance in the ULA and has been ever since the Institute was established two hundred years ago. Cigarettes are traded on a black market, but they are an expensive and lucrative commodity from the outside world. Soldiers smoke, the Greys do too, but not publicly and certainly not at a state ball. But then again, Asher is a prince, and he enjoys impunity from Institute law.

Shauna, the princess and Asher's half-sister, marches over with meaningful strides. The train of her elegant carmine *stola* trails behind her, and the red reminds me of blood. I haven't heard her utter a single word since I have been here. She doesn't speak now either, as she snatches the cigarette from Asher's parted lips.

"I was just—" the prince begins, but the words stick in his mouth as Shauna throws the cigarette to the ground and stomps down hard with her right heel. "Finishing that," he says, unimpressed by his sister's intervention.

"You need to grow up." Her voice is smaller than I expected it to be. If it weren't for her olive wreath crown, you would never think her to be a princess. She is pale-skinned, unlike her father and the prince. It is rumoured the emperor's mistress was Lutetian, at least that is what my *Ornatrix* mentioned in passing. Her lengthy black hair is covered tonight by a red scarf that is held in place by her crown. It makes her seem older than seventeen. She barely has an inch of skin on show, while the rest of the youthful girls in attendance tonight are scantily clad in dresses that bare their bodies from every angle.

The prince wobbles from foot to foot, and Shauna grips him sternly. She is yet to acknowledge my presence. "Ash, you must stop this." Her tone is firm but gentle.

Shauna is genuinely concerned for his welfare. I, however, couldn't care less. He is rich, spoilt and rotten to the core. I can't let myself pity him. Only a fool would ever pity a prince.

She turns to me. Her stare is not scathing in the way that a Patrician's usually is. "I'm sorry about him. I need to find some water; would you mind keeping an eye on him for a minute or two?"

I nod as I have no choice but to oblige. The prince stumbles over to me and all I can do is pray for someone to rescue me. Just as he is about to open his mouth, a man approaches. Dark skin, raven hair and eyes like a mid-winter sky. His resemblance to Ember is uncanny, and I realise he is her father – Marcus Licinius Hadrianus.

"Oh, dear Ash, have you been drinking too much again?" Marcus slaps his palm hard against the prince's back. He has a deep, thundering voice much like the emperor's. He, too, is dressed in Fabian red, and wears a long jacket that touches the floor. The wealth I have heard so much about is on display. He is dripping with all manners of jewels and gold chains.

The prince squints and recognises the figure before him. "Ah, Marcus, good to see you. Have you met Electa Steel?"

The man extends his hand and grasps my wrist a little too tightly. He is lucky that no one will remember Ember's interview after Trinity's sedition, otherwise, I doubt he would have shown face here this evening. "I know who she is. *Salve*, Miss Steel." His eyes scrape over me, much like his daughter's do. "I know your father, Miss Steel. He is a good man, a good soldier."

It is not surprising that he knows my father. Marcus is not only the leader of the Optimates but also the general of Legion I, Latia's most elite warriors. He is a good friend of Director Drusus, too. But I wonder if anyone can truly be friends with a man like Lysander Drusus without being controlled by him in some way.

"Come to think of it, I haven't seen your father in command for the past few days. They must have sent him back to war."

I nod. Of course, Spartaca won't be letting my father run around the Haven. He would know Vel is missing. Crew must have manipulated the military rotations. It would explain the strange notification that Father received on Choosing Day, instructing him to return to the front. Vel warned me he would be returning to war. At least he is safe, as safe as you can be out there. He has survived these many years of war with barely a scratch.

Marcus smiles, and I think he is trying to be kind. He understands the turmoil that war has on families better than most. Shauna hurries back with a goblet of water and forces the drink down her brother's throat. Marcus cackles with laughter as if this is a common occurrence. It probably is.

Suddenly, the room falls silent. Only one sound remains. The clip of a heel on marble stone echoes through the ballroom. Asher and Shauna stare over my shoulder, as does Marcus, and even Crew who stands just metres away. I turn to follow their gaze. A man descends from a spiralling staircase. His head is down as he takes the steps in long strides. I can't yet see his face. His leather-belted robe is forest green, almost black. The man's tenebrous silhouette is similar to the strange spectator I saw earlier at the Victoria. When he finally looks up, his eyes are glowing green in the torchlight. I know little of the Patrician world and its inhabitants, yet this man is recognisable, even to me.

Lysander Drusus walks like he is a god. The effect his entrance has had on the room is remarkable. No one speaks, and the violin plays to the cadence of his step. His ravenous eyes dart about the room and fall on me. Our eye contact is uncomfortable and certainly not brief. I shrink in his spectral presence, unable to look away. He steps up to me, and while conversation resumes elsewhere, I am speechless, silenced by the god-like creature who stands before me.

"I hope you don't mind me saying that you look divine tonight, Miss Steel. The dress is spectacular."

His image has always been distant to me, but now, up close, I see clearly his hauntingly beautiful eyes. Most people here in the Palatine have eyes that are lifeless and dull whatever colour they may be, yet his are piercing and completely alive. There is something inexplicably unearthly about him, his ivory skin and jet-black hair, features that are entirely unusual here, in Latia or anywhere for that matter.

"Thank you," I say, my voice small. I am uncharacteristically quiet and it only now I understand why Lysander Drusus is feared. If he can silence an unruly Plebeian girl, he can silence anyone.

He seems to stare through my soul, not inspecting me as Trixie did. Yet he looks at me in a strange way, one I can't apprehend. "You made quite the impression in the interview. I was pleasantly surprised." As he speaks, I notice his precise elocution, his accent, even more refined than Cosimo's. Lysander's words are clear-cut and delivered with remarkable eloquence.

I am almost ashamed to speak, so I stay silent, hoping he will tire of me and walk away. He doesn't acknowledge the prince or princess who stand at my side, and neither does he depart. He is waiting for me to respond but I can't find my tongue. This is not the man I had expected to meet.

He is not cold, nor monstrous as Spartaca and Calix have painted him to be. He has an incontestable charm, with a manner that ensnares your senses all at once. Yet, there is this darkness in his eyes, a darkness that follows in his wake. He is warm but leaves the air around him cold. He is a demon in the guise of a god. I can't be fooled by him; I know who he is and the things he has done. He stands for all those things that I hate about this world. I should feel revulsion at the sight of the man, but I don't – and this is what terrifies me the most.

"Miss Steel, would you dance with me?" He extends one long arm and overturns his hand in one graceful movement. "With the prince's permission, of course." His eyes fall on the drunken prince. Lysander seems to study him in those short seconds, searching for a flaw. He doesn't look at me in that way. Lysander Drusus stares at me as if I am an open book, one that he has read countless times.

Asher quickly responds after a nudge from Shauna. Her expression barely masks the dismay she must feel at her brother's behaviour. "Yes, yes, of course."

I let my hand be taken by Lysander, who whisks me close to his body. I stumble from the speed of the movement, but he steadies me without a word. It occurs to me now that the centre of this man's attention is a dangerous place to be. His interest in me is vaguely threatening but I can't run away, not this time. His skin is cool to the touch as he places his palm on the small of my back. I don't recoil, as much as I may want to.

"May I call you Electa?" he asks, and I am surprised by his politeness. A man with that much power can get away with calling anyone whatever he wants without reproach.

I nod, still unable to speak.

"Electa, tell me about yourself."

This is it. I have no choice but to engage. I gather my wits. "There isn't much to tell. I'm sure you know who I am." I immediately regret speaking. I can't control my tongue or my bitterness and that is a terrible combination, especially when conversing with someone like Lysander Drusus. I expect him to react in some way, but he doesn't at all. My comment floats into the air, unnoticed by the man whom I dance with, a little too intimately for my liking.

"I certainly do. Forgive me if this seems blunt but how did a girl like you end up here?"

I narrow my eyes, but the words he speaks are not insulting, unlike most of the Patricians I have met here. His tone is flat, and I understand that he is not trying to belittle me.

"I don't know. I suppose I did well on Assay Day." I lie easily, as if it is my natural instinct.

"I reviewed your scores and they were remarkably high for someone with no elite training and especially for someone who fainted."

His words seem to puncture my lungs, snatching all the oxygen away. I struggle to breathe, gulping down the air as if it is water. He knows my secret and he will certainly not take kindly to Spartaca's subversion. I try my best to remain calm and maintain a neutral expression, but if anyone will uncover the conspiracy, it will be Lysander. He knows a liar when he sees one.

"I don't score my own tests so I wouldn't know," I say, taking a breath to steady myself. My shoulders heave as I inhale deeply.

"It is a little odd, but don't get the wrong idea, everything seems in order. I actually quite like your steeliness, excuse the pun," he says, his chameleon eyes transforming once again, becoming soft. "You may even have my vote."

As we sway, I try my best to keep my footing. Lysander is taller than me and it is hard to keep up with his movements. He looks at me again now, but different to before. He looks at me like I am an apparition, and I can't understand why or if I even want to know. It is strange that I feel so nervous and at ease with the same man.

"You don't seem like the type of man who would want a Plebeian on the throne."

He tilts his head and grins in a way that makes me wonder whether he wants to kill me. "It seems you don't understand me at all, Electa. That will have to change. We must spend more time together, get to know each other perhaps."

His interest in me is certainly disconcerting but I can't refuse his desire. My hands are tied, and my enemies are in power, for now. I have to play the game – and well – if I want to survive. I must humour Lysander Drusus or face his wrath.

"Thank you for the dance, Electa. I'm sure I'll be seeing you very soon." And with that he steps out of my arms and leaves me paralysed on the dance floor.

It is only now that I notice the chill of my skin. I look around, searching for a familiar face. Asher stands no longer with his sister but with Ember. He seems to be scolding her, probably for bringing up the marriage proposal in the interview. Ember tugs at his hand but the prince's attention is directed elsewhere. He sees me and takes Lysander's place. The warmth of his skin is a welcome relief after dancing with a demon. His golden complexion has waned to a sickly yellow. It must be the alcohol.

"Lysander stole you away before I got the chance." He is more coherent as he speaks; the water must have cleared his head, if only a little.

"He's very..." I struggle to find the right words to describe such a man. "Sinister."

The prince watches as colour returns to my complexion, I can feel the blood hot against my skin. "That's just Lysander. He has a way of scaring anyone, no matter how powerful they are."

I think this must be the only time that I have ever seen the prince serious. "Are you scared of him?"

The prince hesitates for a moment, and I think he hates me for it. "No," he barks, a little too quickly. This is the first time I have seen him vulnerable, as the boy beneath the façade. His stance stiffens and I know he is lying. "He's been like a brother to me and we get on but..."

"You're afraid."

He doesn't react kindly to my teasing. "I already said that I'm not," he says, gritting his teeth.

The ball continues for what seems like hours. The prince disappears rather quickly after our dance, not to be seen again. Crew is always one step behind me, watching my every move, just as he said he would. I try to sneak away when Cosimo is distracted, but someone follows me. I can hear footsteps behind me as I creep through the deserted halls, lit only by flames. The glass walls are lambent with the firelight, and the Palatine seems to sparkle around me as if it were a palace of the gods. My dress weighs me down and my pace slackens. Soon the shadowy figure is at my side.

"Just where do you think you're going?" Crew's gruff voice is distinctive and unmistakable.

I stop and turn to him. "Back to my room. It's been a long day," I mutter, panting from the speed of my walk.

He narrows his ice eyes. "What did Lysander say to you?"

"He knows about the fainting incident. I think he suspects me of something."

He ponders for a moment but doesn't seem concerned. "There's no evidence. He would never be able to trace the computer records back to us."

His confidence doesn't reassure me; I doubt anything will. I am simply a pawn in their game, and if this all goes to *Tartarus*, I will be the first to be removed from the board. Lysander senses that something strange is afoot, and he is certainly Spartaca's greatest danger. If anyone will uncover the Spartacan plot, it will be him and he will show no mercy.

"That won't stop him from tormenting me. He doesn't seem like the man who would take kindly to treason." The word makes me shiver and my blood run cold. I don't even want to imagine what they would do to me. I take a deep breath to calm myself, but the air seems to shake in my lungs.

"Pander to him, do exactly what he asks of you, perhaps even befriend him. He will ease off then."

I don't know what I expect him to do about Lysander. Even in the ballroom tonight, he was flanked by vigilites at all times. Their gun-metal uniforms, sparse, but present.

"Befriend him? You can't be serious." I almost choke on the words. Lysander Drusus is not the kind of man you are friends with. He is the kind of man that you avoid at all costs.

Crew puts an unwelcome arm around my shoulder as we walk. It is a threatening gesture, one that makes me shudder. "Most girls would leap at the opportunity."

"I'm not most girls, in case you hadn't noticed," I say, shrugging his arm away.

He stops in his tracks, staring me up and down with cool eyes. "Electa." I hate the sound of my name from his mouth. "Don't test me. I am tiring of your defiance. Remember we have your brother," he says, gripping my wrist, and as much as I tug, I can't escape. It is only now that I realise how vulnerable I am here. Everyone is at the ball, and I am alone with Crew and his corrupted Praetorians.

"How could I forget." I dare to be sardonic. "How is he by the way? And my father who you sent back to war. He'll be suspicious if Vel isn't replying to his messages."

Crew scoffs at my statement. "Do you really think we're amateurs at this? Vel is at home with my people and he is responding to your father."

"And the regenerators?"

"We hacked into their software."

That is probably what they did with mine. The regenerators never seemed to have much of an effect on me, the few times I used them.

"I want to see my brother. I want to know he is okay." I hope that some desperate quality in my voice will make him comply.

"That's not possible," he answers immediately.

Vel could be dead for all I know. I would be doing this for nothing. The world outside is nothing but smoke and mirrors and I am not sure whose story to trust. Spartaca is bad, but the Institute is even worse. I suppose you can't defeat a monster without becoming one yourself.

I straighten myself and lift my chin to meet his gaze. "I want to see my brother," I repeat, and the strength in my voice is a shock, even to me.

Crew's voice is equally strong. "I thought I had made myself clear, stupid girl. These are my rules." His grip constricts my ability to move. My skin burns under his touch, and my bones ache with a terrible pain. I feel as though he could snap my wrist at any second.

I breathe through the pain. I sharpen my expression and I feel my eyes steel. "You need me, Crew. Just let me see Vel," I demand, my tone resolute. I expect him to oblige but instead he slams me against the nearest wall, his hands moving from my wrist and closing around my neck. I make a desperate attempt to inhale, but it is futile. My head feels as if it is about to implode and my vision blurs. He releases me before I can pass out. I cough but compose myself. When I stand straight, mustering all my strength, I shove him away from me. To my surprise, he staggers backwards.

"You're stronger than you look, Steel." He laughs at me as if I am some cantankerous child. I wish I could slap his sneering face.

"What's going on here?" A voice echoes from the hallway. I turn quickly, but there are only shadows. A tiger emerges from the darkness, growling, baring its monstrous teeth. It is Atlas. I expect Asher to step into the light, but instead, Shauna stands tall and proud. "Mr Gracchus, I think it would be best if you go now."

Atlas nears Crew, who cowers in his presence. The soft thump of the tiger's paws on the stone is enough to make him jolt. He bows to the princess and turns on his heels, striding off quickly into the darkness.

I can only hope she didn't hear the entirety of our conversation. "He was discussing my sponsorship by the Populares," I say quickly, trying to think of any excuse to explain the situation she has found me in.

"It didn't look much like a discussion to me." She nears me, her steps graceful, precise. She reaches a hand to my neck, examining me for injury. Her touch is soft, unlike Crew's. "Did he hurt you?"

I shake my head, unnerved by the usually silent, stony-faced princess. I jerk away from her by instinct. She doesn't seem to mind. "Please don't tell anyone. It's embarrassing," I plead, knowing full well the implications this could have. No one can know the true nature of my relationship with Crew. I am sure she must see the terror in my eyes.

"If that's what you want, this will stay between us. I doubt he'll bother you again," she says, patting the crown of Atlas's head. He rubs himself against her, affectionately.

I didn't expect such kindness from the princess. Then again, I don't know much about her, other than what I have seen. She is laconic at state events, and usually reticent when in the presence of others.

"Thank you," I say, bowing my head in gratitude. I used to be a girl who bowed to no one, but in this case, I can make an exception.

I think she may struggle to smile, her expression is naturally aquiline, her features bird-like. "No need for that." Her voice is small but fierce. "You should be thanking him, I'm hardly terrifying." She gestures to the tiger at her feet. Atlas glances upwards, his eyes a golden yellow. I suppose he is not that bad after all. I dare to stroke him, reaching out a trembling hand. He pushes against my palm, but I am no longer afraid. "I think he likes you," she says. The corner of her mouth quirks up but she avoids my gaze.

"Why would you help me?" I can't help but ask.

She pauses, adjusting the *palla* that shrouds her head. Her raven locks cascade out at the front; the hair is long, falling below her breast. "I think you would be good for my brother."

111

A small laugh escapes me. "I'm not so sure." I sigh, knowing that if I were to marry him, he would be killed by my hand. As much as I dislike the prince, I am sure he doesn't deserve to die.

Shauna shrugs. "He likes you a lot, you know, I think more than he liked Ember at the beginning."

This is my chance to understand more about the strange dynamic that exists in the Imperial family. I can't say that I am not intrigued.

"Ember?"

The princess strolls to the window, peering out of its obsidian frames. She presses her face against the glass, staring at the night sky. "Yes, he really loved her once."

I didn't believe Asher capable of loving anyone. I knew they were lovers, but I thought it no more than a casual, young and reckless dalliance. "I didn't know," I murmur, letting my words drift away with my breath.

"Ember broke his heart," Shauna says, and her body stiffens. "She was in love with another."

Names run through my mind. "Who?"

Shauna looks me in the eyes for the first time. "Calix."

I nearly gasp. I would never have expected it, but it does explain their strange interaction earlier at the interviews. They had both acted as if they were spurned lovers, and now I realise that they are.

Shauna leans against the window frame in a casual stance. "Lix had feelings for her too, but he would never betray Ash."

That is not how Cosimo told the story. But, then again, he didn't say much about the matter at all. He simply spotted an opportunity to reel off his sententious nonsense.

"I get the impression you're not so fond of Ember."

She rolls her eyes, and a knowing noise passes from her lips. "You would be right. She liked to play Lix and Ash off against each other. It was cruel," she explains in a neutral tone, but I sense her hatred beneath it. Come to think of it, Ember must be the most emotionless female I have ever encountered. I am surprised she has the capacity to love anyone but herself.

Shauna continues, "I do believe she truly loved Calix but knew her father would never allow such a union. She decided the only way to win back my brother's favour was by claiming that Lix had seduced her."

The notion is ridiculous, even to me, who hasn't known the Umbrian prince for long. Lix seems to care for his adoptive brother deeply, despite his juvenile ways.

"Did he believe her?"

"Yes and no. I think he knew never to trust her again." The princess steps up to me, looking me over with her soulless eyes. "But almost everyone on Palatine Hill wants Ember to be his bride. This you already know."

I think back to the chanting in the Victoria earlier this evening, and the overwhelming support she had from the crowds at the Choosing ceremony, days ago now. Latia wants Ember Hadrianus as her empress. I won't be able to canvass the votes that her father has been buying for years with all his money and influence. But maybe I can put her down in that arena. If I want to save Vel, I won't have a choice.

"So, there is an expectation that Ember and Asher will wed?"

"Exactly." She sneers. "My father would be furious if anyone but her wins Imperial Panore. Ash has no say in the matter."

Even here, in the Palatine, sons and daughters bow to their fathers. It is a fact of life, I suppose, to be a vessel of your *pater's* desires. All a child truly wants is to be free, to have liberty, unbound by their father's expectations and the life they have been granted by society. The Havens don't protect us, they trap us. The prince has no escape from his life, much like I have no escape from mine.

"Everyone who supposedly cares about him would have him marry the girl who broke his heart?"

The words leave a little sadness in me. I now see why Asher behaves how he does – swigging on bottles of liquor, burning his throat every day, while his friends spur him on. No one gives a thought to how lonely, empty and lost he had to be to do it in the first place. I suppose alcohol is easier for him to swallow than the fact he will never be free. I felt the same way once. But for the first time in my life, I have hope that things can change.

Shauna nods, sadly. "Yes. Except for me and Calix, of course."

I shake my head, perhaps understanding the prince for the first time.

"That's why he drinks himself into oblivion," Shauna mutters, her voice but a whisper.

"I'm sorry," is all I can think to say.

"Don't be." The princess places a hand on my shoulder as she passes me, then stops. "We all have our demons." And then she walks away.

IX

ODERINT DUM METUANT

Let them hate, so long as they fear

The days that follow are scheduled from dawn to dusk. Signings, photo shoots, public appearances, promotional videos, interviews ... and it never stops. I bear it as much as I can – Cosimo's master plan and all it involves. Mostly, I just do as he tells me. I live on a diet of figs and wine. Figs, of course, being the quickest thing to eat when being hurried from one event to another. And wine, well, that helps with my nerves.

By the week's end, my name and photographs are plastered on every billboard in Ore. *Electa for Empress. Steel for strength.* The days blur into one and the routine quickly becomes monotonous. Cosimo moulds me into a starlet of his own creation with outlandish make-up, outfits and even surgery – straightening out my nose, smoothing my jaw, cutting away excess skin, polishing teeth. I begin to lose count of the procedures. I object, of course, but Cosimo reminds me of my own words. *Whatever it takes.* This goes on for so long that I start to no longer feel like myself.

The little spare time I have, I spend with Lix. He quickly forgives my outburst at the interview, and we grow closer with each passing day. We fish and hunt in the Palatine forest, and more often than not, simply talk. He keeps me sane. Our companionship is easy, unbound by the rules of our society. I forget, in some rare, beautiful moments, that my brother is a hostage and my father is off fighting in a war against the very people I work for.

The first round of voting sees me place third, behind Valentina and Ember. It seems that her dressing down in the interview has been quickly forgotten. Cosimo believes that I am catching up with Ember at a steady place. But while I have the full support of the Plebeians, I lack Senate support.

Cosimo targets moderate Senators, those who dislike Ember and her father, organising meetings in which I must impress them. We have daily lessons in

115

which he coaches me on politics and Patrician culture. For me, it is like learning a foreign language. Patrician parlance is complex and riddled with contradictions. There are times when I think the task ahead of me is impossible, but I persevere. What else can I do?

The big opportunity will come in just two days' time. The Senate's Summit is the next official event of Imperial Panore and it will be a chance for the five Panore girls to converse with Latian politicians, hopefully securing their support for the next round of voting, which will determine our lot for the fights.

Cosimo devises a plan for canvassing as many votes as possible. Instead of continuing with the media-fame route we have focused on, I must be seen with the prince. To win the Patrician's favour, I must first win over the prince. How hard can it be?

I sit across from Cosimo in his office. He peers at me over the stacks of files and clutter on his desk. "Ash will have an interview a few hours before second-round voting begins. He will be asked what he thinks of each girl. Of course, he will be polite in the way he describes you all. But we want him to—"

I break in, unable to bear his verbose chatter any longer than I have to. "Make it clear I'm the obvious favourite?"

Cosimo bobs his chin and grins. "See, you're a fast learner. Now let's put it to practice."

I tilt my head to the side, narrowing my eyes.

"I've organised for you and Ash to spend some time together this afternoon."

I open my mouth to protest but Cosimo cuts me short.

"You don't have much say in the matter," he says in the kindest possible manner. He shoots up from his seat and hustles me from mine, patting me on the back as I turn to leave. "Don't be late. Four o'clock in his private office." His voice is insistent. "And stop spending so much time with Calix."

"*No,*" I say once I have closed the door behind me, to no one but myself.

I change my clothes before meeting Lix in our usual spot by the lake. I find the clothes I would be likely to wear back at home – long hunting boots and a plain, shapeless tunic that I can dirty outside without reproach from my carping *Ornatrix*. I weave my way through the smooth marble palace into the gardens. My head is down as I pass the unnerving statues on either side of the walkway. Suddenly, my body thuds against another, one much sturdier than my own. I look up.

"I'm so—" I begin to apologise, but then I realise exactly who I have walked into. "D-Director Drusus…" I stutter, taking a few steps back.

He grins in the way I imagine a snake might do. "Electa, I have tried to organise a meeting with Mr Falto, but it seems that your schedule is so busy these days. Fame is a wonderful thing."

Wonderful? It is exhausting. I can't remember the last time I had a full meal. I force a smile, unable to speak. There is something about Lysander Drusus that renders me speechless.

"You're free now, I believe. Would you like to have a drink with me?"

I could refuse but that will only arouse suspicion. Lix will have to wait.

"Okay," is all I can manage to say.

Lysander takes me to Helax, the most famous bar in the city. We are transported there by his personal limousine, and although the journey is quick, dread aches in my bones whenever he looks at me.

The bar looks as though it ought to be a temple, and maybe it once was. Monolithic colonnades mark the open doorway. As we emerge from the vehicle, Lysander's vigilites push away the hordes of photographers aside. Helax is frequented by celebrities, and it is no surprise that the press is camped outside. Lysander shields me from the cameras, putting his arm around my shoulder. Cosimo will be pleased. This is the perfect publicity stunt – being seen with someone like Lysander Drusus. I am surprised he hadn't suggested it before. Cosimo must have known Lysander wanted to see me and I can't imagine that my silly lessons or photocalls take precedence.

Inside, the bar is lit by dim candlelight and soft retro music pulses in the background. The place itself reminds me of a cave, with light flooding in from the entrance, and the cool feel of stone walls. A hostess escorts us to a table sectioned off from the others. The vigilites surround us as we sit, to maintain privacy and protection at all times. I realise now just how underdressed I am for such a place. A tunic is not respectable dress for a Chosen woman, and I can only hope Lysander hasn't noticed. But he is the kind of man who notices everything and the fact that he doesn't seem to mind is surprising.

I peer around the vigilites who obstruct my view, recognising the faces of many who sit around crowded tables, gambling, drinking and throwing die. There are gladiators, models and actors, some more famous than others. I hope to see Nemesis at one of the tables, a trivial childhood fantasy of mine, but she is not here. I mask my disappointment from Lysander and put on the fake smile that Cosimo has taught me to perfect. Yet he senses my unease. I still feel out of place in this world that I have been thrust into. So much has changed in the last week – my look, manners and style – but the one thing that hasn't is the tug in my heart and a yearning for home.

"You seem tense," he comments. I fidget on my stool and can't bring myself to look him in the eye.

"Is it that obvious?" I say, not able to prevent the nervous laugh that escapes me.

He casts his eyes over me and I dare not look at his eyes for too long. They seems to have some strange, hypnotic effect on me. Two glasses of amber-coloured liquor are brought to the table. He didn't order but he wouldn't have to, as it seems he is a regular customer.

"No. I just have a good eye." He gestures to his left eye, and I notice now the long pinkish scar that snakes down from his brow. He was in the army once.

As I sip on my drink, faces peer at our table from shadowy corners and the room seems to go quiet.

Lysander sits forward in his chair, crossing his long legs in one swift motion. "They are all looking at you, Electa."

I am a nobody. Or at least I used to be. "I doubt that." I mumble the words. But Lysander may be correct. The Panore girls are now household names and Cosimo's publicity mission must have had some effect. I will never be accustomed to people knowing who I am.

"I can't blame them; you are incredibly beautiful." The words seem to roll off his silver tongue. He must have said the same to hundreds of women, yet I can't help the blush that warms my cheeks. "You don't believe me, do you?"

"No," I say quickly, pouring liquor down my throat to ease the anxiety that is making my skin tingle. As I finish one glass, another takes its place.

Lysander looks me over and studies my expression. A laboured smile trembles on my lips and I am sure he senses my terror. "You must be terribly home sick. Do you have family?"

"A brother and a father."

He bobs his chin. "And mother?"

"She was Unchosen." I bristle, knowing well that his beloved Choosing is the reason she is gone. I almost hope he can hear the hatred in my voice.

"I'm sorry for your loss." I expected him to hesitate, to struggle to respond, but the words come easily to him.

Sorry? My hands ball into fists and my jaw tightens. I feel as though I might burst in my fury. What would he know about loss? He sends thousands of children to their deaths every summer. I have no choice but to restrain myself and soften my tone.

"Do you have a family?" I ask, still sure to avoid his eyes.

Lysander tugs at the clerical-looking collar of his jacket. His entire suit is a dull jade; a colour he often wears. "No. I was orphaned as an infant. I don't remember my parents. They died somehow, I presume." There is no emotion in his voice. It seems strange, as an orphan is a rare thing in our *perfect* world. Lysander doesn't discuss his past often in the media. He is an enigma to the Latian people, and I wonder if he likes it that way.

"It must have been hard for you," I say. But my empathy is fake, as I could never pity a murderer like him.

His face glows in the candlelight. "It never made me sad. How can you mourn someone you never knew?"

My mother left when I was two years old. I don't remember her either. "I suppose that's true."

"I was always determined to make something of my life, in spite of the unfortunate circumstances." He sounds robotic, almost as if he has something to hide. His eyes are deep with secrets, and his mind is an unexplored dimension with depths so dark that it might as well be *Tartarus* itself.

"I would say that becoming the Institute director at twenty is quite the achievement." It never made much sense to me how someone so young could become so powerful. My father used to say that Lysander's promotion happened almost overnight and the Institute directors who had come before him were venerable statesmen, with years of experience behind them.

"I joined the army at seventeen.' It is as if he knows what I am thinking. "Rose through the ranks, saved a legion from certain death, and was awarded the Grass Crown."

The Grass Crown is an ancient war honour; the rarest military decoration someone can receive. The speed at which he speaks is jarring and I can barely keep up.

He continues, "At nineteen I was made general of the ninth legion, the youngest in our history. A year later, my men were taken hostage by the enemy … I was the sole survivor. In reward, the emperor made me director. I must have impressed him."

It seems almost rehearsed., and it is quite a story, but one I don't entirely believe. People whisper about Lysander Drusus and the things that he has done. Some say he butchered a thousand men in a day. Others believe he was a torturer once, the most talented in the Latian army. And I am yet to understand how someone with no political experience could become the director, the senior authority in the ULA.

"The emperor must have believed in you a lot."

Warmth breaks in his face. "He is a good man. The father I never had." His voice wavers now. He cares for the emperor, that much is obvious. But he controls him too, or so I have heard from Lix.

"Excuse me for my audacity, but your story is not the one I've heard," I say gently, my lips trembling with the words. My boldness, however, doesn't seem to rattle him.

"You believe the rumours?" he asks, his manner calm.

"No," I say quickly. "But why not tell your story and make the truth known?"

He sits forward in his seat, edging closer to me. I can't avoid his eyes now, bright, green and venomous.

"The whispering has never bothered me," he murmurs. "I choose not to tell my story, Electa, because it is the very thing that keeps me in power."

"How so?"

"*Oderint dum metuant.*" He quotes the ancient tyrant Caligula. *Let them hate so long as they fear.*

"Then why tell me?" I ask.

"I don't want you to fear me as others do. I somehow believe, Electa, that you and I are similar creatures." There is a glint of recognition in his eyes. I don't know whether I should be flattered or afraid. I know the terrible things he has done and yet I hang on his every word, intrigued and terrified all at once.

Lysander's eyes flicker even in the dim cavernous light. "The mob believes me to be a monster. The Patricians see me as a god. What is the difference between a god and a monster, you say? None. They are but the same, a figment of human imagination."

He surprises me with every word that passes from his lips.

"You aren't religious?"

He doesn't hesitate with his response. "Religion is for fools. I'm sure you would agree."

"But your brooch, the one you always wear," I say, pointing to the golden serpent fastened to his jacket. It is a symbol of Dominus.

He laughs. "It is for show, just as most things are in this shallow little world of ours. And I happen to like snakes. Remarkable creatures."

"If anyone else said this, you would call it treason." I choke out the words.

"Yes, I would," he says without hesitation. "A human being who has nothing to believe in is a dangerous creature. Anarchy, I can assure you, is not beneficial for anyone."

I stare at him in my bewilderment.

"Tell me, Electa, what is an emperor without a mob?"

"No one."

"Exactly." His crooked smile makes the blood freeze in my veins. "People may despise me, Electa, for the things I do and the decisions I make. The truth is, if they were in my position, they become the very monster they fear. I protect my people, even if they hate me for it."

"But you're popular with the public." I know that most Patricians idolise Lysander and worship him like a god. But I realise now, that is just it. People don't adore their gods, they fear them. And that fear drives them to worship, to sacrifice, to idolise. It is all a futile hope that they will be shown mercy in the afterlife.

"There are always cynics, I'm afraid." He lifts his glass up in his palm, letting it glow gold as it catches the light. "The people adore young Prince Ash but if they knew the truth…" He pauses, choosing his words. "Well let's just say they wouldn't be so keen."

"The prince?" My voice quivers, knowing what he will say.

Lysander smirks, mimicking the prince. "The emperor wanted us to work together. Slowly, he has been making more and more decisions. One day, he will be in the position to make them all. But for now, he must remain the innocent, charming prince, with no blood on his conscience. The people must believe that."

Asher is a murderer too. He knows about it all, the culling, the slavery, the bombing. The cool bar is suddenly hot, and I feel as though I am sitting next to a brazier spitting flames. My mind wanders back to the fires of that day in the outside world, and the screams, those anguished, blood-curdling screams. Lysander is not the only monster on Palatine Hill. The prince I have begun to pity is nothing but a viper in the guise of a drunkard.

Lysander returns me to the Palatine and holds my hand in a gesture of farewell. His touch lingers and when he finally leaves, I feel like I can breathe for the first time in hours. I stand on the porch overlooking the Palatine vineyards. A disembodied voice resonates from behind me.

"He seems to like you." It is Warren who watches over me. My silent vigil.

I let out a long sigh. "Spying on me?" I huff.

"Yes." He steps up beside me. "But truthfully, I have better things to do with my time."

"Of course, you do," I mutter, tiring of Spartaca's leash on me. I am being watched at all times, wherever I go and whatever I do. There is no escape from my glass cage.

Warren smirks, patting me on the back. "Some advice," he says. "Stay away from Lysander Drusus."

I think it may be too late for that.

Grudgingly, I make my way to the prince's private office. If I want to win Imperial Panore, first I must conquer Asher's heart. But, after what Lysander told me, I can't play pretend and act like the lady I am supposed to be. He disgusts me and I would rather be anywhere else on this Dominus-forsaken hill than with Asher Ovicula.

His Praetorians acknowledge me at the onyx door. This is a part of the Palatine I have never visited. The Imperial quarter is usually off-limits to guests. Today, the prince has made an exception.

"Please wait for a moment, Miss Steel, the prince is occupied," one of the guards informs me. I am in a half-mind to walk away. Five minutes later, a dark-haired girl emerges from the doors. Ember. She spares me her deadly glare this time, keeping her head down and marching off.

As I enter the office, the prince jerks his head up from the desk and his smirk is firmly in place. But there are swathes of black beneath his eyes and his skin is sallow. He looks as though he has been working through the night. Lysander was right, the prince doesn't just party his days away – he works. I wonder how many people he has sentenced to their deaths just this morning. The prince is still young, but he is capable of being terrible, perhaps even more terrible than Lysander Drusus.

"Electa," he says as he stands from his leather-bound chair. "*Salve.*"

His eyes are soft and entirely deceiving. As he waves me over, I notice how immaculate the study is, with its stacked files, labelled bookshelves and maps on the walls. There are scattered models of antique cars, glittering trophies and crowns in glass cases. There is even a sword, hung on the wall behind the desk; the hilt is gilded and the blade is ruby-red, glinting in the light. The maps show the ULA and all five Leagues – even Etruria, which defected from the ULA in the Great Appian War eighty years ago. There are red pins dotted around, marking the places he has visited. Most never leave their League, but Imperials often depart on state excursions. As expected, there are no pins in Umbria.

"What would you like to do? I've been taking all the girls out, to get to know them individually." He invites me to take the seat across from his. "Saved the best until last," he whispers loudly, puts a finger to his lips and winks. Up close, I can see the stains of red on his lips. Lipstick. It seems as though Ember and the prince's affair is not quite over yet. It frustrates me more than it should. I push the thought away.

I notice the stale smell of cigarettes. But there is no liquor here that I can see, so he may be sober, for once. "You choose," I mutter. "I only came to get Cosimo off my back."

I can no longer conceal my frustration. My manner is curt and unacceptable, but the prince doesn't erupt into a fit of anger, as he usually does. He puts his head in his hands and sighs.

"Why won't you give me a chance, Electa?"

I press my lips together, my mind flickering to a hundred reasons I can think of. "Why, Prince? You're nothing but an arrogant, selfish, drunk and—"

"That's really what you think of me?" His expression falls as he cuts me short.

"Can you blame me?" I gesture to the maps on his desk, battle plans, combat strategies and the causality lists. It seems as though he has been writing condolence letters to families torn apart by this war. His hands are ink-stained, and there is a pile of envelopes, stamped with the Imperial seal. "It seems Ember doesn't mind." I spit the words at him and immediately regret it. His eyebrows arch, his eyes locking onto my embittered expression. He thinks that I am jealous.

"Stop pretending, Electa, I'm tired of this game." His roar sounds like a battle cry.

"What game?" I raise my voice to match his own.

He kicks his feet up onto the desk. "If you hate me, like you say, then why do you care what I choose to do in my free time?"

I scowl at him, and my nostrils flare with fury. "So, you do Ember in your free time?"

He smirks and licks his lips. "Occasionally," he mutters.

I roll my eyes and laugh. "How delightful." After what Shauna told me, it is surprising. But I suppose it is not so easy to fall out of love with someone.

The prince stares at me. "I don't know why you think you're so high and mighty, Electa Steel." He spits out my name. "When I look into your eyes, there is only ice. You are the coldest person I have ever met."

"At least I don't claim to be a nice person," I fire back with twice the rage. My words are biting and sharp like blades.

He wrinkles his nose, throwing his head back. "What is that supposed to mean?"

"Your entire life is just one big charade, Ash," I say, and then my tone softens as I say his name aloud for the first time.

"Wow, the gods give me blessings. Electa Steel knows my name." He mimics a hail to the heavens.

I want to scream. He can't be serious for more than one moment. "Why do you act like you don't care about anything, or anyone?"

"Because I am beyond reproach, Electa. I don't need to care; the people love me anyway." His hubris is amour and he wear it proudly. I lose myself in the wildfire that consumes him and the rage that tumbles out with every word. "I grew up in a world filled with superficial people and how do you expect that I would be any different. I wasn't always this way, maybe you weren't always so cold, but people change, learn to hide their pain so no one can hurt them." He slams his fist on the stone desk, making it tremble under his might. He is trying to convince me of his pain. But I already see it, in everything he does.

"So, drinking, getting high, filling your lungs with smoke, that fixes all your problems? Does it purge your demons, prince?"

"Electa, it is my birthright to relapse, to drown in wine, to set the world on fire and watch it burn. That's what emperors have done since the beginning of time." He says this like it is a mantra that he tells himself over and over. Perhaps it numbs his conscience. "I have no choice but to fulfil my destiny. Much like you have no choice in being here."

"We always have a choice," I mumble. I doubt he even hears me as I say it. It is a reminder to myself that the power is still in my hands. I am helping Spartaca because I choose to. I want to save Vel, of course, but this is about so much more than that.

The prince stands over me now, his gaze alive with fervour. "Do I disgust you, Electa Steel?"

I pause. "No, but I do pity you," I say, eventually.

"Pity me? Who would pity a prince?"

I thought the same once. Not anymore. Asher Ovicula is the most tragic being I have ever encountered. "It is always sad to watch someone destroy themselves." My voice is soft, and I barely recognise it as my own. "I should go." I stand and tip my head, walking back out into the corridor. The guards slam the great stone doors behind me.

Outside, a woman leans against a colonnade in the deserted walkway. She taps the toe of her heel on the marble floor. It is Trixie Merula. It seems she has been waiting for me.

"Cosimo Falto said you would be here." She addresses me without looking up from her *tabella*. She is typing notes on the device. "I couldn't help but overhear."

She refers to my discussion, or rather, argument with the prince. *Great.* This will be front page news on tomorrow's *Acta Diurna*. Cosimo will be furious. "Please don't—"

"Don't fret, Electa, I won't publish the story."

I stare at her, perplexed. Her cropped grey hair sharpens her features, I feel as though if I get too close, she might bite. "Then w-why are you here?" I stammer. It is not like Trixie to let gossip such as this go unannounced.

"Cosimo sent me. He wanted me to report on your *favourable* relationship with the prince," she simpers, and I note her sarcasm.

Thanks for warning me, Cosimo.

"Was it really that loud?"

She nods. "I actually quite like you, Electa. You even remind me of myself when I was your age."

Trixie represents everything about the Patrician world that I have come to hate. The lies, the scandals, the gossip. She feeds off the tragedies of others and yet has chosen to spare me. I am not quite sure that I trust her intentions. Her soured expression barely moves as she speaks, and it makes her a hard person to read. I suppose the surgery has limited her expression to a permanent scowl.

"I know the prince rather well, actually. You two are well-suited."

My eyes widen at her statement. "That's what you got from that?" I can hardly believe what I am hearing. We behave like children when we are around each other.

"You may fight like dogs, but anyone can see you care about each other."

"I don't care about him," I say, hastily. But Trixie is no fool. Could she be right? Do I have a soft spot for the troubled prince?

Trixie studies me, just as she did at the interview. "You impressed me in the interview. I was trying to break you, but I struggled," she explains. "I was a Plebeian once, one of the few who rose through the ranks of society. It took me a long, long time to earn their respect."

Trixie Merula is a Plebeian. This is not something I would have ever expected. It is not common knowledge, and I am sure it is a fact she would rather keep hidden.

"Don't lose sight of yourself, Electa," she continues. "This is not a fairytale. Nothing good ever comes from loving a god. Remember that." Her grey eyes seem to burn through mine. Is this a portent of things to come?

"I don't understand."

"This world has destroyed me, and it will destroy you. If I were you, I would run, while you still can."

She drifts away down the hall, silently and delicately. But her words haunt me. It is almost like she knows what I have agreed to. But it is already too late for running. I am in too deep and there is no turning back. I must be brave, for the first time in my life.

X

FERE LIBENTER HOMINES ID QUOD VOLUNT CREDUNT

Men generally believe what they want to

The Senate Summit was scheduled for today but for some reason, unbeknown to me, it has been postponed until further notice. Cosimo later informs me that the delay has been caused by pressing issues at war, but he can't tell me any more than that, as a matter of national security. He also mentions an invitation of some kind, but I don't pay much attention.

I receive the letter at around half past three the following day. It informs me, in elegant, sloping calligraphy, that I will be picked up at exactly five o'clock and delivered to Lysander Drusus's villa, a little further down Palatine Hill. Short notice, I think. But I should expect nothing less from a man who has the whole of Latia running around at his beck and call. I am a little taken aback by his invitation. When he had mentioned *getting to know me*, I thought it was no more than a joke. But Lysander Drsusus is not the type of man to joke.

I am in half a mind to decline his *generous* invitation but Cosimo advises against it. He tells me to tidy up my hair and dress promptly before the director's *lictor* arrives. Lysander is a dangerous man, that much I have gathered from my brief encounters with him and the stories Lix has told me. He is also a man who is best avoided. It seems even the heroic, courageous Asher Ovicula fears the director. My mind wanders back to the Imperial Ball and the prince's pasty flush at the mere sight of the director. Asher wouldn't be afraid of anyone unless they were worth fearing.

Cosimo, much like me, can't comprehend Lysander's interest in me. The most powerful man in the ULA has taken an unexpected liking to a poor Plebeian girl, or so it seems. But I have to remember just who Lysander is, and what he does. I can't be fooled by his charms, and of course, those eyes, which render me speechless.

A limousine arrives, gleaming white in the aestival sun. An aged man emerges, Lysander's *lictor*, with stark eyes and greying hair. He introduces himself as Julius and ushers me into the vehicle. His suit is velvet and emerald in colour, similar to the one Lysander wears at most occasions.

"Miss Steel, *salve*. It is a pleasure to make your acquaintance." He extends his hand out to me and grips my forearm in a customary greeting. In any other life, I would be nothing but a street rat to this man, but things have changed, and even Patricians take notice of me.

I smile back at him, taking a seat. He holds a tablet in his hands and begins to study it.

"Apologies for this, but there are a few rules I am obliged to run past you – it's procedure," he says, taking a long breath in preparation. "There is an electronics ban at Villa Averna." He holds out a small black box and waves it before me. I place my *tabella* inside. "Never address him by his *praenomen*, it is either sir or Director Drusus to you." Julian squints, as if apologetic for reciting these laughable rules. "When you greet him, do not bow, do not salute. Simply extend your hand. The director can't bear anyone who bows to him."

I nod as he goes on, yawning in my boredom, and Julian catches me with a stern eye.

"Do not eat unless he does. Do not drink until he invites you to do so. Do not sit before he does. And most crucially, Miss Steel, never repeat the conversations that take place within Averna to anyone, is that clear?"

"Yes," I say, the intensity of his voice grating on me. "Anything else?" I joke but the *lictor* simply frowns, quite unimpressed.

The limousine comes to a sudden halt, the hum of the MagLev engine ebbing away. I step out.

A marble path winds its way past a monolithic fountain that seems to reach the skies and through a landscaped garden with sculptures that tower over me. The gods of old stand like titans in their stone form, casting long shadows across the path. And as the artificial sun sets, the villa glows rutilant, as if it is Olympus itself. I cast my mind back to my last interaction with the director. He had blasphemed about religion and mythologies in a causal act of treason. Yet here, his garden is littered with statues of gods he claims not to honour. He is a strange man.

The marble building resembles a temple in its magnificence. A plinth raises the entire building several feet from the earth, with hundreds of stairs leading up to the arched doorway. A gold-plated chariot pulls up in front of the steps as we approach. Two black-haired stallions with gilded bridles make full skyward circles with their muzzles and neigh cheerfully.

Lysander holds black leather reins in his hand. He stands poised atop his chariot, the sun mantling him with golden light. He looks like an angel as he steps down, although the black hair crowning his head looks more like the garland of a dark god. He wears a loose white exercise tunic fastened with a dark green belt. and his skin is dewy with sweat. He wipes his brow and hands the reins to a servant in a white robe.

He addresses Julian now. "Leave us."

Julian nods and quickly departs.

"Welcome, Electa." Lysander takes my palms in his hands, and I shiver at his touch. "I'm honoured by your visit," he says with his typical courtesy.

"I didn't know that you were a charioteer." I note the definition of his arms – it is as though his body has been sculptured by the gods themselves. I have never seen him look so casual, and it eases me a little to know there is human skin beneath those suits he so often wears.

A smile blooms at the corner of Lysander's lips. "It has long been a hobby of mine. But it's a dangerous sport, one I wouldn't recommend."

My father used to say that anyone who rides in a chariot must be a lunatic of some kind. The injuries are gruesome, and the spectacular crashes often result in death for the participant and horse, alike.

Lysander points over the hedgerow. "I have my own racing track, over there. I'll show you another time, perhaps you would even like to see me race."

"Yes, I'd like that." I bite on my tongue, trying to retrain my excitement for fear of embarrassing myself. The tickets for the Circus were always too expensive for my father.

Lysander escorts me inside his villa, and I gasp in awe, surprised by the lack of furnishing. It seems the place is more gallery than a home. There are dyed tapestries hanging on the walls, and smaller statues of the same gods who lingered like marble ghosts outside. At the end of an entrance hall is what seems to be an audience chamber where Lysander would usually receive guests. An ebony throne dominates the back wall; its imposing design is meant to strike fear into those kneeling at the director's feet. I examine the artefacts and artwork on the walls. A golden bident is mounted on the wall, riveted with emeralds. It is an old weapon, one that hasn't been used for centuries.

"What is all this?" I ask.

He stands back to admire the bident from afar, his eyes glinting. "I am a collector of historical artefacts. I have a fascination with the ancient history of Rome."

"The home of Dominus?"

"That's what they say, isn't it," he says with a grin.

His response muddles me, but I dare not question him in his own home. I allow the director to guide me through the villa. Upstairs, he lectures me on the histories he is so enthralled by. He makes the mythology all seem so romantic, and waxes lyrical about the gods of old, the ones that came before Dominus. He makes sure to remind me of his agnostic tendencies and claims that it is their worship that fascinates him so. He discusses the artwork too, which, I gather from his words, is the most exclusive and valuable collection in all of the four Leagues. Lysander mentions several Volscian artists, who I am embarrassed to admit I have never heard of.

"And this tapestry, from the fifteenth century, depicts the abduction of Persephone." He stands beneath the most elaborate tapestry I have ever seen. It takes up the space of an entire wall. Half of the artwork is made with dark threads, and the other with light.

Lysander begins to tell me the story. "Persephone was the daughter of Zeus. A goddess of spring with eyes that flamed with light. The young girl had an adventurous spirit and wandered off into the meadows. Hades, the god of the underworld, was enamoured by the goddess and dragged her down to the infernal abodes to make her his bride." Lysander closes his eyes, immersing himself in the world he has imagined. I never thought that I would find such stories engaging but Lysander has this manner about him, that no matter what he discusses, you can't help but listen intently.

He continues, "Persephone came to love the dark god. He, her darkness, and she, his light. She emerged from the underworld for half the year, returning the light and bloom to the world. But spring and death always come hand in hand. Without life, of course, there would be no death."

Each room has been planned in the most intricate of detail, and there is not a floor left unclean, a chandelier not sparkling, nor a dust-ridden windowpane in sight. Lysander has a room dedicated to each item of clothing he owns, and a display room for his bespoke suits, which are designed by Leonato Latinus, the famed Latian fashion designer. This is a glimpse into the mysterious director's life that few experience. The opulence of it all is unlike anything that I have ever seen before. The halls seem to have a celestial flicker to them, and even the stones appear to glitter beneath my sandals. Yet a hollow fear lingers in my throat as I stand here, in this strange house, this strange world, where I feel unmistakeably out of place and where even my voice is becoming censored and weary with the tide.

We sit on green couches, sipping on tea in a room of books, stacked from floor to ceiling in every direction. He is unchanged from his exercise earlier, and yet there is not a strand of hair out of place nor a single blemish on his skin. I wonder if he always looks so perfect. Does he ever let his image slip?

Probably not, I think.

"Tell me, Electa, what province do you come from?"

"Chrysos, near Hedera."

Lysander smiles to himself. "I know the area well. I grew up not far from Hedera."

No Patrician child grows up in an outer province like Chrysos. Confusion muddles my expression and Lysander is quick to notice.

"As I said, I was adopted."

"So you're a Plebeian?" I dare to ask him. My voice comes more easily to me this time, but I can't allow my boldness to get the better of me.

"Yes, my adoptive family were Plebeians." He meets my gaze with a relentless intensity and speaks without a hint of laughter. He is serious. Lysander Drusus, the Institute director, is a Plebeian. It must be a sensitive topic and it certainly is not something widely publicised. I wonder if anyone even knows that he is adopted. His honesty with me is disconcerting, I am just a stranger after all.

His stare fixates on me, but not on any part of my body in particular. He doesn't examine me as he did when we first met, nor does he flinch when I notice him. My body seems to tremble under his gaze as he continues for several moments more. His eyes turn glassy and shine. He is not admiring me nor scrutinising me, and after a while, I realise that it is sadness hiding behind his eyes.

"So pure," he breathes. It is as though he has forgotten I am here. "You'll end up losing your mind."

"What?"

"This place. It ruins everyone it touches."

"This place?"

He pauses, the only noise between us and the silence is the pendulum swinging in the clock on the wall. "It's getting late; why don't you return tomorrow at the same time. We can discuss *Vici*."

"*Vici?*"

"Yes. It's a novel. The one you slipped into your satchel."

Stercus. He noticed me steal a book from the shelf when we walked in. I believed his back was turned and was sure he didn't see. But Lysander is no regular mortal; he seems almost omniscient at times.

"I'm sorry, I can give it back." My voice sounds pleading. But the director's expression is lax, and there was no bite to his tone. Thievery is something he most likely expected from me.

He lifts his chin, peering down at me. "You can take as many books as you like, Electa. I have little use for them anymore," he says, a smile curling on his lips.

"I'm a fast reader. I'll return it by tomorrow."

He stands to see me out. "I'll look forward to seeing you again."

I leave his house. My hands still tremble and my legs are numb beneath me. Lysander waves me off from his porch. He looks so innocent like that, with his shoulders back and a beatific smile creasing his cheeks. I wonder if he senses my trepidation whenever I am in his company. Stealing that book was reckless, an old habit of mine back in the valley. But maybe it is a sign that Lysander is not as fearsome as everyone believes.

I don't sleep that night. I toss and turn in my silk sheets and pace around my room for hours in the darkness. My mind is on fire, and my strange bruise burns hot against my skin.

I return the next day and the days that follow. Always at five o clock and never a moment later. Lysander spends his days at the Institute building, hard at work, and a part of me forgets the terrible things he does there.

I find myself enjoying the visits to Villa Averna, my hands stop trembling and I find my voice, naturally, with time. It is an escape from the Palatine and all that it entails – the expectations, Spartaca's watchful gaze, and the fatuous rules that exist there. I feel myself sinking into this world that I want no part in. I suppose I am getting used to the life of a Patrician but coming here to Lysander's villa is an escape back to the old Electa, who lived in Chrysos Valley with her brother and father.

Lysander understands me. He listens to me, and even after hours of talking I don't find myself silent nor does his attention ever waver. I tell myself over and over that it is a mistake to be with a man like Lysander, such a bad and dangerous man. It seems I have sympathy for the demon of Appia. And yet, I have more in common with him than anyone else on this Dominus-forsaken hill. He and I are outsiders, thrust into a world that doesn't belong to us, a world where the people are fake, but the money is real.

Lysander's hands are scarred from battle and he doesn't glorify war in the way that the prince does. He doesn't give much away, and I find myself asking him often what it was like to be a soldier. Not once does he mention Spartaca, and I doubt he ever will.

"Did you ever see a thunderstorm, outside?" I ask, watching the way his muscles work as he prepares his stallions. He seems to drift so gently between movements, like it is a dance and doesn't want to disturb the air around him.

"A few times, yes. That is a strange question," he says, laughter bubbling from his throat.

"I know, sorry, I just…" I begin, but the words fall to the wayside as he catches my eyes with his own. Those are the type of eyes I could easily drown in. "I've never seen one. I read about them in books and poetry. I suppose they must be beautiful."

Lysander squints at me, lost in thought. His face turns to stone for a moment and then just as quickly, his smile returns. "They are certainly beautiful," he mutters, but his mind continues to roam through his memories of the world outside, not pleasant ones, I am sure.

The day after, he teaches me to play the piano. We sit side by side on a stool, and my legs brush up against his. I feel my body go tense and my limbs quiver. His touch terrifies me, even now. He reminds me of a snake, pleasing to admire from afar, but get too close and he will bite. His fingers brush against the keys so delicately, a light touch and no more. It is surprising that hands with such strength can be so gentle. I like to see the way his sinews rise and fall with his movements and the way his eyelids flicker at a change in note. He looks peaceful like that. But I am careful not to disturb the beast within him.

That same evening, he takes me to his balcony, overlooking the entire city and the hills of Ore beyond. We stand out there in the typical dry heat of summer. Then, suddenly, hot air catches in my lungs. My skin turns damp, and a low grumbling sound echoes from the heavens. A cool wind whips across my bare shoulders and I shiver all over. *Crack.* A flash of light cleaves the twilight sky, shattering the constellations apart. Then the heavens groan once more, and the stone beneath me seems to shudder at the sound. *Crack.* The bolts flicker, illuminating the earth for a moment, and the peals of thunder rebound in the darkness that follows. The rain comes, and within moments my hair and my dress are soaked through. The water seems to stick to my skin, but it is a welcome feeling. I can't remember the last time there was rain.

"Did you do this for me?" I turn to Lysander. Rivulets of rainwater fall from his hair and run down his face. He towers over me, with a knowing smile.

"Yes, you said you wanted to see a thunderstorm. Is it as beautiful as you imagined?"

I nod, looking around in the fleeting light. "More so." My words are sundered by the screaming sky. I look out over the horizon and think myself lucky. But I remember that it is not real, none of it, even the lightning in the sky and the rain that wets my skin. Lysander created this illusion to please me. This is not nature at work, it is the Institute and a reminder that this place is still no more than a golden cage.

As I look at Lysander now, he seems more holy than ever. He marvels at the storm of his own creation, his green eyes alight.

"Is it the same outside?" I ask him.

"No. It is not."

Moments pass like this with no noise but the pounding of the rain. No words are exchanged as I stare at the man beside me for a little too long. I study him now and begin to doubt my own mind. He is no monster, not to me anyway. I find myself questioning everything that I have ever heard about this man.

"Why do you allow people to believe you're a monster when you're not." I urge him to face me.

His face illuminates in the brief flash of light, and he sighs. "Men generally believe what they want to."

The next day is Lysander's birthday. He is throwing a grand party at his villa and asks me to help with the preparations. There is an excitement in the villa this day, even the unsmiling servants seem more jovial than usual. They walk about the place with purpose, transforming the place into a work of art to rival Lysander's collection. A gold-coloured *velarium* is hung from colonnades in the gardens, and a bandstand is erected at its centre.

I oversee the work and make sure it is to the director's high standards. Torches are lit to line the carpeted walkways as dusk approaches, and I hurry off to dress. Latian high society will be here tonight, and the Imperials, of course. I have not seen the prince since our altercation and Cosimo has urged me to make amends.

'Maybe,' I said. It seemed to satisfy my advisor enough.

Lysander meets me before the guests arrive and thanks me for my efforts. He wears his trademark green velvet suit tonight and has a genial smile that almost makes me forget the serpent disguised beneath. The dress I wear is green too, a colour not dissimilar to his suit – he had it made especially for this evening. The gown is fastened by chains and a metallic serpent back strap.

"Beautiful," he whispers, and red blooms on my cheeks.

"You have good taste," I say, twirling myself around, the silk supple on my skin.

The prince arrives in all his haughty glory. His grin is perhaps even more crooked than the director's. His wine-stained lips blow me a kiss, and I realise he must either be drunk already, or high on Porgy. Ember is on his arm, and they are matching in carmine red. It bothers me more than it should but then I remember where I stand, a vision in green, next to Lysander Drusus, the real king of the Palatine.

We dance all night, wine is poured, music plays into the twilight hours and here, beneath our sky, there are always stars, the fake diamonds of the heavens. This is so close to seeming real, if it weren't for the sheen of the electromagnetic field, undulating in the night sky. Soon it is morning, yet the dark of night seems only to deepen. Exhausted by the company of the hundreds that occupy the villa, I wander about alone, finding sanctuary on Lysander's expansive bedroom balcony where we had watched the storm the night before.

I am sure that I shouldn't be here, not without Lysander, but somehow I am not afraid of being found. I stare out at the party below and the city beyond, its lights glittering in the near distance. For a short while, I feel at peace. But I know this silence can't last for long. Heavy footsteps on the marble stones reverberate behind me. There is no need to turn; I know it is Lysander who approaches, just by the tempo of his steps. Lysander stands beside me while I continue to look over the horizon. He, however, doesn't stare out at the view, but rather, his eyes fall on me.

After a few minutes, he speaks. "Why are you here, Electa?"

My head throbs and the pulse in my blood consumes me. He knows that something is not right. He always has.

"What do you mean?" I say, silencing the quiver in my voice.

"Some of your Assay Day results are missing," he says with a passive expression. I stay quiet, staring out over the balcony. I feel more vulnerable than ever, alone with him on his balcony, his territory. "It's odd. Our system doesn't tend to make mistakes like that. Actually, your entire record seems to have disappeared."

"My whole record?"

Crew must have erased everything after I told him of Lysander's suspicions.

"It's as if you don't exist, Electa Steel." His voice commands me to look at him now and when I do, all the fear that has dissipated over the past days comes flooding back in one great surge. I feel like I could choke on it.

"I have no explanation," I murmur. Lysander reaches out to me, his touch like ice, but I don't recoil. His beauty terrifies me.

"You were a Grey, weren't you?"

How does he know?

"How—"

He interrupts. "That tattoo," he says, tracing the marking on my ribcage. The tattoo is symbolic of the Grey; it is barely visible, a small wolf. "I have one too." His eyes spark with recognition. He moves to stand behind me now, examining the needle scar, and unbuttons the cuff of his shirt to reveal a similar mark on the underside of his wrist. *He was a Grey.*

"What are you going to do? Put me in prison?" I raise my voice a little.

He looks at me as if he would snap my neck, but then a certain softness returns to his features.

"No, Electa, you're already in one."

He takes my hand and we begin to dance, swaying with the faint music from below.

"You needn't be afraid of me," he whispers against my ear, closer than ever. He is a serpent incarnate, and it feels as though a viper has slithered around my neck and is taking its time choking me.

"Well, I am."

He brushes a stray length of hair from my face. It is a gentle movement. "What if I told you that I would like it very much if we could be friends." His voice is dripping with honey, but I don't trust his intentions.

The crescendo of the orchestra heightens and then dwindles into nothingness. The party has ended. "I could be dead in two weeks." Saying this aloud is more terrifying than I could ever imagine. The words die in my throat and we no longer sway. We are still, in the dead of night, and his lips come up against my ear once more.

"You won't be."

And with that, he leaves me stranded above a sea of Patricians. I look down at them as they pass and know that I will never belong here. I used to think pretend was the only thing I could do. Fool people. Lysander and I have that in common – hiding our true selves to survive in a world that is not our own. He once said that we are similar creatures. I know that to be true. And I don't fool him. I never will.

XI

HOSTIS HUMANI GENERIS

Enemy of the human race

The Senate's Summit, according to Cosimo, is the most important event of Imperial Panore. I must, like the other Panore girls, wear a *stola*, the traditional dress of Latia, fastened with a snake-head fibula. The senators must wear purple bordered togas, as they do to all official ceremonies. Cosimo spends the entire journey to the forum spieling the names and politics of each and every senator, in the hope that I will make some sort of impression.

The Senate House is an imposing structure, entirely marble, spare the tiled roof. A frieze carved into the entablature reads: *S.P.Q.O, the Senate and people of Ore*. The white togas in the dark marble hall seem to merge into a horde on indistinguishable figures. There are a few with their distinctive gold trimming, the Imperials, party leaders and generals, who I am able to recognise. Vigilites are posted at each end of the room in their grey armour. I look to Cosimo for comfort, intimidated by the mass of people before me.

"You can do this, El," he says, but his words of encouragement aren't much use. I get lost in the voices that seem to echo all around.

Trinity and her mentor stand close. She, like me, stands frozen. She is not nervous but petulant. Her advisor has a stern face and crossed arms.

"Don't try that *stercus* again, Trinity." The advisor's words are terse, unforgiving. She grips Trinity's arm; even from here, the movement seems violent.

Trinity snatches her arm away quickly, flexing her toned arms. "I'd sooner die than play-act the person you want me to be," she snaps before marching off into the sea of white. Her mentor is left with a gaping mouth as she dashes off after her. I can't help but giggle. I should thank Trinity; her unpopularity is the only thing helping me on my way to the top.

Praetorians surround the emperor and his children who sit on three gilded thrones on a pedestal, lording over the proceedings. I catch Shauna's eye and manage a smile that she returns. My eyes linger on Asher for a moment. He is slumped in his throne, sipping on a flask, which he quickly hides under the folds of his toga. I wouldn't expect any less.

Crew is here too, of course. His glacier eyes follow my movements even as he converses with Valentina. Her efforts will be wasted on him. He is the one sure vote I have. But that has to change. I must win the senators over in some way or another.

Cosimo parades me around the room, with his palm lightly pressing against my back, urging me onwards. I engage with consuls, praetors, magistrates, legates, censors and the senators, of course. Their names roll easily off my tongue after the hours practising with Cosimo and I think I may even manage to charm a few. I agree with their politics and offer my opinions on their *commendable* work in the civil domain. Mostly I just tell them what they want to hear. Cosimo prompts me often, whispering relevant information in my ear, and steers conversation away from topics I know little about. I am grateful for Cosimo in times like these. In some ways he is becoming a friend, offering me praise and encouragement on every step of this journey. No longer does he wear a damning frown when he looks my way.

As I come into contact with more and more senators, I wonder which of them have been corrupted by Spartaca. Crew warned me that there were operatives even here, and I am sure most of them are Populares. Eden Marius, a young censor, said outright that I could count on her vote. A number of similar encounters follow, even a select few Optimates seem to show me favour, raving about my interview and commenting on my friendship with Lysander Drusus.

A familiar touch lands on my shoulder. Lysander is here, and dressed unlike anyone else, in dark-green leather. "Terrific work, Electa. Everyone is singing your praises," he says, his voice resonant with praise. A hot blush creeps onto my cheeks as he addresses me before a crowd of senators. Cosimo is pleased but is never his usual animated self in the presence of the director. He tugs at my *stola*, pressing me to move on. But there is no escape from Lysander. His eyes anchor me to the ground where I stand. I hear whispers all around, a new empress rising, Electa Steel, the companion of the director and the future of the Haven. It is electrifying, standing beside Lysander. *This is what power feels like*, I think.

I mouth a "thank you" for the compliment, too embarrassed to speak. But Lysander, astute as always, notices my apprehension. He guides me away from the safety of Cosimo and invites me to take a seat beside him on the Senate benches. There is a little awkwardness between us; he sits further from me than usual and his expression is hard like a diamond. My mind wanders back to the past week, all the fun that we had, the bond we developed. A part of me hopes that is not lost but perhaps it would be better if I keep my distance from him.

"My contacts tell me that you are currently in second place, right on Ember's heels," he says, his eyes settling on mine. I am certain he shouldn't be disclosing such information to me, but I don't question him. The relief his statement brings me is comfort enough. At once I feel lighter, as if a weight has been lifted. No more sycophancy, for today at least. It seems the Summit has been a success.

Lysander leans forward, nearing me once again. My stomach clenches as I feel the warmth of his breath on my skin. "I'm sorry if I frightened you last night. But you intrigue me," he says, casting his gaze over me.

"Not at all," I lie to appease him. "I invaded your privacy ... I shouldn't have—"

"I have no secrets with you, Electa. You are welcome to stand on my balcony if you so wish."

I nod, but my words stick in my throat. His expression softens once more, and it eases me a little. I glance over at Cosimo, who watches our interaction intently. He mouths something that I can't quite make out. He is confused about our friendliness, no doubt. It must seem strange to him, but we have spent much time together this past week.

"You are also welcome to steal the rest of my library," Lysander jokes and I can't help my laughter. But when I see Lix's expression fall as he passes, all the joy that I feel fades away. I leap up from my seat without saying so much as a word to Lysander. Lix rushes out of the building, through the great archway and down the marbled steps into the forum. I bound after him, catching his arm before he can get any further.

He speaks before I have the chance. "So that's the reason you've been avoiding me?" His voice is harsher than usual. Every step I take towards him, he takes a couple more back.

"I haven't been avoiding you," I say, unable to meet his gaze. "I told you I was taking extra lessons with Cosimo."

That was a lie, of course. I was with Lysander. The very man that left him to rot in Umbria. How could I be so foolish?

"Do you think me a fool, El? It's all over the press. I thought it was just for show, to win votes but it seems it is more than that," he mutters, turning his back. I shout after him, but he doesn't respond. I run to catch him again, clutching at his toga but my fingers strain to get a grip.

He stops, but still doesn't face me. "You lied." His indrawn breath is sharp and my heart lurches with guilt.

"It is for show, Lix, I swear it. I need the votes." It may be the most unconvincing lie I have ever told. I don't even believe myself. Lix can't bring himself to look at me and I don't blame him. I may as well have plunged a knife through his heart.

"I think it is best if we stay away from each other for a while."

I could let him walk away now but my fear of losing him takes over my head and my heart and all in-between. "That's not what I want." But it is too late, and he shakes my grip off.

"It's not what I want either, but you're promised to my brother, Electa, and I can't afford to make the same mistake twice."

He refers to Ember. He disgraced himself once with her, he won't do the same with me. This is not about Lysander at all. He is distancing himself to protect his honour and reputation here in the Palatine, the closest thing to home he has left.

"Ash nearly had me exiled once," he breathes, turning quiet at the memory. "He came around. I don't think he would hesitate a second time."

Shauna never mentioned that. I suppose she wouldn't want her brother to seem a monster to me, his possible bride. I knew Asher had a temper but exile, that is punishment reserved for dissidents, not foreign-born princes.

"How c-could he do that to you?" I stammer.

Lix sighs and shrugs his shoulders. "I deserved it."

All Lix seems to do is make excuses for Asher. I don't push the matter further; it seems a sensitive topic. When Lix walks away this time, I don't stop him. I don't want to cause him pain and suffering, he has had enough of those things for ten lifetimes.

I stand there for what feels like an eternity, watching him melt into the flocks of Patricians hurrying about on their daily business, until I hear the screams. I turn to the Senate House. People flood from the archway and coalesce into a swarm of white. The thunder of hundreds of footsteps on the marble is enough to make my entire body tremble. They push past me in their flight, their screams filling the forum with a dreadful cacophony that rings in my ears. I fight back against the current spilling from the arch, running towards what they are running from. It is a foolish move, but a surge of adrenaline takes a hold of me and I can't stop my feet as they scramble up the incline of steps.

I stand inside the building and the perpetual stream of bodies ceases. Those who remain in the room are still and silent, some cowering in corners, others hiding behind the Senate benches. And then there is me, right in the middle, standing directly before the Imperial's dais. Their thrones are toppled over and the splintered wood is splayed all over the marble floor. On the dais stands a masked figure with the princess in his grasp. Shauna's dull eyes are wide and afraid, as the man presses the barrel of gun against her temple.

"Stand back or I shoot," the man shouts, and the vigilites slowly move away, lowering their weapons.

Asher and the emperor are encircled by their Praetorians at the side of the room, and next to them is Lysander, whose body is perfectly still. He is calm and composed and doesn't blink. Only I stand alone. I am racked with fear as I meet Shauna's pleading eyes.

A vigilite with his arms raised above his head steps out from the bench. "Let her go and you will be spared."

The masked man doesn't respond.

"What do you want?" the vigilite asks, edging towards him.

The assailant waves his gun around, firing off a few rounds in the air in warning. It is now that I understand why the vigilites don't make their shot. The man wears a heavy-looking belt strapped around his waist. It is heavily padded and likely an explosive device. I don't dare move, keeping my eyes on Shauna.

Our eye contact seems to calm her, and her breathing steadies. I mouth to her: "Stay still, it's going to be fine." I pray for an intervention, and even consider distracting the man myself. But then he might blow this entire place to the sky and what good would that do. Lysander notices me at the hall's centre, but the attacker does as well and makes a step in my direction.

"Nobody moves," the attacker yells, now aiming his weapon at me. My skin prickles with cold. I shut my eyes; my breaths are short and ragged.

Lysander ignores the warning and slowly makes his way towards me, his arms in the air to show he is unarmed. He stands in front of me, blocking me from the attacker with his own body.

"There must be something you want. Money? I can get you whatever you want but let the girl go," Lysander says, his tone calm. He speaks with the utmost eloquence and keeps his countenance without so much as a slip of the tongue.

"I don't want your filthy blood money," the masked man cries out. His voice has a metallic clang that seems to stop the blood flowing in my veins. Blind rage overwhelms him as his entire body shakes with his words. He tears away his mask, throwing it to the ground. His face is pock-marked and a thin jagged scar traces across his forehead. I recognise him now, he was standing with Warren only days ago, in Prateorian red. "*Ave Caesar libertatis.*"

A scream ricochets off the stone walls – "*Hail the Caesar of freedom*" – and the gun cracks. One, two, three times, the sound piercing me like a knife. Rapid fire follows from the vigilites. Lysander grips me, his touch my only comfort. I squeeze my eyes shut, unable to bear the sight before me. Blood drips from the dais, and both the attacker and Shauna are slumped, lifeless, on the stone. My vision is blurred red. I turn away and gag. Lysander doesn't let go.

The emperor wails; the sound is deep, harrowing and shakes me to my core. The prince darts to his sister and shakes her as if from sleep. A solitary tear slips down his cheek, and he roars. I can't make out his words. There is only terror. Medics sprint to her, but it is a futile response. Medicine can cure anything, but not a bullet directly in the head. Asher cradles his sister's head in his arms, rocking gently from side to side. When he finally closes her lifeless eyes with trembling fingers, it is a relief.

"You shouldn't see this," Lysander urges, holding me back. But I push past him, nearing the two bodies. It is not Shauna I want to see but the scarred man. I notice the inked marking behind his ear and shudder. It is Warren's tattoo. Two crossed swords. Spartaca's symbol. My senses numb, even with all the commotion around me.

Lysander stands over the man, and a vigilite crouches down, pointing to the tattoo. It seems I am not the only one who recognises the mark.

"They're back," Lysander mutters under his breath. Pure hatred fills his eyes. "No one finds out about this. No one. Understand?" he commands, his voice rattling even me, and the vigilite nods in compliance.

I stare at Shauna's body, a young girl, my brother's age. One of the few here who have shown me kindness. Now, her white *stola* is soaked crimson and her complexion is waxen in death. *I told her everything would be okay.* My chest suddenly feels tighter. Lix told me what Spartaca did in Echos. I never believed that it would do the same here. This was a stunt, choreographed and practised. An act of terrorism to send a message, a warning to Latia and the entire ULA. Spartaca is back and it is not going anywhere.

My throat thickens with my shame. I work with Spartaca. It is my fault the princess is dead. It is no longer a life for a life, my brother for the prince. I could never have imagined the bloodshed that would trail in my wake. Asher has lost his sister today and my heart wrenches for him. It is a feeling I can understand better than most. But my brother still lives, and Shauna is gone. Even the cold-hearted emperor cries for the loss of his daughter.

There is no longer a sense of celebration in the Palatine's halls. The entire hill is under lockdown; the Latian Infantry Division are stationed at the gates and no one is allowed in or out. A curfew is enforced, even for the Imperials. At six o'clock everyone must return to their rooms until sunrise. I pace around my room for what must be hours.

My mind fends off a constant barrage of thoughts and emotions. The sickness in the pit of my stomach doesn't subside. I distract myself with the viewing screen showing old gladiator fights on repeat. The hum of the broadcast is enough to keep me sane, for now. I find myself glancing at the clock every few minutes or so, praying for dawn to come. I won't sleep. Not tonight. Shauna's limp body is forever cast in my memory, and the words of her attacker. *Ave Caesar libertatis.*

At eight o'clock, there is a single knock at my door. I jump up from the couch, my guards informing me of a visitor. But there is a curfew. No one should be out roaming the halls at this time. But no law or rule applies to Lysander Drusus. When he stands in my entrance hall, still in his suit, I feel distinctly bare in comparison, wearing only a small silk robe. I wrap my arms around my body, shielding my embarrassment.

"The curfew doesn't apply to you, I suppose," I say, managing a small laugh. But it is hollow, and any happiness I felt is gone.

Lysander echoes my laughter with his own but is equally devoid of feeling. "How are you holding up?"

It is a customary question after such a horror occurs. "I'm well..." I pause, unable to articulate the emotions swirling within me. "I just feel awful for the prince and the emperor." I can't tell him the truth. That I am afraid of what I have done. Spartaca's presence is recognised now, and I feel more vulnerable than ever.

"It is a terrible tragedy. Shauna had a pure soul," he says, shaking his head. But Lysander is accustomed to war and hardened to the cruel nature of death.

I think of her now, the girl whose blood is on my hands. I feel it dripping from me, making the very ground I walk on unholy.

"Do you think she will go to the Elysian Fields in Rome?" It is a place in death reserved for heroes and Dominus's chosen mortals. I may not believe in religion, but I have always hoped that there might be an afterlife, a place for souls to rest for an eternity.

Lysander mulls my question over before answering, "If such a place existed, she would be worthy." He takes a seat on my couch, splaying his languorous limbs. He seems more tired than usual.

"Who attacked her?" I ask. I know the answer, but it will be interesting to hear Lysander's response. Has he put aside his suspicions of me? Does he trust me yet? I suppose I will find out soon enough.

Lysander hesitates, which is unusual for him. He runs a hand through the dark tresses of his hair. "Truthfully, we have been trying to keep the incident hushed. We can't afford to spark civilian panic. The attack wasn't orchestrated by one man but by an organisation that calls itself Spartaca."

I force a shocked expression, hoping he doesn't examine me too closely. He will surely see through my deceit.

"This is confidential," he warns.

I bob my chin, taking a seat on the coffee table opposite. "I won't tell a soul, I swear it."

He moves his hand and places it over mine, and I don't draw back. He mustn't see my fear. "I know," he says gently. "Spartaca has attacked us before, two decades ago. We thought we had ridden Latia of it for good, but it seems we failed." He unfolds his limbs and exhales, as if frustrated. His voice trembles as he speaks of Spartaca. The very name appears to haunt him. "It has committed the most atrocious massacres in our history. We were forced to cover up its crimes to protect the sanctity of our nation and the peace of our people."

He believes it righteous to deceive the people, to have them believe in this illusion of a perfect world, forever untarnished. Maybe it is better that way. The world before ours was a dark and terrible place, they say. But I don't know what to believe any more.

"Where does it come from?" I test him once more, taken aback by his candour with me.

"Outside the Haven." His eyes latch on to mine, radiant even in the dim light. The room is soundless as I feign another expression of shock and awe.

I lean forward, playing my part. "But there is nothing outside. At least, that's what the Institute says." I lie effortlessly, no more than habit to me now. It was always easy to fool my father, but Lysander Drusus is certainly more of a challenge.

His lip quirks up into a half-smirk. "There is a savage and lawless world governed by those Spartacan heathens." He spits in his rage – this must be the first time that I have ever seen the tempestuous side of his nature. "The people kill each other in the streets, fight over scraps, barter with whatever they can find. The emperor has been trying to restore order and peace. It seems Spartaca doesn't want that." He speaks with conviction as he runs a chain through his deft fingers. It is necklace he often wears, and it seems that it would be more suited to a woman's neck. I catch a brief glimpse of the letter on the triangular locket – *A*.

What he describes of the world beyond ours bears no resemblance to what I had witnessed. I cast my mind back to the mound of earth where I stood and saw the Institute's crimes with my own eyes. I remember the blood, the stray body parts mingled with the dust and rubble of the unpaved streets. To rid myself of the image, I squeeze my eyes shut but it doesn't go away. I don't think it ever will.

"The emperor wants to restore peace?" I ask him. "Most people believe that you control him."

Lysander throws his head back against the cushion. His laughter comes in sudden squalls and his entire body contorts, which confounds me. "It is all hearsay, is it not?" I nod. "Someone must take responsibility for the actions of the state. My job is to shield the emperor of a bad name."

His eyes dart across the room and when they finally settle on mine, they appear almost black in their intensity, making me believe every word he utters, even though I know I shouldn't. He smiles, flashing his bone-white teeth.

"So, you're the scapegoat?"

"Yes," he says.

I realise how pathetic I must sound to him. Basing my opinions on silly rumour. But he must be accustomed to it. He hides behind so many masks that no one person could ever know him entirely.

"Why would you risk your reputation for the emperor?" I can't help but ask.

"He's like family. I would do anything for him." His face falls, and I wonder if it could be the other way around. The emperor controlling Lysander. The perfect bow of his lip twitches and his hand goes cold over mine. There is so much sorrow, so much grief within him, behind his war-torn skin. But I can't afford to pity someone like Lysander. He is, above all, dangerous. Yet I find myself caring for him in ways even I don't yet understand.

He stands up abruptly. "I'm sorry to have bothered you, Electa."

"You haven't," I say, my voice almost urging him to stay. This is one night when I would rather not be alone, but I am too proud to admit it to him.

"I have much work that acquires my attention," he says over his shoulder, as he pauses in his tracks. "Actually, before I go, how would you like to join me at the Imperials' private breakfast tomorrow morning, perhaps to offer your condolences?"

It would be the proper thing to do, I suppose. That is, if I weren't lying through my teeth. "Yes, I'd like that," I say.

"*Vale.*"

I don't sleep that night. I am plagued by terrible visions of Shauna's murder. In my nightmare, it is me holding the gun. And my hands are wet with her blood.

I arrive at the Imperials' private dining room with Lysander at my side. It is in the east wing of the Palatine. I have visited only once before, when I met the prince in his office. The distinctive gilded stucco and mosaic tiles are distinctive to this quarter of the palace although it is no more or less grand than the entirety of the place. The dining room is lit with a morning glow, casting the figures of the prince and Cosimo in a heavenly light. Cosimo often dines with the Imperials as their personal secretary – he must brief them on their schedule for the day. The smell of honey and ripe fruit is thick in the air, yet they don't eat. This doesn't surprise me. Grief seems to have this effect.

Asher, sitting alone on the far end of the long table, looks up from his empty plate, noting my presence. His eyes rake over me and it is hardly welcoming. "Electa?" He mustn't have been expecting me.

Cosimo also looks surprised to see me.

Lysander steps in front of me, taking out a seat, and gestures for me to take a place at the table. "She has come to offer her condolences, as my guest." The servants rush to seat us but Lysander waves them off. I have come to expect such decorum from the director.

A frown creases the prince's forehead, and he looks bemused. "Well, she is here now, isn't she? I didn't know you two were friends." He huffs and I am not sure whether his features convulse with contempt, disdain or another emotion that I can't place.

I fidget in my seat, my skin suddenly taut, letting Lysander speak for me.

"You could call us that. I certainly enjoy her company, as you already know," he says, smirking a little.

Asher looks as though he might throttle Lysander where he stands. The director stares straight back at the unblinking prince with twice the ferocity. My pulse quickens, and I dare not look up from my lap.

"I'm so sorry about Shauna," I say quietly, hoping it will in some way alleviate the tension between them, but it seems the prince's tongue is rough with thorns, and I brace myself for his cutting words.

"We were never close," he snaps. The prince may have the face of angel but certainly not the demeanour of one. I notice that he wears the same toga from the Summit. Yesterday it was a crisp, gleaming white, and now it is stained with dark splotches of what can only be liquor.

Cosimo seems just as uncomfortable, making brief eye contact with me from across the table. He has a hand resting on his forehead, shielding his face. The marble-panelled doors swing open, clanging against the walls. The emperor strides in, with as much movement as his thickset legs will allow. The ground trembles beneath him.

"What is the Pleb doing here?" the emperor bellows, throwing himself onto his throne and kicking his feet up onto a footstool that the servants scrambled to place. His inky eyes latch on to me for no more than a second, and then are quickly averted.

I silence myself, for now. He has lost his daughter and can say what he wishes. But Lysander doesn't seem to agree. He grips my wrist.

"I would prefer if you did *not* address my guest with such a crass appellation," Lysander says. His manner is polite but my jaw drops, and Cosimo gulps down a glass of water, nervously. This is a brazen act of defiance against the emperor, his father figure and mentor. I sink lower and lower into my chair. When Lysander slips his hand onto my shoulder, the emperor watches with tapered eyes.

"Strange taste in friends, dear boy," he mutters but his temper doesn't flare as I expected.

Lysander squeezes my shoulder to appease me or retrain me, or both. "She is here to offer her condolences," he explains. His composure doesn't slip even in his temerity.

Asher is wide-eyed at Lysander's defence of me but remains silent, hunched over his plate.

The emperor takes no time with his response. "I don't want her condolences. She does not belong here, in my home or my kingdom and certainly not at my table." His words are lashing and strip me raw. I shouldn't have come here. This was a mistake. The emperor doesn't mourn like his son. I am not sure he mourns at all.

"I am sorry, my emperor. I was fond of your daughter," I say, hoping in some way to pacify the titan of the man before me.

He slams his fist on the table, the china and silverware rattling with the impact, and the ringing fills my ears. "Keep that mouth of yours shut, Pleb."

"Father!" Asher shouts, coming to my defence at last. *Took him long enough.* "That's enough." The prince has inherited his father's voice; it is imperious and fevered. It is a battle cry, a rallying call. It even makes me want to bow.

"Fools. Both of you," the emperor slurs, his eyes drifting between Lysander and Asher. "You are gods. She is nothing."

I can't bring myself to argue with the emperor. He is not wrong. I am nothing. I deserve to be erased, forgotten, along with the rest of the Unchosen. I would have been, if it weren't for Spartaca.

Lysander and Asher stare back at the emperor with hardened expressions and clenched jaws. They are not afraid of him – not at all.

Asher sits up straighter in his chair. "Not all women are like my mother."

The statement takes me off-guard. It is the first time that I have heard the prince mention his mother. She died soon after Asher's birth and it seems that she was not on good terms with the emperor. He flinches at the mention of her. His son's comment has silenced him.

Cosimo coughs to make himself known. "My emperor, I believe we should begin preparing the funeral rites," he says, softly. It is typical of Cosimo to play the peace monger, changing the tide of conversation with ease.

Asher nods. "Cosimo is right. We should honour her properly." He directs the comment to his father who is busy sucking on figs. His chest heaves and his bronze skin turns red and splotchy. I could even swear that his eyes are damp, as if he has only now realised that his daughter is dead.

I stand. "I think it may be best if I leave," I say, quietly.

"Don't." Lysander's touch lingers on my wrist and Asher's mouth folds into a thin scowl.

I tug my arm away and walk towards the doors. Lysander follows.

"I hope you have enjoyed yourself." The director sneers towards the emperor, and I can hardly believe his audacity.

The doors shut behind us and I can breathe again. "You shouldn't have defended me like that," I murmur, almost embarrassed to have elicited such a reaction from Lysander.

He smiles, nudging me with the crook of his elbow. "You could simply thank me." His laughter manages to soothe me.

"Thank you," I say. "I'm sorry. You shouldn't have taken me in the first place." I hate to think that I have caused discord between Lysander and the emperor.

"We had good intentions."

We stroll the halls of the east wing. Lysander instructs a servant to fetch me food, despite my protestation. The boy returns with a plate stacked high with fruits, pastries and cured meats. I eat as we walk.

"I think it would be best for me to avoid the emperor from now on," I joke.

Lysander lifts his chin and stares up at the ceiling. "He is in mourning," he tells me.

I swallow down a mouthful of honey bread. "Funny way of showing it," I say, my voice muffled. "He has never been my biggest fan."

"True."

"I should just learn to keep my mouth shut." I shake my head as I speak. My words often run away from me. It is a fault that I have tried often to rectify.

"Don't," Lysander says quickly. "It is what I like most about you." He pauses in his tracks so that he can look me in the eye.

"All it does is cause trouble. One day you will hate me for it," I say, staring back at him. Thoughts flash across my mind. The things he would do to me if he uncovered who I truly am. One day we will be enemies, and this will be nothing but a forgotten memory. "It seems that I'm not the only one with a big mouth. Trinity..."

Lysander wears a smug expression, "Yes, the truth is that girl has only been saying those things because her twin brother was Unchosen."

That explains it. A Patrician wouldn't hate the Choosing unless they had good reason and an Unchosen brother seems reason enough.

"Oh. How sad," I comment.

"Yes, it is."

"What are you going to do about it?" I ask.

"About what?" Lysander plays coy but he knows exactly what I am asking.

"Trinity's statements. They undermine the Institute and all it stands for."

The director shrugs, nonchalantly. "I will do nothing. As long as she doesn't win Imperial Panore, it won't be a problem." He seems relaxed about the whole affair, which is surprising. The Lysander I have heard stories about would have had her killed on the spot. "We have had a word with her mentor, I'm sure she will be quieter in the future."

Quieter. The Institute sure knows how to control their citizens.

"You said to me once that it is courageous to stand up for what you believe," I say.

Lysander doesn't flinch or give much away. "Yes, it is. That is why I will take no action against the Messalla girl. One girl's views won't change the opinions of millions. Especially now they know the reasons behind her ideology."

He leaked the story to the press. I would expect nothing less. It could have been much worse for Trinity. I can hardly believe he has taken no action to reprimand her. Perhaps he is not the man Spartaca makes him out to be.

I press the issue. "Did the emperor not believe it to be treason? Surely he wanted action to be taken?"

"No, he did not. Ash did." Lysander speaks with a measured smile.

My mouth hangs open. "He wanted you to—"

Lysander breaks in. "I have already spoken out of turn. I must be getting to the Institute." He kisses my hand as a gesture of farewell before hastening his pace.

"I have one more question," I call after him. "How did Asher's mother die?"

He turns on his heels, the polished marble squeaking beneath his leather shoes. His green eyes fall on mine. "She was executed for treason."

XII

OBSCURIS VERA INVOLVENS

The truth is enveloped by obscurity

Executed. That word plays over in my mind. The rumours say she died after years of ill health or that she went mad and killed herself on top of Capitoline Hill. I suppose it sounds better than *execution*. Asher's mother was the empress of Ore, the last empress, the last winner of Imperial Panore. The emperor never re-married, but took mistresses, one of whom bore him a daughter – Shauna.

It seems strange that the truth of the empress's mysterious death is enveloped by such obscurity. The matter has been concealed for a reason, either by the Institute or the Imperials, or both. Something about it sits like a stone in my stomach, and I can't help but suspect Spartaca. Lysander had said that Spartaca had plagued Latia two decades ago and the prince happens to have just turned twenty-one.

Warren has been included in my guard rotations, thanks to Crew, no doubt. He wants someone keeping an eye on me. It is a shame it has to be Warren. He looks so handsome in his Praetorian armour, and I almost forget all he has done to betray me. *But he saved me, twice,* I am forced to remind myself. At least that way, I can be half-nice to him. I tell him that I need to speak with Crew and that I need his help getting out of the Palatine. I don't give him a reason, but he agrees. Crew's villa is at the bottom of Palatine Hill, a few minutes' walk away. The trickiest part will be escaping the palace, which is under lockdown after yesterday's incident. But if I get the information I need, it will be a worthwhile trip.

Warren cocks his head to one side and squares his body. "Do you know how crazy this sounds?" he says, wrinkling his brow. "I'll be breaking at least a dozen protocols."

Warren won't succeed in dissuading me.

151

"The only reason they're keeping everyone in is for their own safety," I remind him. "It's not like I'm going to be a victim of Spartaca's terrorism."

Warren is displeased by my sarcasm and takes on a defensive stance. "We're not terrorists," he snaps. It seems I have touched a nerve.

"That stunt you pulled yesterday looked a lot like terrorism to me." I step right up to him until I am just under his nose. His hardened expression doesn't waver, and he displays no sign of remorse.

He simply says, "I had nothing to do with that."

I look up, catching his eyes. "Standing on the sidelines and watching it happen is equally bad." It is infuriating that even now, in the face of a dead girl, he doesn't blink. I see the soldier in him now more than I ever have.

His muscles bulge in his fitted armour as he crosses his arms. "You know we just follow orders, right? There are people above us. They send us commands, and we carry them out."

I always knew there must be people who control them – Warren and Crew. Such a big and ruthless organisation must have an equally ruthless leader. Just as I am Spartaca's puppet, Warren and Crew act on the behalf of some man in a far-off land. *Albion.* That is what Warren called the place he came from.

"What? So that makes it acceptable to murder a teenage girl in cold blood." The bitterness in my voice seems to take him offguard, and he tears his eyes away from me.

He falls silent for several moments, staring down at his silver-plated greaves. "No, it doesn't," he murmurs, and I believe he is sorry, even if for just an instant. "But this world needs change and if that is what it takes then, yes, it is necessary but not acceptable." The coldness he exudes is not something I ever expected. He is just like Crew – heartless. They care not of the consequences of their actions, and I should take note. They will just as easily slaughter Vel if I don't cooperate.

I bristle, turning away from him, unable to push my anger away any longer. "I will never forgive you for what you did to her." I want to scream at him. I want to make him feel something, anything for that innocent girl.

He baulks at my comment. "I don't expect you to. I don't expect you to forgive me for taking your brother hostage either, but I'd like us to be friends. And if we can't be friends, we should at least be allies," he says. As he towers over me, he puts a hand on my shoulder. I quickly push it away, which only seems to elicit laughter from him.

"Allies?" I narrow my eyes.

"Yes, allies." He nods, his eyes falling on mine. "Despite what you may think, I'm on your side, Electa." He smiles, as if all is forgotten. The murder of the princess, Vel's kidnapping and my blackmail. I shouldn't fall for his sweet talk.

All he has ever wanted from me is my allegiance to Spartaca's cause. And I can't trust him, but maybe I can use him. Just maybe it is my turn to use, my turn to hurt – they will never see it coming.

I mimic the prince's trademark smirk. It fits well on my face. "Aren't allies supposed to help each other out from time to time?" My mouth curls and my features become pointed. Manipulation has never been my strong suit, but it is time for me to get my hands dirty and make a stand.

"Yes, I suppose," he says.

"Then get me out of the Palatine." It is more an order than a request, and the tone I use tastes foreign on my tongue.

Warren tosses his head back as he laughs, and his flaxen curls ripple with his movements. "I've already saved you skin more times than I can count." He shakes his head.

"Please, Warren. It is important."

"What do you need to ask Crew anyway? He's not exactly cooperative."

"Trust me, I know. It doesn't matter what I want to ask him. Just help me." He quirks his head. "Please." I force the word from my lips once more.

His smile turns smug. "So, you're resorting to begging now?"

"You don't have to come with me."

There is a flash of irritation in his eyes. "Oh, I was never coming with you," he scoffs. "I could lose my job and then where would you be?"

I grin. "Happier."

"Ha, no," he retorts with a huff. "You would be dead."

"Perhaps. But at least I could die happy."

He rolls his eyes. "Very funny. Come on then, let's do this." As he finally gives in, I ponder for a moment what it must be like for him. To face the full brunt of Crew's anger for my actions, to be expected to follow orders without question, without delay. Warren is young, he could still turn his life around, choose another path. But revolution burns like fire within him. It is the only life he has ever known. And I don't think he would choose any other.

Warren fetches me a servant's cape so that no one will recognise me. It is a dullish brown colour and ill-fitting, but it will do. He leads me down to the servants' passageways beneath the ground floor. As a Praetorian, he has access to most parts of the Palatine. The winding walkways flicker in the electric light, and the soft padding of footsteps on the stone is a calming sound. Servants scurry back and forth, carrying plates piled high with food and goblets filled to the brim with wine. I keep my head down and follow Warren.

He takes me to the end of the passage where a heavily armoured door stands between us and the outside. The palace is built into rocks, and this secret exit comes out from under the granite. Warren knows the codes, although I am sure he is not supposed to. He tells me that this is the only way in or out of the Palatine that is not guarded or under video surveillance. It is for emergencies and only the Imperials and select officials know the codes. But it seems that Spartaca has comprised the Palatine's entire security database.

I thank Warren and make my own way outside, following his directions. I take a roundabout route through the gardens to avoid any run-ins with the vigilites or soldiers who now swarm the hill in grey and red. The sun slips into the lower horizon, casting my path ahead in a soft orange glow. There is a sign etched into stone that reads – *Villa Acheron*.

Crew's house sprawls out over one of the many terraced gardens of the hill. It is simple in comparison to Lysander's home but still finer than anything I had seen before coming to the Palatine. Iron-clad gates bar my entrance, and eight *lictors* are patrolling the perimeter, armed with Institute-issued pistols. Wrought-iron fencing encircles the villa. As I scan the area from the hedgerow, it become clear that there is no way in other than through the gates.

I approach the nearest *lictor*, a woman with cropped blonde hair wearing a black girdle, Crew's family colour. "My name is Electa Steel and I'm here to see Mr Gracchus."

There is a glint of recognition in her eyes. "He is not seeing visitors." Her response is curt, but I decide to persist.

"Tell him that I am here, and that I'm not leaving until I see him." I plant my feet firmly on the ground.

She glances at me and then looks away. "I can't do that, Miss Steel." The man to her right nods in agreement but looks almost apologetic. There is no doubt in my mind that these *lictors* are with Spartaca. They must know about my brother. All I seem to do is evoke pity. *Poor little Pleb*, they all think. It is infuriating. I want people to flinch when they look my way. I want them to be afraid. I am tired of being everyone's fool.

I step up to the woman until I am but an inch from her face. And I grin. "Oh, you can. Trust me, he won't want the suspicion of me loitering around his gates."

She seems to understand that. The *lictor* contacts Crew and escorts me inside the premises. The villa's interior is spartan, with a distinct lack of furniture or any personal items at all. There are a few statues, some paintings and a book here and there but that is it. The few items of furniture in the hypostyle hall are covered with dust sheets. It is not surprising. This is not Crew's real home. He lives thousands of miles from here.

The *lictor* delivers me to a salon that has some dashes of colour and usable furnishings. Crew sits in a bathrobe, legs crossed on a long couch, book in hand. It is an antique hardback, its leather binding worn and the font fading. It reminds me of the books in my collection at home. They were my grandfather's and probably my most cherished possessions, although I never had much as a child.

Crew peers over the edge of the book, his cold eyes latching on to me. "What do you want, Electa?" He returns his gaze to the pages, which he thumbs gently. Clearly, I am of interest to him for no more than a few seconds. Provoking him, however, seems to always get his attention.

"Charming welcome. Are you always so friendly?"

He tosses his book aside and lets out a long sigh. "You know how I tire of your wit." He mimics a yawn. "What do you want?"

I may as well get straight to the point. Warren was right, he is not in a cooperative mood. "I have a question for you."

There is a flicker of amusement in his expression. "So, you came all the way here, when the palace is under lockdown, to ask me a question?"

When he says it like that, it sounds utterly nonsensical. "Yes," I answer, meekly.

"In that case, you are complete fool."

So much for pleasantries. "Why was Asher's mother executed?"

Recognition dawns on his face, although he tries his best to conceal it. "That's a strange question to ask someone like me," he mutters, picking up his discarded book once more, feigning disinterest.

I near him. "I think her death had something to do with Spartaca." I stand over him now, and he can longer avoid my gaze or my question.

Indistinct laughter bubbles through his nose. "How did you come to that little conclusion?" He raises his eyebrows.

"I know Spartaca was here before, two decades ago, in Latia." My voice is insistent.

He hesitates for a brief moment and forces his eyes back to the creased pages of his novel. "It was before my time so I wouldn't know."

I fight off the urge to tear his book away. "You're lying."

"Stop wasting my time, Electa. I was having a delightful evening until you appeared."

That's it. I can't take it anymore. I rip the book from his hands and throw it to the floor. "You killed a girl yesterday, Crew." The words come out in a series of shouts, but it doesn't seem to startle him much. I half-expected his hands to be around my throat by now.

"I am aware." His voice is neutral, passive and detached. He doesn't feel pangs of conscience that I do. I am the one suffering for his crimes.

"You don't care, do you?"

"No, I don't." He answers far too quickly, and it is now that I finally understand just how inhuman he is. At least Warren knew it was wrong. "She was an Imperial, a Patrician, a Gold. She is no different to the rest of them."

"She was s-seventeen years old," I stammer, hardly believing his words.

"She would have become a monster," he says. "I did the world a favour by killing her."

A sudden pang of regret ripples through me. It all becomes clear. There must have been hundreds of potential targets at the Summit. But Crew chose Shauna. My mind flickers back to what she did for me all those nights ago and now I realise that it is my fault she is dead.

I look away in shame. "You did it because she humiliated you the other night, didn't you?"

"I don't know what you're talking about." He laughs yet must know exactly what I am referring to.

"She protected me from you, after the Imperial Ball…" My voice dies away as my grief and guilt threaten to overwhelm me.

Crew simply shrugs, even though he can hear the strain in my voice. "I vaguely remember the incident."

I shut my eyes and let the emotions pour out of me. I take one deep breath to steady myself. I won't let a monster like him see me cry. There are a thousand things I want to say to him, but, "You disgust me," is all I can manage.

He chuckles at my feeble words. It is in times like these that I wish I had the courage to plunge a knife through his heart and watch him bleed – the way he made Shauna bleed.

No matter the pain I feel, I need answers. "What happened to the empress? Why was she executed?" I urge him again.

He presses a hand to his forehead, and I can tell he is losing patience. There is only so much I can push him before his violent side manifests itself. "For treason. Can you leave me in peace now?"

"Treason?" She must have done something terrible to end up on the cross.

"Yes, treason."

I fumble for words. "What did she do?"

"I've told you enough." Crew waves me off with his arms.

"No," I say, firmly. "What did she do?" I will *not* let this go.

"She was implicated with a Spartacan operative after killing the emperor's eldest son."

The emperor had another son? It seems strange that no one has mentioned such a thing. Perhaps the regenerators conditioned people to forget the entire incident occurred. An empress committing infanticide is not exactly in keeping with the Institute's beloved *perfection*.

"How long ago was this?" I ask, knowing that the ramifications of this can only spell disaster.

Crew no longer resists my curiosity. "Twenty-one, maybe twenty-two, years ago."

Just after Asher was born. So the prince never knew his mother, much like I never knew mine.

Crew continues, "Skylar, the prince's mother, was recruited by Spartaca in the same way that you have been. She and a number of conspirators were caught and killed. We had to start all over again," he explains in a calmer manner. It seems my persistence has worn him down. Or he is desperate for me to leave his house?

"So, she was like me? She went through the same process? Imperial Panore?" The questions tumble out of me all at once, and I am surprised that Crew can make any sense out of my words.

"More or less. She was recruited after winning the competition."

I came here for reassurance but instead I know what the *Parcae* have in store for me. History repeats itself; it is a constant of mankind. Skylar was like me. A girl recruited by Spartaca and tasked with the destruction of Latia.

"So that's my fate? I am going to be executed for treason and erased from history?" Speaking this thought aloud makes my blood run cold in my veins. My body is frozen by a paralysing fear. Skylar was punished not only with execution, but *Damnatio Memoriae*. The very words would strike fear into any Latian's heart. It is the most feared form of punishment that exists in our world. It is oblivion and reserved only for the most wicked of traitors. Her memory gone, erased from history and the minds of Latian people forever.

"We are all putting our lives on the line, Electa." Crew's voice is lost amid the direful thoughts that swirl in my mind. I imagine my body nailed to a cross and pecked away by carrion birds until there is nothing but bones.

"I wouldn't concern yourself." Crew seems to be attempting to put my mind at rest. "The only reason she was discovered was because she killed her firstborn."

That is the one thing I don't understand. "Why would a mother kill her own son?"

Crew sinks back into the couch. "Skylar was a sociopath, so who knows what she was thinking?"

I still can't make much sense of any of it, and I suspect Crew is holding something back. I won't try my luck by pushing the matter further. For now, I know enough.

I shake off my fear. "Thank you, I'll leave you in peace now." My tone sounds mocking and the smirk that comes with it seems to irritate him.

"How did you even get out?" He is only now catching on that I must have had help escaping the palace.

"Warren."

Crew grumbles and mutters for me to get out of his house. *Happily,* I think.

I trace back my steps to return to the palace. Warren instructed me to return through the service entrance and hope no one questions me. The doorway is in sight when I am spotted.

A vigilite shouts after me, "Do you have identification, Miss?" He breaks into a run. "Miss?" he shouts again. *Stercus.* I can't outrun him, so I stop in my tracks. He lifts up my hood and recognises me instantly. "Miss Steel, how did you—"

I don't know how I will explain my way out of this one. Before I can even find my tongue, a refined voice drifts from behind me.

"She's with me." It is Lysander who speaks. His voice wields command and the vigilite backs away.

"I apologise, sir," he stutters and scurries away into the gardens.

Lysander is going to want an explanation too. And he is far more difficult to lie to. He faces me now, and there are times when I think he knows all my secrets just by looking at me.

"I was wondering just the same thing. How did you get out?"

I hesitate for far too long. "Climbed out a window."

"Why are you out?"

I have to improvise. "I was actually coming to find you."

He raises a single eyebrow in disbelief. "Well, you have…"

"Yes … I…" I stumble over my words. It seems Lysander understands me a little too well. I have been caught in a lie.

"You weren't looking for me, were you?" I expect him to be angry, but his voice is typically calm.

I want to hate him, to see him for the monster he is. But everything Lysander does surprises me. He hasn't yet lived up to my expectations of him and I am starting to doubt that he ever will.

I shake my head. "No. Truthfully, I just need some fresh air. I was feeling upset about Shauna, what I saw, all of it really." Another lie, albeit a more convincing one. But Lysander is no fool and I am sure for a moment he sees through it.

He laughs a little, with the incredulous sort of laughter that can only indicate utter doubt. "That is understandable. I won't mention this again if you do something for me in return."

There is always a catch with Lysander, and I never know what to expect.

"Okay…" I say, hesitantly.

He smiles, and the last bit of sun catches in his eyes, turning them gold. "Would you allow me the honour of escorting you to the voting ceremony tomorrow?"

Not what I was expecting at all. I sigh with relief. "Yes," I answer, but there is something tugging at me. This is my punishment for breaking curfew? I should fear his motives, but something about his voice, the way he conducts himself, makes me want to say yes to everything he asks of me. It is disturbing, the hold he has over my mind. It won't be long until he has stolen my heart too. And then I will have nothing.

"Delightful. I will see you then." He grins and pulls down the hood over my eyes. His touch is gentle as ever. "I'm sure you will have no trouble finding your way back in."

I smirk at him and scamper away.

It is time for my nightly meeting with Cosimo. It is no longer a chore and I find myself looking forward to seeing him. I don't have any other friends here, now that Lix has stopped talking to me. Cosimo is an adequate substitute, although he is often far too verbose for my liking. I knock on his office door and barely put one foot forward before he has his arms locked around me. His embrace is fatherly and reminds me of the days that my father would return from war and lift me from the ground, holding me tight to his chest.

"Congratulations, my dear girl. I am so proud," he says, his head buried into my shoulder.

This sudden outpour of affection takes me by surprise. "What have I done?"

He takes a step back, perching on the edge of his desk, his smile more genuine than usual. "I just received the exit poll. You're second, just behind Ember. They don't believe it will change much between today and tomorrow." He holds his head high, proud of himself for transforming a Pleb into a princess, but prouder of me and all that I have sacrificed to get here.

But I am not proud. I am ashamed. I have lost myself and compromised myself in ways that I never expected to. I am choking on my pride and allowing this world to humble me. It was a promise I made to myself. To not let this world change me. But it has. I should be happy. But I can't bring myself to rejoice in this success. I am one step closer to becoming a murderer and a terrorist.

"That's ... uh ... great news," I murmur, but I am lying to myself. Cosimo can see it and his smile fades. "I couldn't have done it without you." My gratitude for Cosimo, however, is no lie. I don't feel so alone, knowing I have him. But my guilt eats away at me, hollowing my stomach. I yearn to tell him everything, the truth. Maybe he could help me.

No. Don't be a fool, Electa. He is still a Patrician.

Cosimo's eyes narrow, as he detects the slip in the mask Spartaca has painted for me. "You don't really want to win? Do you?" He presses the bridge of his glasses against his nose.

"Of course I do." I answer too quickly. I can lie better than that, but I am tired of fooling people.

"I don't believe you, El." When Cosimo speaks, he reminds me of my father. For all his faults, he is a good, honourable man. They both are. "You have never wanted this, not for one moment."

But I want to live. I want to be free – free to live, to learn, to be wild and have fun. "Maybe I want to win, just not be married to him…"

"Hm, Ash?" Cosimo grimaces. "I know you believe him to be some monster but there is another side to him, I promise." There is such conviction when he speaks, it makes it difficult to doubt his words.

"Another side?"

Cosimo sighs. "It is a side that I haven't seen in a very long time. But I think you could change him. You're the only one of the girls who could."

"I think he's pretty unfixable, Cos." Ash may as well be a ghost. There is no humanity within him.

"Perhaps you are right," Cosimo muses. "But he would be miserable married to Ember. You are just the kind of person he needs." His voice is insistent, and I realise now how much he cares for the prince. It explains his dislike for Calix and all the times he has encouraged me to pursue a relationship with Ash.

"Ash doesn't need anyone. He likes to remind people of that … often."

"Being a prince isn't exactly easy, you know?" There is an edge to Cosimo's voice.

"Shauna tried so hard with him. You could see how much she wanted to help. But Ash just pushed her away." My mention of the princess tugs at my heart. I feel a lurch of guilt. "What makes you think he will be any different with me?"

It seems Cosimo has no answer for that. Moments pass, in an eerie silence that drowns us both.

Cosimo rocks gently in his chair. "You should see the way he looks at you," he says, softly.

His comment riles me more than it should. "He hates me," I snap. But I know that it is not true.

Cosimo leans forward in his chair and shakes me by my shoulders. "No, Electa. He has a real soft spot for you, and I know you feel the same."

I tear my eyes away from him. Cosimo knows me too well, he can see my denial even if I can't. "Trust me, I don't. He is a *bacchant*, and a drunk. I could think of a thousand more unpleasant words to describe him." The words fall from my mouth and I instantly regret them. Cosimo winces, and I can see that my foul language is bothering him. An insult on the prince is an insult to him. His jaw tightens but he still manages to retain his calm demeanour.

He looks over me, and his stare lingers longer than it ever has. "El, you are different. There is something that sets you apart. He would change … for you." He points at me to make himself clear. "Don't let people use you." His voice is suddenly dry and burgeoning into something sinister. I go cold. He knows. Everything.

I begin to speak. "How do you—"

He cuts in. "Don't kill him, Electa. Whatever you do, you can't kill him."

I squeeze my eyes shut, hoping this is all just a terrible nightmare. Is there no one who is not involved in this plot in some way? I want to hate him, for his lies, for the part he has played in this deception. But he stands there with this sad, tragic look in his eye, and I know that he didn't choose this path.

"Are you a part of this?" I have to ask. My tone is more chiding than I had intended and Cosimo flinches as if struck by a fist.

"Holy Dominus, no." He inhales sharply and I notice now that his eyes are wet. "They can't know that I told you. They have killed my wife already. They have my baby daughter and will kill her too."

I step away from him, rubbing my palms against my face. I feel myself choking on my emotion. It seems that Spartaca's *modus operandi* is to use threats and blackmail to achieve its ends. Its cause may be just, but its methods are wrong. What won't it do in pursuit of its goals?

"I'm so sorry, Cosimo. I had no idea," I whisper even though we are alone. My heart aches for him. I could never have suspected that he is a victim of such tragedy. I could count on one hand the times I have seen him without a smile. *We all wear masks.* The silence that envelopes his office allows us both a moment to pull ourselves back together, to position our masks once more.

Cosimo finally raises his head and meets my gaze. "Find another way, El. You're smart. Take my advice, get to know Ash and maybe things could change."

Change. The only thing that would change is my brother dead, gone forever.

My voice cracks. "They have my brother…" I allow myself to be vulnerable. He is the first person I have been able to tell about Vel, and I break down before his eyes. I feel myself crumbling, but I don't fight it. I let my dignity pour away with my tears.

"I know," he says, understanding better than anyone ever could. They have already stolen so much from him. "But you always have a choice. Remember that." Cosimo fights off his own tears, putting on a brave face for me, the young girl, only seventeen, who has no one left to turn to.

161

In the face of his own devastation, he manages to sing my tears away with ancient songs and stories that seem to fill up the entire night. I watch him as he dotes on me and know it can only be a father's instinct. His daughter is gone, for now. I am not exactly a perfect substitute, but it must be nice for him, even for the short moments it lasts, to feel like a father again. He is too good a man to be involved in all this and I can't help but feel responsible for the loss of his wife. Spartaca knew that my only chance of winning was with Cosimo by my side. And so perhaps her blood is on my hands too. I push the thought away. As we chat idly, distancing ourselves from our sad reality, it becomes clear to me what I must do – play the game from both sides.

XIII

SIC EGO NEC SINE TE NEC TECUM VIVERE POSSUM

So, I can't live either with or without you

The twilight hours descend on the Palatine, and there is only the noise of the fire between Cosimo and I. His eyes are half-closed as he drifts off into sleep. I cover his body with a tartan blanket that happens to be draped across the window seat. Only the upper half of his face is visible, and, in the firelight, he looks more peaceful than ever. I leave him like this – content. The administration wing is empty of anything but shadows, and I fumble through the darkness in dread of being caught. I have broken curfew, again, and there are only so many excuses I can think of.

As I wander, with my arms outstretched, I notice a flicker of orange light through the glass windows. I pause for a moment, and stare out into the peristyle. The flare is the burning end of a cigarette, and I know the silhouette slumped against the bough of the olive tree must belong to Asher Ovicula. A cloud of smoke obscures his face, and without his smirk he seems almost human.

I emerge from the glass doors. The rattle of the hinges disturbs him. His head jolts upwards but the rest of his body remains lax against the bark. His linen shirt makes a soft scraping sound against the wood as he angles his body towards me.

"I wasn't expecting company," he drawls, his voice heavy with liquor. I hear even the faintest sniffle and notice now that his eyes are glassy with tears.

I stand still, unsure whether to retreat back inside. "Sorry…" I say, hesitantly. "I can go."

He pulls his body taut and shakes his head. "It's fine. Stay." The prince is aglow in the moonlight, his skin paled silver. He doesn't look me in the eyes, even as I near. He holds out a near-empty bottle. "Want some?"

In spite of my better judgement, I take the bottle from his hand and swig the remaining contents. The burn in my throat is a familiar feeling, and I smile, wistful of better times.

The prince lets out a choked laugh that warms my bones. "I'm impressed, Steel." He raises his eyebrows. "But not surprised."

I tilt my head to one side. "Really?"

He sinks to his haunches, lowering himself onto the grass. "I knew who you were before you were Chosen." He looks up at me and notices the twitch in my expression. "Don't worry, I'm not going to tell on you," he says with a mocking tone.

It seems everyone knows about my past as a Grey. There is little point in denying it.

"Well thanks, I guess," I murmur, the smallness of my voice carried away with the breeze.

Ash puts the cigarette to his lips but pauses. "And I am sorry about this morning. My father is grieving," he says, taking a drag. "He has never been particularly good with emotions."

"It runs in the family," I say, intending for it to be a joke.

"True." He reaches out a hand into the lavender stems, letting his fingers trace the plant. The smell clings to my skin and my hair.

The prince falls into an unexpected silence. He often has many things to say to me, unpleasant things usually. But tonight, he is sad, sadder than I have ever seen him.

I settle myself down beside him, my back against the tree. He doesn't react, nor acknowledge my presence at his side. "What are you doing out here all by yourself?" I finally muster the courage to ask him.

"Couldn't sleep." He takes one last drag of his cigarette and flicks it onto the ground. "I buried my sister today and all I can think is that it should have been me." His voice is stifled by his sorrow and quieter than I have ever heard it. "I imagine death often. Sometimes it feels like I am dead already."

For a moment it seems that he has forgotten my presence. He muses to himself in a haunting whisper. His expression is blank and his eyes cold in the moonlight.

"You're more of a ghost than a person, Asher Ovicula." I angle my body towards him, urging him to face me. "But you are also the most alive person I have ever met."

I think back to the first time I met the prince, in the Institute building, weeks ago now. There was a fire in him that frustrated me incredibly. A fire that I also possess. We had a rare, special kind of rapport that day, and every day since.

He sits up straighter, leaning forward but still can't meet my gaze. "That doesn't make any sense."

I shrug my shoulders. "I suppose it doesn't. But you are a walking contradiction, and I think you like it that way."

One of his eyebrows quirks up. "Is that a compliment, Steel?" His laughter is unnatural, sending a ripple of pain through me. This is the man behind the princely mask. There are no cameras for him to bask in here and although he seems more human, it is not a pretty sight. Asher Ovicula has tragedy etched into his bones.

I sink back against the bark. "Take it how you wish."

He manages a forced smile. "Well then, compliment it is."

The prince reaches into the satchel bag between us and takes out another bottle. His jaw tightens as he rips the metal cap off with his teeth. Without much thought, I quickly snatch the bottle away from him and expect at least some protestation, but he doesn't speak nor move in retaliation. He doesn't have much fight left, I suppose.

"Shauna wouldn't have wanted this," I say sternly, clutching the bottle in my hands, expecting him to wrestle it from me.

He stays perfectly still. "No. She hated me for it."

The words make my stomach heave as my mind traces back to the memory of her. The way she protected me, the way she always protected him. "She didn't hate you, Ash. She wanted you to get better."

It is only now that he takes the bottle back, in one swift motion as if it were never in my hands. "I'm not sick, Electa," he mutters, before pressing the neck of the bottle to his lips. The irony is painful to see. "I have just never seen much point in living."

His words confound me. "How c-can you feel that way?" I stammer. "You have everything." The remark sounds far more critical than I had intended but the prince doesn't flinch.

His shoulders heave as he sighs. "You are only looking with your eyes," he says with a level tone. "I was raised to be admired, not loved. There is a difference. And what is living without love?"

I consider. A life without a brother and father who care for me. The thought is too much to bear. And I suppose that is why I will do whatever it takes to save them.

"Your family loves you."

Ash shakes his head stiffly. "No. They don't." It is a blunt response. "My mother is dead. And to my father, all I am is a ghost of her."

I ache for him more than I believed myself capable. His mother was executed for treason and his father hates him for it. The dullness in his voice is jarring, and it is clear that he has long endured this sad existence.

I attempt to reassure him, offer some limited comfort to the broken man who sits beside me. "You will be loved, Ash. If not by your family then by friends, by your wife."

"You're a fool if you believe any of my friends are real or that any of these girls could love me."

I am no fool. He speaks the truth. Asher Ovicula is a rich boy with fake friends and suitors to match.

I look at him with pleading eyes. "Just because your father doesn't love you doesn't mean that no one else will."

He tugs at the collar of his shirt, staring at nothing in particular. "My father sought solace after my mother's death," he speaks without blinking. "He summoned an oracle from some place where the ancient discipline is still practised. I think he hoped it would bring him peace..." His voice trails off.

I didn't even know that such a profession still existed. The myths of old said that oracles had the gift of foresight and could understand the will of the gods. I neither believe in foresight nor gods but I entertain the prince, for now.

"And did it?" I ask.

"The sibyl offered him no prophecy. But she offered me one."

"What did the prophecy say?" I ask with urgency in my voice.

He looks at me. "That I would die in the arms of the only person who ever loved me."

My eyes crinkle in bewilderment. "And you believe that nonsense?"

His eyes are unblinking. "Why wouldn't I?"

It is surprising that Ash is a believer in the creed of myth and legend. "No one can predict the future," I insist.

But he simply shakes his head. The prince has convinced himself that this self-proclaimed oracle, seer, sibyl or whatever she called herself, has seen his fate. He is haunted by her words, whether he entirely believes them or not.

"Are you sure about that?"

His question throws me. I have never fully understood whether the visions that plague me are representations of the past, future or something else entirely. I push the thought away.

He studies me for a moment, expecting a response but he is met only with my silence. "Whether or not it is true, it has played over my mind since I was a child. I memorised her words and think about them so often that it has become a sort of truth. In my mind, at least."

"I think we make our own fate."

His forehead creases pensively. "Then you believe I can change?"

"I don't know. But I hope so."

166

His eyes examine my expression, as if searching for the faintest indication of doubt. His face folds, his flawless skin crinkling in confusion. "I thought you hated me."

I manage to laugh, hardly the reaction Ash was expecting. "I do sometimes." My voice now goes quiet as the laughter dies in my throat. "But I also care. You lost your sister today."

Ash tears his eyes away from me. "I don't want to think about it anymore," he snaps. "Let's talk about something else."

My mind races to find a topic to distract him from the thought of his sister. But I have never been much good at small talk. "Did you cast your vote?" I ask, finally. *This could be interesting.*

"Yes, not that it counts for much," he mutters, annoyance threaded in his words.

The prince has no real say in who he marries. If he weren't so insufferable, perhaps I might pity him.

"I suppose you voted for Ember," I mumble, my expression stony.

He stifles a laugh. "Why would you think that?"

Why wouldn't I? She is on his arm at every event and scurried out of his office half-naked no more than a week ago. But I don't have the gall to phrase it quite like that. "Well … you are close. You know what I've seen…"

He chuckles without any sense of self-control. It seems he is amused by my naivety. "That doesn't mean I want her as my wife." He narrows his eyes. "She likes me only for my title and I no longer care for her how I used to."

It didn't seem that way at Lysander's birthday celebration. Ember didn't leave his side, and they made a show of things, kissing, revelling, dancing and the like. I can't say it didn't bother me. For what reason, I am not sure.

"Then who did you vote for?" I ask, but my question is tactless and desperate and I am ashamed of my curiosity.

He presses his lips together, anchoring me with his golden eyes. "You." And there is no hesitation in his voice.

I look down, hiding the flush of red that creeps up my face. For a moment, I am sure he must be teasing me. "Why?" I choke on my own question, incredulous and unconvinced by the prince's confession.

But Ash is unsmiling. "Many reasons. The only one I am willing to tell you about is that someone told me that I needed to change, to be a good emperor, a better man. And the only one who could change me is you."

His words are familiar. It seems that Cosimo has been playing matchmaker behind both of our backs. Strangely, I am not annoyed. Cosimo has set this up for a reason and I trust him better than anyone. And for the first time I find myself not entirely hating the prince.

The sky seems to press down upon us. The constellations flicker overhead, and the air itself sticks to my skin. We fall into silence, the only noise between us being the crickets chirping in the undergrowth.

Suddenly, Ash stands. "Look, I need to get out of this place." His body is drawn tight, and his veins twitch under his skin. "Do you want to come?"

The question falls out of his mouth too quickly. He is rash, reckless, wild. All the thing I used to be before I came to this place. Maybe I should refuse, maybe I should follow the rules for once. But I don't want to. This night, I will follow him to the ends of the earth.

"Okay."

The prince and I sneak around the patrol guards, pacing the corridors. I follow his lead, watching his steps. A Praetorian hums, standing watch outside the gymnasium. Our footfall is light, and the listless guard take no notice as we approach. Ash peers around a corner before grabbing my wrist and whisking me away at a speed I am not prepared for. Adrenaline pulses in my veins, and I feel a certain excitement, a feeling I haven't experienced in a long time.

We are in a stairwell, and the torches gutter in the narrow, airless pass. I have never been here before, but the prince has. He doesn't hesitate in his movements as I do. His strides are purposeful, swift, and I am sure this is a place he has come many times before as a child. There are so many crevices to explore in the Palatine, hiding spots and secret passageways. It might be a fun place to grow up if it weren't for the pressures of becoming an emperor.

The stairs seem to descend for an eternity and our pace doesn't slacken. There is an urgency to Ash's steps that makes me think he is eager to escape his home. The stairwell ends and we enter a large, mostly empty room. It is a hangar, with dust sheets covering unidentifiable equipment. Ash doesn't explain why we are here or where we are going but I like the mystery of it all. He approaches one of the blanketed objects, tearing the cover away in one smooth motion, revealing a complex vehicle beneath.

I stare at it in my awe. It is a racing car, something that only exists in the history archives. It is blazing, bright red and untarnished. I lift my jaw, masking my surprise from the prince who beams at it like it is his most prized possession.

"Is this yours?"

"Not exactly." He smirks. "It is my father's, but he never uses it."

The vehicle is roofless, and Ash jumps into the driver's seat without bothering to open the door. Somehow, I don't think the emperor would be too pleased if he ever knew about this. The old me wouldn't have cared, the old me would have been in the passenger seat begging to drive but I can no longer afford to be so reckless. I can't afford to anger anyone here in the Palatine, let alone the emperor.

"Well … are you coming?" Ash hollers, starting up the engine, which roars like a caged lion.

My apprehension subsides and I slip into the seat next to the prince, sinking into the aged leather. He doesn't spare me a glance as he speeds out into a tunnel that emerges from the craggy hill onto the Appian Way. There are no guards, no checkpoints, and I wonder how such a tunnel could exist. It must be a secret escape route, like the one I used earlier to get to Crew's villa. The roads are mostly empty at this hour and there is nothing in the horizon but the silhouette of the marble city and the expanse of the night sky.

The magnetic hum that I am so accustomed to is absent. The engine growls beneath me, and the exhaust rattles in the rear. It is an exhilarating sound, one that makes the hairs on my skin stand on end. With every acceleration and deceleration, my nerves rise into my throat but it is not an uncomfortable feeling. It is as though I have gone back in time to a world where people were free of the Institute's shackles and the Haven's cage. I often wonder what that world was like and whether my romantic visions of it are unfounded. The Institute believes we shouldn't be exposed to the past evils of humanity. There is no such thing as history, only myth, legend and Dominus. I hope one day I can know the truth. It may bring me a peace the regenerators were never able to offer me.

My thoughts are interrupted by the prince who sings along to the radio, but it is more a shout than a melody. He bays like a wolf might at the full moon, and I can't help but snicker. He purposefully amps up his voice, facing me now and over-pronouncing the words. I think he wants me to sing, but I bow my head, shying away from his invitation.

"I think you should be concentrating on driving, Prince." I tease him, but our interaction is more playful than pugnacious. He smiles and turns a dial. The music fades and the sound of the wind takes its place. The air strokes my face and its coolness is unexpected. I shut my eyes, relishing in the sensation. "Where exactly are we going?"

He pulls himself up straighter. "I was actually going to ask you that. I'm sure you know the outer provinces better than I do."

I am not sure I hear him correctly. His voice is drowned out by the breeze lashing against us. "You want to go to the outer provinces?"

Ash nods, his eyes on the road ahead. "Yes, why not? It will be an adventure."

The outer provinces are no place for a prince. "I don't think you will like it."

"Maybe I'll surprise you," he says, effortlessly guiding the gearstick with his right hand. There is a speed to his movements that I have never seen before, it almost seems unnatural. "Why don't I take you home? You can see your family."

His kind offer takes me by surprise. But the kindness doesn't suit him. "That's against the rules," I say quickly.

"Since when did Electa Steel care about breaking the rules?"

He is right, of course. But I had to think of an excuse. My family are not at home because of Spartaca and now I am forced to lie to him. "There is no one there for me. My brother is at Cassida and my father is at war."

He glances over me and the amber in his eyes is ablaze, even in the darkness. "Oh. I'm sorry to hear that."

It is a strange sight, this genuine side of the prince that I have never seen before.

"Well ... you must have friends," he continues.

"You won't like my friends much."

He pauses for a moment and then smiles. "I want to meet them."

My breath catches in my throat. The prince of Ore meeting the Grey. The idea is nonsensical. "It's not a good idea..." I begin.

Ash jumps in, disregarding my comment. "It's settled then. We are going. But you're going to have to direct me."

"Don't say I didn't warn you."

But he can only smirk by means of a response.

As I sit, guiding the prince, I think how terrible this is. I may be forced to kill him in a few weeks, stealing his life away just as the prophecy foretold. He glances over at me a number of times, and in those brief, fleeting moments his eyes do enough smiling for the both of us. I swallow down hard, hoping to rid myself of the guilt that sticks in my throat. Yesterday, I hated him. And it was easier then.

Deep in Chrysos Valley, we leave the vehicle at the end of the track and begin the ascent up a narrow ravine. Our boots become damp with river water as we hop from stone to stone. In the clearing is a deserted cabin, nestled amongst dense woodland that the Grey have called *Popina*. It is a homage to the myth and legends of our ancestors who used to frequent such places, in both the history of Rome and Appia. Such lodges are illegal, as are many of the activities inside. To the Institute, this sacred place is no more than a breeding ground for imperfection, sin and vice. There used to be hundreds of places like this across the Haven, but most have been found and burnt to the ground. This *Popina* is the last of its kind and no one knows how long it will stay.

I haven't been here in what feels like a long time. My jaunt with the Grey at the warehouse weeks ago was the first time since Assay Day that I dared to return to my old way of life. I needed it. One last time. But here I am now, with a prince by my side. And I am sure I must be dreaming. But when I see Lana's long, bony legs swinging from the roof, a bottle of *Posca* in her hand, I know that I am finally home. She hasn't noticed me yet and blithely hums her favourite tune, a silly campfire song that we made up when we were just children. I echo the words back, and the prince looks at me as if I am insane.

Lana jerks her head suddenly, turning to face me. As she jumps to her feet, a smile breaks on her face. She stands above us on the roof and is motionless for what seems like forever, staring, breathing, smiling. When she finally climbs down and runs to me, I pull her into my arms. She is skin and bones as I hold her body close to mine. And as she steps away, I notice the gauntness of her face, her protruding jaw and sunken eyes. I knew this would happen. She was never much good at taking care of herself.

"What in the name of Dominus? How are you here? Am I ... am I dreaming?" she stammers, looking me up and down at least a dozen times.

I simply smile. "I thought I'd drop by and make sure you aren't getting too skinny without me." She is far too skinny, but I don't make a point of it, I won't waste the precious little time we have mothering her.

But she no longer looks my way, her eyes are on the prince. She glowers at him for several seconds, her arms crossed before the realisation comes. And then she gasps. "Holy Dominus. It's him. The prince." She bows low before him; her manners better than mine have ever been.

I put a finger to my mouth and shush her loudly. "Go and tell the whole world, why don't you?"

"Sorry," she mumbles in her small girlish voice. "I didn't know it was a secret."

"Lana, this is Ash."

She gawks at him, her cheeks blushing bright red, and tips her head in deference. "Your Highness."

Her respect pleases Ash, who holds his head high, staring down at her over his nose. It seems he can't quite shake off his princely stature. "Pleasure to meet you, Lana, and there is no need for any of that. Call me Ash."

"You never said that to me." I bristle, giving him a sharp look.

Ash laughs. "You were never so polite."

"That sounds like Electa," Lana chips in, with a huge grin on her face. I shove her gently as she giggles.

"I'm going to take a look inside. Let the two of you catch up." The prince leaves us and saunters over to the cabin. As he struggles to open the door hanging off one of its hinges, the gentle pulse of folk music can be heard from within, and the warm glow of firelight escapes into the darkness of night.

Lana cranes her neck, looking at the people who stand around us drinking, singing, laughing, and makes a point to lower her voice. "El, this is the best thing you've ever done for me. Bringing the prince here. He's so ... good-looking." She mimics fainting, and I see the child in her now more than I ever have. A hand-made daisy chain crowns her head. She always liked making them for me, but I refused to wear them. I said they were silly, childish, girly. I regret that now. The thought of her being taken away to suffer the fate of the Unchosen terrifies me. But I mustn't show her my fear. I have to be strong for her.

I roll my eyes. "He really isn't all that. Trust me."

Lana is smug, pressing her lips together and still blushing like the schoolgirl she is. I am surprised she is so enamoured by the prince, my first impression of him was quite the opposite. "How are you here?"

I am reluctant to answer, as it would mean admitting the prince is capable of kindness, and I have to hate him, to kill him so I can save the people I love. "Ash brought me."

Her eyebrows quirk up, suspecting something. "That was nice of him."

"I suppose it was..." The slightness of my voice drifts away among the sounds of the forest. An ache consumes me, it rattles my bones and sets my flesh alight. I am not sure what it is that I feel. Do I care for the prince? Or is it my guilt?

Lana reaches into her satchel, taking out a handful of posters. She hands them to me, and it is my face on display. "I have been handing these out to everyone in the Province. Everyone is rooting for you here. Those of us that are left anyway."

"Left?"

"A lot went this year."

My blood runs cold as I look around. There are few familiar faces, and the place seems emptier than usual. It can only mean one thing. "A lot?" The question catches in my throat.

Lana looks down at her unlaced boots. "Everyone except you."

All my friends are gone. Felix. Lucilla. Marius. Blake. Mariana. Julia. Their names haunt me. Unchosen. Dead. Executed. And it would have been me too.

Lana pulls in a short, ragged breath and manages a forced smile. "I always knew you could do it. You've always been the smartest among us. And now you may even become the empress." Her words are animated, but they don't distract me from the cold, morbid thoughts that swirl in my mind.

I shake my head. "There is still a long way to go before that happens."

"Yeah, but imagine if you did, you could stop the Choosing." Her zeal is something that I used to encourage. I, myself, used to spend hours on a table, ranting and rabble-rousing the Grey with seditious speeches, my words steeled with liquor. But now I realise just how futile it all was. The resistance we offered existed only in our minds.

I can't bring myself to look her in the eye and blight the childish dreamer that exists within her. I was like that once, I think. "Um ... I could try." But Lana was always the one person I was never much good at lying to.

"Try?" she almost shouts, with a confused expression on her face. "That's all you used to go on about. Ending the Choosing. Stopping the Institute for good."

"It's all a lot more complicated than that, Lana."

She folds her arms. "That's not what you used to say."

"That's because I was a fool. This whole thing is foolish. You need to stop." I let it all out. All that I have been thinking and feeling since I left her. But my words fall on deaf ears.

"What?"

"Stop coming here. Stop running with the Grey. Focus on school, on passing your tests. I don't want you to become like the others, to be erased, forgotten forever." My tone is biting, and I realise how much I sound like my father. He used to say those things to me, and I ignored them. But I won't let Lana. She already has a death sentence.

"Is this the only reason you came here?" She pulls away from me.

As many steps as she takes back, I take forward. "No, I wanted to see you."

"Liar." She spits the word. "You just came to lecture me about being a Grey."

"No. I didn't. I'm just trying to help."

Her earthy eyes are alight in anger and burn through me. We have never argued but now she stares me down as if I am her worst enemy. "Gone for a month and you come back walking, talking and dressing like one of them, like a Patrician."

I look down at myself, my clothes, and touch my hair. She is not wrong. My dress is made from silk, my boots from leather and my hair is held back with a golden circlet. I grimace, knowing exactly what she sees.

"You were a Grey once, but I suppose you're an Institute puppet now. Just like you always said your dad was."

I realise only now that my fists are balled at my sides. I take deep, steadying breaths to calm myself. Lana knows how to rile me better than anyone. I look up at her now, her small body trembling in the breeze. I unclench my fists and it stings. My nails have left small incisions in my skin. We fall into silence now, and she has a sad, empty look in her eye.

"I am trying to protect you; you fool..." My voice is a whisper. How I yearn to tell her the truth, that I am fighting for her, for Vel and for all the Unchosen. But I can't endanger her, I won't.

She rips her eyes away from me. "No, you're just a hypocrite."

I didn't want to do this, but I have to, for her own sake. "Lana ... you've been blacklisted."

"What?" She chokes.

I sigh, struggling to say what I must. "They will come for you, and I don't know how long you have left before they do."

She caves in on herself, staggering backwards. "So that's it? I'm a goner?" Her breaths are shallow. "I still had two years..."

I steady her, gripping my hands on her shoulders, staring right into her eyes. "I am trying to fix it. I will fix it, but you have to stop putting yourself at risk like this."

It is a promise I have to keep. I will not let her die.

"I'm sorry. Those things I said. I didn't mean them."

I pull her upright, shaking my head. "You were right. I am a hypocrite. And I am no longer who I used to be."

And I don't think I ever will be again.

"Electa, I don't know how to live without this. It is all I've ever known." She gestures to the cabin, to the kids sprawled across the deck, pouring alcohol down their throats, spluttering, slurring their words.

"This isn't living. We just drown our sorrows and play at being revolutionaries. But we're just kids, Lana."

She stifles a laugh. "When did you become so wise?"

My eyes drift over to the deck, where Ash now sits on the wooden railing, a bottle in his hand. I didn't become wise. I saw a reflection of myself in the troubled prince who fills the empty, gaping hole in his chest with drink, hoping it will alleviate his pain. It doesn't, and it never will.

Lana tugs at my arm, bringing me back to attention. "Do I have to go home?"

I consider her words for a moment. "No. One last night. How does that sound?"

A smile curls on her lips. "It sounds good."

I put my arm around her, ruffling her hair with my fist. She quickly shakes me off and sprints towards the cabin. I chase after her but stop dead in my tracks, as Ash grabs a handful of a boy's shirt in his fist. *Stercus. Just what I need.* The lanky boy scrambles in the air as the prince raises him up from the deck. His friends stand behind him, ready for a fight, their faces narrowed at Ash. I rush over, pleading Ash to let him go. And he does, without hesitation. The boy staggers backwards and is caught by the others, who steady him.

"You two aren't from these parts. I can smell it." The boy spits on Ash's boots, and strangely he doesn't react. I have never seen these boys before. They must be from another province, but I can see the Grey in them.

The small, stocky boy takes a step towards us. "No Patricians allowed. That includes you, Electa Steel."

Of course, he knows my name. Everyone knows who I am now. Cosimo has seen to that. The others all glance at me and nod in recognition.

"I'm no Patrician," I fire back, stepping up to him. He is about the same height as me; younger, but most definitely stronger.

"You look like a Patrician to me." He smirks.

The urge to punch him is stronger than my patience. He called me a *Patrician* and that is the worst thing you can say to a Pleb. I throw my arm back to punch him square in the jaw, but Ash catches my arm, his reaction faster than my fist.

"I think we can come to some sort of resolution." Ash's manner is calmer than expected. Why he restrains himself, I don't know. His temper is more uneven than my own. "How about I buy you boys some drinks?"

"We don't want anything from the likes of you," the lanky one pipes up again.

"Or maybe some cigarettes?" Ash takes a packet from his trouser pocket and hands it to Lanky whose eyes light up. Such a commodity is impossible to get your hands on, unless of course, you are a prince. He would be a fool to turn down the offer.

The next thing I know we are all drinking, chugging down one bottle of *Posca* after the other. My vision blurs and all my senses numb. We line dance, kicking our legs high in the air. The band plays traditional music that I am sure Ash has never heard before. He catches on quickly, memorising the lyrics the second time around, and belts the song out louder than anyone in the room. The gentle clatter of dice rolled on gambling tables rings in my ears. The clash of bottles slammed together, the shattering of glass, the hiss of liquor on the fireplace, poured in libation. It all blurs into one deafening noise of drunken stupor. Lana twirls me around again and again until I fall into a heap on the ground, dizzy, dazed and confused. Ash pulls me up and extends his hand.

"Want to dance?" A delicate smile tugs at the corner of his mouth.

Our eyes lock and hundreds of emotions hit me all at once. I deliberate whether to take his hand, as best as my inebriated mind will allow. Taking his hand signifies so much more than a dance – it signifies a friendship, a friendship I can't afford.

I place my palm in his and he pulls me close, tight against his body. The floor is crowded, and we brush up against the close-knit bodies that surround us. He spins me around, still close, and I lose myself in the honey of his magical eyes. It is all I see. New friends hand us drinks, small glasses overflowing with peculiar amber liquor. The burn in my throat soothes any apprehension that I had, and I dance with him freely. I let my body be guided by his movements, and the more we drink, the more we stumble about, falling over each other, laughing uncontrollably. I haul myself up onto a table, dragging Ash with me. The percussive tap of our boots on the wood sounds like a drum and then the clapping of the crowd below is all I can hear.

I lose my footing and Ash catches me again before I can crash onto the floor. As he steadies me, our breaths heavy, we stand still. The cheers and rapture of the people clapping, hollering, whistling, drown out any sense, any judgement, that I have left. I glance up at the prince, his deep, dark-set eyes sending my stomach into a whirlwind of anxiety. I should pull away, but I don't. This was my plan, and it is supposed to be an act. The act Spartaca told me I had to play. But it is more than that now. And as his lips press against mine, it is as of no one else exists but us. I forget who I am, what I have to do, and all the weight I have been carrying is suddenly, all at once, lifted from my shoulders. I feel free, truly free, for the first time in my life. He tastes like alcohol and firewood. I pull away, but his warmth lingers.

It is dawn and Ash is in the car, starting up the engine. I say my goodbyes to Lana, who promises to leave this life behind her. It was a night to remember for us both. And I couldn't have asked for a better last time as a Grey. We cut out our tattoos, and all that will be left is a scar of what we once were.

I slump into the passenger seat of the car, still inebriated, waving to Lana wildly as Ash speeds off down the track. As we drive, the sun creeps over the crest of Capitoline Hill, setting alight the Temple of Dominus in a golden flame.

The sudden light prompts the birds to warble in the greenwood. As I look out at the horizon before us, I realise how often this place is taken for granted. Latia, the universal symbol of perfection, is undeniably beautiful. But all I see is a lie. Ash no longer glances at me, and we don't speak. It is better that way. Last night was a mistake. And I feel like a fool. I gladly bask in the silence between us and hope we can pretend it never happened at all. But it did and what it means, for me, for Vel, Lana and the cause I follow, I am not quite sure.

Ash escorts me to my chambers and kisses me on the forehead quickly as means of goodbye. He doesn't utter a word. It puzzles me how he can be so alive one moment and cold like ice the next. I throw myself into bed, my head pounding and my clothes smelling of my foolishness. The bruise on my torso has darkened and aches more than it ever has. I ignore the pain as best I can until it become a dull sensation. As I shut my eyes, darkness descends upon me and so do the voices.

"Don't test me, Cosimo." Crew speaks in his distinctive smoky tone that makes me shudder even as I sleep.

"I beg of you. You must tell her what she is," Cosimo responds, *the usual calmness lacking in his voice.*

"It is too soon."

"You don't want to make an enemy of her, Crew. You know what she will become."

XIV

NUMEN

Divine power

I don't see Ash when I awake. A part of me hoped that I might, to ease the tension between us. Last night was a terrible mistake and this afternoon he will be interviewed by Trixie and reveal what he thinks of us all. I spend the remainder of the day in dread, praying silently that he has kind words for me. Could he have seen through my act? Our intimacy certainly came at a convenient time, just hours before his interview. Perhaps to the prince, I am no better than his old flame.

Cosimo drags me from the comfort of my bed and prepares me for the day ahead. He gets me to try on my *stola* for the voting ceremony. It is silken white with slits on either side, and fastened with an aureate belt. "You look like a goddess." he says. But when I look at myself all I see is a liar.

It is dusk. As the darkness descends, so does my fear. Ash's interview, the voting ceremony, all one step closer to fights, the arena and my fate – to live or to die. Cosimo sits beside me in his office. A broadcasting screen displays the prince live on air, sitting across from Trixie Merula. My heart lurches uneasily in my chest as I await his blessing or his curse.

He begins with Valentina and is polite, as expected, but largely indifferent. There is not much to note apart from her intelligence. Aria receives a glowing review, and the prince favours her humility and kindness, but hints that he hasn't gotten to know her much yet. It is not surprising; Aria likes to keep her distance from almost everybody in the Palatine. You can often find her alone, humming some whimsical tune in the library, her face veiled by her hair and a book. He is reticent at the mention of Trinity, and it is obvious that he has been instructed to say little in the wake of her public outbursts. When Trixie presses him for more, all he can acknowledge is her beauty, which is, of course, undeniable, and how they both share a passion for horse riding.

179

"I heard about your little outing with Ash last night," Cosimo says, turning to me, a sly grin on his face.

"How did you find out?" I hope Cosimo is the only one who knows. We could both get into a lot of trouble for leaving the Palatine in the first place and for where we spent our night.

He laughs. "Everyone knows. Some guards saw you leave. The emperor was less than impressed. In fact, he is furious and blame you for it all."

"That doesn't surprise me." I don't think I could change the emperor's opinion of me even if I bowed down and kissed his feet.

"It's not surprising to the emperor. Ash is becoming more and more rebellious lately. On Assay Day, he was caught stealing Institute files." Cosimo settles back into his armchair, pressing his glasses against his nose, staring intently at the broadcast.

I thought he was there to see the shortlist for Imperial Panore. It seems I was mistaken. "What files?"

He doesn't avert his gaze. "No one knows. He deleted them before anyone could see."

"You know what Ash is like. 'Rules are made to be broken.'" I mimic him, adopting his trademark smirk, and even the lilt of his drunken voice. Ash is always doing things he shouldn't.

"I'm glad you took my advice. Last night went well, I presume?"

"It was fine." My response is curt. If I told him the truth, he would tease me mercilessly. Nor am I ready to say it aloud and admit to myself what I did.

"I suspect you like him more than you care to admit." He speaks in an off-hand manner that I don't take much notice of what he says. "People always follow a veil." These last words, however, catch my attention.

"What do you mean?"

He pauses, mulling over an explanation. I expect some verbose platitude, yet his answer is simple. "Mysterious people are always attractive, and dangerous."

Dangerous. He is warning me about Lysander too, I am sure, in his roundabout way. I don't usually heed anyone's advice, but Cosimo is an exception. And I consider whether my strange attraction to both Lysander and Ash could be a curse.

Cosimo continues, "He has been poisoned by his father and the Institute. But there is still time for him. He can be saved."

"I don't think people can change, not really." But a part of me *hopes* Ash can.

I redirect my attention to the interview where Ash now discusses Ember. I can hardly bear to hear as he makes known their years of history, friendship and more. I wish my seat would swallow me whole. And then he comes to me.

"And Miss Steel?" Trixie asks, an impish glint in her eyes.

"Electa…" Ash stares down the camera, as if he is here, sitting across from me. "She will never let anyone humble her, and she never knows when to keep her mouth shut." He pauses and I think that is all he has to say. "But I suppose that is what I like about her the most. If you left her in the Senate House for a day, she would walk out as their spokesperson. That is just the kind of person she is. There is a wildness in her that I have come to admire, and I will say this – if I could have anyone as my wife, it would be her." His gaze anchors me and his words replace my sense of relief with fear. He is not subtle, by any means, and has just put a target on my back for not only Ember, but the emperor too. Cosimo is right. Ash does have a rebellious streak, and I am just his latest project.

"Well … that was unexpected." Cosimo is transfixed by what he is seeing. "You must have made quite the impression last night."

This is what we wanted. To make me the obvious favourite. But Cosimo knows just as well as I do that Ash's words were not scripted, and I am just some tantalizing prize that he can hang on his trophy wall. He wants to anger his father, to make Ember jealous, hateful, and humiliated, all the things she had once made him feel. The prince is using me just as much as I am using him.

"This is not good, Cos."

"You're right. It isn't." He flicks open his pocket watch, its tuneful ticking a reminder of the passing time. "We must get you dressed and to the ceremony."

Cosimo hurries me along as I slip over the marble tiles in my heeled sandals. We are late, as usual. Punctuality is not his speciality, nor mine. He frets that I don't have an escort and I have to remind him of Lysander's kind offer. He makes a noise of disgust but doesn't argue. He knows that Lysander is the one who has secured my popularity over these past weeks.

We arrive at the mezzanine and stand behind the red curtains, along with the Panore girls, their mentors and escorts. Cosimo is actually organising the entire event, and is remarkably composed, perfumed with pomaded hair despite the rush. How he has the time to mentor me and coordinate the Imperial calendar, I will never understand.

Lysander is already here, standing proud with a gentle grin, in a beautiful suit that accentuates his lean figure. His eyes drift over the faces of those standing in attendance until they finally settle on me. I don't look away as I once did. Now I can't help but stare right back, my hands trembling at my sides. I feel lighter suddenly, and I walk with more purpose than I ever have as I greet him.

Before I can say a word, he folds his arm around mine and whispers, "You look beautiful." It is loud enough so that everyone can hear.

He looks as handsome as he ever has but I can't bring myself to say it. There is still something about him that renders me speechless.

The other girls stand with equally noble and attractive men from their respective Houses. Cousins and distant relatives, all in the colour of their companion's family. Ember's glare burns my skin and every time I lift my head, she looks askance at me from the corner where she stands. The tight braids that hug her scalp seem to stretch her expression into a permanent frown. She knows that I am her competitor, a threat to her throne, her crown and title, and she will show me no mercy.

Cosimo makes an address and announces the order in which we will descend the stairs. Ember will go first, followed by Aria, Trinity, Valentina and finally me. We will dance with our escorts before the voting results are announced. Tomorrow, training will begin. Ember and her escort make their descent, and the other Panore girls, one after the other. They each slip through the red curtain, and gentle applause follows their steps. The Latian anthem sounds from below and then thunders once we stand on top of the staircase, arm in arm. Our names are announced by a faceless commentator, and the eyes of the crowd below flicker to us. I glance over at Lysander for reassurance, who smiles in return. The train of my dress drags behind me, and Lysander guides me down each carpeted step, with slow, secure movements so that I don't trip.

Ash stands beneath us, his figure thick with his martial armour and fur cape. He gawks at us as we descend, a flicker of irritation in his eyes. I am sure he can't be pleased that I am with Lysander. And after his interview, I am not quite sure how to act around him. I tear my eyes away from him, but that doesn't much relieve the trembling feeling in my stomach.

Lysander takes my hand and places his palm against the small of my back. His raven hair darkens against the paleness of his skin, and the sight of him, this close, ensnares all my senses at once. The length of our bodies are pressed together and his scent is familiar to me now. He smells like the earth after rain. I relax into his hold and mimic his steps that meld into the cadence of the orchestra. His lips come up against my ear, sending a shiver through my bones.

"He doesn't deserve you," he breathes.

My body goes still, his words settling like frost on my skin. He doesn't expect a response. And even if he did, what might I say? Lysander is playing a game with me, and I am not sure how much longer we can dance around each other like this. He steps away from me as the music fades, taking his place behind a marbled lectern at the centre of the room. I struggle to find my footing on the mosaic tiles without his arms to hold me. But Cosimo quickly comes to my side and offers a friendly shoulder to lean on.

"Citizens, Ladies and Gentlemen." The words roll off his golden tongue. "Tonight marks the end of the first stage of Imperial Panore. In just ten days' time, one of the beautiful Chosen ladies who stand before me will be crowned as the next empress of Ore, the *Augusta* and the *nobilissima femina. Sit nomine dea.*"

May she be worthy of the name.

Lysander takes a measured breath before continuing, "Without further delay, I will announce the results. The competitor in first place will not fight until the final, and the second-place competitor must choose her opponent."

I glance across at the others, who all stare intently at the director in anticipation. Trinity, however, glares down at her shoes, her back hunched over, looking as though she would rather be anywhere but here. An envelope is delivered to Lysander by a tunic-wearing servant. He breaks the seal and holds the card in his hands, glancing over the names without even the slightest change in expression.

"In first place is Ember Hadrianus."

The encore that follows his announcement drums and echoes in the vaulted room. It is no surprise that Ember is on top. But the sounds of the applause rattle me no less. I hold my breath, in silent prayer that I have come second at least.

"In second place, Electa Steel."

Relief surges through my veins, and I don't attempt to conceal the expression that breaks on my face. Cosimo squeezes my arm in his excitement, his expression blooming like a hyacinth in spring. Valentina is third, Aria fourth and as expected, Trinity is fifth. Although I have heard she is the most skilled fighter out of them all. But any relief that I feel is quickly stolen away.

"Electa Steel. Who do you fight?" Lysander addresses me, and his words seem to snatch the ground from beneath me. I have no answer prepared. But Cosimo whispers a name in my ear, just the name I didn't want to hear. My eyes dart over the girls that stand beside me, unable to bring myself to say what I must.

My voice wobbles. "I challenge Aria Glycias."

The only girl here who has shown me kindness nods to my left. I can't help but feel that I have betrayed her. *What terrible things we do in the name of survival.* But still, she doesn't glare at me as Ember does. She will keep her bitterness to herself. Cosimo believes her to be the weakest in combat, but I know better than to think my task easy. Even the elfin Aria is skilled in the gladiatorial arts. I have seen the brass knuckles she wears as ceremonial armour and the bulk of her arms.

The ceremony may be over, but the festivities will continue long into the night. I make a point of finding Aria, hoping to, in some way, explain myself. She hums some strange tune in an alcove behind the staircase, alone. She wears a neutral expression and stares at nothing in particular, her demeanour typically airy. As I near, she doesn't notice, lost in the mythical world of her own creation.

"Aria, I'm sorry. If it's any consolation, I didn't want to choose you." I speak to her how I might speak to a child, my voice gentle and soft. Aria is unique in her beauty, and there is a certain fragility to her, with her porcelain skin and oversized doll eyes.

The light returns to her eyes, and slowly she turns her head to face me. "I was actually hoping you would."

Hardly the response I was expecting. "Why?"

She fidgets, adjusting her laurel headpiece, stepping lightly from foot to foot. "I don't want to win, Electa. I want to survive. Let's put on a good show and then I will concede."

She is handing me victory on a silver platter. I can't decline her kind offer. This way we both live. "Really?"

She bobs her chin in reassurance. "Yes. Why marry a man that you don't love?"

There is a truth in what she says. We children of Latia don't have much power in our lives except the power to love who we choose to. That is a special kind of freedom reserved for humans alone, and not even the Institute can take that away.

Lysander congratulates me on my success, as do many of the senators here tonight, although I am sure few of them voted for me. Marcus Hadrianus seems to have them all wrapped around one of his slimy fingers.

Lysander affirms my thoughts. "Truthfully, the Senate are the test of any emperor's strength. All looking for any opportunity to further their own political careers. The real war is fought in the Senate House," he explains in the passing seconds as we drift between conversations.

"And the Institute?"

He smiles at that. "There is only so much we can do. The Senate are the hardest subjects to control."

This doesn't much surprise me. The political manoeuvring and subterfuge are enough to make anybody's head spin. It occurs to me that the Palatine is only a lawless state because Lysander allows it to be. "Is that why there are no laws in the Palatine?"

Again, he smiles. "That's how we control them, Electa. They are quite happy with their settlement."

It would be foolish to assume that anything could escape the director's mighty grasp. The Imperials and Senate are but puppets to the Institute. In return, they can *bacchor* all they like.

"Did you hurt yourself?" Lysander reaches a hand to the slit of my *stola*. His gaze falls on my upper thigh, and I notice only now how far the strange bruise has spread from my torso.

I yank his hand away. "It's just a bruise."

He frowns, his fervid green eyes narrowed. "It's a rather large bruise. How did you get it?"

"I tripped in the olive groves, a few days ago."

Weeks ago, actually. But that would only worry him, and I don't like to be fussed over.

"You should see a doctor."

"Yes, I should. Would you excuse me?" I quickly say, scurrying off to the bathroom.

The pain is now a terrible ache that burns at my skin. I fuss with the material of my dress in an attempt to conceal the bruising. In the mirror's reflection, Warren stands just a few steps behind me.

"This is the ladies' bathroom – in case you are lost," I quip.

His shoulders heave as he sighs. "Crew asked me to check on you."

I straighten my spine, quickly twisting my dress back into position. "Spying on me again?"

He shrugs. "Something like that. Although, it doesn't look like you need much protecting with Lysander on your arm all the time."

I detect the bitterness in his voice. "What is that supposed to mean?"

He seems stunned for a moment, unaccustomed to the harshness of my tone. "Ash is one thing but Lysander … He is a monster."

Lysander told me once that he didn't mind what people thought. What is a monster, after all?

"Perhaps. But I suppose we can all be monsters."

I push past Warren, eager to escape his prying eyes. It seems I can't get a moment's peace in this place.

A mass of people has gathered around the bar area, all bustling to get a better look of something that I can't see from this angle. The shouts and the shrill of shattering glass make my stomach heave in remembrance of Shauna's cruel execution. But as I near, it becomes clear that this is not Spartaca's doing. I shove my way through the hordes, with little concern for the others scrambling to get to the front where they can see the spectacle. Two men are fighting. They charge at each other, the larger of the two slamming the other to the ground.

Now I see their faces. Ash and Lix.

They roll around on the shattered glass, tumbling over and over, as each tries to get on top. Ash raises his right forearm and slams his fist into Lix's face and the sudden crack of bones breaking makes me shudder. Lix grabs tufts of Ash's hair, slamming his head down onto the marble stone. They are both on their feet soon after, wrestling each other onto the bar countertop. They jab, some strikes landing on the torso, some on the temple, and grunt as they weather the hits.

Ash has removed all his armour, and his undershirt is stained red. Blood spills from his nose, too. He throws his head forward; the impact makes Lix stagger backwards. Lix gathers himself, and lurches towards Ash, throwing him to the ground. Lix's hands close around Ash's throat. The prince chokes for air, but swiftly brings his kneecap into Lix's stomach. It is Lix's blood that now spills like wine onto the marbled floor. They crawl back towards each other, glass crunching beneath them. But Ash's breathing is steady, unlike the sharp, sudden rasps that escape Lix's throat.

Some boys, friends of the princes, intervene. One grabs Lix by his collar, yanking him away. Two boys restrain Ash, who fights against their grip. The princes stare down each other from a distance, their hair a mess, their faces bloodied, panting in their rage. The room is thick with whispers and gasps.

Lysander stands at the edge of the crowd, chuckling to himself before stepping out of sight. I stand motionless and speechless, my mouth agape. I turn to the servant standing beside me.

"Who started it?"

"Calix," he answers.

The crowds step aside, making an opening, and the emperor storms through. His thundering voice ripples through my skin, shaking me to the core. He orders for them both to be taken to the hospital wing. The anger seems to burn through Ash, and something terrible grumbles within him, no matter how hard he tries to conceal it.

"Stay away from her," he growls before turning his back and marching out of the service entrance.

I can't stay here any longer – in this room, where it seems all the air has been stolen away. I sit in a stairway just outside the ballroom. Through the glass doors, I can see Cosimo flapping his arms around, engaging with the guests. But his efforts will be in vain; the festivities won't resume, for tonight at least.

A woman steps out of the glass doors. The click of her heeled thigh-high boots on the marble is enough to make me jolt. Trixie takes a seat beside me; her distinct rose oil scent is cloying and makes my stomach turn.

"I overheard the entire altercation; it's going to make an exciting cover story." She simpers with her typical vulpine expression. As she cranes her neck, it catches the light for a moment, revealing fingerprint-size bruises that fringe the entire length of her skin, all the way to her collarbone. Their darkness has been subdued by layers of makeup.

"What happened to your neck?"

Her crooked smile doesn't fade. "Marcus wasn't best pleased that I made a fool of his daughter on an Appia-wide broadcast."

I should be surprised, or maybe even disgusted, that such a thing could happen in our *perfect* world. But the Palatine is a lawless state, the director admitted that much himself.

"Marcus did this to you?"

She seems amused by the alarm in my voice. "His little troupe of thugs. He would never dirty his own hands with such business."

"Will you not report him?" I know the question is silly, even as I speak it.

Her laughter is unexpected. "Oh, my dear Electa, you are so naïve. This is not the first time this has happened to me. Just think of how many discriminating articles I have published over the years."

I shrug, adopting her nonchalance. "I suppose that's what happens when you exploit people for fun." It sounds more bitter than I had intended.

"Is that what you think I do?" Her eyebrows arch at my audacity.

"That's what everyone thinks you do."

She settles back against the step, her expression folding in understanding. If she is bothered by my comment, she doesn't show it.

"You know they were fighting over you. The princes," she says, her tone turning excited at the prospect of such a scandal. She clasps a miniature notebook, bound with expensive leather hide, and she has a pen tucked behind her right ear. "Ash seems to think that Lix is madly in love with you. But he doesn't realise that his real threat comes from Lysander Drusus."

"Lysander?" She is saying the very things I don't want to hear.

She grins. "Yes. Isn't it obvious? He instigated their entire spat, playing mind games with the both of them just by escorting you this evening."

I shake my head, tearing my gaze away from her. "I don't think that's true." She is right but I just can't admit it, not to myself and especially not to anyone else. I saw Lysander's sly smirk for myself.

"I don't think you know Lysander as well as you claim to." She presses her lips together, pausing in thought. "Lysander's been watching everything. He knew that Lix defended you that day when you first arrived. He knew that Ash suspected his adoptive brother was attracted to you. It was so easy for him to turn the two of them against each other."

"This is ridiculous." My voice is now indignant. "Speculation. What reason would Lysander have to go to such lengths?"

"Lysander wanted to bring you closer to him. Lix cares for you, of course. But he knows better than to fall in love with someone that could never be his. Lysander is quite the opposite. If he wants something, he will stop at nothing until it is his. And he wants you." Her tone sounds informed, as if her speculations are proven fact.

The obstinate voice in my head has been warding off such thoughts, such admissions. "Lysander wants me?"

"Yes, my dear girl. Can you not see it?" She slaps her palms against her knees and stands. There is a definitiveness to her movements.

I don't answer.

"A part of you wants him too. I can see how intrigued you are by him." Her face contorts as much as the plastic will allow.

She is wrong. I don't want Lysander. I can't. He represents everything I hate about this world. I tuck my hair behind my ears. "How did the fight start, I don't understand? It can't just be because Lysander was my escort."

"Lysander started a rumour that you and Lix had been spending the past week together, alone. Ash was naturally suspicious and confronted Lix, who has quite the temper. Ash mocked him, and one thing led to another."

Cosimo was right all along. I am the wall that will lead to the downfall of the two brothers. Their foundations have been shaken once before, and the second time they will crumble. But this is not my doing, it is Lysander's. "I spent the past week with Lysander, not Lix."

"I know that. But Ash doesn't. If you want to salvage your relationship with the prince, I suggest you convince him that nothing is going on between you and Lix." She bends down, patting my shoulder lightly before drifting into the shadows of the corridor.

Trixie is right. I have to make things right with Ash. The curfew is still in place, and I doubt he would have had time to leave the Palatine already. He must still be in the palace somewhere, but it is a big place and Ash is not an easy person to find. I rush up the stairwell to the first floor of the southern wing. There are only vacant guestrooms and servants scurrying around with trays of food and silverware. No one questions my presence; they are all absorbed in their own affairs.

I search every spare room I pass, knocking a few times to ensure they are empty. There are no signs of the prince. I go to the second floor. The door of the first room on the left yawns open, light escaping from within. I creep inside. The reception hall is empty, and so is the bedroom, but running water sounds from the bathroom. I move silently around the corner. The sliding marble door is wide open, and the prince stands there, facing a large mirror. He stares back at me in the reflection, the fire in his eyes scaring me more than it ever has.

His back is lashed with scars. *Pink scars.* The scars of freshly healed wounds. His blood-stained shirt lies crumpled on the floor, but his torso is not stained red in the same way. I cover my mouth with my hand, muffling a gasp. The prince has dark bruise-like markings etched all over his skin. I stagger backwards until my back is up against the wall.

"You shouldn't have come here." He bares his teeth how I imagine a rabid dog might, the dim light of the mirror framing him against the darkness.

"What are those?" I can't stop my voice from trembling.

He turns, so quickly that I think I imagine it. His strides are fast and, before I know it, he is just inches from my face. My horror grows, and a terrible ache tugs at my heart as I reach out to touch the bruises, only for my hand to be snatched away. The prince has all his weight against me now as he pins me against the wall, a hand over my mouth to stifle my screams.

His breaths are hot against my cheek. "You never saw that," he growls. "You understand?" His words ring loud in my ears.

I nod, as if by instinct, terrified by the prince I thought I knew. But my curiosity overrides any sense of fear. His bruises resemble my own, their darkness, the strange ink-blotch shape. This is no coincidence. His strength knocks all the air out of me, and it is a kind of strength that I have never felt before. I try to find my voice, but all I can manage is a croak as Ash finally takes his hand away from my mouth. I push against him with all my might, but he immobilises me with little effort. He doesn't even have to try to keep me in place. His eyes rage over me like wildfire, an inch closer and I might burn.

"What are they?" The words rise in my throat.

His grip tightens on my wrist. "You don't need to know."

I know that I should just run away, pretend this never happened. But I can't. I have seen something I won't forget.

"Ash, please just hear me out," I plead, my eyes raking over him, hoping there is still something left of the man I knew. But anger has always been the one emotion Ash never had difficulty expressing. There is such rage within him, and it is the kind of rage that can only lead to his destruction, and mine too.

"I swear I'll kill you if you don't keep that mouth of yours shut."

I don't recognise his voice anymore. It is not the voice of a prince, nor a general. It is the roar of a beast.

"I will never mention this again. I swear it. But I need to show you something."

He shakes his head, stiffly. "No. Walk away, Electa, my mercy is wearing thin."

I stand resolute as he releases me. "I can't walk away. You have to see this."

Before he can protest, I tear the fabric of my dress, revealing my own markings. His eyes widen as they settle on my lower torso. He staggers backwards, his breathing heavy, shaking his head over and over again.

"Oh my Dominus…" Terror transcends his expression. "I knew you were different."

"*Different?*"

He doesn't avert his gaze from my bruises as he holds out his arm. "Let me see your wrist."

And I do. We both extend the underside of our arms. The scar on his wrist, the one I saw all those weeks ago, is plain to see.

"They're the same." The tremor in my voice doesn't abate, even now.

The storm in his eyes clears, and he is quiet. "I should have known then what you were."

I am drowning in the chaos of questions that swirl in my mind. "What I am? What do you mean 'different'?"

Ash puts his hand over my mouth once again and hushes me. "I can't talk about this here. They could be watching us. And they can't find out. Especially about you."

But I can't help myself, and I try to speak again.

He shakes me by my shoulders. "Remember what I said. Not here. We will go to your room. You will get dressed. And then we will talk, somewhere away from the palace." He bends down to pick up his discarded carmine jacket. "Put this on. You can't let anyone see the markings, understand me?"

I nod, adopting the quiet in his voice. "Yes." I slip my arms into the oversized sleeves and button the jacket all the way to my neck.

"Good. Let's go."

Ash hurries me from the room, one step behind me all the way to the west wing. Once there, I throw on the first clothes I see. The plain garments don't leave any skin visible, and Ash bobs his chin, satisfied. He wears his blood-stained shirt for lack of any other options. We leave the palace through the same service entrance Warren showed me before.

The woods are unsettling at these hours, without the chirping of swifts and the golden glow of the sun. The northern woods of Palatine Hill are nothing like those where Lix and I would pass our days. The forest is thick, and we stumble on the unkempt trail. The silence is a relief in some ways, as it allows me to gather my thoughts. There is nothing but the sound of our breaths and the snap of branches underfoot.

"I am sorry about how I reacted." Ash's voice disturbs the stillness of the night. "I didn't mean to hurt you."

I believe he may even feel remorse. He may have given me the fright of my life, but I am unscathed. Neither am I unaccustomed to Ash's fits of temper and the violence of his being. He has hubris to rival Icarus.

"You didn't. I'm fine." I brush his apology aside, concentrating on keeping my footing. I am no child, I am not afraid of the dark, but my muscles are tense with thick, raw emotion, and my hands shake at my sides.

"You'll learn quickly that emotions affect us in much more powerful ways than humans," Ash mumbles, his voice still low even though we are alone.

"What?" I stop dead in my tracks, but Ash tugs me along by my sleeve.

"Just wait. I'll explain everything."

After five more minutes of mindless meandering in the forest, my impatience gets the better of me. "Are we far enough?"

Ash nods. "This should be fine." He glances over his shoulder, cautious even now. We are in a small opening, caved in by towering pines. The woods are devoid of life, man or beast.

I tether him with my stare. "What in the name of Dominus is going on?"

He casts his eyes down at the trodden earth beneath him and then back up at me. For the first time I can remember, he is speechless. Ash is never tight-lipped; in fact, quite the opposite, he is the loudest person in the room.

"I have no idea how to explain this." His eyes struggle to settle on mine. "I don't even understand it much myself."

"Just tell me what I am, Ash."

He presses his lips together, deliberating how to begin. "They call us Divines."

"Divines? Like the gods?" *But Divinity exists in myth alone.*

"Yes. I have never met another Divine before. I thought I was the only one left."

"Left?"

He shuffles nervously from foot to foot. It is clear he has never discussed this with anyone before. "Most have been tracked down and killed by the Institute."

"Why?"

He squints, as if searching for an explanation. "They fear people like us, Electa. We are the only subjects they can't control."

I am sure he must grow tired of my ceaseless stream of questions, but I can't stop myself. "I don't understand. What makes us so hard to control?"

"Divines are unbelievably powerful," he says, his amber eyes glinting in the moonlight. "According to myth, they are gods, the new age of gods. The resurrection of the gods of old. The gods that came before Dominus."

As much as I enjoy the myths, I am not foolish enough to consider them history. "Gods don't exist." I shake my head, unable to bring myself to believe what he speaks of.

"But what is a god? Does anyone really know?" Ash says quickly, asking himself the question as much as me. He is met with my silence. "Divines are faster, stronger, smarter than regular humans. They can heal faster, some are geniuses. I have even heard of psychics."

It explains how his wounds had healed, but I am still not convinced. I am not strong, nor fast, and I would have been Unchosen if Spartaca hadn't saved me. "I don't believe it. I can't be a Divine."

"Have you noticed anything different recently?"

I pause to think. "I have been having vivid dreams, fainting."

"Maybe you're a psychic."

"Psychic?" I choke out the word.

"Yes, they can have visions of past, present and future events."

It could explain the strange visions I have been experiencing. But I still can't believe that such things exist, and that I am one of them. "How do you become a Divine?"

He shifts his shoulders, eyes on the ground. "I think it may be some sort of genetic anomaly. I have been trying to get answers. But I can't."

It is so fantastical, what he speaks of. I need to see more. "Prove it."

"Prove what?"

"That what you say is true."

His nose crinkles. "You saw that my wounds had healed."

"I need to see more."

He throws his hands in the air in frustration and steps up to me, lifting up my cotton shirt.

"What do you think you're do—"

The sting of the plaster ripping from my skin is enough to make me yelp. It covers the wound where my tattoo used to be. I cut it out just a night ago. I bend my neck to see what I expect to be a deep gash, still fresh. Instead, there is unblemished skin.

Ash raises his eyebrows, confidently. "Do you really think that would have healed within a day if you weren't a Divine."

I can't bring myself to agree, to believe that any of this is real. "I need to see more."

He sighs, followed by his typical smirk. He rests on his haunches, reaching down to the ground to pick up a stone that tapers to a sharp tip. He tears it across his forearm and blood spills from the slit. Within seconds, new skin grows in its place, meshing the wound together, and the blood retreats to its source. I rub my eyes in disbelief. Now he walks over to the nearest tree and hurls his fist into the bark. His splintered hand heals, too, as if it never happened.

"Do you believe me now?"

I can't speak nor move, nor bring myself to believe that what I see is real. I can't do that. No one should be able to do that. I wipe the sweat from my brow, and stare at Ash's arm where his wounds once were.

"So, this is just some sort of genetic accident?" My mouth moves, but the words I speak are nothing but a low murmur that dies in my mouth.

Ash doesn't hear me and continues to speak. "Do you believe in science, or myth?" he asks.

"Neither. I believe what I see."

"Then what do you see?"

"*Numen.*"

He nods. "*Divine power.*"

I start to make sense of it all in my mind. Cosimo had said Ash had been stealing Institute files that day, and this is why. "This is what you were really doing at the Institute."

"Yes. I was stealing files, looking for answers." He nods. "All I know is that before the Havens were built they were experimenting with genetic engineering. Trying to create the new age of gods, an army of them. But everything to do with the research was destroyed."

I don't believe the research was destroyed, and it is clear Ash doesn't either. "But you think the Institute knows the truth?"

He smirks. "Oh, they do. I am sure of it."

There is one thing I still don't understand. "Why now? My bruises only appeared a few weeks ago."

But Ash has an explanation for that, too. "My abilities didn't start developing until I was your age. Power increases as you age, and the bruises will go."

"But yours?"

"Mine only resurface when I am not in control of my emotions."

"Are our parents Divines?"

"No, well, my father isn't. My mother couldn't have been." His mouth twitches at the mention of his mother.

One last question, I promise myself. Ash doesn't know much himself, and I must be exhausting him with my curiosity. "And you don't know any other Divines?"

He paces up and down the clearing, every footfall steady, secure. "As I said, there are only rumours. Divines are but myth and legend. The one thing I know for certain is that if the Institute … if Drusus … knew what we were, they would kill us."

I frown, doubtful. "They wouldn't kill a prince."

Ash smiles, a small, sad laughter rising in his throat. "They killed an empress once, so what makes you think they wouldn't kill a prince."

"Your mother?"

The slant in his jaw tightens, becoming more defined in the moonlight. "Yes."

It pains him to speak of her. He was young when he lost her. We never knew our mothers, but the memory of them haunts us, even now.

His eyes find mine in the darkness. "You can't tell anyone, Electa. I have spent years hiding who I am. Playing off my abilities as natural skill."

"I won't. I swear it."

He nears me now. "It hasn't been easy. At the beginning, I had no idea how to control it. You won't either and in a few days' time you'll be in the arena. If they see you for what you are, it will be over. You're going to have to learn how to harness your power, control it, hide it, starting with those markings." He points to my torso, and I instinctively put my hands against the blackened, burning skin.

"How?" I look up at him, my eyes searching for some glimmer of hope that I can survive.

"I will help you, train you."

My eyebrows arch in suspicion. Ash is selfish, he never does anything out of kindness, and definitely if he doesn't get anything in return. "In exchange for what?"

"No strings attached. In the arena you could die because you don't know how to fight or because the Institute can see that you're a Divine." He takes a long steadying breath. "I need to make sure that neither of those things happen."

I sigh, the thought of the arena making me shudder. I don't have much time left. Ash puts a hand on my shoulder, but it offers little comfort. I know now why Spartaca chose me. Not because I am a poor Pleb girl, from nowhere, going nowhere. They chose me because I am a Divine.

XV

SERVA ME, SERVABO TE

Save me, I will save you

Ash keeps his word. At dawn, he raps on my door three times and is ready to train me. We keep our meetings secret, of course. But we are both in agreement that we must tell Cosimo, who has prepared another trainer for me. Cosimo doesn't protest; he knows Ash is talented in the gladiatorial arts. We don't tell him that we are Divines. As much as I trust Cosimo, he can't know the truth, no one can. But if Ash is right about my visions, my psychic abilities, then Cosimo already knows.

Spartaca must know of my Divine nature; it is the reason they chose me after all. Yet Warren saw my markings last night and didn't say a word. It is strange that they have kept this from me, and I am determined to find out why. I consider whether they even know about Ash's Divinity.

I must now confide in the prince I once hated. He is saving my life, and in return I will be forced to take his. I shake those thoughts away, concentrating my energy on the arena, on the gladiatorial skills I must learn. We return to the same clearing in the northern woods that we had visited the night before. Ash has a leather satchel slung across his broad shoulders. He carries an array of weapons – swords, daggers, knives, spears and shields – borrowed from the gymnasium.

"I assume you have no experience with weapons," he says, gesturing to the whetted blades that gleam in the filtered daylight.

I nod, meekly.

"Then we must start with the basics. Those markings..." He rakes over me with his eye; my athletic garb is form-fitting and reveals the darkening skin. "Mine took a few months to fade."

I cross my arms. "We don't have that time."

195

"Thanks for stating the obvious." He rolls his eyes in good humour. "Are you going to listen or continue interrupting?"

A smile curls on my lips. "You just love the sound of your own voice."

He mimics my expression and stance, folding his arms and adopting a smirk. "And you don't?"

I nod, unable to stop the words falling from my mouth. "Of course I do, otherwise I wouldn't waste my time taking to you."

He shakes his head with a laugh, admitting defeat for now. "Fighting talk."

As much as I enjoy bickering and fooling around with the prince, this is no time for such childish amusements. I look up at him, a stern expression moulding on my face. He knows the time for fun and games has passed.

"Why are you helping me?"

His cheek twitches. "It is an opportunity to learn more about myself, about Divinity. I have never met another Divine before. I spent four years in the dark and I suppose I want answers." He sounds robotic and unnatural, and it is plain that he is lying. A part of me hopes he is. A part of me hopes he is helping me so that I survive, because he wants me as his wife. But it is a selfish thought so I push it away. Perhaps the truth is, he has always been intrigued by me, and that is all.

He notices my expression fall but doesn't press the issue. Instead, he steps up to me, examining my markings. "Mine resurface whenever I feel any emotion too strongly. I learnt to control my emotions and you must do the same."

"How did you do it?"

"I numbed my senses with alcohol. It helped, although I don't advise it. It's an expensive habit. As a Divine, I need to drink more to feel anything."

"What do you mean?"

"Our bodily functions are more advanced. Alcohol and other substances have a lesser effect."

It makes sense. It always surprised me that Ash was healthy and athletic considering the quantities of liquor he would pour down his throat each day.

"What can I do about this?" I peel the hem of my shorts down to my hip bone, exposing the entire coverage of the ink-coloured skin.

He hesitates, and I know there is not much he can do. "Keep calm, don't let your emotions get the better of you," he proposes. "Now I teach you to fight. Today, you become a gladiator."

He turns, bending down to retrieve a weapon from the ground. I blink, and he hurls a knife at me at incredible speed. Before I can think, the weapon is in my hand, the ivory haft cool against my sweating palms.

"Natural talent, huh?"

The blade could have killed me, and Ash gave me no warning. "How did you know I would catch it?"

"I didn't," he says. His nonchalance flares my temper, but there is no time for quarrelling. "Now it's your turn. Throw the knife at me, I want to see what your aim is like."

I think I might quite enjoy hurling a blade at the prince's head. It's all I've wanted to do since I met him. The adrenaline knotted in my throat bests me, and I don't bother to aim. My carelessness means that I miss by several centimetres.

"You have good instincts but your aim on the other hand..." He makes light of my ineptitude, his back buckling over as he erupts into fits of laughter.

I scowl at him playfully. "How did you harness your abilities?"

He leans back against a tree trunk, his eyes restive with thought. "It came with time. Time we don't have."

I should have expected this from Ash; he doesn't sugar-coat the ugly truth of it all, he never has. But I almost wish he would lie to me. Just this once.

"Race?"

"What?"

He approaches me. "Race me to the lake?"

I don't agree, but still I run without warning. My legs work effortlessly beneath me, and I feel something electric and powerful pulsing through my veins. This is one thing I could always do – run. I used to run from my father shaking his fist in the air when I didn't come home at night. I used to run with the Grey as a child, through the meadows, chasing and bounding blithely. I ran from the Institute, more times than I can count.

Ash shouts from behind me. "Cheater."

I don't let it deter me. I focus on my strides, and my feet seem to tear up the earth beneath me.

Ash is at my side and soon overtakes me, without so much as a pant. I follow on his heels, pushing myself as much as my short limbs will allow. We weave through the trees, our arms shielding our faces from the protruding branches. I chase him, and then the lake is in sight. My breathing is steady, and I feel like I could run for miles. I regain my lead, my legs moving faster than they ever have. He tackles me from behind, submerging us both in the limpid lake water. I flail beneath the cool water's surface, unable to bring myself up for air. My mouth opens, hoping for oxygen, but instead water fills it. Ash hauls me onto the bank. I cough and splutter, my heart pounding hard against my ribs.

"Can you not swim?" he asks, resting my head on his body.

"I don't like water. I nearly drowned once." Rattling coughs make my entire body convulse.

I don't like to think of that day. They found my body on the pebbled banks of Chrysos Reservoir. The medics told my father that I was dead. Hours later, I awoke in a cold, refrigerated room, naked and afraid. I swore never to swim again.

"I'm so sorry, Electa, I didn't know." He fusses over me, sitting me upright, brushing the hair from my face in frantic movements. His touch is not gentle, not at all like Lysander's. I don't think the prince knows how to be gentle. His movements are hungry, desperate, and his skin burns against my own.

I push his hand away. "I'm fine."

The water beads his brow, trickling from his hairline, and I watch as his chest heaves with his breaths. He could kiss me now, and I wouldn't mind. But he doesn't, and it is better that way. I am thinking as a little girl would, and I can longer afford to be so naïve.

He sinks back among the reeds, staring up at the unclouded sky. "I have heard that not all Divines are the same. Some are stronger, some faster. Each has a strength in a particular ability that supersedes the rest."

"Do you think that my strength is my speed?" I ask.

He nods. "It would seem that way."

We return to the clearing, our clothes soaked through. But the mid-morning sun warms us dry in no time. The jubilant festivities of Panore sound from the valley. I was a child full of hatred and rage, yet Panore placated even me once.

It is the one time of year when the Institute's presence can be sensed a little less. People dress in garish costumes, wearing masks of the monsters and heroes from myth. Paints and dyes in all their vibrancy are strewn across the streets. Both Patricians and Plebeians dance, singing ancient songs and Latin hymns. Street performers and marching bands are on every corner. The priests and priestesses lead the sacrificial rites, smoking blood on the altars and burning incense. On the fifth day of Panore, the gladiatorial games begin and blood will be spilled. And the blood is never beautiful like the poets say. The mob is thirsty for it. The blood and the gore. They consider war and violence to be entertainment, and they will watch as we fall, as our blood dries on the arena's sand. They will relish in every moment of it.

Ash and I spend the rest of the day practising defensive techniques. Tomorrow, the real work begins. I will be learning combat skills and swordsmanship. The prince shows me no mercy; he unleashes the full power of his strength until my body can take no more. He tells me it is better this way – "suffer now and survive later" – the arena will be easy in comparison. I heed his words and swallow the pain. In the twilight hours, I stay awake, focusing on my emotions, on my markings just as Ash told me. They fade, for now. It is a small victory that I rejoice in. And I sleep through the night, for the first time.

When Ash said he would try to stimulate my Divine power in a fighting scenario. This is not at all what I had in mind.

He barks at me. "Fight back," he urges, over and over until I can take no more.

I lunge at him, but he side-steps me easily. My abilities could come and go at any time. In the arena, I have to rely on myself, not on my Divinity. So I don't stop. I keep trying and failing, picking myself up and falling. I can't master any of the moves Ash teaches me, even the simplest of them. Yes, I can fight, but not with the technique and the finesse of gladiators, who perform like actors in a play.

By midday my frustration slips into anger. "I can't do this anymore," I finally admit, my breathlessness igniting laughter in the prince.

"I didn't know you were such a coward."

"I'm no coward." Somewhere inside me, I find the energy to stand, hauling myself up onto two shaky feet.

He smirks, standing proud. "Then show me your courage."

I grit my teeth, my fist raised, throwing myself at him one more time. And one more time, I fall to the ground.

"Imagine that I am trying to kill you," he says, offering me a hand, pulling me upright. My palms are sticky with sweat and earth. The prince wipes his hand on his cargo trousers.

"Then actually try," I say, between my rasping breaths.

"You're not much use to me dead." He smiles, stepping up to me, leaving himself open to a frontal attack.

I project my fist. It is as close as I've managed all day. He catches my wrist before I can make contact. But it is improvement – in my mind, at least. Suddenly, his grasp tightens, and no matter how hard I try, I can't snatch my arm away. There is a glint in his eyes, not of malice nor deception, but as if he has had a brilliant idea.

"You really are a coward, weak and foolish." His breath is hot with rage. "Little Pleb." He pushes me to the ground. My head thumps hard against the rock outcrop, and waves of nausea roil within my stomach, washing over me, drowning me in pain. My markings throb with heat and my vision fades. I have experienced this feeling before, many a time. It is the sensation before every vision and every blackout.

"You are no Divine."

Instead of the usual weakness that inhibits my limbs, my muscles and veins surge with power, and it rouses me – my mind and my body. Ash's words strike like a cane against bare skin. I no longer recognise his voice.

"You were nothing before you met me."

I jump to my feet and dash headlong at the prince. I kick and punch at him, and he doesn't expect the blows. He staggers backwards, tripping on a tree root. I pounce on him, but he dodges me, rolling to the side. He is fast and on his feet in seconds.

With twice the force, he knocks me back and slings me like a boomerang at the nearest tree. I land with a thud on the earth and feel my broken bones fuse together, the blood from my wounds retreating to the source. There is no pain, only anger within me.

His satchel is beside me, and from it I take a knife. He wears only a loose-fitting vest, and I slash at his exposed skin. He ducks and swerves, avoiding the blade. Every motion and every sound is heightened; the taste of copper in my mouth, the sound of Ash's quickened heartbeat, it almost overwhelms me. He wrestles me to the ground, knocking the knife from my hand. I bring my knee up into his torso, giving me enough time to escape his snare and crawl towards the knife. But Ash is there first and puts the blade to my throat.

"Nice try, Electa." He speaks softly now. But I can't think, let alone speak. My eyes are unblinking as my mind begs me to kill, to take the knife from him and plunge it into his heart. "Electa, are you okay?" he asks, taking the cool metal away from my skin. He sits me up against the bough of a tree, his mouth forming words I can't hear.

After a few moments, I find my voice, and the tingle on my skin and in my blood abates. "I don't know what happened..." I swallow the urge to vomit. "I had no control over my body, my power, my mind."

"Divinity is a dangerous thing. You have to both harness and control it," Ash explains, his voice steady, fearless.

"What happens if I can't? In the arena, my powers may not come at all and even if they do, I won't be able to control them." The bitter truth of it all hangs in the air between us. We have no time. One more day, and that is all. I lower my head.

Ash lifts my chin with a single finger. "Just focus on keeping your speed down. They will notice – no one is that fast. Don't worry about your strength, only the person you're hitting will notice that."

I anchor myself to him in my fear, his eyes keeping me sane among the terrible brutal thoughts that swirl in my mind. "I'm scared, Ash."

He nods, slowly. "I know, I am too."

Warren comes late that night and informs me that Crew wishes to meet with me. It must be important, as Warren, his lap dog, often delivers messages on his behalf. But tonight, he wishes to see me in person. It is a good thing too, as I have some questions of my own.

Crew's villa is made from the same white stone as all the structures on Palatine Hill. Inside, it is dark, the charcoal-black panelling making the place feel more like a cave than home. Today, he has all the curtains drawn, and the heavy perfume of frankincense makes me choke on the air. He invites both Warren and me to take a seat in his parlour, dismissing the guards and servants in attendance.

His ice eyes settle on me, but they are softer, more human than usual. "Electa, there is something you should know."

Warren shuffles in the seat beside me, his face blanched white, his gaze darting. They are going to finally tell me the truth, I am sure of it.

I lift the hem of my blouse, revealing my faded markings. "Is it about these?"

Recognition dawns on Crew's face, and he nods. "Yes." He takes a sip of his tea, and there is a slight tremor in his hands as he lowers the painted cup from his lips. *Could he be afraid of me; of what I am?*

Crew explains everything, just as Ash did. He makes no mention of other Divines, of Ash. It seems he has no knowledge of the prince's Divinity, so I should keep it that way.

I feign my intrigue. I have to be certain they don't know of the prince's nature. "Are there any more like me?"

He no longer looks at me but at Warren. "Not anymore."

Anymore. Ash had told me that the Divines have been hunted and captured by the Institute since its formation.

I shake my head. "I don't understand why you have kept this from me for so long."

"We needed to trust you," Crew answers. "You wouldn't have believed us at the beginning, your abilities were only just developing. Warren noticed your markings, he thought that it was perhaps the right time."

I don't know whether to believe him. Every word uttered from Crew's glossy lips is dripping with deception, and I would be a fool to trust him.

"How did you even know what I was?"

Crew's stare makes me cold all over. "Your father."

It leaves me breathless. My mouth is agape as I tell myself *no* over and over. It can't be true. My father. A war hero, Institute slave, dedicated to the fatherland. He is a good man, no terrorist. "I don't believe you."

Warren speaks up. "It is true." His tone doesn't falter, as it often does when he lies. His voice is just as even as it is when he informs me of my guard rotations.

201

"That's why I asked you here," Crew interjects.

I shake my head as if hoping to rouse myself from this terrible nightmare. "No, I don't believe it. Not my father."

Crew continues, "The morning of Assay Day he drugged you so you would faint, so we could fabricate your results." His words drift into silence, and the weight of the world seems to collapse on top of me. My father made me breakfast that morning, fresh food from the Chrysos Valley Farm. I remember its taste, bitter and medicated, but I thought nothing more of it at the time.

"No." I say my thought aloud, breaking the stillness of the air.

Warren slips a letter into my hand. "Read for yourself."

The seal is the carmine red of the Latian army. I break it with trembling fingers.

My dearest Electa,

I wish more than anything that I could be with you, to explain this. I have been called away to the war, but I do not fight with the fatherland, I fight with Spartaca. It came to me when I was just a boy, when I lost your mother to the Choosing. I have devoted my life to its cause ever since. The greatest regret of my life is that I was never there for you, or for Vel, but I had hoped I was protecting you, from the Choosing, from the fate of our kind. Fighting with Spartaca, I believed that I could end it all for good, the Institute and its Choosing, so that I would not have to watch my children suffer the same fate as their mother did, all those years ago. But Spartaca needs your help, Electa, more than it ever needed mine. You are blessed by the gods, my girl, you have a gift unlike any other. Use it well. You are ready.

Your loving father,

Cassius

There is no doubt that this is my father's hand, and that these are his words. I fight off the urge to scream, cry, shout in all my fury, my grief and betrayal. My anger swells within me and I don't control it as Ash taught me, instead I let it rage. The markings burn like fire on my skin, but I swallow the pain.

He lied to me all these years, my own father. He let me believe I was ordinary, a Pleb who would have to fight every day to survive the Choosing. When he was home, he would make me study for hours and pray to the old gods. He would scream at me when I was a minute past my curfew and sent me to bathe if I had the slightest speck of dirt on my skin. But all that time, he knew that I would survive, that Spartaca would save me, and that I was Divine. It seems I learnt my skills of deception from my father. I thought I had him fooled, but all along it was him fooling me. Cassius Steel would be well suited to the Palatine.

A small part of me clings on to the desperate hope that this is some cruel deception, another Spartacan lie. "You said everyone has that Institute device in their heads, that implant. It can't be possible that he was helping you," I protest, but I am only fooling myself.

"Spartacan technology is advanced. We have a device of our own that blocks the signal, whether it be from the regenerators or other implants," Crew explains, his voice gentler than I have ever heard it. He is feigning sympathy and I see straight through it.

Warren puts a rough, callused hand on my shoulder. I shrug it away. "Your father wanted you to fight with us, Electa."

"I would like to hear that from his lips, not yours."

Warren and Crew glance at one another. It is brief, and my mouth is suddenly dry.

"That is why I asked you here," Crew says.

My breaths are shallow. "What? I thought you asked me here to tell me that I am a Divine."

"Yes. But there is something else." He slides a slip of paper across the coffee table and I can't bear to look at it. "Your father was killed last night in a raid. He was with Spartacan forces."

I don't blink, nor breathe. The dryness of my throat stifles any sob that might escape me.

Warren reaches out to me again, but I stand, my legs shaking beneath me. "He was the one who wanted us to withhold the truth of your Divine nature. He was worried that it would overwhelm you."

And then Crew speaks once again. "I'm sorry for your loss."

I see red, as if my body is alight in my rage. It feels as though my scream could shatter this world whole. I snatch the carbon revolver from Warren's holster and press the muzzle against Crew's skull. He raises his hands slowly, dropping the china teacup, which smashes on the flagstones. The sound makes him flinch, and there is the slightest trace of terror in his dormant expression.

"Sorry?" I spit. "You are sorry? You're holding his son, my brother, fucking hostage." My voice grows louder at every syllable.

Warren doesn't move an inch, his back straight in his seat.

Crew presses his trembling lips together, scrambling to speak. "You would never do it."

I grit my teeth and place the gun on the table. I can't kill him, not yet. "You're wrong Crew. One day, I will prove it to you."

I don't believe in religion. To revere something you can't see, touch or speak with has never made sense to me. But I find myself in the Palatine Temple, nevertheless. I hope it might bring me peace, as it does Cosimo. But as I kneel on the cold marble, before the altar of Dominus, all I feel is the ache in my knees and the shiver on my skin. I clasp my hands together, blowing breaths into the gap I make with my thumbs, in an effort to warm myself. But the room is not cold. It is my grief.

I stay like this for what could be hours. There are no clocks in the temple, and I think it is supposed to be that way. Worship shouldn't be constrained by the passing of time. And as the hours slip by, my eyelids don't droop in my drowsiness, and my spine remains stiff like wood. I count the seconds as they pass, to distract myself from thoughts of my father, of the fights, and of the mess I find myself in.

After 1,223 seconds, a clip of a shoe on the marble stone sounds behind me. I don't turn to see the visitor as she kneels beside me, golden locks wrapped like a halo around the crown of her head. The moonlight spills from the vaulted glass above, casting the girl in a heavenly glow. I don't recognise the girl as her skin is paled by the light and her face is pressed to the stone floor, like a suppliant sitting at the feet of kings.

"I thought you would have been gone by now." The girl's guttural voice is the only familiarity. A vestal white tunic falls to her ankles, and her femininity is a surprise to me. Trinity doesn't wear a dress unless she has to. "We all knew you didn't want to be here."

"Someone changed my mind." My voice has been out of use from some hours now and I speak with a croak.

She raises herself from the floor but doesn't spare me even a brief glance. "Why are you here, Electa?"

Her question surprises me. Her actions should have led to disqualification in the very least. I turn to her, but her eyes are fixed on the serpentine altar that towers over us. "I could ask you the same question."

She bows her head. "Do you mean here in the temple, or on Palatine Hill itself?"

"Which did you mean?"

Her lip curls. "I am not quite sure."

Trinity has always been a girl of few words. Indeed, I have never had a conversation with her before now. But she is not just the sulky Patrician with an attitude to rival my own. I think I now see her for what she truly is. A girl grieving her brother.

"We have more in common than you know," she says. Her voice is just a whisper, but even so, her words echo around the vaulted structure.

"How so?"

She pauses for a moment, and then looks up at the constellations flickering in the limpid night sky. "We both want revenge."

"Your brother?"

"How did you know?" She looks unsettled by my knowledge of her secret.

"Rumour flies in the Palatine," I lie. She can't know that Lysander told me. "Is that why you are here? To pray for him?"

"Perhaps." She speaks more slowly now.

"You are religious?"

"Sometimes. And you?"

I stare at the altar, the walls painted in fresco, depicting the myth of Dominus, the free-standing statues of the snake and the gods of old. "I think it is absurd."

"*Credo quia absurdum,*" she breathes. *I believe it because it is absurd.* "Do not let this place, these people, humble you, Electa." She looks at me, her green eyes swimming with tears. "I have wasted my life like that and take my word, it is a miserable existence."

"What about your faith?"

She laughs. "Faith is wasted. We all die, Electa, it is how we live our lives that matters."

She is rancorous and defeated, but even so, there is a glimmer of hope in her eyes. Trinity weeps inside for the two people she has lost, her brother and herself. She is the person I will become if I lose Vel.

"Is that why you want to change it all, change the world?"

She tears her eyes away from me and returns to her prayers. "No, it's why I am willing to die for the chance."

XVI

Omnibus Locis Fit Caedes

There is slaughter everywhere

The sun sinks to the lowest vault of the heavens, spilling orange light over the olive grove on the western peak of Palatine Hill. I sit beside Ash, our backs against the fissured bough of a fig tree in the emperor's private vineyard. After a full day of training in weapon techniques, we decided to come here to quench our thirst and sate our appetites. It is our third and final day of training. Tomorrow, the fights begin.

He trained me to use a *gladius* and shield. A simple, yet diverse weapon that would perhaps be the easiest to use in the little time we have. The other girls have signature skills and weapons they have spent years mastering. Aria is trained in the martial arts, and her signature weapons are knives and blades of all kinds. Ember is known for her mastery of the Roman claw and scissor, particularly brutal and bloody weapons that make for a good show. Trinity specialises in archery but is proficient in all martial skills, since she spent three years training at Fort Cassida. Valentina is known for her traps and cunning.

There are many types of gladiator, Ash tells me. Some fight all manner of wild animals and are called the *bestiarii*. Others re-enact the famed battles of mythology. Some gladiators are criminals, sent in without weapons or armour just to die. It is tradition, he explains, sacrificial almost. Honour, the one quality valued above all others in this prideful country, can be gained or stripped away on those bloodied sands.

I stuff grape after grape into my mouth, their sweetness like a tingle on my tongue. Ash swigs on jugs of wine, poured straight from the barrel. I don't stop him. It is the first drink he has had in days, and that is progress, at least. Atlas rests his heavy head on my lap, but I no longer mind it how I used to. The tiger is actually one of the more harmless creatures of Palatine Hill.

"Can I ask you something?"

Ash nods.

"You once said that you had to hide a part of yourself – this part." He will know what I mean. Our shared Divinity is something that scares and unites us both. "So is it all an act – the drunken prince, the fool?"

He laughs, but it sounds hollow, almost sad. "I've got so good at pretending that I can no longer tell the difference."

A pang of shame ripples through me. I was blind to his suffering once. "Is that really how you want to live out your life? Drowning on wine? Pretending to be heartless? Pretending to be an emperor?"

"I am an emperor," he snaps, lurching upright.

"Not yet," I mumble, hoping I haven't roused the beast within him.

"Soon. It is my birthright." His skin is gold in this light, and he looks holier than ever.

"Not all princes were meant to become kings."

"What is that supposed to mean?" There is an edge to his voice, as if I have offended him.

I shake my head, stuffing three grapes into my mouth to muffle my response, hoping he forgets all that I have said. "It doesn't matter."

"No, you're right."

I didn't expect him to agree. We usually bicker like children, but there is something different now, an understanding, a secret, a feeling like we are the only two people who exist in the world. Maybe we are. We could be the last of our kind.

He sharpens his hunting knife with a whetstone, slouched against the trunk. "This place can feel like a prison. All my friends would go off to war and see something of the world, but bound by my duty I was rendered here, taught to sing politics and fight in the arena. It was lonely. I acted out, anything to get my father's attention."

The scrape of the blade whines in my ears, and the sound makes me shiver. "You're better than the throne, and your father."

He stops his movements, and a brief silence settles between us. "Are you starting to like me, Electa Steel?" There is a hint of humour to his tone.

I laugh, putting a finger over my lips. "Don't tell anyone. I like everyone to think I don't have a heart."

His eyes shine like golden jewels and warm me from within. "But you do, I've seen it."

He once said I was the coldest person he has ever met. I didn't deny it. It was true, still is. I am like ice when I want to be. But now he sees the side of me that I try so hard to hide.

"Did you mean it when you kissed me?" *Stercus.* "Sorry, forget I ever said that."

His brow quirks, and that infuriating smirk of his returns. "That was certainly unexpected," he says. "But yes, to answer your question, I did mean it, still do."

I choke on his words, and I am not sure what is more embarrassing, the persistent spluttering sounds that escape me, or the fact I asked about the kiss. But he doesn't laugh, nor even smile. Instead, he puts the knife and whetstone down.

I finally steady myself. "Best of five, huh?"

His smile returns. "Something like that," he jokes, resuming his prior activity. The silence that settles upon us is easy and welcome. He sharpens his blade, its taper glinting in the last bit of flaring light. I stroke Atlas, until I can no longer feel my legs from his weight.

Ash's expression brightens, and he speaks once more. "At first, I liked you because you hated me. You were the only thing that never came easy for me. But recently, I've seen the part of you that you try so hard to hide. And I happen to like it, quite a lot."

He has no idea how much I hide.

"I've heard stories, rumours. That you're a bad man, that you have done terrible things in the name of the fatherland," I say under my breath. In times like these I forget the person he is supposed to be. The murderer, the sadist, everything Spartaca and Lysander have told me.

He makes a noise of agreement. "Do you believe those stories?"

I sigh, unable to look him in the eye. "I don't want to, but I am still scared to trust you, even now."

"Those stories you heard are probably true, I am no saint, Electa, are you?" He steeps his fingers, staring out at the horizon, the vineyard, the olive groves and the rolling expanse of hills in the distance.

I had expected excuses and arrogance; he has surprised me instead, and his question intrigues me. Innocence doesn't exist in a world like ours. Here I am making idle chat with someone I am going to kill. Ash lights his cigarette. As I watch him and the beatific warmth that blooms on his face, I wonder whether I can do what Spartaca asks of me. I think of my father, his wish for me to help. It is a wish I must honour. My eyes water at his memory, but I don't allow the prince to see.

I bury my face in Atlas's fur and hum the song Father used to sing to me. It soothes me, as it always has. But the encroaching thought of killing the boy beside me unsettles me in ways I never thought it could. Ash is Divine, and Crew doesn't know that, but if he did, would he want me to kill him all the same?

I don't sleep that night. Instead, I cry for my father, my brother and the life I have lost forever. Cosimo wakes me at dawn, and the preparations begin. Lucia wheels in my armour on a display rack. It is more decorative than practical. She straps me into thick leather undergarments and fits the white metal cuirass over my head. The material covers my markings, at least. She kneels at my feet, adjusting the greaves that attach over my leather boots, and then the platinum armguards. Finally, she adorns me with a headpiece, a simple metallic wreath that pin my locks back.

Cosimo explains the rules of Imperial Panore one final time. Any competitor can concede by raising her index finger. The emperor will then proceed to either spare you with a thumbs up motion, or signal for execution with a thumbs down motion. I remember Aria's pledge to concede and can only hope the emperor will spare her. The Glycias family are esteemed. The emperor would allow her survival, I am sure.

Cosimo continues with the needless details but my thoughts are elsewhere. I can only think of my father. I imagine his cold, lifeless corpse left to rot on those frosted mounds of earth. A tear slips down my cheek.

"Electa, what is wrong?" Concern tugs at Cosimo's expression.

"I'm fine," I say, quickly, too quickly.

He purses his lips, unconvinced. "I have been concerned for days. You have spent all your training time fooling around with Ash, doing Dominus knows what. You could die today."

"But I won't. I am a Divine." I say this much louder than I should. Lucia is in the next room packing away the paints she has used to decorate my face.

Cosimo removes his glasses, his typical angered response. I know his every mannerism by now. "Keep your voice down, Miss Steel."

I huff like a petulant child. "Thanks for telling me. You knew, didn't you?"

"Of course, I knew. But I had my orders." He paces up and down the room, his hand pressed against his forehead. "I don't think you have been entirely honest with me either."

"And how's that?" I cross my arms.

"Ash. The two of you training together is no coincidence."

How could he know? Does that mean Spartaca knows too? I swallow down a gulp.

"I don't know what you're talking about."

He lifts his head slightly, peering down his nose at me. He knows that I am lying, and he knows whose secret I am trying to protect. "Spartaca doesn't know, and I won't tell, if that is what you are so concerned about."

"How do you know?"

"I have had my suspicions for a long time, Electa."

It is almost a relief that Cosimo knows the truth. I hate lying to him and perhaps he can even help understand more about my Divinity. "I need answers, about what I am. Crew knows more than he is letting on."

His green eyes spark with curiosity. "Of course he does, but you would be a fool to stick your nose where it doesn't belong, especially now, when you're so close."

I know he's right. But soon it will be too late. "Spartaca will be eager for me to kill Ash as soon as the final fight is over. That is in three days' time."

"Yes, but there will be the wedding and coronation. There will be time."

I strain to lift my head under the weight of my armour. "I am not so certain."

He grips me by my shoulders, his expression stern. "Electa, you need to be worrying about the fights, about surviving." He shakes me gently, but the fights are the last thing on my mind. "Fifty thousand people will be in the Flavian Dome this afternoon, watching you fight Aria to the death. And it won't just be Aria that you're facing. The game masters are creative, and they want to put on a good show."

"What are you saying?" I search his eyes for some hope, begging him to tell me what I want to hear – that everything will be okay. But Cosimo hangs his head, scuffing his sandals on the parquet floor.

"You won't just be fighting Aria. It is Imperial Panore. The mob wants to see a lot more than two girls hurling weapons at each other." His voice has harshened in warning. "You are there to entertain them. You need to get the crowd behind you, to perform for them. You are a gladiator now."

I turn to the mirror and don't recognise myself. I run my hand over my face. The white tribal paint is dry against my skin. The reflection depicts the idol of my younger years, Nemesis, the Plebeian, who wore her family colour in the arena proudly. I shall do the same.

My attendants tie ribbons around the wreath, holy fillets that signify my servitude to the nation and Dominus in the arena. These fights are sacred tradition. We, the gladiators, do Dominus's bidding, and offer him the sacrifice of human blood spilled. But, as they tug at my hair, I swat them away as if they are flies. I adjust the ribbons myself; it gives me something to focus on. The Flavian Square has been sectioned off into two corresponding halves. One side for me, my attendants and sponsors. The other for Aria.

The gladiatorial procession will begin here and follow the promenade to the Dome. Thousands line the streets, held back like a herd of cattle with barriers. Vigilites stand in front, keeping order in their pewter armour, unblinking metallic watchmen that seem almost robotic in their stance. The sun-bleached marble of the Promenade gleams in the high-noon sun and the Dome looms in the distance.

I am hoisted onto a white stallion, who has the same fillets braided in his mane. Aria is across from me on a dapple-coated steed. Her armour is dyed blue, the colour of the Claudii, but it seems to fit in the same way mine does. She doesn't so much as glance my way; instead, she holds her head to the sky as if in prayer. Cosimo wraps the reins tightly around my hand and squeezes me, hoping to offer reassurance. I return the gesture with a nod, as this is all I can manage for now.

The Imperial carriage sets off before us. The clatter of horse hooves on the stone is almost a pleasing sound among the tumult that escapes from either side of the street. Trumpeters skirt the crowds, edging along the barriers, and serenade us as they would a triumph. I focus on the cadence of my horse's hooves beneath me, my head down, ignoring the spectacle that rages all around. The electronic billboard, hovering around the Dome ahead, flickers to life. The poster shows Aria and I, arms crossed, staring down each other in a glamorised pose.

The sounding of the hooves is subdued by the soft sand of the arena. I squint in the sunlight and stare up in awe at the blurred haze of bodies packed in archway after archway, tier upon tier, right the way up to the colonnade walkway for standing spectators at the highest level. An official gestures for us to disembark, and we oblige. We climb the steps of the podium set beneath the Imperial box. The emperor settles nicely into his aureate throne, followed by Ash to his left, who offers me a crisp nod, and Mr Institute himself, Lysander, to his right, who even manages a smile.

The telescreen hovers above us, a live video feed of the proceedings, so that even the Plebeians, on the highest level, can see the wounds a blade makes on the skin and watch every drop of blood fall to the sand. The emperor raises his hand, silencing the crowds. And we bow, our fists over our hearts, one knee to the ground, in salute of the emperor and the fatherland.

The senators flag the emperor on both sides, their ministerial togas marking them from the Patrician high society in their furs and ostentatious fashions. They, too, put their fists to their hearts and lower themselves onto one knee. The pageantry of it all is nauseating, but I bite my lip and choke down any urges of resistance.

"Hail, Gladiators," the emperor bellows, returning the salute. He is thinner than the last time I saw him; his cheeks look more sunken and his previously round face seems almost skeletal. "And welcome, Citizens. Today, Aria Glycias and Electa Steel will be the first to fight in this special connubial ceremony in honour of my son and heir, Asher."

The prince stands, playing his part. The applause seems to make him glow like a god. His arrogant eyes are alight with the unceasing encore that spills from every tier. And now I understand what he had meant yesterday in the vineyard. There comes a time when you become the mask you hide behind.

"Gladiators show us your courage," the emperor commands, his voice like a drum in my ear. The crowd rumbles, applauses and cheers. "But first, there will be a test of your virtue."

A creaking of metal comes from cages in the pit of the arena. Vigilites flank two men, stripped bare, other than a rag to protect their modesty. They are shackled at the feet. The jangle of the iron bonds as they stumble across the sand wracks me with fear as I realise what I will be asked to do. They are forced to their knees by the faceless vigilites, one in front of me, the other before Aria.

"You are to execute these men. They have committed treason, a blasphemous act against the fatherland, a crime not committed within the ULA for one hundred years."

Liar. I imagine the Institute lifting puppeteer strings, moving his mouth and limbs as they please.

"A ruler of this great League must be willing to deliver justice by their own hand."

These men could be innocent civilians plucked from the streets. This is a test for me alone, of the emperor's own design. There is a canny glint in his eye as his gaze settles on me. He thinks he has outfoxed me, but I must summon up my courage and prove him wrong.

Aria is first to deal the blow. She slits the criminal's throat with her deer horn knives. I expected more hesitation from the docile girl that I have come to know, but she is still a Patrician, a gladiator, a killer, and I mustn't forget it. As the man's body lies slumped, face downwards, his neck is exposed and I notice a small tattoo that resembles Warren's. He is with Spartaca – this is the emperor's revenge for his daughter.

I take more time than Aria, and my hesitance doesn't go unnoticed by the crowd or the emperor.

"Is there something wrong, Miss Steel?" His voice startles me. I didn't expect him to call me out in front of all these people. I look to Ash for comfort, and he mouths something I can't understand.

"No." I shake my head, taking the *gladius* from the scabbard strapped to my back. My grip on the hilt tightens as I step up to the criminal. I take a breath, squeezing my eyes shut, and mimic Aria's movements as I put the blade to his neck. I don't think, and when I open my eyes again, there is a lifeless body and blood staining my hands. I fight the urge to vomit. I have never killed before, but I am sure I will again.

The games master, Tacitus Nerva, a short man with a lustrous black beard acts as a referee and guides us over to two marbled podiums elevated slightly from the sand, several metres across from each other. We take our places on the markers, and Aria still doesn't look my way. I draw a nervous breath as I realise that our pact may no longer stand. Perhaps her family pressured her, and like any good Patrician girl, she would bend to her *pater's* will. My breaths come more quickly now as panic grips me. Bile rises, hot and burning in my throat. *Pull yourself together*, I tell myself over and over.

Click. Click. Click. The sound of cogs grating against each other, and then the rattle of iron. I turn sharply on my heels, and Aria does the same but in the opposite direction. Metal gates grind upwards at the edge of the pit. I bend my head over my shoulder and see Aria facing an identical gate. Cosimo had warned me that I wouldn't simply be duelling Aria. I had hoped he was wrong.

The dark cavernous cage yawns open, and three silhouettes emerge from its abyss. Wolves prowl towards me, snarling and barking, their teeth bared. A trumpet sounds. The fight has begun.

I shrink behind my shield, but it won't offer me much protection. The beasts flank me. These creatures are no strays; they have been born and bred for the arena. They are muscled, and their fangs have been sharpened to a point. Their trainers would have starved them for days in preparation for the fight and they will be hungry for flesh ... human flesh.

I pray for my Divinity to come, to feel its power coursing through my veins, but instead I am numb, terrified by the sight before me. I wave my sword as a warning, but it doesn't in any way slow their steady approach. My feet are planted firmly on my pedestal, and I have the high ground, for now. They circle me as I spin, brandishing my *gladius*, in a futile hope that they will retreat. Instead, one pounces, and the blade finds its way into the beast's body, if only by chance.

I tug at my weapon with all my might, straining to tear it from the animal's flesh. In that time, another leaps up to the podium, gnawing at my legs. My greaves only offer me so much protection, and I can feel the hot trail of blood leaking from my skin. I kick at the beast, and he cowers for a moment, long enough for me to remove the sword. The third wolf springs up onto the podium, I stagger backwards, crashing to the sand. I jump to my feet, knocking back one with my shield, slashing at the other with the blade. It falls to the ground, dead.

One more to go.

The third wolf, the alpha, is bigger than the others and bounds towards me at a terrifying pace. He drags me down to the sand, and the only thing between us is my shield. It takes all my strength to hold him off, to keep him away from my face. My hands frantically search through the hot sand for my sword. The tip of my finger brushes the cool metal, and I stretch out as far as my limbs will allow. I find the strength to push the wolf away and plunge the blade through his skull.

The three carcasses surround me, their fur discoloured with matted blood. The crowds chant. "Electa." "Electa." "Electa." Over and over. The sound of glory is sweet to my ears and electrifies me. But the fight is not over. Aria struggles against her final wolf, wounded, a bite gouged into her calf. I run over to her, to slay the beast before it can slay her. Her skin is torn and blood spills like wine, dripping onto the sand. My wounds will heal, but hers will remain as scars for an eternity, a testament to what she endured this day.

I drive the blade into the wolf's neck and then wrench it from the limp corpse. Aria remains on the ground. I offer her my hand, but she doesn't take it.

"Aria?" I speak between my panting breaths.

No response. There is nothing left of the girl I knew. Her innocent blue eyes are clouded grey, and she doesn't blink, not even once. My legs are taken from beneath me in an instant. My head thuds against the ground and my vision swirls. I have to get up, fast, if I want to live. Our agreement is over, it seems.

My entire body aches as I drag myself up from the sand. Aria is ready for me, throwing perfectly placed punches to my jaw, arms and torso. I block her as best I can, remembering the moves Ash taught me, but there is only so much I can do.

She is quicker than me without my Divinity. I swing my sword, only for her to duck and dive as if her limbs are made from elastic. A measured kick to my right hand sends the blade flying from my grip. I manage to snatch the shield from the ground beneath me. She knocks me backwards as I cower behind it, forcing me closer and closer to the arena's edge. I swallow down the coppery taste in my mouth. A trickle of warm blood escapes my nose. As the warmth spreads, my entire body goes numb. Black spots fleck my vision. I know what is happening, I can feel it.

I drop my shield and fling both my legs into her stomach. She tumbles backwards but is quickly on her feet again. But now my task is easy. I dodge her every punch, every kick, bending at will. She tires and her movements slow, but mine only quicken. I feel myself losing control of my own body, and my arms reach for her knives that lie beside the dead wolf. With a flourish, they twirl and dance in my hands, as if I have used the weapons for years. But she has my sword. Our weapons lock with a resounding clang that silences the cheering crowds.

She wrestles a knife from me and makes a headlong sprint to her podium. She throws her arm back, preparing to hurl the knife. Her pupils flare, and I know in that moment that she will kill me if I don't kill her first. My reactions are quicker. I launch the blade. It spins in the air before landing in her throat. In that second, the entire world crumbles around me and the cloud lifts from her eyes. They are a beautiful blue once more. And as she sinks to her knees, I can only watch as life pours from her throat, vivid red against ashen skin. A single tear rolls slowly down her cheek and her body folds over onto the sand.

I collapse, unable to tear my eyes away. A single wisp of white hair flutters in the breeze. The sound of the mob drones in my ears. Confetti falls, and I hope it will bury me whole.

XVII

In Perpetuum, Frater,
Ave Atque Vale

Forever and ever, brother, hail and farewell

In my nightmares, the blood that dries on my hands finds its way to my throat and I can no longer breathe. I choke on the red fluid until it drowns me. When I wake, there is an empty feeling in my chest and the blood is still on my hands. I scrub them until they are raw, until there is not a single trace of the girl I knew. Just the thought of her name makes me shudder and my skin cold to touch.

They carried me through the forum on a gilded litter in celebration of my victory, of an innocent girl's death. The people rejoiced, and I became a gladiator – the embodiment of strength, honour and sacrifice. But the only person who has been sacrificed is myself. I fool the people here with a smile and tell them what they want to hear so often that I have forgotten who I was before I became a part of this world. Electa Steel is now a name on the people's lips, and I hate the sound of it.

Aria was not the girl I knew in the arena. She was in a trance-like state, a terrible bloodthirsty monster. I can't help but wonder whether the emperor had some involvement. He didn't want me to win, and hoped to make a fool of me. The Imperials are known for their use of *pharmaca*. Warren told me once that drugging revellers was a common occurrence in the Palatine. Would it be so strange if a son mimicked the behaviour of his father? I don't want to think of it too much.

A Praetorian announces that I have a visitor. Calix strolls into my chambers, his vivid blue toga clinging to him like water. He has come from the party; a party I was supposed to attend.

I sink further into my bathrobe, tucked under my sheets, not even bothering to look his way. "If you're here to drag me to that party, I'm afraid you are wasting your time," I mutter.

He huffs. "Quite a welcome. Nice to see you too, Electa."

"What did you expect?" Sometimes, I want to fight the entire world. "You haven't spoken to me in weeks."

He shifts his eyes and stares at the floor. "I know." I note the sadness in his voice.

"I understand." I allow my voice to fall to a whisper, whether it is my grief for Aria or my shame for the way I have treated him, I am not sure. He deserted me, and I hated him for it. But he is good and kind and all the things that everyone here is not. He was trying to be a better brother, a better man, and who am I to deny him of that. "Before she died, Shauna explained it all to me. I don't want to be the reason you lose your home and your family." I clamber out of bed, my legs still shaking. I reach out to him, but he grimaces at my touch, as if he has been beaten. And I remember that he has, when he was just a boy, by the very people I work with.

"I shouldn't have let my own fear stand in the way of my relationship with you. We are friends, nothing more. Ash will have to accept that." He manages a forced smile. His eyes shine as if to say that everything will be okay. But it won't. Our renewed friendship won't fix the mess I have made of things.

"What are you doing here then?"

He gives me a knowing look. "I am not exactly welcome at the celebration. Ash hasn't forgiven me for what transpired at the voting ceremony."

"I am sorry. I didn't mean to come between the two of you." I can't help but feel responsible for what happened that night. I still can't bear to think of it, even now.

The folds in his toga ripple as he heaves a long sigh. "It is not your fault. Unlike my brother, I live with the mistakes of my past and try to move on from them."

My eyes roll skywards. "Ash is not one for forgiveness."

"No, he is not," he says with a sad nod. "I also came to check on you – your absence didn't go unnoticed."

I was the guest of honour. They are celebrating my victory and the victory of either Valentina or Trinity, I am not sure who. But I couldn't bring myself to revel in the death of an innocent girl, slaughtered like a lamb for sacrifice.

"What are people saying?"

He takes a seat on the edge of the bed, the soft mattress swallowing him up. He pats the space beside him, encouraging me to sit. "Nothing much. Cosimo has dispelled any rumours."

Of course he has.

I sit beside him but keep a little distance between us. The conversation is strained, and it makes me sad because I know it can never go back to how it used to be. "And the other fight? Who won?"

"Trinity."

It is not surprising. She is rumoured to be the best fighter of us all. In two days, I will face her in the arena. She could easily devour me whole. I almost hope she will. If I survive, my fate could be far worse.

The silence is taut like a knife edge. I rub my eyes, dry from the countless tears I have cried. Lix eases himself closer to me, as if noticing my pain.

"Have you ever killed someone, Lix?"

He hesitates. "Yes, escaping Echos," he says finally.

"How did it make you feel?"

He recoils. "I don't like to think of it, but I suppose I felt angry … empty."

I feel all those things, and more. Crew has made me into a monster. "I don't know who I am anymore Lix…"

I expect his typical reassurance, a cheery smile to brighten my day, but he seems sadder than he has ever been. Instead, he asks, "Why are you doing this, Electa? Do you love Ash?"

"No." I almost scoff. "But I love my family."

"You are trying to save them?"

I latch onto his eyes, an abyss of blue that makes me want to be truthful, to be good, just like him. "Of course. Wouldn't you, if you had the chance?"

I already know his answer. If he could go back in time and save his family from their fate, he would.

"Yes. Yes, I would."

We sit together, calmly. He distracts me with stories of mythology, the ones my father used to read to me every night when he returned from the war. But I don't sleep, and it feels like I never will again.

Warren is in an uncooperative mood. His expression hardens into a firm scowl as he says *no*, for the hundredth time. I need to sneak into Crew's mansion and understand for myself what I am. It may bring me a little peace. But Warren, ever the loyal and dutiful servant, won't help me this time.

"Please. I deserve to know the truth."

He squares his shoulders, his gaze steadfast. "I can't, Electa. If we were to be caught—"

"We won't be, I swear." He doesn't respond but his fists stiffen into balls. "You said yourself that Crew is in meetings all day."

His jaw tightens. "There will be servants and guards."

A smirk tugs on the corner of my lip. "You owe me."

"I owe you nothing."

The coldness of his voice shocks me. Only now do I notice the bruising creeping past the stiff collar of his uniform, the purple as bright as the red cloth. He helped me once before, and it cost him, it seems. But his words still anger me.

"You have singlehandedly ruined my life, and my brother's, forever."

But my ire doesn't provoke any sympathy or musings of regret. Instead, his response is harsh and knocks all the air from my lungs. "It wasn't much of a life, now, was it?"

He is not wrong. We may survive the Choosing, only for our children to suffer the same dreadful fate. We live our lives in fear, and that is not much of a life at all. The truth of his words leaves me cold. My eyes flash to the unsecured gun in his holster. He must have forgotten to re-arm the lock.

My hand seizes the weapon, and I press the barrel into his ribs. "I am not asking."

He winces at the force. "I suppose arrogance is the price to pay for Divinity."

My voice steels. "Take me to his villa."

He presses his lips firmly together, shaking his head, every muscle and sinew taut. "I'll get you in and out, that is all."

"That's all I need."

We return to the Palatine archive room, where this conspiracy began. It is harder to breathe in here than I remember. The oxygen levels are lowered so that the books and records aren't damaged, Warren tells me. Labyrinthine passageways wind out from the dank cavern where they held my brother captive. Warren explains that the tunnels are, in fact, catacombs of the old city that existed before the Havens did. It is the burial place of the emperors of old, while their mysterious and marble statues loom above the forum like ghosts.

We have only a flashlight to guide us. The crack of an old dry bone underfoot is an unnerving but frequent sound. Warren uses no map; he navigates the tunnels effortlessly, not placing a single foot wrong. He tells me that only Spartaca uses these passages, and no Imperial, vigilite or Praetorian dare come down here for fear of stirring the souls of the dead. Miles of subterranean tunnels branch out across the entire city, comprised of old hypocaust systems and burial grounds like these. The passage narrows until Warren's broad shoulders brush against the crumbling walls. The plaster disintegrates as he walks past, and I cough as a cloud of dust blows in my face.

Warren clambers on top of a granite boulder, pushing up against the ceiling with his arms, which bulge against his tight uniform. He pushes the slab aside, and I squint as light spills into the tunnel. He clambers out through the gap in the ceiling and hauls me up too, using only one hand. It seems we are in a small closet. Warren shoves fur robes and coats aside to reveal the door, which no doubt leads out to the ground floor of Crew's villa.

Warren pushes lightly against the small of my back. "I'm waiting here, make it quick."

"No, I need your help with something," I say, resisting the pressure from his arm.

He scowls at me. "That is not what we agreed."

"I know, but you're here now." I flash him a pearly white smile, which I hope he can't resist. He is kinder than I am. If our roles were reversed, I am sure I wouldn't have offered the help he has given me.

He relents with a sigh. "What do you need?"

"Crew's office. I need to access the computer records."

I don't know what exactly I am looking for, what answers I am hoping to find, but computer records seem like a good place to start.

The villa is quiet. Dawn broke only moments ago, and the servants will be preparing a morning meal for the master of the house. I follow Warren's steps tentatively, my footing light on the dark marble flagstones, as he leads the way to Crew's office.

The room is bare, lacking in trappings or personal items of any sort. I suppose it is safer that way. I often forget that Crew Gracchus is just an elaborate guise. Warren takes a seat behind the desk. I watch as he works past the layers of security, biometric scanning and passwords. Warren doesn't fear Crew like I do, yet he is a cog in the Spartacan murdering machine that could easily be replaced. As that realisation washes over me, the slow warmth of guilt rises like bile in my throat.

"You're going to get in trouble for this, aren't you?"

His eyes are focused on the screen as his fingers move at pace over the keyboard. "I thought you wanted my help. Are you trying to scare me away?"

The hint of humour in his tone calms me, and I shove a bony elbow into his ribs, playfully. "I do need your help, and I appreciate it, but..."

"Crew wouldn't lay a hand on me."

The certainty with which he speaks both confuses and reassures me. "Are we talking about the same person?"

Warren narrows his eyes in concentration. "Just let me get on with this. You want answers, don't you?"

"Yes." I nod.

"Then, *tace*."

Be quiet. And I oblige him. Within minutes, he has cracked the system and the entire Spartacan database is at my disposal. I am awestruck by his talent. But he shies away from my compliments, explaining that his father was the one who created the Spartacan tech and from time to time Warren would help.

Files upon files of Spartacan secrets are laid out before me. I don't know what to look for. Perhaps my own name is a good place to start. I type *Electa Steel* into the search bar, and an icon pops up – *732 results*. I scroll down the list of files. So many catch my attention, but I don't have time to read them all. There is one that strikes both curiosity and fear into me all at once. It reads – *Latia Intiative/1998/Divine Implantation*.

This is the year Ash was born, the year his mother Skylar was executed for treason. I click on the file and realise I have been holding my breath. Warren leans over me; it seems he, too, is curious. There is list of twenty-five names, none I recognise apart from my own. It makes no sense how this could be, as 1998 was four years before I had even been born. And then there is a paragraph beneath it, with a number of names that are familiar to me.

Skylar Tucca Ovicula – ELIMINATED – initiates phase one
Alder Ovicula – ELIMINATED – HUMAN
Darius Ovicula – ELIMINATED – DIVINE
Asher Ovicula – ALIVE – HUMAN

There were three Ovicula sons, not two. It seems Crew wasn't lying when he told me that Skylar had been recruited by Spartaca, just like me. According to this, Asher is the only surviving Ovicula son.

I click on the links attached to the file. I make sense of what I can, and my first impression is that Skylar's mission may not have been the failure it seemed. She succeeded in killing the firstborn, Alder, so that a Divine child named Darius, provided by Spartaca, would be first in line to the throne. The Divine child would be swapped at birth with her real son, Asher. The file reports that Darius, too, was murdered by Skylar, and only the human child, Asher, survived.

But there must have been a mistake, a deceit of some kind. Ash is the Divine. He is the Divine that Spartaca believe to be lost, dead forever. He was the original conspiracy, not me. Spartaca would have had no need for me; they would already have an heir to the Empire that they could control. I turn to Warren, breathless, but he looks just as confounded. Of course, he doesn't know what I do – that Ash is a Divine. And I don't tell him, because I swore to Ash I would protect his secret.

"Do you understand any of this?" My mind spins hopelessly over the names and dates on the screen. "My name is listed here but I wasn't even born."

Warren shakes his head stiffly. "I am not sure." And I genuinely believe him.

"And this?" I point to the paragraph outlining the mission Skylar was tasked with. "Why did she ruin Spartaca's plan?"

He pauses, peering over my shoulder to get a better look. Eventually, he says. "That, I do know something about."

"Tell me."

"Castel is our leader, Spartaca's leader, and was to Skylar what Crew is to you," he says.

"A handler?"

He nods. "Castel seduced Skylar to convince her to do Spartaca's bidding. They had an affair while Skylar was married to the emperor."

That would explain the emperor's bitterness; a man spurned, a man brought under the yoke by his own wife.

"Did Romulus find out?"

"Eventually. But Skylar realised that Castel was using her as a pawn," he says.

Just like they are using me.

"She decided to turn her back on Spartaca. But she had already killed her eldest son on Catsel's orders, and the conspiracy was nearly complete," he continues. "So, she decided to thwart the plan in the only way she could, by killing the Divine child Spartaca had intended to place as the first in line to the Latian throne."

"And she was successful?"

"Yes. And Castel, in his fury, told Romulus about their affair, about the murder of Alder, and how she had been working with Spartaca. He, of course, didn't implicate himself, and fled."

But Warren is wrong. She didn't kill the Divine; she gave him the chance to live. I understand it now, and the images of that day stir, lucid in my mind. She pretended to kill the Divine child and attempted to escape Latia with her real son. Asher was left behind, and Spartaca believed him to be the human child and blood heir. I am sure Skylar couldn't have acted alone. Someone in the Palatine must have helped her escape, but I wonder who, and what was the fate of her newborn son.

"And so, she was executed?"

Warren bobs his chin. "Exactly."

And what of me? Shall I meet her tragic end? I am too fearful of the answer. And what of Ash? Do I let him believe that he is simply a product of a freak genetic mutation or reveal his true heritage, as a Spartacan operative believed to be lost? Will he forgive me for my lies? And where will he place his loyalties? Surely not with me, not with Spartaca who was responsible for the slaughter of his sister. Yet a part of me longs to tell him the truth. Spartaca would no longer need me to kill him, and his life would be saved, but at what cost?

The heavy thud of leather training boots on the stone floor shudders through me. I jolt out of the seat.

"*Stercus,*" Warren breathes.

He quickly shuts down the computer and hauls me into the closet to the left, his hand over my mouth to stifle any sounds I might make in protestation. I push his large, soldierly hands away from my face and peer through the wooden shutters of the closet door. He huffs silently in disapproval.

It is Crew, returning from his morning jog. He has a damp towel slung around his neck and dons white athletic garb that is certainly meant for more youthful models. He strolls over to a cabinet and pours himself a drink from a liquor bottle, half-full. I feel Warren's fingers tremble beside me, vibrating against the fabric of my shirt. Crew pauses as he approaches the closet where we hide. He must hear the rustle of fabrics hanging on the rail as they rub up against our bodies. I hold my breath and shut my eyes, expecting the worst.

"Sir, Director Drusus is in the parlour and has requested to see you. I tried to stop him." The servant's voice echoes from the doorway.

Crew sighs heavily. "Lysander *fucking* Drusus," he grumbles before storming out of the room.

Lysander Drusus may have just saved us a very unpleasant encounter. I burst out of the closet, grateful for the air and light of the open space. Warren curses like a maniac and urges that we must return to the tunnels. But I have another urge, one I can't control. I dash from the room before Warren can say much more than, "El, where in the god's name are you going?"

I am light on my feet, luckily, so I don't make much of a sound as I creep towards the parlour that I have visited once before. Warren hasn't followed, knowing well the risk I have taken. I hide behind the tawdry red curtain of the dark stone archway. The men's voices sound from inside.

"Trinity Messalla is dead." Lysander speaks with a voice cut from diamonds.

"How?" Crew demands, genuine surprise in his tone.

There is haunting laughter. "Suicide, apparently. We both know otherwise."

Trinity was on a warpath with the Institute and the Choosing. She wouldn't have given up her chance to change things, not for one moment.

"Spartaca?" Crew's tone gives nothing away.

"The raid yesterday on our fortification in Romont was a bold move, they lost thousands of men. Does that not seem foolish to you?" Lysander asks.

"It sounds like they are wasting lives," Crew says.

"Indeed. Something bigger is coming, I can feel it."

It seems that Lysander, while he has his suspicions of me, doesn't have any of Crew. It is a relief in some ways. He couldn't possibly piece together the intricate, complex fragments of this conspiracy.

"Why have you come to me with this information?" Crew asks.

"I am here because you are Electa Steel's sponsor," Lysander begins. "This is good news for her, and you. She is now in the final. And I want her to win."

My jaw drops, my mouth turns dry.

"I didn't expect a man like you to take such a liking to the girl. May I ask why?"

This same question sits on my tongue. I peek around the curtain for a moment and see Lysander's dangerous smile. "Let's just say, I don't want her to die."

I scamper back to the safety of the tunnels where Warren waits.

His reaction is as expected. "Are you trying to get yourself killed?"

I don't humour him with a response. Instead, I relay what I heard. "Trinity is dead."

Another dead girl. More blood on my hands. No doubt Spartaca killed her so that I would be in the final and one step closer to the crown. Crew obviously didn't believe that I could defeat her in combat, and she is dead because of it.

Warren's face turns bright red. "What?" He almost chokes on the word.

"Don't play dumb with me, Warren. I know it was Spartaca's doing." I barge past him into the darkness.

He is quickly on my heels with his flashlight. "Trinity?

"You think me a fool," I growl.

"No, Electa, I swear, I didn't know about this."

He said the same about Shauna, and I didn't believe him then any more than I do now. "You seem to say that every time someone is brutally murdered."

He stops in his tracks, unbuttoning the top collar of his martial suit as if he is too hot. For the briefest moment as the torchlight flickers to his face, I think I see a tear slip from his eye. "Perhaps Crew just never told me…"

I examine him, scrutiny in my eyes. He is as composed as always, soldierly and steadfast. Maybe I'm seeing things – it's been a long day. "You're his senior operative."

"I know." He sighs. "But he can be reckless, ruthless and well, and I am none of those things."

It is true. Warren is measured in his actions, calculating every situation until he understands his advantages and the consequences. And he is certainly not ruthless. His sweet spot for me could easily lead to his downfall, and as I study the bruises that fringe his neck once more, I realise that maybe it already has.

"You really didn't know?"

He nods, and this time I believe him.

The Palatine gates have been barricaded on Director Drusus's orders. Outside, members of the press and news correspondents flood the forum, as the Institute makes a statement from the Basilicia Julia, the courthouse of the city. The vigilites tell the world that Trinity's death was a suicide, while the truth will remain hidden within the enclaves of the Institute forever. The semi-final has been cancelled, and the final has been brought forward in its place. The day after tomorrow, I will fight Ember for the crown.

I return to my chambers, where a note has been left in my stead. It is from Lix. He asks me to meet him in the woods as soon as I can. It is unlike Lix to leave notes. There is a certain urgency to the written letters, his usual cursive script replaced by bold, unjointed capitals that shout off the page.

I go to the lake where we once met. For a moment, I consider returning to fetch a hat, as the sun beats down on me with a fiery vengeance. But there is no time for that. Lix is desperate to meet me.

The cicadas buzz in the shrubbery and their ugly song is unusually loud this day. Lix is not here, nobody is. I call for him. No response. My throat turns hoarse the louder I shout, until there is no breath left within me. I pace around the water bank, searching for any sign of him, perhaps his favourite purple vest or even a discarded novel. But there is nothing.

I walk down the track that leads further into the coppice. And I see bright splashes of crimson on the arid soil. I crouch down and run my fingers through the earth. It is wet with blood. I struggle to stand as my legs quake beneath me and my throat thickens with fear. I follow the blood trail, my steps frantic, my limbs failing me many times over. My Divinity courses through me; I can feel it now. The power of it stirs inside of me, rousing me, and I sprint. The woodland thickens, branches scrape against my arms, and my shirt catches against the knotted bark of a tree. I trip, falling out into a small clearing. And then I see him.

Lix clutches onto the haft of the knife lodged into his stomach. His white cotton shirt is red. It is unbuttoned at the top, and his chest is bare and raw, steaming. He has been branded with two crossed swords. A breath catches in my throat. I scream for help until my lungs burn and my throat dries. But there is no one coming. We are a mile from the Palatine.

I caress his face, his angelic face that always wore an easy smile now pale and damp to touch. His breaths are shallow, too shallow. And a slow, sickening feeling rises from my stomach. I tear the shirt from my body and press the cloth onto his wound with all my weight. It is quickly soaked through. A fire churns inside me, anger, guilt and anguish all at once. I curse and shriek, but the words, the sounds, die in my mouth. And my lungs don't fill with blood as they did in my dream; instead, I drown on my own tears.

His eyelids flutter. On my knees, I pray to the gods. I pray for them to save him, to keep the light in his bright blue eyes. But gods don't answer my prayers, they never have. He makes a small choking sound, his mouth trembling open.

"Alder isn't dead," he croaks, his voice faint.

Alder. Skylar's firstborn. "What do you mean?"

But his hand is already limp in mine. I can't bring myself to look at his beautiful eyes, their light stolen away by the cruel, selfish gods. My entire body numbs as I collapse onto his, sobbing into his bloodied clothes. His skin is cold against my own as I clutch it, never wanting to let go.

I don't know how much time passes, but I am not alone anymore. Voices echo, over and over, a cacophony of voices roaring above me. Someone drags me away from his lifeless body. I kick and scream but cry no more. Instead, a fury burns through me like wildfire. I will have my vengeance.

XVIII

ANCHERONTA MOVEBO

I will raise hell

His blue eyes haunt me. I shut my eyes to rid myself of the vision, but it lingers. I loved Lix like a brother. It is my fault he is dead, and he is not the only casualty of my ignorance. Shauna, Aria, Trinity and soon Ash will meet the same fate because of my selfish wish to save my brother, my selfish belief that things could actually change. I am no better than Ash or Lysander. I have caused death and left behind destruction in my wake. I used to see this world in black and white, but now I realise there is only grey.

I have been undressed and wrapped in the silk sheets of my bed. I peek under the covers to check I am not entirely naked. A slight, shapeless nightdress clings to my body. In my hysteria, they took me away from the woods and sealed me up here, away from the world. I have little recollection of the hours that followed.

I venture from the sleeping chamber into the reception room, hoping for a familiar face, perhaps Ash or even Cosimo. Instead, Lysander reclines on the *lectus*, his long limbs extended and a book in hand. He hasn't yet noticed me, and I examine him from afar. He seems peaceful, harmless, like this. But I know better than to think such things of a man like him.

I sit beside his feet and only then does he glance up from the creased pages of his antique book. He smiles. In moments like these, I forget the evil that lurks within him, an evil that may not exist at all. His eyes flicker over me, studying me, and I crumble. Tears spill – limpid rivulets that glitter against reddened skin. I can't hide my pain any longer and I let myself be consumed by it. I bow my head in shame of my weakness, of the salty water that streaks my face, but Lysander, with a delicate finger, props up my chin and wipes the tears from my cheeks. He draws me close into his strong arms. I shouldn't feel safe in the clutches of a serpent, but I do.

229

I have never let him come so near, and now I understand why. My small body pressed against his makes me feel things that I can't comprehend, things I can't afford to feel. Grief has made me tender and vulnerable. It has made me weak.

"I am sorry; I know how fond you were of him." His voice is like a dark lullaby, and it soothes us both back to silence. But then he looks at me, the green in his eyes dancing in the light, and I look back at him. His hand is folded over mine, and his breath is hot on my cheek. I stand quickly, before I can do anything foolish.

"Why are you here?"

He settles back onto the *lectus* with a sigh. "You were with his body for five hours before anyone found you. I brought you back."

I nod, unable to make sense of the emotions and thoughts in my mind. *Five hours.* It felt as though seconds had passed. "Are the funeral rites prepared?"

"Ash has asked me to take you away for the day. He thought it would be best."

Ash would never ask a favour of Lysander; there is too much bitterness between them. Lysander is here of his own accord.

I shake my head. "No. I want to honour him properly. I have to be there."

Lysander adopts a stern tone. "Electa."

"I beg you, let me say goodbye." Tears are welling in my eyes.

"The emperor has forbidden your attendance. There is nothing I can do."

Of course he did. His hatred for me knows no bounds; he is not even above drugging a girl to kill me. But to deny me attendance to Lix's funeral is cruel beyond anything I have known.

"You're the Institute director, surely there is something you can do?"

Lysander seems taken off-guard at the dry anger in my voice. "This is Imperial business," he says. "I have no remit nor ground for denial of the emperor's wishes."

He had defied the emperor before in my defence, at the Imperial breakfast after Shauna had died. I don't see why he can't do the same again.

"But Lix was my friend, I cared for him, more than his supposed family," I mutter. But my words are futile, the decision has been made, and the emperor has given his orders.

"I wish I could help you, Electa, I truly do." Lysander reaches out to me as he speaks, standing up and taking both my hands in his own. "I will find the monsters who did this and kill every last one of them, I can swear that to you. And this time, I will end Spartaca once and for all." His voice quivers with a quiet rage that frightens me, and I have to look away.

"Where are you taking me?" I ask.

His features soften again. "Somewhere peaceful, far from the Palatine and all the tragedy that has occurred here."

The peaceful place he speaks of is Capitoline Hill in the outer province of Accensus, with far-flung meadows and farmland that stretches for miles, right up to the Haven's skeleton. Lysander has a small villa at the foot of the hill while the Temple of Dominus looms above, a monolithic marble construction that is suffused with sunlight by day and moonlight by night. I stare up at the spectacle in awe. The temple's walls seem to glow gold, and glitter as if enchanted by the gods.

Lysander's servants bring out a stallion. They fit a saddle over its lustrous black coat, and Lysander effortlessly swings his leg over and pulls himself up onto the horse as if he has practiced the same mount for years. I remember that he has; he is an avid charioteer and was once a general who lost a lot to the war. He offers me a hand, his open collar flapping in the breeze. My eyes flitter to his bare chest, and I notice his godly, unblemished skin.

I take his hand, and he lifts me like a feather, up and behind him.

"You might want to hold on," he says with a chuckle.

I wrap my arms around him, tentatively, and I can feel the muscles beneath his skin. He kicks the horse lightly, urging the stallion onwards. At a trot, we roam the wheat fields of the valley. There are streams with wildflowers sprouting on the banks and cork trees offering shade from the beating sun. The taller plants tickle my bare legs as we pass, and I shut my eyes, basking in the light's warmth and the silence.

The thought of Lix doesn't leave me, even now, and sorrow aches in my bones. His final words don't leave me either, I haven't stopped thinking of them. I remember the way his eyes looked just before the light left them, just before the blue dulled grey.

When Lysander senses I am comfortable, he brings the horse into a gallop. I cling on to him even tighter, but he doesn't seem to care. He bends his head to catch my eyes, and smirks. At once, he kicks faster and faster, and the stallion speeds until the air lashes against my face with punishing blows. I relax into the moment, letting my hands loose, as they catch the air either side of me.

We dismount beside a colossal cork oak that has framed the horizon of this unbroken plain since we began our journey. These lands are untouched, sacred to the temple that sits like some holy palace in the clouds above. Lysander unbuckles the saddlebag and takes out a discoloured book. The plain blue cover fades to white at the edges.

"I remembered you liked to read." The lightness of his voice reminds me of my foolish thievery. I laugh at the memory.

He sits with his back against the russet bough. I take a seat beside him, keeping some distance between us. The Aeneid is a book I have read many a time. It is compulsory reading for students, of course, but I read it long before we did in the academy. My father read it to me on those few nights he was home, making silly faces and a voice for each character. Instead of making friends with the girls at school, I lost myself in books. I always found that they were kinder than people.

He reads the book aloud. His voice almost lulls me to sleep. It is sweet to the ears and how I would expect an angel might sound. Yet the story is of violence and war; two princes going to war over Lavinia, the daughter of a king whose name gave us ours, *Latinus.*

He reads my favourite line: "*Flectere si nequeo superos Acheronta movebo.*"
If I cannot move heaven, I will raise hell.

It terrifies me more than I remember. And I think it is because it comes from Lysander's lips. He will destroy everything in the world if it means ending Spartaca, tearing it apart until there is nothing left of the precious world he tries to protect. And there is more than hatred in those green eyes of his whenever he speaks of them. Spartaca made a monster of Lysander Drusus a long time ago.

The sun sinks, and the summer sky is dull without its light. We walk among the wheat that shudders in the evening breeze. But he doesn't walk with the confident strides I am accustomed too. It is as if my sadness has blighted him, too. He swallows his voice, trying to speak, to find the words.

"I know how you feel, Electa," he says, finally. "I lost someone I loved too."

I stop walking and look at him. His eyes are unmistakably damp.

"Who?" I ask.

"My fiancée." A breath rasps in his throat. "I was twenty. She was taken hostage with my Legion. Spartaca made me watch as they slaughtered her." Horror consumes his features, and the poised man I have come to know crumbles before me. He brushes a finger over his scar at the memory.

I recognised the poison in his voice whenever he spoke of Spartaca. It is the kind of hatred that is coupled with a thirst for revenge. "I am so sorry." Warm, nauseous guilt rises in my throat. Spartaca did that to him. The people I work with tore apart his life and murdered another innocent girl.

"Her name was Persephone." He winces. "She was my first love. And I never thought I could love again." There is a flash of memory in his eyes as he looks at me. "You look just like her."

My spine stiffens, and suddenly I am cold, even in the blazing summer heat. He has looked at me strangely ever since we met, as if I was a ghost, and now I understand why. I am Persephone's ghost.

I embrace him, not caring for the feelings that stir inside me. "I am sorry," I say again, and it is a whisper against his chest. He smells like wood and earth.

"You shouldn't be sorry. Be glad. You have her light," he says.

But he is wrong. I have a lot to be sorry for. I am an imposter and every word out of my mouth is a lie. I tear myself away from him, my body brushing against his hand. A silver chain falls to the ground. It is a necklace I have seen him wear before. I kneel to the ground to retrieve it. On the locket, a single letter is embossed – A.

I stare at the chain cupped in my hands. I swallow the lump in my throat as a cold realisation washes over me. Lysander told me once that he was adopted and never knew his birthmother. I allow myself to think back to Lix's final words. *Alder is not dead.* There is no mistake. *A* stands for *Alder*, and Lysander is the emperor's son, his firstborn son.

I want to tell someone, I must tell someone, but who would believe me, it is outlandish and absurd, more than that, it is an accusation against the most dangerous man in Latia. I wonder if Lysander even knows himself. If he does, that can only spell trouble for Ash, his throne and his title. Skylar hid Lysander away, gave him a new name and family, and erased any memory of his true parentage. She was protecting him from Spartaca, just like she tried to protect Ash.

Lysander returns me to the Palatine.

"*Placideque quiescas,*" he says, bidding me goodnight. *May you rest well and peacefully.*

I won't.

I am thankful to be alone with my chaotic thoughts. I no longer cry for Lix; instead, I make a promise to myself in his memory. I must make things right; fix the mess I have made. Until my last breath, I will defy the path that fate has laid before me and the will of the men who try to control me. I will save Ash's life, even if he hates me for what I have done. It is what Lix would have wanted.

Lucia has run me a steaming bath, fragranced and lit with candles at its rim. She has added milk to the hot water, and oils to help soothe my aching muscles before the fight tomorrow. I lower myself into the sunken stone tub, slowly, to accustom myself to the temperature. The white liquid swallows my body and relieves the ache of the bruising on my side.

"*Salve,* Electa." A disembodied voice sounds from the archway, but I can't see clearly in the steam. A dark silhouette emerges from the haze, and I jump at the sight of him.

I clutch my knees, trying to cover my naked body as best I can. "What are you doing here?"

Crew smirks and sits on the edge of the tub, far too close for my liking. "The people love you, Electa, they are chanting your name in the forum as we speak."

I want to kill him, to watch him bleed, how he made Calix bleed. "How flattering," I say through gritted teeth.

He licks his lips, a smug expression sharpening his features. "You should be pleased. Victory is within our reach."

"I still have to fight Ember," I remind him, sinking lower and lower into the water.

His ice eyes pierce me, and the warmth of the bath ebbs away. "You will win."

"And Trinity, Lix, that was your doing, I suppose?" There is an edge to my voice that he doesn't expect, and he flinches for a short moment, as if afraid. I am a Divine, and I could eat him raw.

He looks away. "Perhaps."

"You are a murderer."

"So are you, remember that; violence is the very core of your being." He leans over the water, leering. "And you will always be a killer, no matter how beloved."

A low growl rises from my stomach. "I am no killer."

"Aria. The criminal. Ash." He counts the dead with his fingers, making a point of it.

"Ash is still alive," I bristle, still clutching at my knees.

He smirks. "For now."

In my dreams, I kill him every time. Maybe Crew is right. I am a born killer, a weapon. It is my nature and that will never change.

I want to scream. "Lix. Why did you kill him?"

"I suggest you don't step foot in my house without my approval. Next time it will be your brother who pays for your insolence." He stands, turning his back on me. "And as for Warren…"

"Don't hurt him. I forced him. It was all me." I am not sure why I leap to Warren's defence with such an outburst. He doesn't deserve my compassion after his betrayals but equally I dread the thought of him suffering because of me – my actions and my words.

"He is alive. But you won't see him again, I assure you."

He has probably sent him away from Latia, back to the war, to fight with the Spartacan army. His life will be in danger, more danger than it ever was here. And as for Lix, I am the reason he is dead. If it hadn't been for my terrible curiosity, he would still be here now. The thought brings tears to my eyes. For a moment, I swear Crew looks at me with pity in his eyes, as if I am a tragedy just waiting to unfold.

"Get out!" I scream at him.

"Electa, you forget your manners." He pats me on the head. I quickly swat his hand away, hoping it hurts. He chuckles at my meagre defiance. "You should treat me with the respect I deserve. After all, I am the one who can give you a new life, when Spartaca has invaded and the people of Latia are freed."

Freedom. The abstract thing I have always dreamed of. But Crew is not motivated by freedom. It is power and greed that drive the men of this world. I keep quiet, refusing to rise to his intimidation.

He raises a rigid arm, fingers outstretched in a strange salute. *"Ave Caesar libertatis."* And with that, he marches from my room.

I sit for hours. The bath water cools until I shiver, but I can't move.

Every time I think of Lix, it destroys me all over again. I throw the covers over my head, hoping the darkness will swallow me whole. But I can't sleep. I think of all the mistakes I have made and hate myself for what I have done, who I have become, and for how I feel about both Ash and Lysander. I hear footsteps from the hall, and a head pokes around the corner.

"Can't sleep?" Ash's smirk has been replaced by a grimace that hollows me from the inside out. It is always a strange sight to see the prince sad.

I crawl out from the mountain of soft bed sheets and plump pillows, piled high like a burial mound. I nod.

"Me neither," he mutters.

"How are you feeling?" It is a stupid question. He grieves, like me, for the loss of a soul so pure, a soul the world didn't deserve.

He sits at the foot of my bed, hunched over, head hung. "Like a fool." He is quieter than I've ever heard him. "I loved him, Electa, and I never told him."

I smile softly to comfort him. "He knew."

He forces his eyes shut to rid himself of the tears that gloss his eyes. "I wish I could have said goodbye."

I remember the way Lix looked in his last moments, the exact curve of his brow, the colours of his eyes, the way his chest heaved with shallow breaths. The memory of it makes me want to retch.

"Sometimes goodbyes hurt more," I say.

His jaw tightens. "Spartaca will burn, I will see to that myself."

I don't doubt his conviction. Spartaca has taken much from him. A sister and now a brother. And yet I get to keep mine. I was foolish to think I could tell him the truth and he wouldn't hate me. I am the reason half his family is dead. But I won't be the reason he dies too.

"Get in line." I sigh as the lie tastes stale on my tongue. I am tired of the deceit, the pretending.

He climbs up beside me. We don't touch and yet he comforts me in a way I never knew a person could. I was always so good at being on my own that I never imagined I would need anyone other than myself. But sometimes it is nice to have company, even that of an arrogant prince.

He rests against the upholstered headboard. "You knew we used to be close, like real brothers before Ember came along. We did everything together. I used to idolise him, worshipped the ground he walked on."

I look at him, his honey eyes like molten gold. "You were wrong, you know."

"Wrong?"

"When you said nobody loved you. Lix did, always."

I remember the times he excused Ash when nobody else could. He always protected him, even to his last breath. He tried to warn me that the real heir still lived. He was trying to protect Ash and his title, I think, as he always did.

He shakes his head, but his movements are weary, as if he is Atlas and the weight of the world is on his shoulders. "I was blind to it, too proud, young and headstrong. I thought myself king of the world."

"And still do," I say with a laugh, hoping to lighten the mood.

But still, Ash hangs his head. "All these years wasted, over a girl, a girl who I never really loved to begin with."

I was always under the impression Ash had been heartbroken by Ember and her betrayal. "I thought you said—"

He silences me. "It doesn't matter what I said. It wasn't love, it was pride, not wanting someone to take what was mine."

"Lix truly loved her," I say with sadness in my voice. I wish Lix could have had the happiness he deserved. His life was one of violence and grief, yet he carried himself with a gentleness unlike any I have ever seen. I hope, now, he has finally found peace.

"I know. And I should have let him have her." Ash's laugh sounds hollow, unfeeling.

We talk about Lix and all the moments they shared. The hours go by, but neither of us tires. Ash tells me of the mischief they caused in the Palatine – whether terrifying servants with the tiger, racing chariots through the gardens, or throwing wild *bacchanals* that the entire city used to attend. We laugh together and cry together, and I think Lix would look down at us from Elysium with a smile on his angel face. But the bliss can't last for long, it never does with Ash. We return to our old ways, bickering like schoolchildren.

"You and Lysander seem close," he says. His manner is offhand, but I sense there is an edge to his words, a bitterness concealed with an easy smile.

I don't lie to him. "I suppose. I wouldn't go so far to call us friends. I don't really know what we are."

He sits up a little straighter. "He certainly seems to have an interest in you." His tone makes me smirk. "Are you jealous?"

"Yes. But you don't mind."

"You're right, I don't."

Again, we laugh. And a part of me forgets where I am and who I am with and all that has happened.

He turns serious again. "It is strange. I've seen the way he looks at you. He has never showed much interest in girls. I always thought he liked men, before you came along."

"I just remind him of someone, that is all."

"Who?"

"He had a fiancée when he was young. She died," I say, expecting Ash to already know.

Instead, his brow creases in surprise. "I have known Lysander a long time and never heard that. How do you know?"

"He told me."

"Well … that says everything I need to know," he huffs, turning his body away.

"What do you mean?"

"Lysander never discusses his personal life with anyone."

What he says only confirms my fears. Trixie was right, Lysander wants me, he has all along. I have denied it for so long but now I see the truth and it makes me shudder.

"Perhaps no one has given him the chance to." Even now I can't admit it, not aloud.

"You care about him, don't you?"

Ash's terse, unforgiving question makes my body stiffen. "No. Not like that," I say quickly, another lie I can't take back. "I don't like what you are implying."

He rolls his eyes, unconvinced. "Be careful. Lysander Drusus is used to getting what he wants."

I have nothing to say to that. I roll over, putting my head against the pillow. "Night."

"Goodnight, Electa."

His presence has been welcome, despite the spat. I don't think I could bear being alone, not tonight. When I am with him, I feel whole. I am not sure if it is because he is Divine or because of something else entirely. Dizziness returns and I don't fight the sensation.

A stranger holds me at gunpoint, his face shrouded by darkness and shadows. Crew stands behind the stranger, roaring with laughter as the gun cracks. My body is numb, and warmth spreads until there is only darkness.

XIX

INTAMINATIS FULGET
HONORIBUS

Untarnished, she shines with honour

I wrap my hands with tape so tightly that I can no longer feel them. Cosimo sits opposite me in the training room. It is morning, and in just a few hours I will fight Ember. One of us will walk away a champion and engaged to the future emperor of Ore. The other will most likely be dead. Cosimo has enlisted the help of a gladiator named Cacus, a former champion, to help me with some techniques before this afternoon. He is bald and brawny, more giant than man.

"I need to tell you something," I say under my breath, conscious of Cacus who is waiting for me in the wrestling pit.

Cosimo bobs one of his knees in impatience. I have been taking my time with the tape, stalling. "Now is not the time. You were lucky to have won the last fight. I sense that Dame Fortune is not feeling so kind today."

I lean forward, my voice a harsh whisper. "Lix told me something before he died."

Cosimo stares at his pocket watch and then points to the tape. "*Festina.*"

Hurry. He clearly doesn't want to listen to me. I look around and am glad when I see that we are now alone. Cacus is bored of waiting and hurls javelins outside the glass doors.

"Alder isn't dead." The words fall out my mouth before I have the chance to stop them.

I have never seen Cosimo's eyes so wide. "Keep your voice down!" But he soon realises that Cacus is no longer here and is oddly annoyed by it.

I throw my hands in the air like a cantankerous child. "You wouldn't listen."

He runs his fingers through his hair, which is now greying. He has suffered much loss; it is no surprise. "Lix told you this?" he finally asks.

I nod, putting the tape aside. "It was the last thing he said to me."

He shakes his head, making a noise of bewilderment. "I saw Alder's body. I was young, but I saw it plain as day. Twenty-one years ago."

I think of the Viscom, a device that could make anyone look like anyone. Skylar had everyone fooled. She made the entire world believe her son was dead.

"Lysander is Alder." Again, the words burst out before I can think.

I swear Cosimo almost faints. His complexion wanes to a sickly yellow. "Dominus, I need a drink," he says, taking a breath. "Have you forgotten all the manners I have taught you? What has possessed you to make up such silly, childish accusations."

He is right, such accusations could get me into a lot of trouble. It is not the place of a girl to accuse or question the most powerful men of the League.

"It is not accusation if I can prove it is true," I say, defiance in my eyes and my heart.

Cosimo scratches his beard and taps his foot against the flagstones. "And how is that?"

I think about how to justify myself, how to explain this all to him. It sounded far more convincing in my head. "It makes sense. He told me he was adopted at a young age and has no recollection of his birth parents, and he also wears a necklace with the letter A—"

He cuts me short with a shout. "Silence." I have never heard my advisor like this before.

Fury burns through me, sweat beading on my fevered brow. "No. I have stayed quiet all my life. I will not let men silence me anymore."

My words startle him. He cowers, his weight shifting from foot to foot, mouth agape.

I take a breath to calm myself. "I will not,' I repeat, my voice gentler now.

"And rightly so," he says. "I apologise, but to accuse Lysander Drusus of falsities is to sign your own death sentence."

I understand now. Lysander frightens him. But he doesn't frighten me, not anymore.

"He told you of his past?" Cosimo asks, his manner calmer than before. I nod, even though I don't know what he means. "If he confided in you, told you of his past, his story, he must see you in his future. Lysander doesn't open up so easily."

I look away to hide the flush of red that warms the apple of my cheeks. Does Cosimo speak the truth? Do Lysander's feelings run so deep? I think of the man they call the destroyer of armies, best of the Appians, and so many more. Surely such a man couldn't have feelings for someone like me. But behind his cool exterior, Lysander Drusus is fiercely alive. He wants his revenge, his twisted vision of justice. A broken man, who never let another soul see him, but me.

"And you care for him too…" Cosimo's voice trails away. The silence presses upon us, crushing me until I can't breathe. He doesn't make light of his disapproval; his features are hardened in disgust. "You are walking down a very dark and dangerous path, Electa. Especially if what you say is true."

"You believe me?"

"I don't know," he breathes, having to steady himself on the ropes of the wrestling pit. "But if Lysander is Alder, as you say, and if he knows, he could destroy everything."

Frustration spills into my speech. "Don't you think I know that? That is why I had to tell you. I know what he is."

Oh the devil, how he makes me weak.

I proceed to tell Cosimo all I learned from Crew's database. He listens silently, and I am not sure if he believes any of it.

"You must tell Ash the truth," he says.

If I don't tell Ash the truth, Cosimo will, I can see it in his eyes. Light filters down from the vaulted glass roof and somehow makes him seem wiser, like the words he speaks are the words of gods.

"No, I can't. He despises Spartaca." Still I find it in me to fight – I think I will until my final breath.

He crouches down, gripping me with both hands. "And you do, too. Convince him off that, fight back against both sides."

"Two against the world. Good plan, Cosimo." I laugh bitterly.

"Two Divines," he reminds me, unperturbed. "You are the only people in the world with the power to change things. Do *not* waste your chance."

I push him away. "I can't do it. Not yet, he isn't ready."

Cosimo stands firm, pressing the frame of his glasses against his nose. "He will never be ready, Electa. But you must finish what you started."

I must right my wrongs. But I am afraid, just as I have always been. I was never brave, or strong or smart. I was just an ordinary girl, destined to be Unchosen, a mindless slave to the Empire. "I am a coward, Cosimo, always have been, this fate was not meant for me," I say.

He smiles, hope in his eyes. "And yet the fates chose this path for you, nevertheless. Ash cares for you, and you for him. It is more than blood that bonds you."

I have tried to deny it, every day since we met, but there is something that exists between us, and it is blossoming. But how do I tell Ash that his entire life is a lie without him hating me for it?

I heave a sigh. "I will tell him after the fight."

Cosimo doesn't allow me to look away. His eyes follow me as I fidget in my seat. "Swear it."

"I swear it."

The metallic armour is cool against my baked skin. It is lightweight and white, but it won't be for much longer. There is something spectacular planned for the arena today and the game master has outfitted me accordingly, with redesigned armour. I trained with Cacus all morning, yet I feel no more prepared. Cosimo looks ill, sipping on his third glass of red wine in the cavern-like dressing-room I have been assigned. We are underneath the arena, and the ceiling tremors with the roistering of the crowds above.

Cosimo hasn't said a word. And when the attendants have left, when even Lucia has finished with my battle paint, he still doesn't speak.

"What happened?" I ask, my voice unsteady and thick with nerves.

His face turns ashen with what can only be fear. He gulps down the wine until there is nothing but residue in the glass. "I did some research of my own. You were right, Electa."

My stomach lurches as if I have thrown myself off a cliff. This is the one time I wish I was wrong.

"As the *Princeps Officius*, I have access to the emperor's personal files and privy to his communication," he explains with a trembling voice.

"And?"

He sighs. "There was a letter from Lysander with blood test results."

"He knows…" My legs go weak. Above, I can hear the groan of the *velarium* as it stretches out over the *Cavea*. I don't have much time left.

"Yes," Cosimo admits with a shaky nod. "I don't know what he is planning, but this could change everything for Latia and Spartaca both."

I gulp away the lump that has formed in my throat. "The entire ULA."

Lysander is going to tell the world that he is the emperor's firstborn, just a matter of days before Ash's coronation. The throne will be his, and Ash will be cast aside. And as for me, I will be tasked with killing Lysander instead.

"Yes, indeed, the entire ULA," Cosimo reluctantly agrees. "There was something else."

But before Cosimo can finish, there is a knock on the arched door of the dressing room. I have a last-minute visitor. A dark-haired man emerges, and the sight of him terrifies me more than it ever has.

"May I speak with Electa for a moment?" He is no less polite than usual but Cosimo is just the opposite, unable to conceal his disgust.

"I suppose so, Director," he says with a huff.

I stare daggers at my advisor as he stays in his seat, not moving an inch.

Lysander coughs, the toe of his leather boots making a soft padding sound on the cobbled floor. "Privately."

Cosimo stomps out of the room, the way I used to when I first came to the Palatine. My bad habits have rubbed off on him, I see. It almost brings a smile to my face. Almost. But reality is brought back into sharp focus when I hear the crowds scream so loud that I imagine their throats bleeding raw. Ember is making her entrance, and the people love her. Only the elite can afford to be here tonight, and she will have the momentum of the crowd behind her.

Lysander holds my gaze, his eyes flickering with emotions I can't understand. He is white like snow, and there is a coolness to his presence that radiates until the room feels like ice. His jaw stiffens until his entire face is but harsh lines and pale skin. "El, we need to speak, after this all over. There is much I wish to tell you," he finally says, reaching out to me with a gloved hand.

Is he going to finally tell me the truth? Is this an end to his elaborate game?

I clear my throat, trying my best to sound normal in front of him. "I may not live long enough."

He fiddles with a serpent fibula that attaches a cape to his martial armour. It is green, like his eyes. He pulls me close into an embrace, the metal hard against my body.

"I can't lose you today," he whispers, his mouth trailing my ear. And it feels like goodbye. He presses his lips against my forehead, and then he is gone, as if he was never there at all.

I stare down at my bare feet as the attendant attaches a button-sized monitor to the back of my neck so the audience can see my health stats on the live feed. The games master hasn't provided me with footwear, luckily. I have always liked the feeling of the earth beneath my feet.

"May fortune be with you, Miss Steel," the attendant says.

I always imagined the attendants that organise such a bloody sport would be robotic, unfeeling creatures. They are not all like that. But his kind words don't placate me. The iron gates open with an electrical, blood-curdling whine, and sunlight pours over me from the cracks of the *velarium*. I look up at the golden portals, casting the glow of the heavens on me. It fills me with hope for the smallest moment. But it is soon stolen away.

The podium set before me towers above the pit of the arena, level with the emperor's box. We will fight up there, not on the ground. The tannoy announces my name and the attendant thrusts me onto the powdery sand of the arena. I squint at the brightness of it all – the sun, the cameras, the light dancing off floating telescreens. When my eyes adjust, there are a thousand faces, mouths moving, but I hear nothing but the sound of my own heart in my chest.

Torches line my path to the stairs that reach the lofty podium. Attendants wearing theatrical stone masks, a tradition of Panore, stand in between each flame like living statues. I wave and bow as I go, emulating all the histrionics Cosimo taught me. Such is the way of a gladiator. It is a performance, after all.

I steady my breathing as I climb the steps and slowly make my ascent, careful not to trip. I push my fillet braids back with the white-gold wreath, I want the world to see me for what I am, the Pleb with over-tanned skin, a bony, protruding jaw and the long hair of a peasant. They will never underestimate me again.

Inside, I am terrified, terrified they will see what I am, terrified to die but I can't show them my fear. I must show them my courage. The pain of my bruising abates as I focus on the steps ahead of me and nothing else. I reach the top, where Ember already stands in armour identical to mine but in a bright Fabian red. She, like me, is barefoot. Black raven's feathers have been woven into her hair to form an ostentatious headdress that makes her look like a terrible bird. Attached to her hands are mechanic Roman claws, which look like they could rip me to sheds. I look at my own hands. I hold a simple snakeskin shield and *gladius* in my scabbard. They must think me boring in comparison.

"Civilians." The emperor's voice rattles me, just as it always has. But now I look at him and see him for the murderer he is. I wonder if he has used the same dirty tricks this time round. But then again, Ember is a bloodthirsty monster already, she needs no encouragement. "Electa Steel." He looks to me directly, and when he says my name, it sounds like a slur. "And Ember Hadrianus will fight for glory, for honour and most importantly for love."

A ripple of applause spreads, the Patricians adoring the pageantry of it all. But Ash and Lysander are motionless on their gilded thrones. Ash can't even manage a smile as the cameras home in on his face.

"Gladiators." Light hits the emperor's eyes at such an angle that I realise they are not black, as I had believed. They are green, the green eyes of a liar, the green eyes of Lysander Drusus. "When the trumpet sounds, the fight will begin. Take your places," he commands.

Golden rings are etched into the marble podium as starting positions. I plant my feet firmly in the circle and take the *gladius* from its sheath. Ember's gaze falls on my trembling hands, and she leers over me like a flesh-eating beast. I expect the low drone of the trumpet but instead there is the gushing sound of … water. I look down over the edge of the podium and see it for myself. A jet of clear water is spilling onto the arena's sands from gaping pipes jutting out of the pit's metal walls. The water rises rapidly until it stops just short of the elevated podium on which we stand. And all I can think is: *I can't swim.*

It is as if the emperor knew. Water is the perfect death trap for me. Ember will barely break a sweat. No. I won't let my fear kill me. The trumpet sounds, the shrill piercing me. Before I have time to brace myself, Ember lunges, dragging me down into the water. She claws at me, snagging my thigh, ripping the skin apart. The sting of water crawling into raw flesh is unbearable. I try to keep my head above water, flailing like a fish might on dry land. Ember, too, struggles to swim, her metal claws weighing her down. She slings the weapons onto the podium, where my sword and shield lie, knocked from my hands as Ember tackled me down. I need to swim back to the podium, to my weapon.

The water pounds against me as I thrash, and mouthfuls of the clear liquid spill over into my mouth and my throat. It feels like poison. Ember is at my legs, trying to drag me down further and further into the abyss. We are equals now, without weapons to defend ourselves. But memories sting, memories of something I can't understand. Fear pulses through me, freezing the blood in my veins. *I can't breathe, the water pours into my throat, coming down over me like an axe.*

I nearly drowned once – I won't do so again.

Ember is strong, with limbs like iron and hands that hammer me down with each measured blow. She grips my hair, forcing my face under the surface. I fight back as much as I can, forcing my head against her hand. My legs are numb from treading water. When I manage to hold myself up long enough, I gulp down the air and hold my breath. She rams me down, and I dive, deep, to escape her clutches. I claw at the water, fighting my way back to the podium, each desperate kick at a time.

I pray for my Divinity, to feel its power coursing through me, but there is nothing but the lonely beat of my heart as I run out of air. The water chokes me, filling my throat and my lungs, and it tastes like death. Ember grips my leg, holding me back. The water stings my eyes, but I see the shadow of the podium in front of me, a glimmer of hope in the eternal darkness. But I am drowning, sinking as the water fills me up. *I close my eyes, and my body is cold.* I reach out, and a fingertip brushes against something solid, something made of stone.

I haul myself up onto the podium with the little strength I have. Coughs and splutters rattle through me, shaking my bones. Ember is behind me, clutching at my armour, but I swing my legs over, collapsing onto the platform, letting the water spill from my mouth.

I can't stay like this for long. Ember will have her talons in me soon. The hum of the crowds cheering and chanting is enough to spur me on. I must stand. I must fight. But when I finally steady myself on two shaky legs, Ember already faces me. She lunges, her fist landing in my throat, knocking the air from me just as the water did. I stagger backwards, but dodge her next attack, stepping to the side. Her momentum carries her forward, nearly off the edge of the podium, but she steadies herself and turns with a movement so quick that she is but a blur as she charges at me.

Her nails are in the gash on my thigh, slowly ripping it apart. The blood streams, warm against my leg, mingling with the water that beads my skin. I yelp as pain floods me. She kicks me back. All I can do is shield my face with my forearm, as her punches come thick and fast. She wants me back in the water where I am at my weakest. This time, she will drown me. I can't allow her the chance.

My sword is at her feet, I glance down, and her eyes train my movements. With one effortless twitch of her leg, my weapon is in the water, sinking to the sand. She purses her lips, satisfied she has disarmed me. I curse under my breath as she edges closer. One step back and I'll be in the water. This time, I dive of my own accord.

I go deeper and deeper, the weight of the water crushing me. The blade glints in the sunlight that beats down from above. My own body fights against me, screaming for me to go up and find the air my lungs so desperately need. But there is a small, obstinate voice urging me onwards. My fingers close around the haft. I kick against the ground, propelling myself upwards to the light, to the air.

I emerge and gasp, devouring oxygen like a starving beggar. Ember leans over the podium, staring down at me with violence in her eyes. This time I am quicker, and with one sharp tug at her legs, she stumbles, toppling over into the water. I clamber out, but she is at my feet. She strains to get a grip on the slippery stone, and I kick her square in the nose. The audience gasp in horror as her nose shatters under my foot. If she survives, at least I will have the pleasure of knowing she will need surgery before her wedding.

Her fury rages, angered by my assault on her beauty. She pulls herself up with ease, sliding beneath my legs. I wave my sword about, hoping to ward her away, but it only serves to fuel her fire. A perfectly placed kick sends the weapon flying from my hands, and she charges at me headlong. Her bony knees pin my arms to the stone, the weight of her body on mine restricting any movement.

Her hands may look delicate, but they don't feel that way as they slither around my throat, her grasp firm enough to bruise, tight enough to kill. My vision blurs as she pants and grunts above me, teeth bared like some ungodly beast. I can't breathe. A burning numbness surges through me like fire and water all at once. It is unlike any pain I have ever felt, and I am not even sure if it is pain at all. Maybe it is peace. I shut my eyes, succumbing to it. *Images and voices flash in the darkness. Lysander's last words. Ash's smile. Vel's caramel eyes. My father's goodbye. Lix's corpse. Cosimo's glasses.*

I can feel my body, even see it, but can't move, speak or even breathe. The piercing squeal of a heart flatlining rings out above. My monitor says I am dead and yet I am not. Ember releases me. But I am painfully aware of what occurs around me. The mob cheers, the sound leaving me cold. They believe the fight to be over, the victory to have been won. But it can't be. It can't.

Suddenly every sense is clear, pure, as if reborn. The events that transpire around me are heightened, the smell of my own blood, the sound of the conversations within the crowds, the feel of my own body heavy like a corpse. And my eyes, even closed, can see clearer than ever before.

"I can't watch this." Ash's voice is an anchor among the sea of noise that submerges me. He sits metres away in a box, out of hearing range for any ordinary person. But I am not quite ordinary. I know that now.

"Don't you dare make a scene here," the emperor commands, imperious and unforgiving.

Confetti rains from the sky, covering my body like snow. Ember prances around the podium, waving and bowing low to her emperor and her prize. This rouses the audience. They stand, raising up flags with the Fabian colours, their palms meeting with a resounding clap a thousand times over. She basks in her glory, roaring some strange and foreign battle cry of gladiators past.

"Lysander, where are you going?" The emperor speaks again, but the man he addresses offers no reply. He has already gone, unable to watch me die. I scream for him to stop, to wait, but my mouth doesn't open, and he doesn't hear me.

This is not over. I am alive. I know it.

And then comes a surge of what can only be power, godly and visceral. Divinity seizes me. I am incandescent, glowing gold, if only in my mind. And I rise.

The heart monitor sounds. The crowds are silent, and I shove Ember to the ground. Her skull thuds against the stone, cracking, splintering into bone dust. I am too strong for her to withstand. The urge to see her blood spill, staining the marble red, is stronger than my control. I will slice her body, twist her limbs, break her bones.

The sword is my hand, and I raise it up, over my head, ready to bring it down over her with a single punishing blow. She raises a solitary, trembling finger, a signal of surrender, of defeat. But I won't spare her. She didn't spare me.

The blade lodges between her ribs, red streams from her like ribbons. A half-breath escapes her and her arms fall futilely to her sides. But there are no cheers for me. Lysander stops dead in his tracks, his green eyes falling on me. I can feel them. A twisted grin forms on my bloody lips as my stare meets his. And then there is darkness.

VERITAS NUNQUAM PERIT

The truth never dies

Dark shapes flash across my half-closed eyes. There are voices too, but I can't make any sense of them. The voices slip away and are replaced by the dull hum of electricity. I open my eyes, and light returns to the world. I am in a room of white tiles and fluorescent lamps. Sleep has leeched into the corner of my eyes, crusted with dried tears. I rub it away and my vision clears.

"You should be dead," a voice says, his accent one I have heard before.

"I wish I was," I reply, weakly.

It seems in the confusion of it all, they managed to keep me alive. *It is a shame*, I think. They should have let me die. They will weep one day that I burned their kingdom down. A man leans over me. He has Umbrian skin but wears the green epaulettes of the Institute on his shoulders. A *Peregrinus*.

He scribbles notes on a large *tabella*. "They're calling it a miracle, a sign from Dominus himself."

I don't know what transpired in the arena. It was like a dream I can't remember when I wake. "What happened?"

He drifts from my bedside to the monitor in the corner of the square-shaped room with a purposeful walk. "Your heart stopped for several minutes, the fight was won, and then suddenly, as if resurrected, you rose from the grave."

It is not the first time. I died once before as a little girl. My father believed me to be gone, only for me to return the next day. There was Divinity in me then, too, and it saved me.

"It isn't the first time such a miracle has occurred, I gather."

How does he know?

"Excuse me?" I almost choke.

"I am Doctor Galen ... pleasure," he says, bowing low. "Your Highness."

My confused stare tells him all he needs to know.

He smiles, smugly. "You won, Electa. In a few days' time, you will be empress of Ore."

I can hardly believe it. I won but at what cost? All the girls I came here with are dead, and their ghosts will haunt me for an eternity. I know that if I close my eyes, I will be greeted by them, so I keep my eyes wide open, unblinking.

"How did you know about—" I begin to ask.

He bends over me. "*Ave Caesar libertatis,*" he whispers. He is another Spartacan loyalist. They must know what happened to me all those years ago. "It seems your Divinity is the only thing keeping you alive."

It is, and I hate it. The brief moments of death I experienced were pleasant, a respite from all that I have endured and all the suffering I have caused.

"I have bandaged your wounds. They have healed, of course, but we must keep up appearances," he says, tucking a pen behind his ear.

I peek under the thin sheets that cover me. My thigh has been wrapped where Ember tore me apart. I am glad there will be no scarring. Today is not a day I wish to remember. But there is a nagging thought in my mind. I lost control in the arena, my Divinity consumed me, and I am scared that Lysander and the Institute saw what I was.

"Did they see? Did they see what I am?" I ask, my voice hoarse from hours of disuse.

He looks at me like I am a fool. "Do you really think you would still be alive if they did?"

No. I am sure the Institute has creative ways of killing people like me. We can endure much, survive most things, but I imagine not a bullet to the head, or being burnt at the stake.

I straighten my back, propping myself up on my elbows, but my entire body feels weak. "What now?"

"The emperor wants to see you," he says.

I knew he would.

A Praetorian stops me outside the emperor's audience chamber. Ash told me once that it was a glittering vaulted room of statues, regalia and portraits. I wait outside for several minutes before the red-suited guard returns. He ushers me through the obsidian-framed door. The room is longer than it is wide, and the emperor sits on his white marble throne, elevated at the back of room. He looks like a titan, and then there is me, a mere mortal cowering at his feet.

My footsteps echo in the vaulted chamber, and as I stand before him, I realise that we are alone. I could kill him if I wanted to. Weapons sharpened and shone by servants are hung on the walls, glinting in the torchlight. He could kill me too; Dominus knows he wants to.

His eyes fall on me, and he scrunches up his face. "Electa."

It is expected, as a visitor to the audience chamber, to make a deep obeisance and kneel at the emperor's feet for the duration. But I won't bow, I won't kneel, I will never go under the yoke again.

I purse my lips. "My Emperor." Coming from my mouth, it is more an insult than address.

His face is set with a sternness I have come to expect. The years have not been kind to the emperor. The portrait that hangs behind him shows a younger and kinder-looking man. "There is something we must discuss," he says.

The emperor is never without his guards so it is a strange sight to see him without his entourage of Praetorians and servants. Alone, like this, he seems only a little more human. I wonder why he has sent them all away. Perhaps he is trying to trick me out of the title I have won. "Is this the part where you tell me I can't be empress even after I passed all your silly tests?" I ask, with bitterness in my tone.

"I wish that was something I was able to do, but unfortunately there are laws in place to prevent such a thing."

Institute laws. The emperor sold his soul to the Institute a long time ago. It is strange that the institution I have hated my entire life is the only thing keeping me alive.

A smile curls on my lips. "That is a shame."

"But you are not empress yet, remember that," he growls. His voice doesn't make me shake as it once did, and as he searches my eyes for fear he finds none.

"Do you expect me to bow down and kiss your feet after what you did?" My words echo off the walls, each sound harsher than the last. I should remember who I am talking to. But I don't care.

He laughs with that cruel laugh of his. "Quite a tongue you have, Pleb."

I don't even flinch at the nickname anymore. But my anger is something I can't contain. I think of Aria and what he did to her. He turned her into a monster. And she wasn't the first Glycias he killed. "You poisoned an innocent girl against me. You tried to kill me!"

He shifts on his throne, his red robes creasing as he leans forwards, and he throws one of his stout arms up and down. "But here you are, alive, a miracle they are calling it."

It was no miracle. Laughter bubbles up from my throat. "You failed and now you will be made to watch as a Pleb sits on your throne."

When he meets my eyes, a spark of rage turns him red. "I see Mr Falto failed to teach you any propriety during your time here."

I am not here to trade blows with the titan. This is the room where he receives suppliants and legates. Official business is conducted here, not petty squabbling.

"Why did you summon me?" I finally ask.

"As I said, there is something confidential we must discuss." His imperious voice fills the room. "I think we both know I don't like you, Electa. But it seems my son does." The words that come next seem to wrap themselves around my throat and choke me of air. "There has been a change to the line of succession." The emperor's shoulders rise and fall as he speaks, his beard scraping against the leather buckles of his cape. His breathing is heavy, and there is a nervousness in the way he speaks.

"It recently transpired that my firstborn son believed to be murdered is in fact alive. Ash will not be the next emperor of Ore," he continues, and I know the name he will say next. "Lysander Drusus is my son and heir. He will be emperor."

My stomach lurches as if I were learning this truth for the first time. I already knew who Lysander was and what he planned, but I didn't take the emperor for such a fool. He forgets his other son who is consumed by a fire so strong that it will burn this entire kingdom down until there is nothing but the ashes and dust of what it once was.

He coughs, clearing his throat. "The coronation will take place in two days' time and he has made a special demand. He wants you, Electa Steel, to be his wife and take your rightfully earned position as empress by his side."

I sense his irritation. The emperor will not have swallowed such a request easily. But he would never deny his favourite, his lost son, the golden boy who enjoyed the favour Ash never did. And Lysander wants to marry me. That terrifies me, but for all the wrong reasons. Spartaca will want me to kill him instead of Ash. *Could I do it?* I would be lying if I said yes.

"You can't do this to Ash, it will destroy him," I say, and cold sadness envelopes me as I realise the emperor doesn't care, he never has.

"It is already done." He slams his fist against the marble. "Ash was never suited to the throne. It is better this way for the League, for the entire ULA."

Perhaps he is right. Lysander is the perfect choice. He was born to rule, born to be an emperor. He has played us all for fools and stolen a throne as easily as snatching an apple from a farmer's tree.

"Have you told him?"

He tears his eyes away from me, and for a moment I believe he feels regret for the way he has treated his other son. "No. But I must be the one to deliver the news. I suggest that you keep that mouth of yours shut for the time being."

This is no request. If I don't stay quiet, he will find some way of punishing me, I am sure. "Someone once taught me never to slight a prince. If I was you, Emperor, I would watch my back," I say, remembering Cosimo's words an eternity ago now. Ash won't step aside so easily.

The emperor tosses his legs carelessly onto the footstool laid before him, adopting a casual stance. "This wasn't Lysander's choice or my own; it was the Senate's. The firstborn son must rule; it is written in the legal codes that have governed us for centuries." He speaks of laws and government as if they were as simple as a farmer ploughing fields with an ox. But I detect the tremor in his voice. Beneath all that indifference, there is fear. I see the emperor for what he truly he is – a coward.

My throat tightens, disgusted by the man that sits on the throne. "You would face censure from the Senate, your reputation would be destroyed. You don't care about your sons, you only care for yourself."

He sighs, his eyes half-closed. "Ash will have the freedom he always wanted."

Freedom. The great lie we are told. "There is no freedom here. I see your Institute shackles as much as you try to hide them."

He waves his hand, dismissively. "I will deliver the news to Ash myself tomorrow. You will go along with this evening's proceedings as usual. That is all."

Ignave. Coward. But who am I to judge? My own heart wants me dead.

Cosimo links his arm to mine so it fits neatly within the crook of my elbow. The light of day has leeched away to darkness, and through the great glass windows of the Palatine I can see the inviting warmth of flickering torchlight. I am outside, breathing the much-needed air I have been deprived of all day. The palace feels hot and tight today, as if the walls will crumble down and the vaulted ceilings will cave in. I couldn't stay there. Cosimo found me here in the rose gardens by following the scent of hibiscus perfume Lucia often uses in my baths.

"You heard the news?" he asks, with a coldness to his voice.

I know what he means. *Lysander.* There is a reason why Cosimo has been occupied in meetings all afternoon. And this is it. I often forget of his duties that don't revolve around me.

"Yes."

We speak no more of it, for there is nothing to be done. Ash will be replaced, and Lysander will rule. I suppose Cosimo is glad for it. Spartaca will no longer wish me to kill his precious prince.

"You certainly look the part," he remarks, looking me up and down. I wear a dress, all white; in the moonlight, I am sure I must look like a ghost. A thick cape trails behind me. It is heavy, and all I can think is that it would stop me from running if I wanted to. But what good would running do?

"There will be a wedding dress fitting tomorrow, with Royce."

The famed *Ornatrix*. She used to dress Trinity, when she was still alive.

"Okay," is all I can manage. A wedding is something joyous, something to be celebrated, but dread strings me up like a puppet and my body is no longer my own. I scuff my feet against the flowerbed, my pearly shoes splattered with dirt. I expect Cosimo to scold me as he always does for such trivial things. But he is quiet, marking my actions with a silent displeasure.

"Are you really going to go through with this?" he asks.

I don't have an answer for him. I need to talk to both Ash and Lysander. And so, I simply say, "What choice do I have?"

His brow furrows, as he tightens the leather strap of his toga and brushes my gown with his hands to rid it of dust and dirt. "We must go. They are waiting for you at the reception."

Cosimo mutters indistinct prayers behind me as he holds up the train of the gown. *He's probably praying I don't trip and embarrass myself,* I think. We come to the room that adjoins the stairwell of the southern ballroom. Chatter can be heard from the crowds below. They are here to celebrate my victory as champion of Imperial Panore and my engagement to Ash. But that won't last for long.

Cosimo presses his palm lightly against the small of my back, encouraging me onwards down the great stone steps. I emerge from the curtains, Cosimo in tow, and polite clapping ensues. Ash stands directly below, standing tall and proud, an olive wreath crowning his chocolate hair. My eyes lock on his as I descend; despite the distractions raging around us, all we see is each other. A sense of calm washes over me for the first time in this dreadful day. A small peace before the storm.

The hall is thick with whispers. The people talk of a new empress rising. They call me *monstrum*, but they don't mean monster. They believe me to be a divine omen from their god. I have evoked both wonder and fear. What is a monster? Because I think I am that too.

I expect a subtle display of affection, but Ash likes to make a show of things. And so he kisses me, but it doesn't feel like before. It is a performance to show the entire world who I belong to now. When he pulls away, he doesn't spare me a glance. Instead his eyes fall on the dark-haired man in the corner of the room.

Lysander. I follow Ash's stare, and when I see him, my heart flounders and my pulse quickens. I have to look away.

The guests in attendance are eager to congratulate me, eager to pander to their new empress. I am sure most of them had hoped to see Ember in my place. But they would never express such sentiments. It is strange to see Patricians revere me in this way. But they are vapid and fickle creatures. I was a Pleb once, just not anymore, not to them or to anyone. When they look at me, they see an empress, a god. It is a small victory that I rejoice in. They bow to me now.

Ash is at my side, conversing with the guests desperate to speak to us. He does the talking, sparing me of embarrassment. I am a no better diplomat than I was when I first arrived. They mostly say the same, wishing us well for the *confarreatio.* "*Congratuliones vobis agimus,*" they say, "*Congratulations to you both.*"

I stay quiet, wishing I were invisible. But a familiar face greets me. Trixie is dressed in all her usual splendour; beautiful flowing fabrics spill from her corseted body. But her face is a spectral shade of pale. I immediately recognise the two muscled Praetorians that flank her. They were with Warren.

"Still waiting for that happy ending of yours?" she croaks. She is careful to ensure that I am the only one who hears. Ash is out of earshot, encircled by fawning senators.

She knew all along what was in store for me. Something stirs inside me, fear and understanding all at once. But I can't make a scene, not here in front of all these people.

"What is going on?" I ask, my voice equally quiet.

Her vulpine features twitch, as if afraid, as a Praetorian closes his hand over her shoulder. "Knowledge is often a curse. And it seems I knew too much."

Trixie Merula, a Spartacan loyalist? But it doesn't look that way. Whatever she was doing for them, it was under duress, that much is clear.

"You were helping them?"

She nods briskly as the Praetorian pushes her away. "Yes. But they won't kill me yet. They still need me."

A thousand questions flash across my mind. But in the blink of an eye, Trixie is gone, the golden epaulettes of her towering escorts just visible above the crowds. Spartaca is not hiding any more. It is in plain sight. Crew knows the end is near and is bringing in reinforcements ready for the takeover. He lurks, his cold eyes trained on me. But tonight, he smiles and laugh with all the joy in the world. I have delivered his kingdom on a silver platter.

The sound of the duduk sends shivers all over my skin. A hand brushes past my own. I uncurl my fingers to see a small paper note. It is from Lysander; I can tell from the elegant cursive alone. The note instructs me to meet him on the terrace in ten minutes. I quickly tuck it away as my breath catches in my throat.

Ash nudges me. "El, what in Dominus's name are you playing at?" The whisper is harsh against my ear. Senators are trying to engage me in conversation, but my mind is elsewhere. I need to get away. Now.

"I am sorry. I need some air."

I push my way through the throngs of bodies that cling together in the humid summer air. The veranda doors have been opened, spilling twilight onto the marble floors. But Lysander didn't mean on the balcony here, so close to the event. I use a winding corridor that leads to the feasting hall, following the scent of truffles and roasted meat. The terrace of the dining hall is quieter, and there is no sound but the scurrying footsteps of servants preparing the feast.

The breeze that whips across my shoulders catches me by surprise. But in an instant a jacket is wrapped around my shoulders. It is forest green and belongs to Lysander himself. His touch lingers on my skin, and the warmth of it spreads all over, like leaking blood. Squinting in the shadows I see him, his squared jaw and green eyes. He grins, and the simple gesture leaves me breathless, as it always does.

"You lied to me." The words come quickly, and there is a bite to them that I hadn't intended.

But Lysander doesn't flinch as I expect. Instead, his grin fades and his dark brows draw together as if confused. "I did no such thing. I simply withheld the truth."

I fold my arms, stepping away from him. "I see no difference." He could have told me the truth that day we spent together in Accensus. He should have been honest with me then.

He counteracts my step backwards with his own step forward. "I was afraid to tell you, afraid you would hate me, afraid of what you might think."

"It doesn't matter what I think." I bristle, closing my body off from him. "Think of Ash, think of all you are taking from him."

I think he senses my feelings for Ash, but he also senses my feelings for him. I don't know which is more dangerous.

His fervent eyes sing like a hymn in the starlight. "I didn't want it to happen like this. It was the Senate's decision not mine."

His words sweep me away just as they always have. I believe them, even when I shouldn't. He has this magic way of bewitching people, crawling into their minds until the only truth is him. "That is what your father said," I say, only as a way of placating myself.

"It is true. Marcus made the ruling the morning of the fight."

Marcus is the leader of the Optimates. I am sure Lysander would have promised him much in return for such compliance. Then, Marcus believed that his daughter would be the next empress of Ore, and that she would marry

Lysander Drusus in Asher's stead. Lysander would become the most powerful man in the ULA, director and emperor both. A more than suitable companion for his beloved daughter. What more could he have wanted? But I ruined his little power play.

That same morning Lysander came to me in the Dome, he was fraught, not at all like his usual composed self. "That is why you wanted to talk to me, why you came to see me in the arena?"

He nods. "Yes."

There are a thousand reasons why I should turn away and refuse his explanation, but I won't, not now, not ever, because Lysander Drusus is a creature designed to torment me for an eternity. He never treated me like a Pleb, a girl, as others did. To him, I was an equal, a grown-up. He bought me cocktails and gifts, made storms in the sky and waxed lyrical about the old mythologies I once adored.

"You could have said no … refused the title." My words are weak, even as I speak them. I can't resist this urge any longer. I can't fight against my own mind, my own heart.

He is a safe distance away and I pray he doesn't step closer. "Perhaps, but the truth is, I didn't want to lose you," he says.

And suddenly it all makes horrible sense. "You're d-doing all this just so I don't marry Ash?" I stammer.

A smirk tugs on the corner of his perfect bow lips. "Of course," he says, his voice like a song. "I had hoped my feelings for you were plain enough to see by now."

"You are a confusing man, Lysander Drusus," I breathe, my body collapsing against the stone pillar, my heart like a drumroll in my chest.

"Electa, I will not force this on you. If you don't want to marry me, you are free to leave this place behind. I will see to it that you are looked after," he says, edging closer. "Equally, I would run away with you, if that is what you so desired. I don't care much for thrones and titles." *That is a lie*, I think, but I don't say it. "The choice is entirely your own. But I am at the mercy of you, as long as you allow me to be."

In this moment, he is ancient and godly. The moonlight hits his face in such a way that he glows and glitters in its milky shade. He looks at me with a softness in his eyes, and it is different to the way he looks at everyone else, as if I am the only person he sees.

I notice now how my hands tremble at my sides. I clench my fists to hide my nerves. "Lysander … I don't know what to say."

"All I ask is that you consider my proposal," he says.

I pause, struggling to find my tongue. "I will, of course."

He reaches out to me, his hand grazing my shoulder lightly, but it is careful movement. When he touches me something visceral burn inside of me, something powerful, something dangerous. "I would give you all that is mine, Electa, my heart and kingdom both, it could all be yours if you wanted."

No one has ever asked me what I want before, so the question takes me by surprise. I have become so accustomed to a life of fear, a life of control, that I have no answer for him. "I don't know what I want, Lysander, and it terrifies me."

I blink once, and his lips are on mine. They taste sweeter than honey and carve into mine with the strength and passion of a god. His hands run over the folds of my gown, every moment delicate and as reverent as worship. I expect myself to crumble under his touch, but instead, I feel whole.

I find the strength to pull away.

His heightened breathing is akin to my own. "Does it still terrify you?"

"It…" But the words die in my throat, and I feel the hot flush of my skin. "I should get back before anyone notices I am gone."

He smiles kindly. "Yes, you go first. I will follow."

I do as he commands, willing myself back inside, but my legs shake beneath me as I walk. I hurriedly flatten out the new creases in my dress. In the shadows of the candlelit feasting room, a hulking figure steps out in front of me. I jump backwards in my fright.

"Have you gone entirely mad?" Warren's tone expresses revulsion. I am glad to see him. I thought Crew had sent him back to war. But here he is, still my shadow, and it seems he saw me moments ago on the terrace.

"Spare me the lecture." I barge past him, hardly in the mood for such a conversation but he catches my arm.

He shakes his head, his expression growing more severe by the second. "Do you even realise what you have done?"

He doesn't know yet of the change in succession, and I suddenly understand his abhorrence. In other circumstances, this could tear Spartaca's plan apart. But instead, I am saving it.

"What Spartaca wanted," I say, matching my contempt with his own.

His eyes bulge in surprise. "Excuse me?"

"You will see."

He opens his mouth, thinking of some snarky response, but no words come out. Instead, screams pierce the air. We both run towards it without hesitation, Lysander quickly on our heels. He grips onto my arm, but I need no protection. I am already a weapon.

There is a stampede of hurried footsteps. They thud hard against the marbled flagstones, sounding from inside. People burst through the doors of the ballroom, piling on top of each other, spilling over. In their desperation, they yell and scream, frenzied and afraid. Hordes of people filter past us, and we fight against the current as best we can. There are splashes of red on their clothes, and they limp – injured by what, I don't know.

Praetorians follow them, fleeing, their weapons holstered. But Warren has a hand on his pistol, playing the part of the brave soldier.

"Fall back. Fall back," one of his comrades urges, but soon he is just another turned back among a sea. Gunshots bounce off the stone walls, deafening my ears.

"What is happening?" I yell but not loudly enough for anyone to hear.

Strong arms pull me back and I realise that it is Ash. It must be, for this is the kind of strength that only a Divine can possess.

"Electa, we have to go," he shouts, dragging me away from Warren and Lysander.

Lysander is reluctant to let me go; the crook of his finger still linked to my own. "Look after her."

Ash nods in acknowledgement. And we run.

Shots ring out in the hallways, and I realise that the enemy is among us. They wear the same togas of any unassuming guest. Ash takes them down with a pistol, and they fall to the ground, dead. He throws me against a wall, shielding me from the bullets that come thick and fast from a doorway further down. Another shot, and the heavy sound of a corpse crashing to the floor follows. His aim doesn't falter, not even once.

"Where are your guards?" I ask, in the chaos of it all. We edge our way along the corridor, our backs firmly pressed against the wall.

"I sent them away to safety. I can look after myself." He elbows through a pile of people, servants and guests alike. They could be dangerous, armed, but Ash doesn't much seem to mind.

I trip over a corpse; my quick feet unsteady in my confusion and fear. The Praetorian's blood is the same colour as his uniform and only noticeable against his now-pale skin. I try not to look at him as I take the weapon lodged under his back.

The skill comes naturally to me. I mimic Ash's movements and take down those who attack us with measured shots. Like him, my aim is unfaltering. I follow closely on his heels, and soon he finds a corridor empty of people and a deserted office that we can lock ourselves in. He shakes with what can only be anger.

"What happened?"

Ash grits his teeth. "Spartaca." His breaths come quickly. "It all happened so quickly."

"Another terrorist attack?" I ask, collapsing against the nearest wall, sinking onto my haunches.

"Not exactly," he mumbles. "Trixie stood up on a table and tried to make some sort of an announcement. She said she had a list of Spartacan operatives undercover in Latia. She began to read off names, and then there were shots. It was chaos. Everyone turned on each other, people ran, and all I could think was that I had to find you."

She was outing Spartaca. She discovered all of those people involved, in deep cover. It was the only way she could reveal the names. There are Spartacan loyalists entrenched in every facet of Latian society, publishing such information would have been an impossibility. When I saw her earlier this evening, she looked ill and conflicted. She knew what she had to do and knew she would die for it. I silently pray that she uttered Crew's name.

"Is Trixie ... dead?" I ask, already knowing the answer.

His expression says enough. "Electa, it was a blood bath." The memory of it flashes across his face for the briefest moment, and I see his fear.

This can't have been planned. Trixie either used to work with Spartaca but came to hate it as I do, or used her sleuthing skills to uncover the bare bones of the conspiracy. I wonder how many were compromised; I wonder if Warren is in danger.

"The strange thing is, I found her list." He holds up a half-burnt piece of paper. "And your name is on it."

My body feels like ice. I can feel my heart shattering against my ribcage. The tremor on my lips can't be concealed by my hand, because they shake too. I feel as though I could implode. I wish I would. I didn't want it to be like this. But my time is up. I have to come clean; it is now or never.

"Ash..." My voice is weak. "There is something you need to know."

XXI

IRA FUROR BREVIS EST

Anger is a brief madness

I can't believe this is happening. My breaths are shallow, too shallow, and I feel as though I might faint. "I…" But the words don't come as I hoped they would. There is a terrible ache in my lungs. I need to tell him the truth, but how? I have to just come out with it. "I work for Spartaca."

His breath catches in his throat. "You what?"

Panic rises inside me. "They have my brother. They will kill him; they will kill me unless I kill you."

His hand is tight around my throat. I am against a wall. A pistol is rammed against my skull. I don't know how I expected him to react, but I certainly hoped it wouldn't be like this. And I can't fight back. Ash is stronger than me, much stronger.

His breaths are rasping and burn my skin like flames. "Are you going to beg for your life, traitor?" There is pain in his voice. I am the reason his sister and brother are dead. And I would have been the reason he died too. The prophecy – he must believe it is true, that it is playing out just as the seer foretold.

"I am not scared of you, Ash. Go on. Pull the trigger." I know he won't. But I am in no position to test him. I need him to listen – to understand.

I choke as his hand closes around my throat for the second time. "You have some nerve, Steel."

My legs go weak as I feel all the blood rushing from my head. "I was going to do it. I would have killed you. Before I saw what you were," I croak. I see hurt in his eyes, but I won't stop, not until he understands. "At first I thought it was coincidence. But it isn't. Spartaca put you here, Ash, gave you a family and an identity so that when the time came it could use you to bring down Latia."

He doesn't believe me. I am a traitor and terrorist, all in the world that he hates.

"Your mother, Skylar, was one of them. But she was not your mother at all. She was pregnant with another boy. Spartaca wanted to make a swap – you, the Divine, for her son." Only now saying these things aloud do I realise how ridiculous I sound – like I am begging for salvation. He will understand. *He will.*

"She wanted to save her son, so she turned on Spartaca. She said that she had killed the Divine child, and that you, Ash, were her real son, not the Divine it had intended to install within the Imperial family."

Each word is a blow that knocks him backwards. He releases me, stepping away, breathing hard and fast.

But I don't stop. I can't. "I assume Skylar sent her child far away, somewhere safe. And of course, as you know, she was executed." At the memory of her death, he flinches. I realise my mistake, but it is too late. Ash is ablaze, a wildfire of rage and anguish.

My voice is small as I cower in a corner. "You're from the world outside the Havens. Spartaca thought you were dead all these years, so they chose me instead to carry out their plans. They wanted me to kill you so I would be the reigning Imperial."

Still he says nothing.

I turn over my wrist, the scar we share now on full display. "It explains everything. Why we are Divines. Our scars."

He has turned from me now. He can't even bring himself to look at me. His Divinity has spun him taller than other boys. Even now, when shaken, he holds himself up with all the pride and strength of a god.

I pant, exhausted from the rush of my words, my desperation to make him listen and understand. "I wasn't going to tell you. I was scared you would hate me and that Spartaca would use you, just like it used me."

I am met once more with his silence. If he weren't standing upright, I might think him dead.

"Can't you see? I was trying to protect you!" I shout now, shaking my fist. But he doesn't see me. I am not even sure he hears me.

My throat is hoarse. "Ash, please! Say something, I beg of you."

Silence presses down upon us until I can no longer breathe. It is as if the world itself is punishing me for my sins. *I deserve it*, I think. *Ash would be a fool not to hate me.*

"But you would have killed me," he whispers.

His words shock me in the way electricity might, and I don't know what to say.

"Would you have done it?" he asks, louder this time.

"Yes, there was a time when I would have killed you."

His laugh stings me like poison. "That is brave of you to admit."

"It is the truth," I murmur, the strength of my voice dying in the air between us. "But I don't feel that way anymore."

He looks at me. The emptiness in his eyes is terrifying, his face very still. "You are the reason Lix and Shauna are dead."

I open my mouth to speak but quickly close it again. There are no excuses for what I have done, for the destruction I have caused. Eventually I say, "And I will suffer for it every day of my life."

"Did you know?"

"No." I sigh. "You know how much I cared for Lix."

His legs buckle and he rests against the desktop. Moments pass, and I wish he would just shoot me. Get it over with. Then his face brightens. He digs his hand into the fold of his toga and uncurls his fingers to reveal a locket. "It all makes sense now…"

"What?" I dare to step closer.

"Trixie gave this to me tonight." He holds it out for me to see. There are a set of initials engraved in the gold. *S. G.* and *C. S.* "It was Skylar's; Trixie was her best friend."

"Whose initials are they?" I examine the trinket more closely.

His hands shake, the remnants of his fury coursing through him. "Skylar Glycias, and Castel Shademoore." I recognise the name. Warren talked of him once, and of his affair with Skylar. But Warren didn't mention that he was a relation. "Castel is the Institute's most wanted criminal. Spartaca's leader."

And now I understand. It made no sense at first, what Trixie did tonight, but she had planned her stunt for years. She wanted to ruin Spartaca, even if it meant her own death.

"This was Trixie's way of avenging Skylar," I breathe, the realisation leaving me cold. Her revenge cost her life. I will not make the same mistake.

"I have been searching for answers all my life." He runs his trembling hands through his hair. "My entire life is a lie."

"I am so sorry that you had to find out like this." I reach out to him, but there is no warmth left on his skin.

He pulls his hand away. "How are you doing this, Electa? Working with those terrorists? They have killed so many."

My throat thickens in fear as I realise I haven't spared a thought for Cosimo, Warren, even Lysander. In the confusion of the ballroom, I was separated from them all. They could be dead. In my selfishness, I have forgotten them. Ash is right. I know he is. But my mind flashes to that day when I saw the world that exists outside ours, and any guilt I feel is quickly replaced with a burning anger.

"And you have not done the same? I've seen it, Ash, all of it. Bombing hospitals, woman and children, entire villages." The rage I have felt my entire life spill from me now, and I couldn't contain it, even if I wanted to.

Ash shakes his head, moving closer. Now it is him pleading with *me*, trying to make *me* understand the terrible things he has done. "I wish things didn't have to be this way. I wish those villages weren't infested with Spartacan loyalists. I wish Spartaca wasn't turning those women and children into soldiers."

I scream, and it is like a battle cry. "And what of the Unchosen? Do you kill them for the same reasons?"

He goes quiet. "What?"

I stride towards him, backing him into a corner. "Don't play dumb, Ash."

"I am not, I swear. I would never authorise that."

I don't believe him.

"Stop lying to me," I growl, my entire body trembling.

He grips me but gently this time as if not to rouse the beast inside me. "El, look at me. I am telling the truth. I swear to Dominus."

But I can't stop my words. "Why should I believe you? You, the drunkard, the pretend hero. You say your life is a lie, but it is you who is a fake. No wonder your father doesn't want you on the throne. You deserve what is coming to you."

He swallows hard, all the colour draining from his face. Words can hurt even a prince, it seems. "What do I deserve, Electa? What do I deserve?" He pushes me away.

I stagger backwards, my back smacking hard against the marbled wall. I let out a cruel laugh. "Lysander is going to be emperor, not you. He is the firstborn, the one who Skylar supposedly murdered. He wants me to be his wife. And I will marry him and end this once and for all. I will kill him." Though I am lying to myself, I must finish what I started.

Ash's fists ball at his sides. His entire life, entire destiny, is crumbling before his eyes, and there is nothing he can do to stop it.

"The emperor made me promise not to tell you." I speak softly now as my rage abates. And it is time the prince saw his father for what he is – a coward. "It is your choice, Ash. Carry on living your worthless life or become someone who matters."

He has no response and his eyes are vacant. The fire is gone, replaced with the sorrow of a thousand lies and betrayals. And I am not the only one to blame – his family is too. He sees that now.

There is a sharp, rhythmic knock at the door, as if it is some sort of signal. I take Ash's gun from the desk. He waves for me to put it away, then unlocks the door and opens it. It is one of his security detail, a Praetorian. I wonder if he works with Spartaca, too.

"My Prince. Miss Steel." He bows low, a fist over his heart. "The emperor has commanded that you should remain in this secure location for the night. We believe the worst of it is over, but the security services will be working overnight to ensure the Palatine is safe by tomorrow."

"How many casualties?" I ask, tentatively.

"Forty-three dead, sixty-seven injured."

I shudder. "Cosimo Falto?" I need to know he is alive.

"Safe, in another secure location."

Thank Dominus for that. I think of Lysander too, but I dare not ask after him with Ash here. If he were dead, we would certainly know about it. The Praetorian leaves us, advising sleep, and I lock the door behind him.

The Institute will cover this up, pretend this day never existed. Trixie Merula, the famous fox, will be erased out of history, forgotten forever. I wonder just how many incidents like these they have concealed over the years. Many, I am sure. But I will remember what happened here tonight. And it will torment me for an eternity.

Ash gives me a fleeting glance, and then looks at me as though I ought to apologise. But I lower myself onto the couch, sprawling my small body across it, while he busies himself with the fire.

He crouches down on the hearth and lights a flame that slowly consumes the wood. From his pocket, he takes the piece of paper that has torn his entire life apart. Trixie's list. He tosses it into the fire. It curls and withers until there is nothing but smoke and embers. Does that mean he is on our side – my side? I hope so. He has a cause of his own now – revenge.

I break the uncomfortable silence that has settled between us. "He is right. Sleep would be best for both of us."

He walks over to the cabinet built into the wall behind the desk. "I have a different idea." There is a rattling sound. He slams the liquor onto the desk, and two glasses. He has clearly decided not to swig straight from the bottle tonight.

"You haven't had a drink in weeks."

He rolls his eyes. "A drink would be best – for both of us."

I am hardly in a mood to argue with him about his drinking habits. "Fine. Just one."

But it is never just one drink with Ash, and within the hour the bottle is empty. It numbs the guilt that weighs down on me a little, and that is enough for now. We don't speak. But I feel comforted knowing he is beside me, even if he is on the floor.

He lies back, body outstretched, eyes closed. He looks almost peaceful. The firelight casts him a warm glow, and the heat envelopes me like an embrace. I wish to have him close, to feel the strength of his body pressed against mine.

But that was another lifetime, it seems. What has transpired tonight will change us forever.

"So how much of it was an act?" he finally says, once the last flickers of the fire have died away.

I fidget at his question. "Some but not all."

"Glad to hear it."

"Do you hate me?"

His cheek twitches, and I think he almost smiles. "I don't think I could ever hate you."

I shouldn't believe him. This is just the beginning. I am sure there are worse things that I will do. I think of my lips now soaked with alcohol, and how they were kissing Lysander just hours ago. He would hate me then.

"I am sorry ... for those things I said." My voice falters. "I didn't mean them."

"You weren't wrong," he mutters.

"I am sorry nevertheless."

He hoists himself up onto the couch but keeps a little distance between us. "Sleep, Electa. After tonight, you won't get much."

I don't know who Ash fights for. Will he fight with Spartaca? With me? I should ask myself that same question. Maybe we both just fight for ourselves. Cosimo once said that together we could change the world and I am starting to believe him.

I am woken by the silence. The warmth of Ash's body beside me is gone, replaced by a startling cold. My stomach heaves. I should have known this would happen. I rub the sleep from my eyes, jumping to my feet. *He must have gone to fetch food*, I try to convince myself.

The door is unlocked. I try to open it, but something heavy is blocking it. I shove with all my might until the door bursts open. I trip, falling face first to the floor. Beside me is a body; Ash's Praetorian lies unconscious. *Stercus.*

The terrible ache rises into my throat and I gasp for air. I have to find him. My bare feet pad against the stone as I sprint through the Palatine halls. They sting, but I breathe through the pain as my speed increases.

I find Institute officials and vigilites at every turn. I avoid them as best I can, but notice the security devices they are installing. Lysander must have ordered it. The emperor values his privacy, but now Lysander will take his place and the Palatine as I know it will change forever.

I climb the stairs to the Imperial quarter. The sight that greets me knocks all the air from my lungs. Four of the emperor's Praetorians are on the ground. They are the colour of corpses, and blood spills from their slit necks. I stumble over, clinging to the pillars that mark the entrance to the emperor's chambers. I steady myself against the cold marble, squeezing my eyes shut as I push against the heavy doors.

The familiar metallic taste of blood is soon on my tongue. Bile burns in my mouth, and I put my hands over my lips to muffle the imminent scream that escapes me.

The flick of a striped tail confirms my worst fears. Ash kneels beside his pet, frozen like some eerie statue. The sound of my steps startles the tiger, but Ash doesn't move. Atlas turns. The underside of his jaw, usually white fur, is now discoloured with shades of red. Ash told me once that Atlas did nothing unless it was by his command. The docile creature that I have come to known chuffs at me in the way an old friend might.

I approach the body, unable to blink, until I stand over it. This is not murder, it is butchery. The sight alone makes me gag. I swallow down the metallic saliva. The mangled body of the emperor lies before me. His organs are on full display, sprouting from his body like ghoulish flowers. His face has been torn apart by claws. If I weren't here in the emperor's bedchamber, I wouldn't recognise the corpse before me. I have to turn away.

My legs buckle and I collapse to the blood-soaked ground beside Ash. The look in his eyes is not one of contempt, or even regret. He is vacant and unresponsive, and this frightens me more than anything else ever could. I say his name over and over. I even shake him until my arms grow weak. *Nothing.*

I have to think fast, move fast. A part of me knows what I must do. All my efforts to shield him will be undone. But there is no other way. Not now. Ash has committed treason. He will be executed, and I will be too. There is only one man who I can call on to fix this. *Crew.*

Ash is drenched with blood, not even an inch of his skin clean of this sin. I shout his name, louder and louder. I haul him up from the ground with all my strength, leading him to the bathroom. He falls into the shower, and I tear the clothes from his body, throwing them into the bath. My own gown is blood-stained, but I don't have time to change.

I run the water over him, and still he doesn't move. The water cleans away what he has done, but it doesn't rinse me of my sins. I am to blame for the brutal end of a man I hated. Perhaps if I had just kept my mouth shut about Lysander, this never would have happened. And now I will pay the price.

I search for the prince's *tabella*, his jacket is soaked with blood, and my fingers tremble as I retrieve the device from the inside pocket. The *tabella* slips from my hands, which are now shaking and slick with the blood of the emperor. I curse under my breath, crashing to the floor and recovering the *tabella* which has cracked on impact. I call Crew, praying that he answers. After my third attempt, he does. I tell him all that has happened. How I compromised Ash and his Divinity that I swore to protect. Crew agrees to fix the mess. He arrives promptly with Warren in tow. They set alight Ash's clothes and my beautiful gown. The emperor's body will have to burn too, I suppose. No one can know it was Atlas that did this, as Ash would be implicated too.

I reluctantly tell Warren that there is an unconscious Praetorian outside the study downstairs. He says it will be dealt with, and I know what he means. Crew will leave no loose ends untied. Warren escorts us to my chambers, unseen, far from the Imperial floor, which will soon be in chaos. Atlas follows, of course, Ash unable to leave his beloved companion behind.

Ash doesn't speak, even here in the safety of my room. I kneel before him, anger and sorrow heavy in my chest. What was he thinking? All I can manage is a simple, "I'm sorry." It is not the death of his father that I console him for, but instead for how I have betrayed him. Ash no longer has a choice; he fights with Spartaca now. Crew will threaten Ash with exposure of his treason if he fails to comply, just as he threatened me with my brother. I am sorry because I sold his soul to the devil and we will both suffer for it.

XXII

SUMMUM IUS,
SUMMA INIURIA

Supreme law, supreme injustice

It is as if the horrors of the night before never existed. The incident will be forgotten; the regenerators will see to that. All memories of the lives lost will be gone forever. The emperor is dead, and I am told that someone has been arrested for the crime.

There are rumours that the emperor's murderer was a Spartacan terrorist involved in the attack last night. No doubt Crew found one of his disposable lackeys to pin the blame on. But I know the truth. The emperor was killed by his own son, and the world will never know.

Cosimo has summoned both Ash and me to his office. We sit in silence like naughty schoolchildren, as we await Cosimo's arrival. The slam of a door behind us makes me squirm in my seat.

"What in Dominus's name were you thinking, both of you?" He brings his fist down hard against the desk. I have never seen Cosimo like this before. It as if I am thirteen years old again, sitting in front of my father as he screams at me for breaking curfew, but I am older now and we have committed a much more serious offence. He leans over the wooden surface, his eyes narrowing at Ash.

Normally Ash wouldn't stand to be talked to in such a manner but, unsurprisingly, he has drunken himself into stupor. He stayed the night in my room, but didn't sleep despite my all my insistence. Instead, he downed the entire contents of my untouched liquor cabinet.

I give him a sideways glance, mimicking Cosimo's disapproval. "He hasn't said anything for hours, so don't expect much by means of response."

Cosimo huffs in his typical flustered fashion. He takes the glass of water from the desk and throws the liquid in Ash's face. But the disgraced prince barely flinches. This only angers Cosimo more.

269

"Ash, you will explain yourself!" But his words continue to fall on deaf ears.

I take another look at Ash, water dripping from his hair, running into his shirt until it is soaked through. He doesn't even bother to wipe the water from his eyes. He is catatonic.

"You're wasting your time." I sigh, edging my seat away from his as he slumps dangerously towards me. He tries to pull himself upright but ends up toppling over onto the floor.

Exasperation runs over Cosimo's face. "Oh well, that's just brilliant."

"Told you." I smirk.

Cosimo collapses into his chair, running a hand over his face. I notice the darkness beneath his eyes and consider the many sleepless nights he has endured. The murder of an emperor has sent shock waves through the Palatine but soon it will be another forgotten day erased from the records and from the minds of the people. It is the one thing I wish I could forget. My mind flashes to his blood that puddled on the gleaming marble floors, and the way bones stuck out from his skin.

"Do you know what they are saying about him?" Cosimo asks.

I shake my head. "No."

Cosimo holds the *Acta Diurna* up to my face. The headline reads "Drunken Prince ousted by his father's dying wish".

"He is not doing his reputation any favours with this sort of behaviour." Cosimo's gaze trails to the prince. There is a sadness in him that I understand. Ash is no longer the boy he knew; he never will be again.

Cosimo straightens his collar, brushing himself off, and puts on his fakest smile. He is trying to be brave, even now. I suppose someone has to be. He props up his chin with his hand, and I notice the gold of his wedding ring glinting in the firelight. He has lost more than any of us. "Crew is untroubled by the change in succession. Marcus Hadrianus read out the Imperial decree pronouncing Lysander emperor this morning in the Senate. There will have to be an official ceremony, of course, which will take place tomorrow, alongside the wedding."

I can't hide the grimace that settles on my face. It hasn't quite sunk in. Tomorrow I will be wed. It is not unusual in Latia to marry at a young age. A girl who has survived the Choosing is expected to be wed within the year. It is tradition that has been with our people for centuries. But as with most traditions, they originated from greed. A husband will often profit from a dowry.

He continues, drawing in a sharp breath. "Crew has said we will proceed with the plan as if nothing has changed. And if we are honest, this has done us all a favour. Ash keeps his life, Electa, you save your brother, and life goes on."

"Life goes on?" I almost choke.

Ash rumbles beneath me, making soft moaning noises, an amalgamation of slurred murmurings.

Cosimo clasps his hands together. "Electa, every man is the architect of his own fortune."

I am certain Cosimo is going to run out of clever maxims eventually and everyone will be better off for it. I roll my eyes. "We just go on with our lives as if nothing happened?"

"Exactly." He nods fervently as if this is something he says to himself every night to help him sleep. "Last night was a setback, but fortunately a man named Warren Shademoore has been arrested and imprisoned this morning for the emperor's murder."

I am sure I can't have heard him right. Crew surely wouldn't sacrifice the life of his chief operative in Ore. "Warren Shademoore?"

"Yes, he was a Praetorian in the palace."

Like a shadow, I slip past the hordes of officials and vigilites that swarm the halls. My stomach is churning. Instead of taking a left towards the servant's quarters, I make a sharp right, dashing down the narrow stairway that seems almost naked in comparison to the rest of the Palatine. There are no paintings or stucco carvings here. Ash told me once of the palace cells. He said he used to hide down there as a child because no one would ever come looking. And I can see why.

The stone is dark, unlike the smooth marble of the palace above, and the air is thick with a smell I can't describe. A vigilite is posted outside the iron-barred threshold. He bends low at the sight of me. A few weeks ago, even servants forgot my name. It is strange how much has changed.

"Miss Steel." The vigilite slides his visor up so I can see his face. He has tiny little eyes that remind me of a rat.

"I demand to see the prisoner." I force out a voice that I barely recognise. It is strangely empowering.

One of his tiny eyes twitches as he cowers before me. "We have orders from the director. No one is allowed in or out," he squeaks.

This is no time for the manners that Cosimo taught me. I never listened much to him anyway. It is my nature to be cruel. "Tomorrow I will be empress, who are you to refuse me?"

"Let her in."

Lysander steps out from the shadows of the staircase, his eyes red. He cries for the father he has lost. He must have known Warren was my guard. But why would he let me in to see a dangerous terrorist, the murderer of his father? Is this his way of warning me to stay in line? The faintest smile touches on his lips. I turn and walk into the darkness.

Warren is bound by iron fetters. The skin that fringes the metal chains is bright red, and he winces in pain at the slightest movement. His head is hung; he seems embarrassed for me to see him like this. His hands have been tied behind him, and his shoulders protrude at an unnatural angle. The muscled boy I once knew is as gaunt as a beggar on the streets.

"Why did you come here?" The low growl of his voice makes me shudder. I am not welcome.

"I had to…" The words stick in my throat, and I can't say any more.

He strains to lift his chin, and all the colour has drained from his cheeks. His skin is bloody and his eyes swollen, threaded with purple veins. There are no cameras. I suppose they don't want anyone to know the terrible things that happen here.

"You had to what? Check I was still alive? Well … I am, and I am sorry for it." His anger frightens me. His blue eyes shine, even now in the darkness. I search them for the tiniest glimmer of hope but find nothing. He wants to die, and I think he feels like he might deserve it.

This is Crew's punishment. Warren helped me and betrayed his cause. Warren is here because of me, because of what I made him do. "This is my fault, isn't it?" My guilt will drown me soon. I have been treading water for a long time.

Every time Warren goes to open his mouth, the skin on his lips cracks a little more. Blood slips from his bottom lip, running down his chin. I want to wipe it away but there are bars between us. "No. It is mine. I fell for your act, I pitied you. I have no one to blame but myself."

I swallow down the lump that has formed in my throat. "Warren … I am so sorry."

"Ironic, isn't it?" He laughs painfully. "I saved your life, and because of you, mine will end."

His words sting.

"I'm going to fix this, to get you out of here, I swear," I say, a newfound resolve igniting within me.

He grunts, shifting in his chains. "Don't make promises you can't keep. Don't give me hope."

My fingers snake around the iron bars. I cling to them as if this will in some way bring me closer to him. "I won't let you die."

But he takes no notice and his head sinks into his lap.

"I can't believe he would do this to me. My own brother…" he mutters.

"Your brother?"

He bobs his head.

I should have known. "Crew is your brother?"

"This is his sick way of punishing me … I choose you before him … you before our family … before his beloved Castel." His words tumble out between hacking coughs that shake his entire body.

I can't believe Crew would do this. I knew he was cruel, but Warren is his brother, his blood. He mentioned Castel, the leader of Spartaca who Warren told me of once before.

"Castel is your brother too?"

"Yes. An evil bastard. I hope one day you have the pleasure of meeting him."

I can't blame him for hating me. The thought of him being nailed to a cross and knowing I would be the reason for it makes my blood run cold. I may as well have signed the sentencing document myself. But my hatred for Crew burns more fiercely than ever before. I will do his bidding no more. I fight for the people I love, and that is stronger than any cause.

"I am going to right this wrong," I thunder, and the bars rattle under my touch. As I turn to leave him behind, I make a promise to myself. This won't be the last time I see him. Before I return through the narrow passage, the sound of his voice pulls me back.

"Don't trust them, El, any of them."

I don't.

Lysander is waiting for me when I return from the cells. He is unchanged from the night before, and darkness edges under his eyes. I am used to him looking like a god, so it saddens me to see him like this. But I can't afford to feel these things. I must kill him after all. I smile at him as I pass, eager to be away and gather my thoughts, make some sort of plan to free Warren and still save Lana and my brother.

Lysander catches my wrist, dragging me back in front of him. I should have known I wouldn't have gotten away so easily. "He will be sentenced this afternoon, and we will both be attending. Supreme law will reign, and that boy will pay with his life for his crime." His words are harshened in warning, as if he suspects me of harbouring sympathy for my guard.

"He deserves it." The lie rolls off my tongue.

He brushes his hand over my temple, drawing me close. "I knew he was your guard. I am sorry for it." His tone softens. But even now, I must tread carefully.

I press my lips together, trying to think of some excuse not to attend the trial of my friend, my ally, but none come to mind. "And what of Ash, will he be attending the trial?"

Lysander looks amused. "He is welcome. He is still a prince, after all." His response is measured, as he doesn't wish to offend me. Behind his words I sense that he likes Ash just about as much as Ash likes him. Which is not much at all.

I put aside my hatred for the emperor and comfort the grieving man who stands before me. He finally had the father he always wanted, only for all of that to be taken away. Tragedy runs in the veins of the Ovicula men.

Tentatively, I slip my hand into his and squeeze it lightly. "I am sorry for your loss."

He sighs, my skin burning under his touch. "My father never approved of my feelings for you."

No, he wanted me dead, I think. "If you are having second thoughts—"

He cuts me off, the sweetness of his voice swallowing my words. "I am not. My father was the bravest man I knew, but he was never the cleverest."

He stares at me for a moment, and I can feel my bones crawl. I think of last night, his lips on mine and the terrible thing I have done. His father's blood is on my hands.

"He didn't want you marry me." My voice is low.

He runs his hand over the marble bust beside him. I think it might be Romulus, as the sculpture has the same curved nose. "No, he didn't. He told me once that you had the power to destroy me."

And he was right.

"Do you believe that?"

His eyes sweep over me in one fluid motion. "*Dulce puella malum est.*" *The girl is a sweet poison.* "The last time I loved, it ruined me. I don't think I could endure that pain a second time."

He stares into the space between us, and then something snaps inside him, his entire body is drawn tight. I put my hand to his shoulder, but he recoils as if I have hit him.

"My mother, she hid me away from the world, erased my memories of her and my father," he says, his voice as soft as a whisper. "A Plebeian family raised me, but they were unkind. The father used to beat me, worked me in the fields until my hands were raw."

"But the regenerators?" The brutality he describes is not supposed to exist in our *perfect* world. The regenerators eliminate destructive thoughts that could pose a threat to our society. They cleanse the mind, condition it until a perfect citizen exists.

"Regenerators can cure many things, but they can't make a person kind," he breathes. "There is an old proverb. A fox may change its skin, but never its character. I am sure you have heard it."

"My father used to say it." When he said it, I used to cry. I cried because I was the fox he described. I wanted to be a gladiator, a goddess, but my father liked to remind me of who I was, and who I will always be. *A Pleb.* The Patricians can dress me up in their silk gowns and hand-stitched *stolas*, but I will never be one of them. It used to make me sad, but now it makes me proud.

Lysander continues, laying his heart bare. "When I was thirteen, I ran away to Cassida and begged to become a soldier. I was too young, they said. But I returned every day for a month, banging on their gates until they tired of me. They made me their errand boy. I would prepare the meals for the cadets, chop firewood, fetch water, wash uniforms."

Every word sounds fresh and new. These are things he has never said before. But I see the composure, the character he has so cleverly played, slipping away. He is slowly unravelling. And as I look upon him now, I see a boy deprived of a life that was rightfully his, a life another lived in his place. Once I thought him a god, but he is painfully, tragically human.

"I proved myself, and a year later I was a cadet. The emperor visited Cassida and liked what he saw. He sent me to the front when I was just fifteen."

Fifteen-year-old boys don't often become soldiers. My brother was only supposed to train at Cassida this year, at seventeen. He would have to complete two years' mandatory training before he ever stepped foot on the front.

"You haven't spoke of this before, have you?"

The green light in his eyes flickers and dies. "No." Sadness envelopes him, and it makes me ache. Lysander is not the man he pretends to be. But he is still the man who sends innocent children to their deaths. He is still the man that steals freedom from his people. I must remember that.

I try to reassure him. "Do not let your past define you. Tomorrow, you will be emperor, and the world will bow down at your feet. They will kneel. They will write legends after you."

He throws his head back in sour, cynical laughter that makes me shudder. "Legends are full of lies. I thought you knew that by now."

The whole world believes him to be a hero, a saviour, a protector. But underneath it all there is pain and suffering, a childhood of cruel parents and calloused hands. Those are the things a legend will never tell. Just as he says, legends are full of lies.

He takes my hand, folding it into his own. He holds me like I am his truth, his past and future. "Last night I don't remember you telling me your decision."

I bite my lip. I don't think I will ever be ready to give him my answer, knowing it will be his destruction. "I didn't."

Suddenly he kneels, still cupping my hands. "Electa Steel, will you do me the honour of becoming my wife?"

The way he says my name makes me think I have been pronouncing it wrong my entire life. I know what I have to say, I know what I have to do.

I can't stop my voice from shaking. "Yes, I will."

The next thing I know are his lips. He kisses me just as he did on the balcony. I am an anchor in his storm of grief.

But I feel the burning stare of another's eyes laid upon us. Ash storms down the corridor, his eyes raking over us, and I feel myself catch fire. He has been standing there far longer than I would have liked. I step away, instinctively, knowing better to stand between a drunken prince and the emperor of Ore.

Ash shoulders his way past me, before grabbing handfuls of Lysander's jacket in balled fists, slamming him hard against the wall. The sound is so loud I expect the marble to crack and dent. Lysander doesn't so much as flinch. His expression is neutral, and I think that angers Ash more. I hope Lysander doesn't feel his godly strength.

Ash spits, and the saliva makes a loud smacking noise as it lands on Lysander's face. "You bastard. Not enough to steal my throne, was it? You had to steal her, too." He speaks like some frenzied beast. He is losing his mind.

With one swift movement, Lysander twists the prince's arm and holds him against the wall. Ash is not so drunk that he reveals his Divinity. *Thank Dominus for that.* Lysander is strong, I know that, but the only reason Ash is up against the wall is because he wants to be. The commotion has sent an entire troupe of vigilites flying around the corner. Lysander releases the prince, who is swiftly restrained by his guards.

"My Lord, should we take him to the cells?" says one of the men.

Lysander wipes the saliva from his face with a handkerchief.

"He's drunk. Please ... he just needs to sleep it off," I blurt out, unable to stop myself from protecting the prince. Weeks ago, I would have rejoiced in seeing Ash in a cell. But not now, as we still have a long fight ahead of us. I plead for Lysander's mercy, and he grants it to me. His guards are shocked; to them he is a god, and I make him weak.

"Take him to his chambers." He waves the vigilites away.

Ash doesn't look at me as he is dragged from sight. I am glad he doesn't. I can't bear to see him like this. Lysander has no idea yet, but he has created a monster.

The Imperial courthouse has only been used once before, to sentence an empress to death. I sit on a balcony above the spectator area, Lysander at my side. We are both dressed in black, the colour of mourning. It is not the emperor I mourn, but Warren, the innocent boy who will be sentenced to death here today. It should be Ash; it should be me.

My engagement to Lysander was announced in a broadcast this afternoon. It has sent Latia into a frenzy. There have been calls for interviews and press conferences. But Ash is in no state for such things, and neither is Lysander, who weeps silently beside me for his father. The damning press reports haven't done Ash's foul mood any favours, and he is not even here, at the trial of his father's murderer. Cosimo tells me he is drinking himself into oblivion. I almost wish Lysander put him in that cell.

Reporters and senators are seated in the assembly chairs below. They stood as we made our entrance, chanting our names and soon-to-be titles. It made me squirm. Soon they will be dead, and Spartaca will reign. Crew is already grooming Ash to take over Spartaca's kingdom in the east, or so Cosimo tells me. I am sure he leapt at the opportunity. At least he will have somewhere to rule, a throne to sit on and a crown of his own to wear. Power has always ruled his heart, as much as it pains me, and I don't think even I can change that.

As for me, I will kill Lysander, because as long as he lives, no one will be free. Next, I will kill Crew for all he has cost me, all he has cost his brother and Cosimo too. As empress, I will order Warren's release if they don't kill him first, and flee the Haven with Lana and my brother. At least, that is the plan.

Warren is lead in by armoured vigilites, still wearing his chains. But they have done him a small mercy by bathing him and painting his face to hide the horrors he has suffered. They won't let him die ugly. Angry murmurs rumble through the crowd as his chains clatter against the polished marble floor. To them, he is a cold-blooded killer who didn't even leave behind a body to bury. To desecrate the dead is a crime worse than murder.

I can't see his eyes, and I am glad for it. The vision of him in those cells, beaten within an inch of death, will haunt me every day so long as I live. His fate is one worse than torture. The judge, an elderly woman with cropped grey hair and a mean stare, orders him to stand behind the marbled lectern on the dais set beneath her. He abides, shuffling up the two steps of the dais in his manacles.

Whispers ripple through the crowds. "Did you know he is Castel's brother?" I hear one senator say. "He deserves a punishment worse than death." A female reporter clutches a serpent emblem, her head bowed in prayer. "Dominus will make him suffer."

Warren pleads guilty, of course. The trial is for show, a demonstration of supreme power, justice and law, or rather, in my mind, supreme injustice. The verdict has been preselected by none other than Lysander himself, the man famous in four Leagues for his lies, and soon to be emperor and director of them all.

He proceeds to recite a manufactured story, in which he claims that Trixie Merula was serving as a distraction so he could slip away and murder the isolated emperor, many of his guards having been killed in the earlier attack. It is believable to everyone here but me. I know the truth, and Trixie Merula was no distraction. *He didn't do it,* I want to scream. But I must play my part – the cold and powerful empress who would kill a traitor with her bare hands.

There is no prosecutor to interrogate him, nor a lawyer to defend him. He has never looked so alone, standing in a room full of people. His voice trembles when he speaks, and I realise that even a soldier born and bred can be afraid. They would have tortured him all day, trying to uncover Spartaca's secrets. But they will have found none. Like my father, Warren has an implant in his brain that blocks the magical power of the regenerators.

The judge stands to deliver the verdict. There is a coppery taste in my mouth, and I realise I have drawn blood from biting my lip. I want to shut my eyes, but I feel the cameras on me, their electricity dancing on my skin. My senses are heightened as a Divine, and this is one of those times when I am not thankful for it.

"Warren Tanner Shademoore," she addresses him. "You are hereby found guilty of treason and sentenced to death."

It is no surprise, but I feel like there is a heavy stone in the pit of my stomach, nevertheless.

"The execution is date is set two days from now, *post-meridiem*. Death by *Crucifixus*."

Crucifixion. An ancient punishment reserved for the most heinous of criminals. The thought of it makes me sick. Warren will be stripped bare and scourged. He will be made to walk the Via Sacra into the forum and will carry a heavy stone *titulus* that describes his crime. Finally, he will be nailed to a wooden cross and left to die slowly. His body will be devoured by terrible birds, and there will be no one to collect his bones. And I will be forced to watch.

The vigilites lead him out. His eyes find mine, and all I can do is stare back. I know what he thinks as he looks at me: *She can't save me.* He has known it all along that I can't become the murderer they want me to be. I once told Ash that goodbyes hurt more, and watching Warren walk away from me to his death is the hardest farewell of them all.

XXIII

DUCUNT VOLENTEM FATA, NOLENTEM TRAHUNT

The fates lead the willing and drag the unwilling

The half-light of dusk paints the city in a sepia glow. It reminds me of an old photograph that my father used to keep in his bedside drawer. When he went to war, I would steal the photograph and pin it to my wall and put it back in the drawer upon his return. It is the only picture I have of my mother. Maybe she is out there somewhere still, and maybe one day I will find her.

I await the arrival of Royce. She has her own studio in the Palatine, since her services have often been solicited by members of the Imperial family. Racks of ivory cloth crowd me into the centre of the room, on a rather lonely chair facing the unframed window that overlooks the city.

I hear the sound of a door flinging open. A petite woman wearing oversized spectacles and an ankle-length fur coat storms into the room. In one fluid movement, she wiggles out of the coat and chucks it to the floor. I can't stop my jaw from dropping.

"You must be Electa." She dips her head, looking me up and down. Her arms are folded, and she wears a pensive expression that evokes judgement. But I still can't see her eyes. "You're prettier on the broadcasts."

"Um … thanks," I mumble, finally finding my tongue.

She ruffles her short black bob with a jewelled hand. "It looks like I have a lot of work to do, better get started."

She removes her dark frames and flings them across the room. They land on a sewing desk littered with all sorts of junk: crumpled paper balls, half-written letters, threads, thimbles and needles. She measures me first, sighing after every reading as if disgruntled. I keep my mouth shut when I usually wouldn't, as I am tired and don't have much fight left.

She spends more time gossiping than dressing me. I still know little of the Patrician world and the people that inhabit it. She spills their secrets, and I begin to wonder how she could possibly know so much about so many. From senators having affairs, to noble-born Patrician woman becoming expensive concubines, she tells it to me freely. I don't encourage her, rather quite the opposite. The gossip goes over my head, and her voice eventually is reduced to an annoying drone in my ear.

Finally, my prayers are answered and she dresses me silently. Each gown is beautiful in its own right, and I will have trouble choosing only one for tomorrow. But when I look at myself in the mirror, all in white like some chaste being, dread crawls into my bones. This is not a wedding dress. It is more suited for a funeral – *my* funeral.

"You dressed Trinity, didn't you?" I say aloud without meaning to.

Just the tiniest bit of conversation and she comes to life. "Yes. Her parents paid me a lofty sum." In her excitement, she draws one of the shoulder straps too tight, and I yelp in pain. She quickly adjusts it, a rather unapologetic smile on her face. "Do you know how she really died?"

Yes, actually, I am one of the few people who does, I think. But, instead, I repeat the lie the world has been told. "She committed suicide."

A rattling laughter seizes her body. "You believe that?"

Royce does seem to know everything that happens here in the Palatine. Perhaps she has heard the truth. She glares at me, expecting an answer.

"I have heard rumours that Spartaca may have been involved," I mumble, almost hoping she doesn't hear. I shouldn't know this, and neither should she.

Again she cackles, the shrill sound of it piercing through me. "Oh no, my dear, it was not Spartaca, nor was it suicide." She seems to take pleasure in conjecture like this. It seems that she almost breathes it.

I furrow my brow, unconvinced. If not Spartaca, then who? "And you know this how?"

Royce cocks her head to the side, bemused by my question. "I know everything, sweet, can't you tell?" A twang to her voice makes my bones shiver. She is certainly not Latian.

"I am surprised they haven't taken your tongue," I say, bitterness edging into my voice.

If she notices it, she doesn't react. "One day they will, but at least I have my looks."

I now look at her properly as she faces me, altering the hemline of my dress. She is beautiful in an unusual, almost striking way. Her red lips are pursed as she concentrates on the task at hand. She would be much more tolerable without her tongue.

I don't much like the insipid gossip she spouts, but my curiosity is getting the better of me. "Who killed her then?"

Her blue eyes light up like a beacon. "I was on my way to prepare her for the celebration, the night after she fought Valentina. But you'll never believe who I walked straight into when I left to fetch some fabrics for her gown."

I humour her. "Who?"

"Lysander Drusus." Just the mention of my betrothed's name sparks my attention. "I thought it strange to see him in Trinity's corridor. After all, what business could he possibly have with her?"

I don't know where she is going with this, but my silence encourages her to continue. She has put aside the needle and thread, so I know what she says must be of some importance.

"I followed him, of course. He went into Trinity's room. I hid behind the bathroom door and heard the whole thing."

"What did he say?"

"He said he would retrieve her brother from the outside world if she conceded from Imperial Panore."

I nearly fall off my stool as I jerk. The sound of the restricting fabric of my gown tearing at my waist makes her scowl. "What?"

But her displeasure quickly subsides as she eagerly continues her story. "I know. Scandalous, isn't it?" She sits a little forward on her footstool. "You could say I was surprised when Trinity turned down the offer since all she could do was moan about her bloody brother." Every word she speaks seems to smack me around the face.

"She said no to Lysander?"

"Yes. A brave and foolish thing to do." My thoughts exactly – no one says no to Lysander Drusus. "She said she was going to win, and when she did, she would end the Choosing forever."

I almost respect Trinity for standing by her convictions. But surely Lysander had other ways of keeping her quiet. He has multitudes of Institute technology at his fingertips, and silencing her would be little trouble at all. But a terrifying realisation overwhelms me. This was not about him silencing her. It was about her not fighting *me*.

Cosimo once told me that Nemesis had trained Trinity herself. Ember had a lot of talk, but no one had technique like Trinity. I don't want to believe it, but Royce's suggestion is clear.

"And your point is?"

"Darling, no offence intended, but she would have easily put you down in that arena."

She is not wrong. Trinity would have bested me in the time it took Ember to tackle me into that water.

She moves to sit beside me and begins work on repairing the mess I have made of her masterpiece. "Lysander didn't want her to fight you, because he knew you would lose."

Suddenly my entire body freezes over. But I still can't bring myself to believe what she is intimating. I am a liar, always have been, my tongue was made to deceive. But I am the greatest victim of my lies. I have fooled myself into thinking that Lysander is not the monster he seems.

I still find it in me to protest, though. "That's a bit of stretch, don't you think?"

"I don't know, is it?" she says with a shrug. "Love drives people to do terrible things."

"So, what you are saying is—"

She interrupts me. "He killed her, almost certainly."

I think of the conversation I overheard at Crew's villa only days ago. Lysander's words play over in mind – "Let's just say I don't want her to die." Oh, I knew Lysander was clever, but this is genius.

Spartaca was the perfect scapegoat for his crime, and Crew would never deny that he was one responsible for such an act. He wanted to scare people, he wanted to scare me. And then there was the added brilliance of labelling her death as a suicide to appease the masses. The Latian state would descend into chaos if the horrors of Spartaca were ever to come to light.

But this is silly rumour, and I would be a fool to believe her. Spreading salacious lies is what gives this woman life. "I don't believe it. Lysander … he wouldn't do that." But even my own body fights against the lies I tell myself. My stomach clenches, and my body is damp with a cold sweat.

She licks her lips, as if pleased with the trouble she has caused. "But say he did; would you still want to marry him?"

"I don't think that is any of your business," I snap, tired of her stirring.

She makes a clucking sound with her tongue that only serves to anger me more. "There, there, Electa, you are not empress yet."

But I will be soon, and it is not me she should fear.

I tilt my head, mimicking her. "Royce, a piece of advice from a rather naïve and out-of-place Plebeian girl. Keep that to yourself, or he will take your tongue, almost certainly."

She doesn't speak again, and I welcome the silence. I dismiss her and undress myself. The end is near, and I must do the only thing I know how – lie, trick and deceive – better than Lysander, better than them all.

The day slips away faster than I am prepared for. Stars stud the unspoilt night sky, but they are about as real as the people that walk these halls. For the first time, I consider Lysander's offer. I could run from this place and no one would stop me. But I remember my brother, Lana and all the lives I have sworn to protect. And what good would running do?

Instead, I go to a place that will renew my faith and give me the clarity I so desperately need. Ash has gone mad, and Cosimo is preoccupied with the wedding preparations. There is no one for me here. And so I run – through the woods, down the hill, past the bend in the river where Ash taught me to fight. I run until my legs are weary, until my breaths dry my throat.

My nightgown fluttering in the breeze is the only sound in the forest this night. It is as if the place itself mourns for the ashes buried here under the dirt. The earth is soft under my bare feet, slipping through my toes like silk. The stone tomb is modest, not at all like the ungodly monuments in the Imperial Gardens that mark the resting place of the emperors gone.

Lix told me he wanted to be buried in a place where no one would come to mourn him. He didn't want to be mourned. In our religion, mourners spill blood onto earth that covers the dead. It is a sacrifice to keep the soul alive. But Lix didn't like the taste of blood – he had tasted enough for one lifetime, he told me once.

I sit before him, hoping he somehow feels me there, the weight of me above him. I may not believe in gods, but ghosts are real, and I know this because they haunt me even in sleep, even in death. As I exhale, the coolness of the night turns my breath into a fog that dances in the air. And then I feel him, a warmth in my bones, a light in my eyes, and finally his voice, soft, inaudible murmurings in my ears.

I don't know what he says, but I feel him all the same. "I am sorry," I breathe. He understands. The dead see all – he knows what I am and the terrible things I have done. But his warmth doesn't leave, and I believe it is forgiveness.

"I thought you might be here." The voice startles me, and suddenly I am cold again. "I hope I haven't disturbed your mourning."

I am not mourning, you silly fool, I think. Lix wouldn't have wanted me to mourn.

Lysander emerges from the shadows of the forest. Sometimes I think a shadow is all he is, a shadow of a good man that existed a long time ago. "Cosimo told me you haven't eaten a bite today. The kitchen staff told me you like pomegranates."

He places the fruit in my palms.

"Thank you," I mumble, only now realising the ache of hunger that growls inside me. I tear into the fruit's skin with my teeth, not much caring how I must look to my betrothed. The red juice runs down my chin. It is thinner than blood, but in twilight it is just as dark.

He stands above me, looming like some terrible monster of the night. "Your servants told me you were gone. I thought you might have run away."

I nearly did after I found out what you had done. "I just needed to be alone."

He tips his head and turns his back. "Then I will go."

But I can't let him leave. Anger burns through me, and this time it is out of my control.

"Did you kill Trinity?" The words fly from my mouth like knives to his throat.

He stops, a branch snapping under the toe of his boot, and smiles. "Yes," he says.

The pomegranate falls from my hands and crashes to the earth. "Why?"

He doesn't flinch. "I wanted to ensure your place in the final." His eyes, green as the leaves that whisper overhead, study my reaction.

My heart rises into my throat, my voice thwarted by emotion. "You can't kill someone so that I live. The fates are not kind to men who play god."

But he doesn't believe in the fates or the gods, and I now understand why. He doesn't need religion; he has created a religion of his own. I remember a proverb from a book I read once when I was young: *in regione caecorum rex est luscus*, in the land of the blind the one-eyed man is king.

When he nears me, my legs go weak. "I am a god, Electa. If I want someone dead, they die the next day. My word is the law. And when I breathe, the whole world watches. How could I be anything but a god?"

His slender hands reach out to me.

I stumble backwards, falling to the ground. "Lysander, this is madness!" I am sure the entire city hears my scream.

"Know I did it for you." There is a softness in his voice now.

"Did it for me?" I don't know where I find the strength inside me to shout, but rage pours from me and thunders like the storm he once created. "How dare you say such a thing."

His eyes sweep over my body, and I feel smaller than I ever have. My back is against the cool marble of the tomb; I have nowhere left to hide.

"Finally, you have found that tongue I have heard so much about." He laughs.

This is what he was waiting for, what he wanted. He never saw the Pleb in me, but he does now.

I tear my eyes away from him. I can't bear to see him like this. *Nothing good ever comes from loving a god.* "I will never forgive you for what you did to her."

He crouches down. "You asked for my honesty, and I gave it to you." His breath is like ice on my cheeks. "Can you say the same?"

He leans towards me, cupping my face in his hands, and kisses my brow. And I see the understanding in his eyes.

But I say nothing.

"Don't stay out here too long. I can't have my bride being late to her own wedding."

He returns to the shadows. I squeeze my eyes shut. *It was a dream.* Then I see the half-eaten pomegranate on the ground, the seeds spilling from the flesh.

EPILOGUE

The silk makes me look soft, feminine and all the things I am not. They call this place the room of mirrors. *Not very original*, I think. I am greeted by my reflection at every glance. In another life, I might look beautiful. But when I look at myself, all I see is a monster. I take the pins from my hair, undoing the hours of work that Royce's servants spent making me pretty. The curls fall loosely on my shoulders and, for a moment, I look human, I look like myself again.

"You can't go through with this." A familiar voice echoes in the vaulted room. I look up at the gold-plated ceiling – this place is a pretty cage.

"I have to," I whisper. "You know I do."

Ash no longer looks like a prince. The crowns he used to wear are gone, replaced by a head of matted chocolate-brown hair. "He is dangerous, El."

"So am I."

I tug at the belt Royce used to cinch my waist. They call it the knot of Hercules, and it can only be undone by a husband. I want to tear it apart.

"Don't do this. We will find a way out, a way to save your brother and survive." His face is like iron, and I almost forget who he was before he killed his father. I miss the Ash I came to know. He was fun, carefree and reckless – though reckless still rings true.

"We both know you can't survive without a throne to sit on. I am afraid Spartaca is your last hope."

The bite of his anger doesn't come as I expect it. He grimaces, and the cold sea of his sadness swallows me whole. "You still don't know me at all, do you?"

But I have enough rage for the both of us. "You have been drinking yourself into oblivion, Ash. You left me to suffer this fate alone. There hasn't been a *we* since the night you murdered your father."

And he can't argue with that.

He hangs his head, not daring to touch me, but I wish he would one last time. "This isn't the man I want to be…" The words die in the stale air between us. "I am not going to watch you marry him."

I didn't expect him to.

The Temple of Dominus on Capitoline Hill is a rather unholy structure. Its vastness leaves me aghast, even now, as I see it for the hundredth time. The horse-drawn carriage rocks beneath me as it moves along the road that winds its way up the hill. People pour over the roped barriers that line the verge of the track. Flowers cover my body as they rain from the cloudless sky.

I see the girl who greeted me once in the forum. She smiles at me, reaching her tiny hand into a basket of flowers. Among all the faces, she is the only one I see, and when I shut my eyes, her smile remains in the darkness that envelopes me.

The three guardsmen bear torches and lift me from the carriage. I cling to the liveried guard in fear my legs will collapse. Each step I take brings a new kind of fear, but I fool the world with a smile that aches on my painted lips.

The seats on either side of the aisle are carved into marble. I pretend they are empty. I focus on the green of Lysander's eyes. There was always something about his eyes, something beautiful, something terrifying. My breathing steadies, even as my limbs tremble, not with nerves but with an innate power that surges inside me. Divinity is a strange thing.

A blade is delivered to us by a purple-robed *Pontifex*. We cut into our palms, letting red blood spill onto the holy stone at our feet. I make sure my wound is deep; it won't heal so quickly that way. The *Pontifex* joins our hands, the blood coalescing until it is one, heralding the union of two families and two bloodlines. The thick warmth of it clings to my skin. It reminds me of all the blood I have spilled, and the blood that is to come.

Lysander caresses my torn skin, slipping a golden band onto my finger. I wonder how many men he has killed with those hands. And then we say our vows.

"*Quando tu Gaius, ego Gaia,*" I say.

"*Quando tu Gaia, ego Gaius,*" he says.

We kiss, and I feel the world crack open.

The *Pontifex* blesses us with holy water as we sit on our thrones. A priestess with fillets in her hair crowns us with olive wreaths. They pronounce us the empress and emperor of Ore. And the deed is done.

We walk, hand in hand, to the steps of the altar below the temple, and the cameras follow us still. It is not hard to fake being in love with Lysander – it might actually be the easiest thing in the world.

He sweeps me into an embrace. I breathe the heavy scent of death and war as I nestle myself into the curve of his neck. I can't distance my head from my heart as he holds me like this. Lysander Drusus jars my sense of right and wrong and all that lies in between.

The honeyed words that I am so accustomed to never come. I feel as though I may never breathe again.

His lips come up against my ear. When he speaks, the entire world stands still, but I am the only one who hears. "I know what you are."

GLOSSARY

Acta Diurna: *Daily Acts* – Latia's version of a newspaper

Aquilo: the north wind

Augusta: another word for empress

Bacchanal: a wild and drunken celebration

Bacchant: a worshipper of Bacchus, the Roman god of agriculture, wine and fertility. Literally translates as "raving ones". This is often used as a derogatory term for drunks and drug users.

Bacchor: to revel/rave/riot

Bident: a two-pronged implement resembling a pitchfork. It is a weapon associated with the god of the underworld, Hades.

Cavea: literally "enclosure". Refers to the seating section in the Roman colosseum

Cithara: a musical instrument

Cognomen: a surname

Confarreatio: a traditional marriage ceremony

Cornu: a horn used by the army

Cursus Honorum: the traditional order of political and military offices in Latia

Damnatio memoriae: literally "condemnation of memory". When a person is erased from history.

Fibula: a brooch for fastening garments

Gladius: a sword

Haven: a dome-shaped electromagnetic shield that protects the civilisation within

Horreum: a warehouse/granary

Lectus: a couch

Lictor: a civil servant, assistant and bodyguard to important political figures

Ludi: public games

Lyre: an instrument

Nobilissima femina: literally "most noble woman". This is another way of addressing an empress.

Ornatrix: a hairdresser, stylist, make-up artist and personal attendant

Palaestra: a wrestling and boxing area in a gymnasium

Palla: a traditional mantle worn by women

Parcae: the Roman equivalent of the Fates. Divine goddesses of destiny.

Pater: father

Peregrinus: a foreigner

Pharmaca: drugs, medicines and herbs

Pontifex: a priest

Posca: a drink made by mixing vinegar, water and herbs. Sometimes, alcohol is added. Typically drunk by the lower classes.

Praenomen: first name

Quando tu Gaia, ego Gaius: a vow recited by the groom at a Latian marriage ceremony, literally "when and where you are Gaia, I then and there am Gaius"

Quando tu Gaius, ego Gaia: a vow recited by the bride at a Latian marriage ceremony, literally "when and where you are Gaius, I then and there am Gaia"

Salve: a greeting meaning *hello*

(Bovis) Stercus: (bull) shit (slang)

Stola: a traditional garment worn by Latian women that corresponds to the toga for men

Stultus: stupid

Tabella: literally a "small board" or "writing tablet". An electronic device similar to a smart phone or tablet.

Tace: literally "be quiet!" or more colloquially "shut up!"

Tartarus: a place in the underworld where souls are judged after death and receive divine punishment

Titulus: a piece of wood tied around the neck which labels a person's crime

ULA: an acronym – United Leagues of Appia. The Leagues are Latia, Umbria, Lutetia, Volscia and formerly Etruria

Vale: goodbye

Velarium: a type of awning that stretches over the seating area in theatres and arenas

ABOUT THE AUTHOR

M.J. Woodman is a student of Ancient History and Archaeology and debut author of Divine. A Classics enthusiast and self-proclaimed book-nerd, M.J. began writing Divine when she was thirteen. She revisited the untouched manuscript several years later, re-writing the novel with a clear, and mature voice.

M.J. grew up on isolated Dartmoor, in England, surrounded by nature, and as an only child, there wasn't much to do but read. Books soon became her best friend, so it was only natural that she should develop a passion for creative writing at school.

Inspired by a creative writing course at the University of Toronto, and by her studies of the Ancient World, her writing has culminated in Divine, an alternative-history, YA novel set in a rich and detailed world where the Roman Empire never fell.

She spends her time reading, studying, writing, and developing new projects inspired by the enigmatic and mythical world of history. She hopes one day to use her platform as an author to engage young people with history, which she believes, is crucial to building a better, brighter future.

Made in the USA
Monee, IL
22 May 2021